A More Perfect Union

HARPER'S
MAGAZINE
PRESS

A
MORE
PERFECT
UNION

a novel by

ROBERT STAPP

A HARPER'S MAGAZINE PRESS BOOK
Published in Association with Harper & Row
New York and Evanston

Part One

Chapter One

The white city was swathed in dirty gray gauze. Winter-stripped trees were skeletons wading through a spectral swamp. A fine mist glistened on the asphalt and swirled around the black limousine.

The Secretary of State raised his lean, lined face from the portfolio on his lap and gazed somberly out at the shrouded banks of Rock Creek Park. The bleak landscape matched his mood, although Donald Barringer would never acknowledge that the Secretary of State was subject to moods. Annoyed, he bent his head to the paper and resumed reading at his accustomed eighteen-hundred-words-a-minute cruising speed.

As the car slowed for the Parkway exit, he flipped the stapled pages closed and fitted them into the center compartment of his red-bordered dispatch case. He fished a tiny key from his lower vest pocket, locked the case and placed it upright behind his legs.

The limousine emerged from the ramp and edged into the outside lane of the traffic circle girdling the steel-mesh fence. Inside the enclosure, helmeted and holstered MP's flanked four cars lined up on the approach to the Abraham Lincoln Brotherhood Bridge. Beyond them, two domed concrete blockhouses anchored massive steel barricades, one of which was pointed skyward like a missile launcher.

Varnum, the driver, angled onto another cloverleaf. Atop

3

the overpass spanning the approach to the bridge, the mist thinned slightly. Donald Barringer looked out the window at the sluggish brown river. Involuntarily, his gaze lifted to the Virginia shore. Dimly, at the far end of the bridge, he could make out the squat, ugly contours of two blockhouses similar to those beneath him. He stared at them impassively as the car turned onto Constitution Avenue and swept past the graceful Kennedy Memorial on his right.

Varnum eased the limousine into the left lane and slowed for his accustomed turn on Twenty-third Street. Barringer's programed mind recorded the deviation and rejected it. He pressed the intercom button on the arm rest.

"No, Arthur," he said, a trace of apology in his tone. "We're going to the White House. Cellar entrance," he added dryly.

The driver responded with a nod and steered the car back on course. Opposite the Ellipse he turned right off Constitution Avenue, circled through the underpass and surfaced on the Parkway of the States, connecting the White House and the Monument grounds. Geometrically spaced along the center strip were thirty-five trees—each of a different species, each from a different state.

As always, the Secretary subconsciously catalogued them by species and origin—Vermont maple, Oregon spruce, Wisconsin elm, Illinois oak. Ordinarily it gave him a comforting sense of the vast resources and immense diversity of the great nation whose destiny he helped to guide. Today their forlorn appearance merely deepened his sense of futility.

The Parkway diverged at Zero Milestone, separating the Ellipse from the White House grounds. It encircled an intricately fashioned wrought-iron fence, combining the delicate filigree of a New Orleans gallery with the elaborate curlicues and jailhouse construction of a Newport estate. The fence was a gift to the people of the United States from the Iron

and Steel Foundation. It was designed by the eminent archi-
tect Werner Gehrhardt under a commission from the National
Society of Arts and Crafts. It was constructed, however, to
the basic specifications of the Army Corps of Engineers. It
was sunk in reinforced concrete and topped by graceful three-
bladed halberd heads, modeled on those carried by medieval
pikemen. It was both ornamental and practical, and was a
favorite backdrop for tourist photos.

Two Marines in dress uniform wearing ponchos and side
arms stood at attention behind the massive South Gate. They
peered through the scrollwork at the Secretary and his driver,
then, with drill-like precision, swung open the gates to admit
the car. It rolled slowly up a graveled driveway and stopped
under a curved green awning, extending out from the entrance
of a modest red-brick colonial-style cottage. In the center
of the oak-paneled door hung the green and white emblem
of the National Park Service.

The Secretary alighted without waiting for Varnum to assist him and strode up three steps to the doorway. From a
panel on the side of his dispatch case, he extracted a metal
plate, which he inserted in a concealed slot in the Park
Service shield. After a five-second interval, the door slowly
revolved inward to the hum of an electric motor. The Secretary stepped inside. The door closed behind him and the
sound ceased.

He stood in a vestibule approximately six feet square, bare
except for a bas-relief of the Great Seal of the United States,
inset into the wall on his left. He turned and faced the seal,
idly wondering what would happen if he faced the other way
and the back of his head showed up on the television screen.
Silently the wall opposite the door slid back. The Secretary
stepped through into a warmly decorated living room, richly
furnished with brown leather couches and chairs. Four brawny

men in civilian clothes stood at attention facing him. As the door behind him closed, the one on the right stepped forward.

"Good morning, Mr. Secretary," he said, extending his hand. "George Boronski."

"Of course, George. Nice to see you." He shook hands and nodded to the others, who murmured, "Mr. Secretary."

"I understand we are to dispense with the log today," Boronski said, with only a trace of disapproval in his voice. "The others are here. I'll take you on down."

He wheeled and led the way through a low archway, down a short corridor into a round, vaulted room where two glass-enclosed electric carts stood side by side on twin tracks.

Boronski motioned him toward the padded bench forward of one and seated himself opposite. He pushed a lever and the car glided noiselessly into a brightly lighted curving tunnel. Barringer felt pressure against his shoulder blades. "The Well"—as it was vaguely referred to by the few who knew of its existence—was intended primarily as a deep shelter for second-echelon officials not included in the Nucevac Plan. Secondarily, it was conceived as a temporary refuge or escape route for the President in the event of a civil uprising or attempted coup.

President Lander had found it useful, on very rare occasions, for meetings he preferred to conceal from the White House staff and the press. Donald Barringer had "been to the Well" twice before—once when the President had revealed his incredible plan to deal with the Brazilian invasion and two weeks ago when he had confided the fearful peril confronting the United States of America. On such brief acquaintance, Barringer already dreaded the lead-lined caverns like an execution chamber.

The car automatically braked itself and rolled soundlessly to a stop in a room slightly larger than the one they had left.

It was similar in all other respects except for five evenly spaced archways from which corridors radiated in different directions.

Boronski touched a button. The glass door slid back and Secretary Barringer stepped onto a platform which gave off a faintly luminous glow. Boronski glanced at the reflectorized numbers over the archways and moved ahead of the Secretary into No. 5. A hollow, metallic echo followed them.

The corridor appeared to have no exit. It extended for some thirty yards and ended at a blank, smooth wall. Boronski halted halfway, reached overhead and felt along the ceiling. From an aperture only slightly larger than his fist, he pulled a tapered handle, to which was attached a flat iron bar, notched at the end. He fitted the notch into a waist-high slot in the wall, invisible in the dim light to Barringer's eyes. He pumped down on it like a tire jack. A crack opened in the solid wall alongside. Boronski reached out a massive hand, gave an effortless push and stepped back. The heavy door silently swung open and Barringer saw a layer of inch-thick steel sandwiched between lead slabs.

As the Secretary moved past Boronski, he caught, behind his dark appraising look, a surprising glimpse of a worried small boy. He had a fleeting impulse to give Boronski a reassuring pat on the arm. Instead, he held out his hand and said with a shade less than his customary reserve, "Thank you, George. Thank you very much."

Boronski dipped his head. "Thank *you*, Mr. Secretary," he said. "Good luck."

Donald Barringer stepped over the raised threshold into a long, low-ceilinged room which gave an impression of being more spacious than it was. Subdued overhead lights brought out the friendly warmth of the rich mahogany paneling. In the center of the room a silver walnut table was surrounded by padded captain's chairs with blue leather backs and seats. At the far end, easy chairs and couches were clustered in the corners, set apart by a shoulder-high divider.

Two men, seated on a sofa facing him, looked up as Barringer entered. Lawrence Tazewell, Director of the Central Intelligence Agency, rose and walked briskly across the room. "Mr. Secretary," he said formally, extending a long-fingered hand.

"Good to see you, Lawrence," Barringer replied, equally formal. He removed his black raincoat, shifting the dispatch case from one hand to the other. Tazewell helped him off with it and carefully draped it on a hanger in the rack by the entrance.

Barringer paced across the room to the couch where Harmon Thomas, Secretary of Defense, sat puffing languidly on a stubby pipe. With his round, ruddy face and rumpled gray-brown hair, he looked more like an amiable brewmaster than the custodian of an arsenal that could destroy the world.

He stood up as Barringer approached and waved his pipe in a casual greeting. "Mr. Secretary," he said with mock deference.

"Hi, Harm," Barringer responded, not shaking hands. "Miserable day."

"Aren't they all?" replied the Secretary of Defense, resuming his seat and motioning Barringer into the easy chair beside him.

After a preliminary period of aloof assessment, dictated by the sometimes conflicting nature of their duties, Donald Barringer had acquired an unaccustomed affection for the bluff Secretary of Defense—both personally and professionally. He soon concluded that Harmon Thomas was not what he seemed to be. His pugnacious manner and his offhand retorts to criticism periodically aroused the peacemongers to horrified clamors for his dismissal. The inside-leak columnists alternately portrayed him as a bumbling amateur strategist and a bloodthirsty egomaniac, bent on plunging the country into a nuclear holocaust. Frequently they called upon the Secretary of State to repudiate his colleague's bellicose utterances. Occasionally Barringer did, after first apprising Thomas of his intentions and clearing the statement with him.

Thomas's reaction invariably was gleefully profane. "All right, you marshmallow-assed appeaser," he would chortle, " go ahead. Be a chicken shit."

Privately, the Secretary of State took pains to impress upon the President that Thomas's irascibility was an invaluable instrument of foreign policy. The President was well aware that in moments of real crisis the Secretary of Defense was among the most cautious and coolheaded members of his Cabinet. He also was aware that a military machine which must, perforce, move so openly and so ponderously sorely needs an element of erraticism. Or at least the reputation for one.

Thomas emptied the ashes of his pipe in a heavy brass tray with crimped edges and revolved his nondescript face in the direction of the Secretary of State.

"Tell me, Donald, how's our international posture these days?"

"Not too good, I gather from the morning paper."

"Well, just you remember that the world's mightiest fighting force stands poised to back up our commitments—wherever they may be."

"That's very comforting to know," the Secretary of State replied gravely.

Lawrence Tazewell listened to the exchange with the studied blankness of an unintentional eavesdropper tuning out a private conversation. Long, carefully combed strands of blond hair framed a nude, pink scalp and a bony, oblong face. His habitual expression of lugubrious disdain fairly mirrored a lugubrious and disdainful nature. Lawrence Tazewell was a born fanatic. Whatever he dedicated himself to would obsess and eventually consume him.

An intelligence agent for twenty years, he had acquired an implacable mistrust of the human species and a thinly veiled contempt for its individual components. In addition to those qualifications, he was a meticulous planner and a genius at organization. He was not in great demand socially.

Allowing a sufficient interval to dissociate himself from the previous remarks, he suggested in a meeting-come-to-order tone, "Should we not, perhaps, compare views before the President arrives? It might be helpful to him if we could offer him some collective recommendations."

Thomas sucked on his empty pipe and gazed vacantly at the CIA Director. "I don't know how it works in your shop," he said, "but my experience with 'collective recommendations' hasn't been too productive. Every time I ask my four-stars to sit down and draw up a joint recommendation, they come back with the old military axiom 'Do unto them before they do unto us.' Sometimes I think this integration of the armed forces was a mistake. When they were busy fighting each other, they weren't so damned eager to fight somebody else."

Tazewell forced a small smile of sympathy. "Fortunately, I don't have to cope with the military mold. We discourage regimented thinking in the Agency. I insist that my people explore every approach to a problem, no matter how impractical it may seem."

Thomas shifted in his chair. "Uh-huh," he grunted. "I figured that. Fortunately, you've got my people to cover you when you back off from some of those approaches."

"Oh, I didn't mean to disparage the military. Certainly their presence is what enforces respect for our diplomatic and intelligence activities. That's why I feel it's important that we correlate our thinking on this problem." He looked at Barringer for corroboration.

Barringer hesitated. As a former professor of international law, he had learned to temper his normally definite opinions of right and wrong. As Secretary of State, he had grudgingly adopted the attitude that "Diplomacy is the art of not taking sides." He disliked being put in the position of supporting his Cabinet colleague against the CIA Director, who, he suspected, was more sensitive to personal affront than he let on.

"I imagine," he said placatingly, "if the President had wanted us to integrate our thinking he would have asked us to submit a position paper. I got the impression he would prefer each of us to express our own views. However, I have no objection to sharing my thoughts with you."

"I'm sure we're probably all thinking along the same lines," Tazewell persisted. "I just felt it might be easier for the President to arrive at a decision if he knew we were in agreement."

Thomas rattled his pipe against his teeth, then clamped his lips firmly around it.

Barringer saw that Tazewell was not to be diverted. "Well," he said, "what is your thinking?"

"As I see it," the CIA Director observed didactically, "we have gone about as far as we can go from a diplomatic standpoint. Certainly we would not resort to a military solution until all other possibilities have been exhausted. That leaves the area in between."

"Your area," Thomas grunted.

"That's the way it looks to me," Tazewell replied unctuously. "I believe we have a number of options, which I plan to outline to the President. I would appreciate your judgment and support if you feel it is warranted."

Barringer darted a glance at the Secretary of Defense and saw that he was beginning to fume. Turning to the CIA Director, he said, "I confess I don't have any pat answer. If you do, I will certainly be receptive."

"Don't misunderstand me," Tazewell said hastily. "I don't have any pat answers. I don't think there are any. I just think there are certain steps we can take which might relieve the situation."

Thomas heaved himself up on the couch. The other two focused their eyes on him. He reached into his side pocket for his tobacco pouch and deliberately filled his pipe.

"I'll give you a pat answer," he said, concentrating on his chore. "Sooner or later we're going to have to exterminate the Confederate States of America."

Chapter Two

A muffled click, followed by a faint whirring in the corner across from them, swung the three heads around. A narrow aperture opened in the wall to admit a Secret Service man. He nodded to them, swept the room with a glance and stepped aside. The President entered.

He waved a casual hand at the three as they rose. Turning to the Secret Service man, he said, "All right, Jerry. I'll ring when I want Dr. Corfmann."

His escort vanished through the opening and it closed behind him.

President Gordon James Lander advanced across the room with the familiar springy step that magically infected the nation with its buoyancy, lifting men's spirits in times of crisis and despair. Early in his career, when he first ran for Governor of Illinois, the image-makers had recognized its subliminal possibilities. Gordon James Lander was never on stage when the meeting started or when the television cameras began to roll. Invariably he walked on from the wings, rising jauntily on the balls of his feet—a natural, unaffected stride, the stride of a man who knew where he was going and who was enjoying the trip. Magnetically, it impelled others to follow after him.

His three lieutenants rose at his approach. Though he saw each of them several times a week, he gave them the quick handshake, the first name, the boyish half-smile that out-weighed all his other qualities with millions of female voters.

He was medium tall—five feet eleven—slender but sinewy, well proportioned. His physique served him well. Barringer had occasionally puzzled over his seeming chameleon ability to project himself as frail or sturdy as the situation demanded. In fact, he was an enigma in many ways to the Secretary of State, who prided himself on being able to read a man's character by his appearance. President Lander's appearance, he had perceived, was misleading if not downright deceptive.

Disarming brown eyes, a quiet voice, an almost diffident manner masked a carbon-tough mind, tempered by thirty years of political infighting, and a fierce competitive drive. Indeed, it was generally conceded by friend and foe alike that President Lander had been elected under false pretenses.

A nation, wearied by forty years of intermittent strife and incessant abuse, had renounced the role of world policeman—or so it thought. It had turned to the friendly man with the gentle eyes and told him, "Get us out of all these senseless squabbles and let us go about our business."

Probably President Lander took office with every intention of carrying out that mandate. The Politburo, at any rate, took him at face value and immediately set about touching off wars of liberation in scattered areas of the globe.

Their success inspired a number of local psychopaths to save their countries from Communism, and presently Fascism was again flaming throughout the world. The United Nations deplored the breakdown of world order, but with diminishing vehemence as more and more totalitarian regimes succeeded to the seats formerly occupied by their decadent democratic predecessors.

Inevitably, friction developed between rival dictators, particularly in Africa and South America, where they blossomed in profusion. While publicly condemning the archaic medieval concept of neighborhood wars, the two great power blocs refrained from intervening in them for fear of precipitating the cataclysm that would render the earth nonhabitable.

Actually, most of the regional disagreements were settled more or less peacefully after one of the parties had demonstrated to the satisfaction of the other that it had the means and the resolution to utterly destroy it. Throughout this period of international unrest, President Lander issued numerous pleas for peace and understanding. When war did break out, he volunteered his good offices as mediator. As soon as the outcome was fairly well ordained, the prospective loser promptly accepted his offer. The peace negotiations usually resulted in prolonging the conflict several months beyond the date it would normally have ended had it been fought to a finish.

This unsatisfactory but tolerable state of affairs rocked along until the Supreme Potentate of Ulandi breached the unwritten code of good conduct by dropping a crude but serviceable atomic bomb on the neighboring capital of Rfada. The two rival factions within the exclusive nuclear club heatedly accused each other of opening the gates to the rabble. The response from both parties was so outraged as to persuade each of the other's innocence. Separate investigations turned up an unregistered consortium of nonaligned physicists, dedicated to the ideology of making a pile of money in a hurry. The business was quickly and quietly liquidated. But the products were now on the open market, and a score of backward nations were frantically funneling 75 percent of their GNP into atomic weapons.

For the first time in twenty years the United Nations acted with resolution and dispatch—since, for the first time in twenty years, the vital interests of the major power blocs coincided. The previous holders of the franchise, loudly extolling the sacrifices they were making, agreed to a reduction in nuclear arsenals, a ban on the manufacture of additional nuclear devices and an effective system of inspection and control.

In essence, it provided:

1. That the manufacture and assembly of nuclear weapons should cease on the effective date of the treaty.

2. That all existing nuclear devices with an explosive force of more than 5 megatons be dismantled under the supervision of United Nations inspectors within eighteen months of the effective date of the treaty.

3. That existing stockpiles of 5-megaton bombs be reduced to not more than 5,000 in number within eighteen months of the effective date of the treaty.

4. That those nations not possessing nuclear devices be guaranteed immunity from atomic attack by all other signatories to the treaty.

5. That all missiles constructed after the effective date of the treaty be limited to a range of 1,000 miles, except those designed for space exploration or interplanetary travel.

In effect, the treaty established parity in nuclear weapons for those nations already possessing them in quantity. It also assured them of permanent though reduced superiority over the late-comers. Despite the strenuous objections of a dozen have-not countries, the pact was pushed through the General Assembly in the astonishing period of three months. Eventually, it was ratified by all member nations, though with varying degrees of enthusiasm.

"Treaty Day" was celebrated with appropriate ceremony throughout the world. Statesmen hailed it as the "end of the era of fear." With much fanfare, the principal nuclear powers converted their plants to peaceful production "for the benefit of all mankind." The weaker nations availed themselves of the occasion to call for the abolition of all nuclear armaments and the renunciation of force as an instrument of international policy.

There was no formal observance of the historic day in the Confederate States of America. Under the professional scrutiny of a team of international scientists, the nuclear weapons plant near Winslow, Arizona, shut down after turning out its 3,142nd 5-megaton warhead. Its 5,615 employees were given three weeks' vacation as a reward for working around the clock for the past six months. They were instructed to report to the missile plant nearing completion at Huntsville, Alabama.

In an unprecedented telecast, linking the networks of all nations, President Howie Ray Spearman joined twenty-six other assorted chiefs of state in proclaiming the "rebirth of reason." He spoke in subdued sincere tones, with no hysteria and hardly any histrionics. The contrast moved many of his followers to tears, and moved Harmon Thomas to wonder aloud "what that pious son-of-a-bitch is up to."

The thrust of his remarks was unexceptionable—indeed, significantly temperate. Donald Barringer and his rhetorical analysis section did, however, devote one hour-long session to contemplation of his concluding phrase.

"Consummation of the treaty," the dictator observed, "removes the honest adjudication of just grievances from the barred cell of nuclear monopoly."

Twelve months had elapsed since the signing of the treaty. The United States, along with all the other nuclear nations, was proceeding with the phased dismantling of its weapons system. To be sure, each was saving its neutron bombs till last. But that was merely a conditioned salute to the passing of the age of naked force. "Peaceful equilibrium" would be established on the first of August, 1981.

But the United States of America might not survive long enough to enjoy it.

From force of habit, Donald Barringer moved toward the table in the middle of the room.

The President touched his arm. "Why don't we just sit here? I don't think it will be necessary to take notes."

He settled himself into an easy chair. His advisers arranged themselves around him.

"Well," he said cheerfully, "I trust you have figured out a way to deal with this little dilemma we seem to be faced with." He looked fleetingly around the circle. The unresponsive faces gave him his answer.

"I think," he continued, his manner serious but not concerned, "it might be well if each of you outlined the situation, as of now, in his own province. Perhaps the rest of us can bring some fresh thinking to bear on it. Donald, would you lead off?"

Barringer avoided glancing at Tazewell as he unlocked his dispatch case and placed the "Eyes Only" document on his lap. He did not refer to it throughout his presentation, but papers were his pacifier, as Thomas's pipe was his.

"I'm afraid, Mr. President, the situation hasn't changed much since our discussion two weeks ago. I've asked Langwell and Jenkins for independent appraisals and their projections are pretty much the same as mine.

"As you know, President Spearman was a little more restrained in his speech last Thursday than he has been on some occasions." The Secretary tilted his head slightly and raised an eyebrow but continued in the same detached tone. "He did not, for example, refer to you as an unwitting tool of the Communist conspiracy."

A corner of the President's mouth twitched. Harmon Thomas snorted. Tazewell remained impassive.

"He, of course, reiterated the 'incontestable right' of the Confederacy to an outlet to the Pacific. He did mention—significantly perhaps—that their peaceful atomic research would enable them to create a deep-water port. I take that to mean," he added dryly, "they may not insist on the cession of San Diego or Ensenada.

"On the other hand, there has been a slight step-up in the number of incidents along the Colorado and Utah borders in the four-corners region. They may have been deliberately provoked, or they may be attributable to a growing militancy in the Southwest.

"There have been no charges of atrocities or espionage in the past three weeks. President Spearman hasn't called our ambassador in for a dressing-down in more than a month. That bothers me a little bit. You can usually get some idea of what he is thinking from what he says.

"In summary, I would say our relations are about *in statu quo.* I don't anticipate any immediate crisis, but I see no long-range hope for improvement."

The Secretary of State folded his hands over his papers and gazed impassively at the President. Lander jiggled his head up and down, a mannerism that bespoke neither impatience nor agreement, merely an acknowledgment that he had heard and understood.

"Let's lay out the problem first," he said. "Then we can look for the answers. Harmon, would you give us a rundown on where we stand from the military angle."

The Secretary of Defense pushed himself upright on the sofa, shifted his legs from right to left and his pipe from left to right. He had several pages of handwritten notes on a yellow, lined tablet which he consulted from time to time.

"Well, Mr. President, our evaluations haven't changed much either. To put it in a nutshell, my people think they're going to hit us whenever they're ready. That won't be until after the treaty is implemented, of course. They're no match for us now.

"The Joint Chiefs naturally would prefer to hit them first. From a tactical standpoint, I would have to go along with them."

He paused and looked into the President's eyes. When he resumed, his words came out in a harsh, almost raspy, voice. "This much I can promise you. Whether we hit them first or last, we will wipe the Confederacy off the map."

A wave of despair surged over Donald Barringer. In a flash he saw his hopes and accomplishments of the past four years disintegrating into a wasteland of ashes and rubble. He blinked twice, effacing the vision. Lawrence Tazewell cleared his throat and looked down at his polished shoes.

President Lander folded his arms and said matter-of-factly, "We will consider that eventuality when and if we must."

The Secretary of Defense glanced at his notes. "They were working night and day while the treaty was under discussion. Our best estimates are that they have a stockpile of between three and four thousand warheads—two-thirds of them in the five-megaton range. They are not all emplaced yet. I don't think we'll have too much trouble spotting the nests. The devices they were turning out at Winslow are pretty ungainly, but serviceable."

He raised his head and ran a stubby hand over his coarse russet mane. "I might say, parenthetically, if we were to take

. . . uh . . . preventive measures in time, I doubt if one hundred of them would get off the ground."

The President gave no indication the comment had registered. Thomas resumed his auditor's report.

"They're concentrating on the delivery system now." A trace of his characteristic cynicism seeped into his tone. "As I mentioned to you at the time, the treaty might have been written to their specifications. Under the thousand-mile limitation, it's open season everywhere except Hawaii and Alaska. Our laser screen will be largely ineffective against anything under four hundred miles. We would just about have to write off everything south of Chicago and Boston.

"I'm sure they realize they can't knock out our retaliatory capabilities. I don't think they'll be shooting for the missile sites. I expect they'll hit the population centers and take the consequences. It'd be worth the gamble to them to reduce the numerical odds. They're pretty well dispersed already, and of course they can draw up an evacuation schedule in advance. If we wait for them to hit us, I'd figure on an initial casualty ratio of three to one. Something on the order of forty million to fifteen million.

"They're counting on stunning us with the nuke strike. Then they'll shove every man they've got across the border, on the assumption we won't bomb them on our own territory. They'll use low-radiation weapons on the key cities and figure on occupying them while the panic is still on. There again they'd put us in the position of having to slaughter our own people to get at them.

"Of course that would leave them wide-open to a counter-invasion, but they reason they have a lot less to lose than we have. And if it comes down to living off the country, they'll be living better than we are.

"Essentially, though, they're counting on knocking us out

with one punch. If it lasts more than a month, I expect Spearman will throw in his hand and leave us to pick up the pieces."

The Secretary of Defense leaned back on the couch, clamped his pipe in his teeth and looked reflectively at the President. Lander's face gave no insight into his thoughts.

"What you mean," he said levelly, "is that he doesn't think we have the will or the fortitude to fight."

"I guess that's about what it comes down to."

"What do you think?"

"Speaking for the military, you haven't got anything to worry about. As to the civilian population, I just don't know. The way I laid it out to you, you can see they're going to bear the brunt of it."

"Forty million casualties at the outset?" For the first time the President's voice betrayed emotion.

"Well, that may be a little strong. Actually we have a couple of things going for us. Spearman can't afford to throw in all his chips as openers. Thank God the Mexicans got into production before the ban went into effect. They've got maybe five, six hundred two- and three-meg bombs stashed away. They're pretty crude, but the Confeds can't afford to ignore 'em. Assuming Mexico will be on our side."

He cocked an eyebrow at the Secretary of State. Barringer smiled wanly. "I think we may assume that Mexico will be—involved. If we are."

Thomas turned back to the President.

"Unless Spearman is completely insane—and I'm not sure he isn't—he wouldn't dare strip himself of his whole atomic arsenal. I can think of several people who would just as soon pluck his tail feathers if his wings were clipped. That's one thing the goddamned treaty is good for. Nobody's going to shoot off all his firecrackers if he has no way to replenish them.

"So, assuming the Confeds have three thousand five hundred warheads, they would just about have to hold a thousand in reserve. They'll need another thousand for second-strike and follow-on contingencies. Say they deploy another three hundred against Mexico. That leaves 'em with maybe a thousand on the first go-round. I think we could safely scratch off three hundred due to functional failures—either of the missile or the device itself. You can't turn those things out on an assembly line like they've been doing. I have doubts, too, about their accuracy. They just about have to saturate all major targets. I think I can pretty well guarantee we'll knock down a fourth of those that get in the air, and I would hope we could nail half that many on the ground. So we're talking about five or six hundred nuclear impacts. That's a lot of megatons. But this is a big country. I have no doubt it will survive—if the people want it to."

The President removed his half-rimmed glasses and scanned the sober faces of his advisers. "We can't let it happen," he said with finality.

"You're damned right we can't," Harmon Thomas muttered.

Gordon James Lander took a neatly folded handkerchief from his breast pocket and meticulously polished his glasses as though that were the top-priority project of the moment. He replaced the handkerchief in his pocket and the glasses on his nose. He turned to the CIA Director. "Lawrence, could you give us your evaluation of the Confederacy's intentions and capabilities?"

"Yes, sir, Mr. President," Tazewell said crisply. With measured deliberation he opened his attaché case, removed a cloth-bound document, refastened the clasp on his case and deposited it on an end table beside the couch.

"Pursuant to your request of two weeks ago," he recited, sitting at attention and gazing directly at the President, "I ordered an all-agency, in-depth analysis and projection of

Contingency K. Let me say at the outset that our conclusions are substantially in accord with those of the Secretary of State and the Secretary of Defense in their respective areas."

Barringer suppressed a twinge of annoyance. Thomas sucked stolidly on his pipe and gazed inscrutably at the ceiling.

Tazewell dropped his eyes to the manuscript on his lap and read in a flat, precise voice: "All relevant data were collated and programed through the prognosis and predictability computer. Considering the diversity of the input data, an exceptional degree of unanimity was recorded in respect to the indicated course of action."

The President stirred in his chair but offered no comment.

Tazewell raised his head. "You have a question, sir?"

"No, no. I'm not familiar with some of your terms, but I'm sure you will clarify them as you go along. Please proceed."

"From the diplomatic standpoint," Tazewell intoned, sitting stiffly upright, "our projections show that any further attempts to appease President Spearman not only would prove futile in the long run but would weaken our position in the international community. All indications are that he is committed to a course of militaristic aggression. His peaceful professions are, in our judgment, mere camouflage, designed to mask his real intentions and justify his future actions.

"In the military sphere, nearly all relevant indices portend a nuclear attack on this country by the Confederacy. We discount the likelihood of a conventional land, sea or air assault. Its resources, though formidable, are vastly inferior to ours, and it appears unlikely that the Confederacy could sustain a prolonged war.

"It might therefore be inferred that our diplomatic and military options are severely limited. In the final analysis, neither diplomatic flexibility nor military adamance would seem to hold forth much promise of bringing about a mutually acceptable détente."

Tazewell paused and looked across at the President to emphasize the point. A perceptible shadow of annoyance lingered on Lander's face.

"I wonder, Lawrence," he said mildly, "if it wouldn't perhaps be better for you just to outline the situation in your own words. No doubt Mr. Barringer and Mr. Thomas understand what you are saying, but I'm just a simple politician."

Tazewell accepted the rebuke with a perfunctory smile. "I'll try, sir," he said. He scanned several pages of his manuscript, marked his place with a knobby finger and launched into his translation.

"Assuming, then, that the external resources at our command would be insufficient to avert a military confrontation, we are left with one alternative—internal subversion. Our appraisals indicate that any overt attempt to overthrow the Spearman regime would almost certainly fail. He has forged a most effective police state. Inherent in such a structure are manifest strengths and weaknesses. The populace as a whole is either nominally committed or passively resigned to the regime. Any large-scale rebellion is out of the question.

"As in any totalitarian state, however, there are dissident elements which, properly cultivated, could create much stress and turmoil and eventually might undermine the existing order of the Confederacy. These elements, in our judgment, offer the most promising possibilities for fruitful action."

Tazewell swept his eyes over his audience like a classroom lecturer. Their expressions were attentive but uncommunicative. He studied his presentation for a minute, then resumed.

"There are five distinct categories which we regard as fertile grounds for sowing disaffection. Some are fairly well organized. Some are not. We have cadres within each group which are capable of influencing, if not controlling, its direction. Some groups have a real potential for positive action. Others are largely forums for philosophical dissent. We are prepared to utilize whatever capabilities exist.

"The most reliable, but perhaps the least effective, is the remnants of the North American League. As you know, the League was founded in the early days of the Confederacy with the aim of promoting reunification with the United States. Its influence has ebbed and flowed, depending on the attitude of the government in power. In the 1940's it exerted very strenuous efforts to align the Confederacy with us in World War II and very nearly succeeded. Its strength has dwindled over the last three decades with the erosion of democracy in the South. When Spearman outlawed the League in 1969, he eliminated it as a political force, but he also stiffened the backbone of the stalwarts. More than fifty underground chapters still exist. The membership is composed largely of intellectuals and do-gooders who wouldn't be much help on the barricades. Still, they have proved their dedication and they are the people we would have to rely on for ideological leadership.

"The Communists are probably the best organized, but of course are basically hostile to us and not to be trusted. We would not attempt to work with them openly, but we are in a position to . . . uh . . . guide them, as it were. They would not be averse to an open conflict between us and the Confederacy, but they could not afford for either of us to win a clear-cut victory. The most fertile grounds for them would be a prostrate Confederacy and an exhausted United States. From that standpoint, we probably could count on them for a certain amount of sabotage and subversion. While they might be of some help to us, we would certainly have to take steps to prevent a Communist takeover—with or without war. No doubt Spearman will use them as window dressing for his attack on us. They have very little popular support and no military strength in themselves. They have, however, heavily infiltrated both the Prives and the Blacks and will undoubtedly try to use them to their advantage.

"The Prives would join in any kind of an uprising, but would be completely useless as an organized force. They have no ethnic, intellectual or emotional ties, aside from being outcasts. All they have in common is a personal resentment against the regime, which could come in handy, of course, in stirring up isolated outbreaks. But they're so honeycombed with Communists and Seepees and just natural-born informers it would be impossible to mobilize them secretly."

Harmon Thomas removed his pipe from his mouth and grunted. "Would they know how to use the weapons if they had 'em?"

"Oh, yes," the CIA Director quickly replied. "They're not all stupid, you know. They're all misfits in a totalitarian society. For that reason they were 'deprived' of their citizenship. Most of them, of course, would be dregs in any society. But a good many of them are merely nonconformists. And in any collection of nonconformists you get a high percentage of geniuses."

"It would seem to me," Thomas drawled, "you would have a good potential for leadership there."

"I think you will find," Tazewell said with a trace of condescension, "that intellectual brilliance seldom manifests itself in high qualities of leadership. I would doubt if your generals and admirals are men of outstanding intellect."

"I'd go along with you there," Thomas rumbled, "but I don't consider them necessarily incompatible."

"Not necessarily," Tazewell conceded. "But Spearman sees to it that no leadership sprouts up among the Prives. Or the

Blacks either for that matter. You must realize," he continued animatedly, "Spearman's crowd has made a science of subjugation. They know the book—from Genghis Khan to Adolf Hitler. They've had to. Because they are dealing with an essentially spirited and independent people. They know when to tighten the rein and when to loosen it.

"Look how they've handled the Blacks. They abolished slavery eight years after secession because they realized it was no longer practicable. Then for a hundred years they kept them in economic and social bondage. After Spearman came to power he saw that he couldn't build a monolithic nation if 25 percent of its people were dragging their feet. He also saw the scars inflicted by the civil rights struggle in the United States. So overnight he raised the economic status of Negroes to the median-income level. That put them ahead of most of the Negroes in the North and made the Blacks his staunchest supporters.

"It's true, he closed the door of opportunity to them. But it had never been open to them anyway, so they didn't know it had been closed. He built comfortable 'Cloisters' for them, and scattered them around the cities. Sure, they couldn't live anywhere else. But they had been segregated all their lives. And here they were segregated in the midst of decent white neighborhoods, with television sets and dishwashers. It didn't matter to them that they had been split up so they would be more defenseless. They had always been defenseless. And a ninth-grade education with a good-paying job in a factory was a lot better than a high school education with no job at all."

Tazewell's voice had taken on a tinge of admiration—the enthusiasm of an engineer explaining the workings of a finely crafted machine.

"You've got to hand it to Spearman. He's done a masterful job with the race problem. He's given the Blacks equality—

at least among themselves, which is where it counts. He's given them security and eliminated ambition. He's given them enough education to make them productive and not enough to make them discontented. And his real psychological stroke is that he has given them something to lose and not much to gain by rocking the boat. They resent any of their own people who stir up trouble."

"I gather," the President said, "you see little evidence of disaffection among the Negro populace."

Barringer thought he detected a trace of asperity in Lander's tone, perhaps because he was looking for it. If so, it escaped the CIA Director. His manner seemed almost puzzled.

"Strangely enough," he said, "that doesn't appear to be the case. Our sources are in substantial agreement that there is considerable unrest in the Black communities. It seems to have no particular focal point, and so far as we have been able to ascertain, it has not been incited."

"Could it be," the President inquired, "that you can't domesticate human beings?" This time there was no mistaking the sardonic note in his voice.

"It could be that, of course." Tazewell sounded slightly miffed by the injection of an unknown factor into the equation. "In any event we are prepared to nurture it. If we can touch off a few demonstrations and riots in selected areas, they conceivably could ignite a large-scale racial conflict, such as our own country experienced in the sixties."

"With what consequences?" the President asked coldly.

"I should think it might be extremely helpful," Tazewell replied, ignoring the tone of the question. "Despite the recent improvement in relations between the races, the whites are uneasy. They still have their ancient sense of guilt. And I suspect the Blacks are somewhat ashamed of their docility.

The combination could easily result in bloodshed. Once that happens, there's no telling where it might end."

"Where do you think it would end?"

Tazewell pondered the question as a tactical exercise.

"Well, I would expect the Seepees—the Citizens Protection Force—to respond rather savagely. Spearman would undoubtedly regard any kind of demonstration by the Blacks as the basest ingratitude as well as a threat to his whole structure. I'm sure he would feel he must make an example of them. Of course, that might collapse the whole movement. But at any rate it would intensify the feeling that already exists and make it easier for us to capitalize on it. The important thing would be for us to foment a number of riots simultaneously so they couldn't be passed off as isolated incidents."

"Don't you think Spearman would slaughter everybody involved?"

"Yes, he probably would. But he can't wipe out all the Negroes in the South. Even if he could, he couldn't afford to. They're the ones who keep the factories running. If we could promote a really sizable Negro uprising, it would paralyze the Confederacy."

"You are suggesting that we dump the war on them?"

Tazewell finally grasped the gist of the President's interrogation. "The Negroes in the North didn't gain their rights without bloodshed," he said defensively. "They can hardly expect to do it in the South. And they might be better off shedding it all at once, rather than drop by drop over a hundred years."

The President eyed his intelligence chief quizzically. "Might be," he said resignedly. "I believe," he resumed in his normal businesslike tone, "you suggested there was a fifth group that might serve our purpose."

"Yes, the military." Tazewell consulted his dossier again.

"They would be our most effective ally, but, of course, they also would be the most difficult to subvert. However, I do not rule out that possibility. Aside from the usual jealousy and animosity you find in any military organization, there would appear to be an inordinate amount of dissension among the higher echelons. It could be attributable to several causes. Throughout its existence the Confederacy has had no sharply defined system of government. It has veered from constitutional democracy to semisocialism to neo-fascism. The allegiance, not only of the military but of the people, may be a little fuzzy.

"For the same reason it has built up no real military tradition. The army was originally a gentleman's profession. But Spearman has turned it into a power scramble. The top officers are loyal to him, but the other ranks are filled with opportunists who are clawing to move up. They're so suspicious of each other it would be extremely difficult to organize a coup. Spearman has no doubt encouraged those rivalries.

"I believe the real professionals realize the folly of a nuclear war with us. But they don't dare speak out because they know they would be dumped. If we can get to them, we might be able to reason with them. But they're pretty skittish. The military, as well as all the other groups, is infested with Seepees."

Tazewell flipped his manuscript shut and riveted his eyes on the President's. "That's the way the Agency sizes up the situation, Mr. President. As I see it, we have only one course open to us—"

The President silenced him with a movement of his hand. "As I see it, Lawrence," he said brusquely, "we have several courses open to us. None of them very attractive, it's true. Nevertheless, I think we must consider them all and select the least unpalatable."

He leaned back in his chair and paired off his fingertips.

"Naturally, we must first exhaust every avenue of negotiation." He turned his deceptively gentle brown eyes on the Secretary of State. "You are convinced there is no hope there, Donald? What would be Spearman's bottom price for an accommodation?"

Barringer answered without hesitation. "Mr. President, I am convinced Spearman does not want an accommodation. Oh, right now he would settle for an outlet to the Pacific. Either at our expense or Mexico's. But in two years or three or five there would be other demands. He's bent on proving the Confederacy is a world power. And I think he is also fanatically convinced their system is right.

"Unfortunately, we are not the only two nations on this earth. In the past four years I believe we have restored a semblance of stability to the world by giving everyone to understand we will not stand still for conquest by threats or blackmail. If we let it happen to us—or to our ally—we have forfeited our credibility everywhere, as well as our influence for peace."

"Would he accept an internationalized corridor and a free port?"

"He says he won't, but he might. He keeps insisting the Confederacy has an historic claim to all the Western territories south of the Plebiscite line. Farcical as it was, the Plebiscite pact contained no such provision as that. If the line were extended from the northern borders of Arizona, it would slice off the tip of Nevada and cut California in half. Spearman knows that isn't going to happen. So he has magnanimously offered to settle for a twenty-mile-wide strip to the sea. But he demands full sovereignty over the corridor and the port."

"Well, that's out," Lander said quietly. "We should never

have let them bamboozle us out of Oklahoma, New Mexico and Arizona. But that was ninety years ago. It's one thing to give up a couple hundred thousand square miles of barren, unsettled territory and quite another to slice off a sliver of an existing state. Especially California. Can you imagine the uproar?"

A slow grin spread over Harmon Thomas's chunky face. "If you're going to give away my state, Mr. President, I would feel obliged to transfer my allegiance with it. If 'Power-Mad' Thomas ever lines up with Howie Ray Spearman, look out."

The President smiled. "That puts a different light on things. Donald, tell them they can have California if they'll take Harmon too."

"I'm afraid, Mr. President," Barringer replied straight-faced, "those conditions would be totally unacceptable. It would mean war."

With no change in his expression or his tone, the President returned to the topic of discussion. "You feel, then, we have gone as far as we can go?"

The Secretary of State weighed the question. "As far as we can honorably go, I would say." He paused. The words came reluctantly. "We could, I'm sure, appease him at the expense of Mexico."

Lander did not recoil at the suggestion. "For how long?" he said.

Barringer shrugged. "Once you start down that road, you never know where it will lead. I suppose we could put off a confrontation indefinitely if we were willing to pay the price."

Harmon Thomas's florid complexion had been growing progressively redder. His fleshy neck seemed to have overflowed his collar. His normally sleepy eyes were smoldering. His rumbling voice had a reedy quality. "Mr. President," he burst out, "we know the price of appeasement. We've been paying it for a hundred and twenty years. It's too high."

An incongruous flicker of amusement twitched the corner of Gordon James Lander's lips. He turned his calm brown eyes on his apoplectic Secretary of Defense.

"We'll never be in a stronger position than we are now," Thomas said heatedly. "If we sell Mexico down the river, Spearman will make a sanctuary out of it. He'll roll right on down to the Canal. We'd have to stop him there, but it would be too late.

"Mr. President, if we don't live up to our commitments when our own vital interests are at stake, who in Christ's name is ever going to trust us again? We've got to hit them now. The treaty be damned."

He hunched tensely forward on the couch, his pipe clutched in a tight fist. Slowly the color receded from his face. He leaned back and glared from under shaggy brows at the President, then at the Secretary of State. The room was silent.

"You can see no other way out?" The President's voice was neutral. "You think an ultimatum to stop arming would have any effect?"

"Not a damned bit. Spearman has gone too far down the runway. He's either got to take off or crack up. He hasn't got any more choice than we have."

The President looked slowly around at the three grim faces. His eyes stopped on Donald Barringer. "Mr. Secretary?"

Still wearing his diplomatic poker face, Barringer folded his hand and tossed it in. "I'm afraid it may well be that we have reached that stage," he said. "We still have six months' leeway before the treaty has to be implemented. I think we must use as much of that time as we can to seek another solution. But I am not optimistic about finding one."

"Lawrence?"

Tazewell drew his ungainly figure to attention. "Certainly we must be prepared to accept the Secretary's recommendation as a last resort. I would, however, like your permission to pursue the course I outlined to you."

"Do you have any real hope it would divert the attack on us?"

Tazewell hesitated. When he answered, his voice lacked its customary assurance. "No. I'm afraid I don't. But at least it would soften them up a bit. The situation being as it is, it can't do any harm."

"It could give Spearman the pretext he needs. If we force a showdown with the South, we are going to have to justify ourselves in the eyes of the world. We cannot afford to weaken our case."

Lander pushed himself up from his chair and paced to the far end of the room, hands clasped behind his back. As he turned and started back, Barringer noted irrelevantly that the spring was still in his step. Not so pronounced, perhaps, but still there.

He halted in front of them and peered gravely through his unobtrusive spectacles. "Let me put one question to you. Although it entails a subjective judgment, I would ask you to consider it as objectively as you can.

"If Howie Ray Spearman were not President of the Confederacy, do you think the differences between our two countries could be settled peacefully?"

The Secretary of State responded instantly. "Mr. President, that's the most maddening aspect of the whole situation. We have no quarrel with the Confederacy, and they have no real quarrel with us. The grievances of a hundred years ago are dead and buried. Economically we would both be better off if we knocked down all the barriers. Most important, we come from the same stock. We have a common heritage, common culture and basically, I feel, the same goals. It's ridiculous that we should be at each other's throats."

"Do you believe, though," the President persisted, "that Spearman is the only obstacle to peace between us?"

"Not the only obstacle, of course. But he is responsible in large measure for the other obstacles. With him out of the way, I'm sure we could iron out our differences. We've had conflicts with the Confederacy off and on through the years, but they've never reached this point before. And there's no reason why they should now. We've offered Spearman free transit to the Pacific. But that isn't really what he wants. He wants a showdown."

"Why?"

Barringer weighed the question. Heedlessly, he sliced through all the carefully accumulated layers of diplomatic euphemism and equivocation. "Because he's an egomaniac."

"No question about it," Thomas growled. "Without Spearman egging 'em on, the military wouldn't think of attacking us. They know it's suicidal. They couldn't do it, even if they wanted to. You can't drive a country to war. You've got to lead 'em.

"I agree with Donald. He's insane. If he wasn't, he would never have been able to get the grip on those people that he has. Reasonable people can understand a reasonable man. And they'll only go along with him as long as he acts reasonably. But a loony doesn't act according to any rational pattern. Sensible people follow him only because they figure he knows something they don't.

"We've got more than our share of egomaniacs here in Washington, and maybe that's what saves us. They understand each other. Each of them knows that he's the real Messiah, so they aren't going to be taken in by the other phonies.

"To answer your question: yes. Get rid of Spearman and you get rid of your problem."

The President looked at Tazewell.

"I would agree," the CIA Director said, "that if you eliminate Spearman you eliminate the immediate threat. We have no assurance, though, that another Spearman won't arise. The only way to guard against that is to eliminate the totalitarian system. It can be done, I believe, if—"

The President cut him off. "Right now we are concerned with the immediate threat. Do you think the people now in power would carry out the planned attack on us if Spearman were removed from office?"

"Nnnno, I don't." The unqualified answer obviously was painful. "He's the only one who could drag them into it. Of course," he added, "it would be better to get rid of his whole gang."

President Lander's eyes searched the faces of his lieutenants. What he saw was, in a way, comforting but not reassuring: competence, resolution, fidelity—and, underneath, a hint of sympathy, each man secretly relieved that the decision was not his to make.

The President thrust his hands into his pockets, walked briskly to his chair and sat down. He crossed his legs and stared pensively at the low ceiling. For half a minute he said nothing. When he spoke his voice was calm but decisive.

"It would appear," he said, "the choice lies between one life or fifty million. It is clear we must dispose of President Spearman."

The President bowed his head for a moment. A muscle in his jaw twitched. When he looked up, his face was composed but his eyes were troubled. He leaned forward, hands folded on one knee.

"I realize what I am suggesting violates every standard of

international conduct and civilized behavior. It is more abhorrent to murder a man in cold blood than it is to kill a million men on the battlefield.

"I am not going to ask your advice. This is a decision which I must make myself, and I don't want to make you a party to it. I need not tell you how repugnant it is to me. In my years in public office I have always believed—perhaps because I wanted to believe it—that there could be no basic conflict between a man's conscience and his public duty. I'm afraid I was wrong. I can see now there must have been numerous instances throughout history when a man had to make a choice.

"I suppose," he added, "Abraham Lincoln had to make such a choice in 1861. He followed his conscience and so today I have the same choice to make. I'm not going to pass it on to another President."

Harmon Thomas's lips drew back from his square teeth in an animal snarl. "God damn Abraham Lincoln," he exploded. "If he'd had the guts of a goat, he'd have settled this thing once and for all."

The President looked at him gratefully. "I suppose he thought he was doing the right thing. God help me. I hope I am."

Chapter Three

President Lander leaned back in his chair, hands dangling loosely. His incisive tone contrasted with his relaxed manner. "I am fully aware, of course, that the odds are always heavily against any assassination's being carried out successfully. They are even greater in the present case. Nevertheless, I feel we are compelled to make the attempt. You will continue your own efforts and preparations on the assumption that the attempt will fail. Meanwhile, I have—"

"Mr. President," Tazewell broke in. "If I might, I would like to . . . As you know, it's our business in the Agency to try to anticipate all contingencies. . . . As a matter of fact we . . . uh . . . have explored the possibilities of eliminating President Spearman." A note of self-congratulation crept into his voice. "Strictly on a hypothetical basis, of course."

His professorial manner reasserted itself. "While we would be confronted with some formidable obstacles in an operation of this type, we do not regard them as insurmountable. We have drawn up, in some detail, several alternative approaches, which I feel—"

The President raised a restraining hand. "Just a minute, Lawrence." His voice held a hint of apology but also one of impatience. "I realize that this sort of thing would normally fall in your sphere. However, you can appreciate that it would be . . . unthinkable for this government to be involved in a plot to assassinate the chief of state of another country."

Tazewell stared at him in open bewilderment. "I assure you we would—"

"No, Lawrence, I don't question your ability to do the job. But it is simply inconceivable that a large-scale conspiracy could remain undiscovered—after the fact if not before. Even if it were not conclusive, there would certainly be enough circumstantial evidence to convict us in the eyes of the world." He shook his head. "For the most powerful nation in the world to stoop to the murder of one man would be even more heinous than to. overthrow his government. There, at least, we could show some justification. But you can't justify assassination. And I don't intend to try."

Barringer and Thomas looked questioningly at the President. Tazewell continued to gape at him. "Maybe I misunderstood you, but I thought—"

"Excuse me," the President said. "I didn't mean to be cryptic. We have two problems here. One: Spearman must be eliminated. Two: we must have nothing to do with it. The second is as important as the first. If we are linked with the assassination, however tenuously, Spearman's henchmen would be forced to avenge him, whether they wanted to or not. We would precipitate the very thing we're trying to avert."

The creases on Tazewell's freckled scalp smoothed. His voice regained its assurance. "Mr. President, we have given very careful attention to that aspect of the operation. We had concluded that the deed itself should be carried out by citizens of the Confederacy. We will have no difficulty in recruiting and organizing such a group. Men who will be willing to sacrifice their lives if necessary. In fact, the nucleus already exists among several factions. I promise you it will appear to be— and in fact will be—strictly an internal conspiracy."

"No doubt that would be the logical approach, Lawrence," the President said patiently. "I wish you would continue to develop a specific plan along those lines. We may have to resort to it. But it seems to me there are two objections to the classic conspiracy method. In the first place, it rarely succeeds. There are too many things that can go wrong. In the second place, once a conspiracy is exposed, it is virtually impossible to conceal its origins. I have no doubt," he added grimly, "Spearman's Seepees would be very efficient at that."

He glanced at Barringer and Thomas, including them in his dissertation. "I suppose every President has a somewhat more than casual interest in assassination. I confess," he said dryly, "that I find the subject rather fascinating and I have done a good deal of reading on it. In fact, I consider myself a bit of an authority.

"If you study the history of assassination, one singular thing stands out. The more elaborate the plot, the less likely it is to succeed. Practically all the successful assassination attempts in this century have been carried out by one man, acting alone and, to a large extent, without any carefully thought-out plan. It strikes me that that may be the essence of the thing."

"Theoretically, you may be right, Mr. President," Thomas said. "But you're relying primarily on chance—on opportunity. With all we've got at stake, we certainly couldn't afford that."

"Of course not," the President agreed. He stood up and walked to the silver walnut table in the center of the room. "We naturally would try to eliminate as many variables as possible—without compromising the element of flexibility."

He hesitated, running one hand over the smooth surface of the table. "The whole idea may be . . . impractical, indeed irrational. Yet you can't ignore the fact that every successful attempt of this nature *has* been irrational. The question is whether you can harness irrationality.

"I have discussed this subject with Dr. Corfmann, our director of psychological analysis in the Department of Health, Education and Welfare. On the pretext that we are trying to strengthen our own precautions, I have asked him to do an analysis of the ingredients involved in a successful assassination. Also the psychological characteristics of an assassin. Maybe his research could help us decide whether it would be worthwhile to pursue the course I have suggested."

He reached under the table and pressed a silent buzzer. Almost immediately the door through which he had entered slid open and the Secret Service man stepped through.

"Will you bring Dr. Corfmann in, Jerry."

The Secret Service man nodded, disappeared through the opening and the door clicked shut.

"I don't think it would serve any purpose at this stage to tell Dr. Corfmann what we are contemplating," the President said. "If we decide to proceed with it, we probably will need his services."

He strolled back to the circle of chairs and couches but remained standing. The concealed door slid open again, and the Secret Service man escorted Dr. Corfmann into the room. He was medium-tall, skeletally thin, swarthy-faced, with a prominent, narrow-ridged nose. Behind thick-lensed spectacles, his dark eyes were sharply focused. His sparse, black hair lay in limp horizontal strips across his sloping skull. The fingers of his right hand were curled loosely over the handle of a battered brown briefcase.

He glanced cursorily around the room, the preoccupied look of a man indifferent to his surroundings. The President advanced toward him and thrust out his hand. Simultaneously the psychologist essayed an awkward bow from the waist, leaving the President standing empty-handed. He straightened up with a jerk, fumblingly transferred the briefcase to his left hand and finally effected the handclasp. The President chuckled. Dr. Corfmann, with a quick, embarrassed smile, nodded to the others.

"Sorry to have kept you waiting, Dr. Corfmann," the President said, guiding him across the room. "Momentous affairs of state. You know Mr. Barringer, Mr. Thomas, Mr. Tazewell."

They rose and shook hands. Dr. Corfmann bobbed his head to each of them, his eyes not meeting theirs. Lander motioned the newcomer to a chair and resumed his seat.

"As you know, Dr. Corfmann, there have been a number of assassination attempts in scattered areas of the world in the past nine or ten months. It appears that these things run in cycles. We had a rash of them in this country in the mid-sixties. I realize it is impossible to anticipate the actions of a maniac. Still there must be a pattern of sorts. It has been suggested that if we could establish some kind of a common denominator, we might at least set up some safeguards. We are not so much interested in the mechanics of assassination. The Secret Service is well equipped to handle those aspects. What we want to know is what are the personality traits of an assassin? What motivates him?"

The slightly dazed expression on Dr. Corfmann's face abruptly vanished. He was transported back into his element. Deftly he unfastened the briefcase and withdrew a sheaf of papers.

"As you know, Mr. President, I had done a good deal of research in this field before you asked me to draw up this report. It is a fascinating subject, about which there are many misconceptions." His voice bore a barely discernible trace of middle European accent. His obvious enthusiasm overrode his natural diffidence, imparting an odd, stuttering cadence to his words.

"You spoke of maniacs. All the assassins I am acquainted with"—his tone implied he had known them personally— "were perhaps psychopathic to a degree. Maniacs they were not. It would be most difficult, if not impossible, for a real maniac to carry out an assassination."

He shook his head reprovingly at the President.

The President smiled. "I beg your pardon," he said. "I am not too familiar with the terms of your profession."

"So," the psychologist went on, "it is not so simple that you round up all the crazy people and put them in asylums. You will excuse me. In the course of history there are many sane people who would have wished a President dead—is it not? But it is not easy. Only three times it has happened. Garfield, McKinley and Kennedy. Each time they say the assassin is demented. Could be. But that is not why he succeeded. He succeeded because he did it the only way it could be done. He did not make elaborate plans so they can fall apart. He did not tell anyone so they can inform on him. He did it himself, in the most direct way, when the opportunity presented. Perhaps it takes an irrational person to behave so rationally."

"But of course," Tazewell interjected condescendingly, "they were all caught. They disregarded the consequences, which is evidence of insanity in itself."

"Maybe so, maybe not. I am convinced they wanted to be caught. They did not disregard the consequences; they invited them. Many murderers are not caught. So we do not say they were insane."

"Aside from the question of insanity," Harmon Thomas inquired, "is there any way of telling whether a man has the capacity to kill? That is, of course, one of the unpredictable qualities of a soldier. Some people, it seems, just can't bring themselves to do it. They don't contribute much in a war," he added dryly.

"You cannot know for sure that a man will kill until he has killed," Dr. Corfmann replied. "Once he has done it, he is more likely to do it again. Like anything else. But yes, Mr. Thomas, there are certain criteria by which we can calculate the probability of a man committing murder.

"And also, Mr. President, it would be possible to compile a catalogue of the most likely assassins in the United States. We now have, of course, fairly definitive psychological evaluations of all the people who have taken the Psych-Qual examination. It was intended primarily to determine their employment aptitude, but it gives a remarkably accurate insight into their basic personalities. Any marked departure from the norm in the areas with which we are concerned would not be difficult to detect."

"To get down to specifics, Dr. Corfmann," the President said, "would there be certain, well-defined characteristics that might identify a potential assassin?"

"To a certain extent, yes. He would, in all likelihood, manifest some antisocial tendencies. That is to say, he probably would not be a pronounced extrovert. He might be of a rather volatile temperament, subject to fits of passion. On the other hand he would have to be a person of tenacity—stubborn—who would have the persistence to carry out his purpose. Unquestionably there would be an element of mental instability, but it would not necessarily be reflected in his intelligence level. In fact, the more intelligent he was, the better chance he would have of accomplishing his end. As you know, some of the most brilliant intellects are subject to aberrations that make them incompatible with our society. These qualities it would not be difficult to identify. But they are not uncommon and they would not be incriminating in themselves.

"The intangible factor would be his motivation. To evaluate that, we would have to study his environment, his background, his philosophy, his achievements, his failures. Unless they are simple fanatics or constitutional psychopaths, most assassins —indeed, most murderers—have a grudge against society which they focus on an individual. In a sense it is an extreme form of envy. Everyone probably feels it to some degree. Normally we repress such sentiments because there is not much to be gained by satisfying them. To the assassin, though, expressing them may be worthwhile if it will bring him the recognition he craves."

Oblivious of his audience, Dr. Corfmann bent his scrawny neck and thumbed through his papers, which were typed in outline form as though for a lecture. He paused and placed his finger under one subheading. He raised his head and peered through his thick glasses.

"One category I have passed over. The hired killer. It would be very difficult to spot him because he would be atypical. Also, he would be part of a conspiracy, which I consider to be outside my area of competence. Also, there have been, throughout history, many political assassinations which were inspired by ambition, patriotism, greed or hatred. These you cannot categorize because they are objectively motivated."

Donald Barringer was surprised to discover he had become engrossed in the doctor's dissertation. "What would you say," he asked tentatively, "is the decisive factor in triggering an assassination? Behind every positive action there is usually one consideration that tips the balance. Is it the mental aberration? The craving for recognition? What?"

The psychologist regarded him reflectively as he would a

mathematical formula on a blackboard. "I would say the indispensable ingredient is resolution. That is frequently a compound of the other factors—motivation, basic personality, the mental state of the subject at the time. One universal characteristic of assassins is despair. Usually induced by personal failure. They are so consumed by a sense of their own inadequacy, they seek to compensate by destroying an obvious symbol of success. It is a form of suicidal sublimation. But unless they reach the point of resolution, they never carry it out."

"Is it," Barringer probed, "an impulsive or a deliberate decision?"

"Neither," Dr. Corfmann replied without hesitation. "Or rather a little of each. A completely unpremeditated assassination never comes off successfully. One that has been carefully planned over a long period of time rarely comes off at all. 'The native hue of resolution is sicklied o'er with the pale cast of thought.' Usually the assassin has a vague idea of what he intends to do. If the opportunity doesn't arise, he doesn't do anything."

"But," Tazewell pointed out, "an assassin needs more than some vague intent. He needs some preparation and skill to carry it out."

"Not necessarily," Dr. Corfmann corrected him. "Leon Czolgosz just 'went to Buffalo to do something.' He 'didn't know what.' He bought a gun three days before he shot McKinley. He didn't know how to use it. He wrapped it up in a bandage and wandered into a reception and killed a President. During World War II top members of the German General Staff, with all the know-how and deadly weapons at their command, spent two years plotting to assassinate Hitler and they never did pull it off."

The President had been listening silently but intently to

the discussion. "Are you saying, then, Dr. Corfmann, that a more or less extemporaneous approach is more likely to succeed than a well-conceived plot?"

"No, sir." The doctor's tone was deferential but authoritative. "I would say that, given the same motivation, a trained and determined killer would have a better chance of succeeding than an ignorant amateur. But it is unlikely he would be as strongly motivated."

"And if he was genuinely concerned with escaping, his chances of accomplishing his purpose would be greatly diminished?"

"Infinitely. Not only would it double the likelihood of something going wrong, it would restrict his flexibility and freedom of action. It would deprive him of his one big advantage—the ability to seize an unexpected opportunity. Besides, he wouldn't have the singleness of purpose which I would consider almost indispensable to such an undertaking. So you see, Mr. President, you would be in not too much danger from such a person." He essayed a tight, reassuring smile.

The President gazed at him reflectively for a long moment, then flicked a glance at the other three. Dr. Corfmann sensed the tension. His poise crumbled. He peered nervously at the President, fearful he had said something wrong.

"Dr. Corfmann," the President said, "I think we will need your help. I must ask your solemn promise that you will not divulge this to anyone. . . ."

Part Two

Chapter Four

Cordell Vance tilted his glass and forced a swallow more than he wanted. He gazed into the fire and waited as the whisky began to dissolve the sodden lump of despair in his chest.

The woman's remote, husky monotone blended into the flickering yellow flames; her words skipped along the smoldering log and drifted up the chimney with the wisps of gray-blue smoke.

"It wasn't really unbearable. . . . There wasn't any big dramatic crisis. . . . I suppose the thing that bothered me most was that we just gradually grew to dislike each other. . . ."

Vance turned his head and looked at Jo-Anne Christopher-son. A strand of auburn hair dangled across her cheek. She was half-reclining on the studio couch, her head tilted back, her legs loosely parted. Her eyes were half-closed, distantly focused on a dimly lit corridor of her past. Vance felt a ripple of desire; he leaned back in his chair, savoring it and nurturing it.

"I imagine it's always kind of traumatic the first few months. You're never sure you've done the right thing. You either sit and brood or you go out and do things you're . . . not proud of."

He sorted out her words mechanically, arranged them on the slide, and peered at them through his decodifier. Confession is a form of mental housecleaning. Women have to vacuum the rug before a party so it will be clean before it gets dirty again.

Oh, for Chrissake, he snarled at himself. You have to pick it to pieces?

Abruptly he stood up and strode across the room. Jo-Anne Christopherson's monologue ended in mid-sentence. Her eyes widened in astonishment as he hurled himself on her. Her body tensed reflexively, but after the initial shock she relaxed. She did not respond overtly, but her breathing deepened.

He broke away and sat looking down at her. A smile tugged at her lips.

"I was beginning to wonder about you," she said. "Whether you were a gentleman or a queer."

He hadn't thought about it that way, but he supposed maybe they all did. It was an unplanned technique he had adopted in the years since his ardor had begun to cool. It had some drawbacks, but by and large it served his purpose.

He disliked the mating dance—the ritualistic sparring that women seemed to regard as absolution for the surrender of their virtue. He had evolved a hands-off approach, refraining from any overtures whatsoever until the moment of decision came. The moratorium eliminated the boring preliminaries and at the same time provided a decent interval for the woman to assuage her conscience. It also gave him a psychological edge, he suspected, though that was not a major consideration. He had been out with Jo-Anne Christopherson three times and had not laid a finger on her.

He kissed her again with conviction. She responded less than passionately, but more than passively. He was pleased. He regarded an exaggerated show of wantonness as unfavorably as an excess of modesty. He placed his hand on her breast and squeezed it gently. She squirmed, but did not move to displace it.

He raised his head and said, "You are changing your opinion of me, I hope."

She gave a low, throaty giggle and nodded her head.

"But you can't take my word for it," he said. "I'm no gentleman."

"I'm not taking your word for it. I'm convinced."

"You shouldn't be so easily convinced. You're too trusting. People will take advantage of you."

"I wouldn't be surprised," she said.

He put his hand on her shoulder and toppled her over on the couch. She lay curled around him, her legs still dangling over the side. He sat up, inspecting her features. She returned his appraisal.

She saw a well-formed head framing a lean, angular face and topped by wiry black hair flecked with gray; a sharply defined oblong forehead; thin lips set in a hard, straight line, bracketed by thinner lines slicing through taut-stretched cheeks; a narrow, slightly crooked nose; olive-dark skin; close-set ears; a muscular neck supporting an incongruously rounded jaw that contrasted with the stern symmetry of his other features. Deliberately she evaded his eyes. She was building a mood of tenderness. She knew she would see in them a fierce, bitter glint that lurked there even in his rare moments of merriment. As he bent to kiss her, he slid his hand under her form-clinging sweater and burrowed his fingers under her brassiere. He could feel her heartbeat beneath his palm.

With his lips still brushing hers, he said, "You seem to have a little fibrillation there. You should avoid any undue excitement."

"Whatever you say, Doctor," she murmured, pulling his mouth down on hers.

When she released him, her brassiere had been unhooked and his hand had taken full possession of her breast.

"That's pretty slick," she said. "You must have had quite a bit of practice."

"Something I learned in the Boy Scouts," he said, "while the rest of 'em were tying knots."

He moved his hand down past her navel and deftly unfastened the snaps on her green plaid wool skirt. He reached for the zipper on the side. She arched her back and he slipped the skirt down over her stocking feet.

She watched him with amusement as he surveyed the panty girdle, tight-stretched over her rounded hips. "Now for the real challenge," she said. "Let's see you get me out of that alive."

He stood up and began to unbutton his heavy wool shirt. "It's time you showed some evidence of good faith," he said. "So far I've done all the work."

"What's worth doing is worth doing well."

"I don't know yet whether it's worth doing."

"Hoo-boy," she snorted, swinging herself upright. She snatched up her skirt and stalked toward the bathroom with as much queenly dignity as a woman in her stocking feet could muster. She closed the door firmly behind her.

Vance stripped to his shorts, mixed two drinks and stirred up the fire. He threw back the spread and slipped in between the sheets. He felt no tingling sense of anticipation, but the ever-present cloud of oppression had lifted. His mind was a placid void—which was as close to happiness as Cordell Vance had come in the past two years.

He was sipping his drink as the bathroom door opened and the light clicked off. Jo-Anne Christopherson padded into the room, silhouetted by the shimmering light of the fire. She was stark-naked. She walked unself-consciously across the room and settled herself beside him. He wrapped his arms around her and thrust his chest against her breasts.

She slipped an arm under his waist and fitted her body against his. She drew back as she brushed against his shorts.

"You decided it was maybe not worth doing?"

He chuckled and pulled them off. He strained her to him. A pleasurable excitement broke through the crust of desolation.

Jo-Anne uttered a soft grunt of satisfaction and gave him a quick, triumphant squeeze. "Ah," she said. "I finally have your attention."

"That you do," he said hoarsely.

They lay side by side on the Acratuft rug in front of the fire, heads propped on separate pillows from the couch. Cordell Vance watched the play of the firelight on the rough-hewn ceiling beam and sought to shroud his thoughts in the dancing shadows. Jo-Anne took a sip of her drink, hunched up to a semisitting position and said lightly, "Time for the question-and-answer period. I've told you my gripping life story. All I know about you is you're not a gentleman . . . or a queer. I wouldn't even know what to tell the newspapers if they called me for your obituary. Like where were you born?"

"I was born in an oak tree, at night, on top of a mountain."

"Really, Cord. I'd like to know something about you."

Christ, he thought, why can't they let it lie? "White, male, thirty-six," he recited tonelessly. "Six feet one, one hundred and ninety pounds, medium build, scars on upper legs and torso. No previous record. This man may be dangerous."

Jo-Anne gulped the rest of her drink and rose lithely to her feet, brushing her skirt. "I'd better go."

"Don't." Vance was surprised and annoyed at the note of appeal in his voice.

She stood, looking down at him. "Why not? We're not getting anywhere."

"Where do you want to go?"

"Home."

He struggled with the words and finally forced them out. "Stay a while. I need you."

"You don't need anybody," she said.

He reached up and grasped her hand. "I like you very much."

"No, you don't. You don't like anybody very much."

"At least I don't *dislike* anybody very much."

"Don't you?"

"No."

"How about yourself?"

"Ah, well. That's what happens when you get to know someone too well."

"So you're not going to take a chance with anybody else."

The statement irritated him; not because it was true, but because she did not recognize that it was valid. He let go of her hand and rose to his feet.

"Women are always looking for lost souls to rescue from the wilderness," he said. "They don't realize that some souls prefer the wilderness."

"Do you really think so?"

"No, I suppose not."

"How did you get lost?" she asked bluntly.

"If I knew, I'd probably go back and take another route."

"Why don't you go on from here?"

"From here," he said grimly, "there's nowhere to go."

She reached out for his hand. He looked at her dourly. "One thing I don't need is pity."

"I know it," she said quickly. "It's just that . . . I like you very much."

"All right," he said roughly. "That makes us even. Let's leave it that way."

She walked toward the bathroom, then turned and said with studied casualness, "Have you ever been married?"

The remark focused his annoyance—at her for prying into his feelings, at himself for exposing them. It was the old female nostrum—the solution to all hang-ups, the key to all psychoses, the cure for all afflictions of the human spirit: the unselfish love of a good woman.

"No," he said cuttingly. "And if I had, I wouldn't be a damned bit different than I am now."

Jo-Anne ignored the tone. "I think everything has something to do with what we are," she said simply.

In the cold, dark depths of his eyes, she glimpsed a flicker of warmth.

"You know," he said, "for a woman with such a shapely behind, you've got a pretty good head on you."

The frigid air knifed into their lungs as they stepped out onto the flagstoned porch. The small cabin stood on an outcropping of rock, halfway up the mountain. Across the narrow graveled road, the tree-studded slope dropped off at a sixty-degree declivity. Far below and off in the distance, a sparse cluster of lights marked the winter boundaries of the Settlement. In the summer it spread over half the valley.

Beyond the village, an irregular ring of squat, glowering foothills kept sullen watch over the snow-blanketed plain. Behind them, an ashen quarter-moon silhouetted the majestic towering peaks of the front range.

Jo-Anne moved to the low stone parapet guarding the porch. "How can you stand to live up here alone?"

"How can you stand to live in Denver with all those people?"

"You get used to them. You don't even notice them. Nobody but a hermit could get used to this."

"That's me. Cordell Vance, P.H.—professional hermit." He

stepped up behind her and wrapped his arms around her, nuzzling her hair with his nose.

"Some hermit."

"Even a hermit has to take a night off now and then."

"Why here? You told me you had never lived around real mountains before. You don't seem to have any great affection for them."

"It's about as far as you can get from a rice paddy." He turned abruptly and started toward his car.

When they reached the bottom of the icy, twisting road down the mountain, Jo-Anne Christopherson pressed the button to lower the window. Although it was rimed on the outside with frost, she was sweating. Not since the nameless fears of childhood had she known real terror. But she had been terrified coming down the mountain. Cordell Vance had driven with skilled, suicidal calculation; skidding around horseshoe curves, the rear wheel digging for traction an inch from the abyss, grazing the jagged edge of the rocks on her side, then swinging wide to slice through a sharp-angled turn. He was engaged in a life-or-death contest with the mountain—or with himself.

As they leveled out on the valley floor, he reduced his speed to a sedate pace, not looking at her to see if she was shaken. They chatted desultorily. She told him an amusing story about her recent trip to New York. She was head buyer for a department store, and she had an easy facility for shallow, sophisticated patter. Curiously, she reflected, she had not indulged it with Cordell before. He listened with seeming attention, occasionally interjecting an ironic comment. She had the feeling, though, that they had been closer when they were not talking.

The low-slung sports car suddenly emerged from the mouth

of a canyon onto an uneven plateau. Spread out before them were the myriad lights of Denver. Jo-Anne felt as though she had returned to earth from a distant planet. She turned to speak to Cordell Vance. He was scowling.

He pulled into the parking lot at her apartment, switched off the engine and draped his arm loosely around her shoulders. He pulled off his fur-lined mittens and reached for her gloved hand. They looked at each other, not speaking.

He drew her to him and kissed her passively. Suddenly she threw her arms around his neck and pressed her mouth fiercely against his. He reacted without surprise and without restraint. Finally, she pushed him away and reached for her bag.

"That was good-bye," she said.

He looked at her inquiringly.

"I don't think it would be good for me to go on seeing you," she said.

"How about me?"

"You can look after yourself."

"I would be sorry to lose you."

"To hell with your being sorry," she exploded. "I'm falling in love with you and I'm not going to let it happen. I don't see any future in it. My ex-husband was a pretty heavy drinker. I knew that when I married him, but I thought I could cope with it. At least I understood his problem. Yours I don't understand at all. I know I couldn't cope with it."

His lips tightened and the cold glint was back in his eyes. "I'm not looking for anybody to cope with my problems," he said. "Why can't a woman just be a woman? Why does she have to be a goddamn psychiatrist?"

They had said all there was to say. He walked her to the elevator and kissed her lightly on the lips. They parted strangers.

Chapter Five

Vance skidded to a halt, slammed the car into reverse and backed it into the inclined driveway beside the cabin. He opened the door and took a deep breath of arctic air. The temperature, he calculated, must be at least twenty below. The car probably wouldn't start in the morning, but somewhere down the mountain it would. If he was still here next summer, he might build a garage. If he was still here.

He entered through the back door—which he never bothered to lock—and switched on the kitchen light. He paused in front of the refrigerator, discarded the idea and walked on through the arched doorway into the living room.

As he did so, his conditioned instinct for danger sounded an alarm. Too late. A massive arm locked around his neck and jerked his head back, lifting him off the floor. He hung there, unresisting, his eyes irrelevantly fixed on the flickering firelight reflected on the ceiling. After the first moment of panic, his mind detached itself from his helpless body and paralyzed nerves. He found himself probing his reaction rather than his peril.

He was back in the fetid blackness of an Asian swamp. The mortar flashes lit up the tangled bushes like the firelight marching across the ceiling beam. He felt the clutching fear, heard the uncoordinated chatter of automatic weapons, smelled the stench of death. With an odd sense of relief, he tensed his muscles to grapple with a flesh-and-bone enemy.

The pounding in his ears and the hazy outlines of the ceiling beam warned him he was on the verge of blacking out. His shoulders sagged. Deliberately he shifted his weight from the balls of his feet to the steely clamp around his neck. The pressure on his throat eased a trifle. The throbbing in his ears subsided to the point where he could make out the heavy, measured breathing of his assailant. The breathing was overridden by a thick drawl: "Jess you stan' quiet an' nobody get hurt."

Peering down out of the corner of his eye, he glimpsed a sinewy black wrist, confirming the testimony of the voice.

He took three or four slow deep breaths. His toes were on the floor, but his knees were bent, still hanging his weight on the encircling arm. He inched his right heel over to locate his attacker's toe. As they touched, he lifted his foot and lashed it into his assailant's shin, regretting that he was not wearing combat boots.

The maneuver fetched a grunt from behind his ear and a fist like an iron ball clubbing into his kidney. The blow nearly paralyzed him. But it also spun him half around, loosening the stranglehold on his neck.

He drove an elbow into a rock-hard belly. Following through with his shoulders, he tore himself free and staggered toward the center of the room. Crouching, he whirled to face his antagonist.

The hulking Negro appeared to block the whole archway. A torn sheepskin coat hung loosely from muscular, sloping shoulders. Tight khaki pants accentuated the slender hips and bulging thighs. Dark brown skin stretched taut over high cheekbones. He glowered at Vance but made no move toward him.

"Ah tol' you not to make no trouble," he said. "Now ah got to kill you."

He rocked once on his heels and sprang like a panther, covering the distance between them in one bound. Vance leaped sideways toward the fireplace and reached for the three-pronged poker. Before he could snatch it from its holder, iron fingers clamped around his wrist. The black vise twisted. Vance felt his bones starting to snap. Like a caged ferret, he whipped his whole body around. He threw all his weight behind his left shoulder and drove it into the Negro's mid-section.

His wrist wrenched free; the poker sailed through the air; the Negro nearly toppled into the fire. He flung out his hand and grasped the mantel. Before he could recover, Vance dove through the doorway to his bedroom. He yanked out a drawer in his nightstand and snatched up the snub-nosed automatic pistol he had taken from the body of a Chinese guerrilla.

He stumbled back into the living room, gun clutched in his left hand, safety off, finger on the trigger. The Negro was moving toward the outside door, but with no frantic haste.

"Right there," Vance gasped. "Right where you are." He gulped a breath of air. His right calf was trembling. His body felt drained. He motioned the intruder away from the door with the gun. The Negro stood where he was and glared at him through half-closed eyes.

"Over there. Hands on the mantel," Vance commanded, his voice at last under control.

"I goin' out that door."

"You'll go out that door dead."

"You lemme go. I won' cause you no mo' trouble."

"Move away from that door."

"I ain' goin' jail." The Negro took a tentative step toward the door. "You wouldn' shoot an unarmed man."

"See if I would. And I don't shoot too straight with my left hand, so I'm not going for your leg either."

The Negro stared at him dully. Vance stared back at him. He had no idea what he intended to do. He had considered—and discarded—calling the sheriff. Too many questions. Too many papers to sign. Reporters, photographers. Eventually he probably would turn the man loose, but he was not going to let him escape. In man-to-man combat you didn't settle for a draw.

"I said move," he barked.

The Negro moved. In three quick strides he was at the door, reaching for the latch. Without thought or hesitation, Vance pulled the trigger. The hammer clicked on an empty chamber. Three more times the gun clicked before the Negro vanished into the night.

Vance unlocked his elbow and looked stonily at the weapon. "You son-of-a-bitch!"

A heavy, unguarded tread on the flagstone porch realerted Vance's nerves. He tensed in his chair, eyes riveted on the door. Three quick, light raps sounded on the panel. He plucked the impotent automatic from his lap and slid it under the cushion. He was rising from the chair as the door swung open and the big Negro stepped over the threshold. Frozen in a half-crouch, Vance gaped at him for a fraction of a second. Then he dove for the poker, still lying on the rug at the far end of the room. He seized it in his good left hand and turned to face his persistent tormentor.

The Negro grinned. "You won't need that," he said softly. All traces of the cotton-field dialect had disappeared. "Let me introduce myself."

"By God, you've already introduced yourself." Vance held the poker at the ready.

The Negro closed the door behind him and moved a couple of paces into the room. "Could we sit down?" he said. "I've had a pretty strenuous evening."

The situation began to seem almost absurd to Vance. He advanced a step, still clenching the poker. "Who are you?"

Deliberately, the Negro unbuttoned the pocket of his soiled green corduroy shirt and extracted a single card. He moved forward and extended it at arm's length. "My name is Robert Dorsey."

Vance took it clumsily between the numbed fingers of his right hand. Stamped over an engraving of the Great Seal was the terse inscription: "Robert Dorsey. Special Envoy. United States Government." Handwritten in purple ink in the lower left corner were the initials "GJL."

Vance passed the card back to him without comment. Dorsey replaced it in his pocket and buttoned the flap. He offered no further explanation. Abruptly, Vance lowered the poker, strode to the fireplace and hooked it on its stanchion.

He sank into a wing-backed chair and motioned Dorsey to its twin opposite. Dorsey shucked off the tattered sheepskin and dropped it on the floor. He sat down wearily and leaned back, his enormous arms dangling over the side rests.

"I suppose," Vance said, "I'm expected to ask, 'What's this all about?'"

Dorsey nodded. "That would be a logical question. It may take a while to answer. I wonder if it would be out of order to ask you for a drink."

"Not at all," Vance replied. "Forgive me for being such a poor host. What'll it be?"

He pulled himself up painfully from the chair. His neck was sore. His kidney ached. His shoulder throbbed. His right wrist was virtually paralyzed. His heel was bruised. He felt as though he had been run through by a hay bailer.

Robert Dorsey watched him limp stiffly to the bar. "You put up a pretty good scrap, White Man," he said judicially.

Vance did not answer. He returned with the drinks, handed one to Dorsey and took a long swallow from his before he sat down. Dorsey drank half of his in one swig and set it on the floor beside him.

"First of all, I want to apologize for my—boorish behavior. It was necessary. I had to find out a couple of things about you."

He hunched forward, elbows on knees, hands hanging loosely between his legs. He peered at Vance, studying his face.

"I wanted to see how you would react in an unexpected situation. Secondly—" his voice was deliberately casual—"I wanted to know if you could kill a man in cold blood."

Vance eyed him narrowly. "You damn well would have found out if that gun had gone off."

Dorsey's lips curled in a wraith of a smile. "I took the precaution of removing the cartridges. Just in case . . ."

"You could have saved yourself some trouble if you'd looked up my record," Vance said icily. "I've done some killing in my day. But I didn't kill Sid Rogenstein. He was my best friend. I've been over it ten times with the sheriff and the district attorney and I'm not going to answer any more questions. What the hell has the United States Government got to do with it anyway?"

"I know you didn't kill Sid Rogenstein, and the United States Government isn't interested in the kind of killing you've done," the Negro replied. "I know a good deal about you, Mr. Vance—in some ways more than you know about yourself. Let me say, if you hadn't reacted the way you did, you would simply have been the victim of a burglary and assault. You would never have seen me again."

"Maybe we ought to run through it again," Vance said, "now that I know my cue."

"You may wish we had," Dorsey said. He drained the remainder of his drink and squared his huge shoulders. "I have to ask you, Mr. Vance, to swear that you will never divulge what I am going to tell you, or reveal any knowledge of this conversation or even that it took place. Ever."

"Don't tell me any secrets. I don't want to hear them. And whatever your proposition is, the answer is no."

"All right. I'm not going to force you to do anything, and I won't tell you anything you don't want to listen to. I would like to mention just two things. This might be the most vital service any man ever performed for his country. And you have been picked as the man best qualified to do it."

"That's lovely. That's touching. Once before I was picked to perform a little job for my country. I wound up like Benedict Arnold."

"Chances are," Dorsey said, "you'd wind up worse this time. Dead as well as disgraced. If you *were* successful, you'd get no glory. And probably you'd be hunted the rest of your life."

"You're a hell of a salesman, Dorsey. You want another drink?"

"Make it water instead of soda. If you've got it."

For Christ's sake, Vance thought as he mixed the drinks, what kind of a sucker do they take me for? They think they can run me through one more time after what they did to me? He knew he should be enraged. But the situation was so ludicrous he laughed. The sound of his laughter startled him. He realized he hadn't laughed aloud in years.

He looked pensive when he returned with the drinks. It did

not escape the scrutiny of Dr. Robert Dorsey, chief of the Abnormal Psychology Section of the Institute of Behavioral Sciences.

Vance handed Dorsey his drink and sat back warily awaiting the recruiting spiel. He had been recruited before and he was for damned sure not going to be again. He didn't bother to marshal his defenses. He had had it with the U.S. of A.

Dorsey looked around at the rough-paneled walls and sparsely furnished room. "Cozy place," he said. "I imagine you're very happy here."

Vance circled the bait disinterestedly. "It's adequate."

"Ideal, I should think. For a man who likes to be alone."

Vance suddenly recalled the interlude with Jo-Anne. Dorsey must have been lurking outside, but there was no smirk in either his voice or his face.

"Let's see," Dorsey reflected, pulling at his drink. "You're thirty-six, I believe. That's a little young for a man to retire. But then you've led a pretty active life."

"Yeah."

Dorsey finished his drink and abruptly stood up. "Well, if you're not interested in my proposition, I'd better be shoving off. I want to apologize again for disturbing you. I'd appreciate it if you'd just forget all about it."

He stooped to pick up his torn jacket. Vance remained seated, holding his glass loosely in his lap. "One thing I am interested in. Why'd you pick me?"

Dorsey tugged the sheepskin over his bulging shoulders. Two inches of wrist extended below the sleeves. "That ties in with what we picked you for," he said. "I don't think we'd better go into it if you're just curious."

He moved toward the door. Vance realized that he was being used. But to be used at least implied usefulness. Hopelessly he reached for the mirage of hope.

"Look," he said testily to cover any hint of eagerness, "I don't suppose you came here just for the workout. If you've got something to say, I'm listening."

Dorsey turned and peered searchingly into Vance's shadowed face. "I will have to have your word of honor, Mr. Vance, that if you don't accept the assignment, you will forget I ever spoke to you."

"All right," Vance said, impressed by the gravity of the other's tone. "You have it. For what it's worth."

"I know what it's worth." Dorsey moved back toward the fire and removed his coat. "As I told you, I know a lot about you. But there are a few things I have to find out before I tell you what we want you to do."

Absently he picked up a log in one huge hand and deposited it on the fire. He eased himself into the chair and hitched it around so he was facing Vance directly.

"I know you came to this country from the Confederacy at the age of twelve. I know who your parents were and why you left there. I know the North American League looked after you when you were growing up. That you went to college for two years; you were a pretty good baseball player. You left school and joined the army in 1965. I know everything that happened to you there. Almost everything. There are a few points I would like to clear up. But more important, I want to know everything about you during those first twelve years."

"What the hell is this?" Vance snorted. "Third degree or psychoanalysis?"

"A little of both," Dorsey responded amiably. "Perhaps I should tell you, so you can be on guard, that I am a psychiatrist. Ah know you've had some experience with them folks," he drawled.

"Uh-huh," Vance grunted.

"Suppose you just start with your earliest recollections and tell me everything you can remember."

"You want the unhappy-childhood version or the happy one? I can oblige you either way."

"From my standpoint," Dorsey replied, "the unhappy one would probably be preferable. But let's just tell it like it was. You were an only child, I believe. You got along all right with your father?" he prompted.

Vance considered the question. Offhand, he supposed, the answer would be yes. If it would be correct to say that you got along all right with God. A God who spent five days a week battling against the avarice, moral infirmities and downright perversity of men, and who sat down every night at the dinner table to describe with gleeful relish and high indignation that day's skirmish with the forces of evil and ignorance. A God who romped with him as a child and talked with him as an equal. A high-spirited God, filled with right-eousness, passion, wrath, tenderness and, above all, a zest for life and combat . . .

Royston Vance was a lawyer with an abiding faith in the fallibility of man and a penchant for pointing it out. He was born in Baton Rouge, Louisiana, a relatively obscure member of the Southern aristocracy. He never considered moving else-where because he found ample scope for his avocation in his home town.

His favorite target, though not an exclusive one, was the local establishment, of which he was unapologetically a member. It was convenient to his purpose, inasmuch as it gave him the opportunity to pursue his courtroom battles on the Country Club veranda. He won few clear-cut victories in either arena. As an apostle of lost causes, he had an active, though not too lucrative practice.

He was constantly embroiled in battle with one or more elements of the financial hierarchy, as well as the two newspapers, the Chamber of Commerce, city and parish officials, the Daughters of the Confederacy and the gamut of outraged public opinion. Among his notable defeats were:

An attempt to block the Bayou Chemical Corporation from constructing a sixty-million-dollar sulfide-processing plant, utilizing the Mississippi as a sewage system.

An attack on the loyalty oath as a prerequisite to admission to any institution of higher learning, public or private.

A suit questioning the authority of the East Baton Rouge Parish Board of Zoning Adjustment to establish rigid boundaries for black residential areas.

A demand for impeachment—and failing that, commitment —of Governor Earl Long.

At home, he did not dwell on his victories or defeats. Frequently he did not bother to announce the verdict in his summary of a trial. It was not really necessary. If he had lost, he included the judge and jury in the scorn and maledictions he heaped on the heads of his adversaries. If he had won, he poured himself an extra measure of bourbon and branch as a tribute to the triumph of justice and the consternation of his enemies.

Despite his contentious ways, Royston Vance was generally regarded as a community asset—a sort of self-appointed public prosecutor. He was greatly cherished by his few close friends, widely admired by the dispossessed and warily respected by his adversaries. His wife, Cathy-June, bore her role of consort to an ordained gadfly with exasperated affection in private, with a sort of rueful pride in public. Though she did not share her husband's dedication to righting the wrongs of the world, she indulged his idiosyncrasy as she would have a weakness for gambling or golf. She even en-

joyed being cast in the role of a tame anarchist by her com-
patriots in the Junior Cotillion. As a manor-born aristocrat
she did not feel obliged to apologize for the unorthodox behavior of her husband. Occasionally she would parrot his
views with considerable fervor in bridge-table debates at the
Country Club, more to confirm her identity than to defend
his principles.

Cordell Vance absorbed without questioning both the avowed
radicalism of his father and the implicit conservatism of his
mother. Unconsciously, he assumed that his mission in life
would be to fight the forces of greed, injustice, entrenched
privilege and official arrogance without disturbing the status
quo. From his father he had acquired a genuine sympathy and
compassion for the downtrodden and the incompetent. From
his mother he had assimilated an awareness of the family's
social standing and intrinsic superiority to the common run
of people. He had not yet discerned any basic discrepancies
between the two concepts.

Although he had already imbibed the fundamental beliefs
of his disparate parents by his tenth birthday, he seemed to
have inherited few of their physical characteristics. He was
tall for his age, thin, delicate-featured and dark enough to
provoke comment whenever he was placed under scrutiny by
relatives. To be sure, his father was dark-complexioned, with
a thick, unruly mop of brownish hair, and his mother had a
small-boned fragility about her that gave her an aura of
gentility. But in him, feature by feature, nothing quite
matched.

Not so noticeable to outsiders was the difference between
his temperament and theirs. He displayed neither his father's
intense exuberance nor his mother's restrained vivacity.
Though pleasant and not unduly shy, even in the presence of
strangers, his normal manner was reserved, almost withdrawn.

In combination with his somber, deep-set eyes and swarthy color, this imparted a misleading impression of sullenness to his personality.

As an only child, he spent much of his time alone. But he was a full participant in his father's contests and his mother's confidences. His boyhood was infused with the feeling that life was filled with momentous enterprises and fascinating trivialities. He was developing into an exceptional athlete and was popular with his schoolmates. He was gifted with a quick intelligence and endowed with a stubborn tenacity that earned him good grades and marked him as "a young man of great promise." He loved his mother, worshiped his father and enjoyed himself.

One of the secondary targets of Royston Vance's wide-ranging antipathies during the early 1950's was the Party of National Resurgence; secondary, because he did not regard it so much a threat as he did a cesspool for bitterness and frustration—useful emotions which might be diverted into more constructive channels. Royston Vance, in most respects a pragmatic idealist, had one great delusion—that right and reason must eventually prevail, despite all the evidence to the contrary.

Founded by a small-time piny-woods politician, the Party of National Resurgence gradually accumulated a scruffy following of wool-hat demagogues, white-trash supremacists, Bible-pounding fundamentalists and a scattering of fleecy businessmen. It meandered across the Confederacy for nearly ten years, sprouting up mostly in red-clay soil and dingy tenement districts. In 1952 it nominated a candidate for President—a fire-breathing, Commie-hating, flag-waving superpatriot from Memphis, who polled a surprising 18 percent of the vote. More significant than the support it gained was the attention it attracted from a squint-eyed Texas oilman, who employed a regiment of geologists, engineers and technicians to locate likely strata, but who relied on divine guidance for the ultimate decision to drill.

In that year, D. J. Cawthorn had received the go-ahead from on high to consummate the purchase of a string of television and radio stations scattered throughout the Southwest and along the Gulf Coast. Other than the obvious tax advantages and apparent profit potential, he did not know what had impelled him to plunge into a business with which he was totally unfamiliar. Suddenly the inscrutable wisdom of the Lord was made manifest to him.

By the time the Party of National Resurgence came to power in 1956, it had undergone a complete metamorphosis, both internally and externally. So had Royston Vance. He was no longer tilting zestfully at windmills. He was fighting with deadly earnestness against the epidemic of insanity that had seized the Confederacy. The community, his friends, antagonists and erstwhile allies no longer looked upon him as a well-meaning crusader. By degrees he became an eccentric nuisance, a misguided zealot and, inevitably, a dangerous obstructionist.

At home, his slashing tirades against the blind stupidity of the voters took on a note of bitter frenzy. His fury against the regime expanded to include the entire populace. His practice withered; he was excluded from the public forums; one by one, his friends stopped coming to the house. His Socratic dialogues against greed and evil deteriorated into fierce diatribes against the diabolical designs of the PNR, the criminal complicity of the country's industrial and intellectual leaders and the brutish ignorance of the masses.

Finally, in a torrent of tears, Cathy-June capitulated. Cordell Vance watched in smoldering silence as she begged his father to come to his senses and stop banging his head against the wall. For his family's sake if not his own. "You can't even be a martyr," she had sobbed, "because nobody respects you any more."

Royston Vance never uttered another word about politics or the Party in the presence of his wife and son. Occasionally he made an effort to converse with Cord about trivial subjects. But the boy never knew what to say and the man was not interested.

At school, Cord began to feel that his friends were avoiding him. It may have been because he was looking for affront, or because he himself had become sulky and withdrawn. Or it may have been that they really were avoiding him, as their parents avoided his father. Sensing that the world about him was shutting him out, he shut himself in. He tried to direct his resentment against the Party and the President, Martin Ponceford. But he found himself blaming his father.

Unfortunately for Royston Vance, Cathy-June had accurately if mistakenly foreboded his dilemma. He couldn't even be a martyr—not because he didn't have the capacity for it, but because Howie Ray Spearman was not in the business of creating martyrs.

Unlike Vance, Howie Ray could distinguish an infinite series of gradations between right and wrong, good and evil and even life and death. While recognizing the diversity and seeming inconsistency of men and events, he had conceived a theory as a very young man that there was one proper and specific place for everything in the universe; that the Creator or First Cause or Whoever had spilled everything out like a great, jumbled mass of building blocks—and had left it to his creatures to assemble them in their proper place.

As a student of botany, biology and anthropology, and later as a professor of biophysics and biometrics, his theory had congealed into conviction. At first he had contented himself with observing, classifying and cataloguing the functions of various species of lower animals and insects. As his research continued to confirm his hypothesis, he began to look around at his acquaintances and to speculate on their assigned niche in the scheme of things.

When he was tapped by D. J. Cawthorn's talent task force to help formulate a philosophy and a program for the Party of National Resurgence, his own role in the vast universal complex suddenly became clear to him. It was not enough to classify and catalogue. His function was to help bring about the harmonious correlation of all things in nature, toward which all sentient beings secretly yearned.

He did not regard himself as the Messiah, merely as an apostle of order. A place for each thing, each thing in its place. He did not expect to achieve that goal—nor even to make perceptible progress toward it. But he could make a beginning. He could point the way. The way was nature's way: to let each species, each individual, adapt itself to the environment or the station best suited to it. Those that could not adapt must of necessity perish. But in so doing they would contribute to the purification and evolution of the whole.

Howie Ray chose as his laboratory the Department of Internal Development and Security. He delegated to himself the direction of two new divisions: the Citizens Protection Force and the Classification Section.

He explained to President Ponceford—and President Ponceford explained to the people—his plan to provide congenial and satisfying work for every citizen, compatible with his talents and abilities. The proposal was well received by an overwhelming majority of the citizenry, who considered their jobs neither very congenial nor worthy of their abilities.

In a follow-up announcement, Spearman himself outlined the "process of natural selection," by which every individual over the age of twelve would be tested, classified and assigned to the vocational area for which he was best fitted, thus achieving happiness and contentment for himself as well as maximum productivity for the State. To guarantee equal opportunity to all, every man, woman and adolescent child would be classified at the outset as a "Trustworthy" citizen of the Confederate States of America—regardless of present status or color or previous record.

Thereafter he would advance, by virtue of his own efforts and abilities, through a succession of merit stages: "Deserving," "Respected," "Accomplished," "Distinguished," "Exemplary." Each step up would entitle him to additional benefits and perquisites, although actual wages and salaries would be based on the specific job performed, and would be established by government "Compensation Engineers."

Free enterprise would continue to operate as before, so long as it did not conflict with the "Evolution of Civilization." Free speech would in no way be inhibited and constructive criticism would be encouraged.

As a part of the Selection Process, it would be necessary, of course, to identify and weed out the unfit. Depending on their degree of unfitness, they would be classified as "Accepted," "Undisciplined" or "Noncooperative" citizens. In rare and extreme instances of outright obstructionism, they might be "Deprived" of their citizenship entirely. No one, however, would be subject to criminal prosecution merely because he opposed the regime or resisted the Selection Process.

Five months after the Process went into effect, Royston Vance received a registered letter regretfully informing him that he had been downgraded from "Trustworthy" to "Accepted" citizen. It emphasized that in his particular case the "adjustment" had been made on the basis that he had failed to progress satisfactorily toward his "capability potential."

It urged him to intensify his efforts and assured him that this temporary setback would in no way preclude his future advancement.

His name was embossed on the "Accepted Citizen" card. At the bottom it carried the notation: "Must be in possession of holder at all times."

Cordell was at home with his mother when the letter arrived. Her hand trembled as she signed for it. She slithered it onto the hall table as if it were contaminated. She stood, staring down at it, unable to pick it up, unable to turn away. Wrenched by her helpless expression, he snatched it up, ripped it open and thrust it at her. He watched the blood drain from her face as she read it. Haltingly, she walked to the couch and sat down. Slowly her body crumpled before his eyes— broken, defeated.

All the misery of the past months suddenly welled up into Cord's throat, and he buried his head in his mother's lap. He was twelve years old. It was the last time in his life he wept.

When Royston Vance came home, the letter and a stiff drink of bourbon were sitting side by side on the coffee table in front of his chair. He opened it, read it, wordlessly tore it and the card into small fragments, walked across the room and sprinkled them into the wastebasket. He returned to his chair, took a gulp of his drink and launched into his nightly harangue: "Do you know what that son-of-a-bitch Ponceford did today? . . ."

The second letter arrived six months later, after Royston Vance had entered into his period of brooding silence. It informed him he had been reclassified from "Accepted" to "Undisciplined." It was still solicitous, but couched in somewhat more admonitory terms.

This time he did not tear it up. He read it through, absently replaced the letter and the card in the envelope, and, surprisingly, began quizzing Cord about how things were going at school. The boy replied guardedly. He had rebuilt his reserves and would not risk tearing them down again.

That night, after he had gone to bed, Cord heard, for the first time in weeks, the murmur of his parents' voices in the living room. He had an impulse to eavesdrop. But then he thought resentfully, it didn't concern him. Nothing much concerned him any more.

The next day, though, he detected a change in their attitude toward him. His mother seemed to want to touch him, to hold him. Not the affectionate, joyous, impulsive squeeze she smothered him with at unexpected moments in the time before the trouble; more the tender, wistful pat on the cheek she gave him when he first went off to school or when she left him overnight with his grandparents.

His father made an effort to recapture the easy man-boy relationship they had previously enjoyed, even going so far as to dig his old glove out of the closet and invite him to the park for a game of catch. Cord politely declined those overtures he could and stolidly suffered those he couldn't. He sensed the happy days were gone and any attempt to recover them would only renew the ache of their loss.

Still, in the weeks that followed, both his mother and his father seemed to regain some of the vitality that had drained away over the past year. His mother bestirred herself to give the house a thorough cleaning instead of aimlessly puttering about. His father resumed his accustomed office hours, though his office was now reduced to one room with a part-time secretary. Occasionally there was conversation at the dinner table. Not the lively discussions and indignant perorations of the old times. Mostly carefully screened and somewhat labored trivia. But an improvement over the listless exchanges and oppressive silences of the past months.

One relatively cool evening toward the end of July, Cathy-June called Cord down from his room to set the table—a childhood chore which he continued to perform as a symbol of his nominal participation in family ritual. As he wandered into the kitchen, she tilted her head and looked at him with the shy, flirtatious glance of her debutante period.

"We're having shrimp creole. How would you like to eat on the patio?"

Shrimp creole—on the patio—had always been one of the minor, unscheduled delights of his existence. "All right," he said.

The animation faded from Cathy-June's eyes.

Near the end of the meal his father took a sip of his iced coffee, looked across the table at Cord and said matter-of-factly, "I've got to go into New Orleans tomorrow. May be there a couple of days. Like to go with me?"

There was something in his tone that told Cord it was not just a casual question. "I dunno," he said. "I've got a game on Friday."

He looked up and caught a glimpse of his mother's strained face. His father said with forced heartiness, "I never knew you to turn down a chance to go to New Orleans."

"I'm not turning it down," Cord said indifferently. "Yeah, okay. I'll go."

His mother was ironing his shirts when he got up the next morning. "Sit here and talk to me a minute," she said as he finished his breakfast and started for the door.

"Can't. I gotta go."

"Just a minute?" Her tone was nearly pleading.

He turned back and slouched down at the table, picking tentatively at a scab on his elbow.

"It hasn't been too good for you around here the last year or so. Not for any of us." Cathy-June's voice broke. Cord looked up sharply into her face, but it was composed.

"Ah, it's all right."

"Do you know what your father's going through?"

"Yeah, I guess."

"What do you think he should do?" The tone was that of a troubled adult asking another for advice. Cord's sullen expression softened.

"Well, I guess . . . whatever he thinks is right."

"It's sometimes hard to tell what *is* right."

Cord pondered that recent anomaly. His father had always been so positive, it had never occurred to Cord, until the last year, that moral issues were even debatable. A thing was either right or wrong. He knew that wrong frequently triumphed, but that did not make it right.

"Well," he said in defense of his father, "I guess Papa knows what's right. . . . But why does he always have to be against everybody else?"

His mother sniffled as she bent over the ironing board. "That's just the way he is."

Fearful that he might be forced into taking sides, Cord jumped up, gave his mother an awkward pat on the back and hurried from the room.

He did not come back until late afternoon. He was surprised to find his three suits packed in his father's large suitcase, along with an inordinate supply of shirts, underwear, socks and handkerchiefs.

"Holy cow," he said, "we're not going to Afghanistan."

"You never know," his mother said. "You might get stuck there for a week. Your father doesn't know how long his business may take. You can wear your jeans in the car so the other things don't get wrinkled."

He saw his second-best pair of jeans and a worn, long-sleeved sport shirt laid out on the bed. He noted with mild surprise but without comment that they had not been washed.

Royston Vance did not arrive home until after six. Even then he appeared in no great hurry to get started. "We'll wait until dark. It'll be cooler then."

Cordell knew that he did not like to drive after dark. During the evening his mother and father talked sparingly to him and not at all to each other. The normal atmosphere of silent futility seemed, however, to be charged with an undercurrent of hostility. His mother, he sensed, was on the verge of tears.

At ten o'clock his father came down the stairs, carrying the big suitcase and a small overnight bag. He headed for the door without pausing in the hall.

"Say good-bye to your mother," he said tersely as he passed the living room.

Cordell put down his book, rose and started across the room to where his mother had been silently knitting a half-finished sweater for him. He stood beside her chair, waiting for her to raise her head for his dutiful kiss. She sat, staring apathetically at the garment on her lap. With no change in the frozen expression on her face, she picked up a pair of scissors lying in the chair beside her. Methodically, starting at the neck, she cut the sweater in half.

Still impassive, she rose slowly from the chair, spilling sweater, scissors, yarn and needles on the floor. She looked into Cordell's puzzled eyes as if he were a stranger. Then she wrapped her arms around him and held him with a strength he would not have believed she possessed.

She relaxed and gave him a long firm kiss.

"Good-bye," she said. She stepped back, her hands on his arms. He stared, bewildered, at the anguish in her eyes. Her voice trembled. "You must believe—we must both believe— that your father is right. Otherwise it's all so . . . senseless."

She turned away and walked quickly out of the room.

Cordell stood for a moment staring after her. Not knowing what to do, he went out and got in the car beside his father. They drove down the street without speaking.

As they turned onto the New Orleans turnpike, Royston Vance twisted his head and looked at his son, sitting tight-lipped in the far corner of the seat. He reached over and squeezed his knee. "You know you're not coming back here." His voice was husky but controlled. "I've made arrangements to put you on a boat tonight. Friends of mine will take you to New York. There'll be somebody there to look after you. I won't·kid you that you'll be able to come back. So you'll probably be better off if you just forget me and your mother and the goddamned Confederate States of America."

His harsh tone, even more than his words, stabbed at Cordell's heart. He took a quick breath and held it, gazing straight ahead at the jumble of neon signs and sleazy roadside honky-tonks. He refused to digest the meaning of what his father was saying.

Sentiment came hard to Royston Vance, though he was at heart a sentimentalist. He had shown in a thousand ways his deep affection for his son, but he had never spoken it openly. Now he groped for the words.

"I don't know if I can make you understand why we are doing this. You probably think we don't love you. But it's because we do love you that we're sending you away. I'd do anything to keep you with me. I'd even knuckle under. But it wouldn't be good for you in the long run, Cordy. A man can't live with his head bowed.

"But you shouldn't have to spend your whole life fighting either. Oh, I know I've always posed as a big crusader, but I kind of enjoyed it. I did it because I wanted to—not because I had to. That makes all the difference. If you're fighting for survival, you can't help hating. If you stay here, you'll end up with a choice between hate and subservience, and that's no kind of a choice."

Struggling to maintain his self-mastery, Cordell said in a small voice, "Why can't you come with me?"

Royston Vance shook his head. "No good for either of us. I'm in too deep. I can't walk away from it now. But even if I could, it would be bad for you to have me around. Hate is contagious. This is not your battle, and I don't want you to feel it is. Besides, you've seen what it's done to me. I don't want you to grow up like that. I want you to put this last year out of your mind and just remember the way it used to be."

Royston Vance drove the remainder of the journey in silence. They left the car on a side street near the French Quarter and walked five blocks through dark, decaying warehouses to the waterfront. They waited in a shadowy doorway opposite a rusty freighter, loading at a rickety pier. As the longshoremen filed down the forward gangplank, Royston Vance led Cordell up the boarding plank astern. He left the big suitcase in the doorway.

An officer in a soiled shirt and a crumpled cap awaited them on deck.

"Mr. Garrison?" His tone and manner were neutral.

Royston Vance nodded. The mate led them to the captain's quarters, opened the door without knocking and closed it from the outside. The captain rose from his desk, glanced sharply at Royston Vance and fastened his gaze on Cordell.

"This the cargo?" He had a guttural accent which heightened the boy's apprehension.

Again Royston Vance nodded, not speaking.

"There'll be someone in New York to take delivery?"

"He'll be at the shipping office."

"He'll have papers?"

"Yes."

"That'll be three hundred dollars U.S. Prepaid."

Royston Vance pulled a sheaf of bills from an inside pocket and counted them out on the desk. Cordell looked at the strange currency, his curiosity momentarily overcoming his sense of dazed terror. He knew it was forbidden for citizens of the Confederacy to possess foreign money. For the first time, it dawned on him that his father was a criminal.

The captain counted the money again, then opened the door and scowled at the mate, who was lounging in the passageway outside. The mate walked away.

Royston Vance put both hands on his son's shoulders and squeezed them.

"Cordy . . ." Royston Vance's voice broke. Tears welled in his eyes and dripped down his cheeks. "Cordy . . ." He pulled the boy to him, clasped his arms around him and sobbed— one great convulsive sob. Cordell stood rigid, his arms imprisoned, his throat filled with a lump that blocked breath, speech and tears. He felt his father's bristles on his cheek. He strove to close off his mind.

The door opened and a boy slightly older than he stepped through, looked at them curiously and walked past them to the captain's desk. The captain stood up. Not looking at the weeping man, he said, "You'd better go now. We're ready to cast off. This boy will go with you. You bring one aboard, you'd better take one off. Your baggage has been stowed."

Royston Vance stepped back. His voice sounded like a faulty tape recording. "A man named Sievers will meet you in New York. He'll look after you. He's with the North American League. I've been working with them down here. They've got funds to take care of your education.

"You forget your mother and I ever existed. If the Seepees trace you, they'll try to put pressure on you by threatening us. Don't fall for it. You can't help us. We've helped you the only way we can. Don't ruin it."

Royston Vance gave his son one agonized look and walked out of his life.

The Sievers took good care of Cordell Vance. They welcomed him into their family and treated him with the same constrained affection they bestowed on their own children—two girls and a boy—the youngest six years older than Cord. He was grateful to them. He responded as demonstratively as his increasingly introspective nature would permit. He never felt as though he belonged to the family. But the other members never acted as if they did either.

Both Mr. and Mrs. Sievers were engaged in a multitude of good works, which left them little time for family amenities. Everyone in the household was polite to everyone else, preoccupied with his own affairs and disposed to keep his feelings—if he had any—to himself. Cordell Vance had no trouble adapting himself to the prevailing climate.

Every two weeks, Mr. Sievers would sit him down for a "man-to-man talk." He would inquire about his health, his grades, his extracurricular activities and occasionally he would probe gingerly for any untoward adolescent problems. He always appeared slightly relieved that Cord had none. His manner, during the sessions, was that of a sympathetic case worker, obliged to conduct bimonthly interviews, but not wishing to intrude into the client's privacy.

Cord was therefore surprised when, toward the end of his first year's residence, Mr. Sievers suggested rather apologetically that perhaps it might be well for them to institute formal adoption proceedings. To the boy's startled look, he explained that it would be necessary in order for him to become a citizen of the United States. Disregarding the effect on his benefactor's feelings, Cord flatly refused. Though he never spoke of it, he firmly intended to return to his home and to his parents.

Mr. Sievers did not persist. Indeed, he did not mention the subject again until a week after Cord's eighteenth birthday, when he was eligible to take out naturalization papers himself. Then he personally escorted the young man to the immigration service office and helped him fill out the papers. He seemed so insistent, Cord did not resist. Besides, his resolve had faded, as had his memories of his mother and father and his homeland. For the first two years he frequently asked Mr. Sievers if he had heard anything about them. The answer was always vaguely negative. Finally, Cord stopped asking, though he thought about them sometimes. . . .

Vance told his story objectively, without emotion, except when Dorsey interrupted to ask how he felt, how he thought his mother felt, how he thought his father felt. Under Dorsey's questioning, he dredged up several long-forgotten incidents: the time he hit his head on the raft and nearly drowned; the time Eric Garner and Jodie Carstairs lured him into the shed and took his pants down; the time he shot his first rabbit and threw up.

Dorsey probed at some length into the deterioration of the family relationship during the final year. Vance described the change in his father and his mother, but he could not delineate any change in himself. The happy times had blended into the unhappy times, leaving no emotional residue, either of pleasure or of pain.

The recital brought him no sense of relief. In the early days of his despair he had thought about consulting a psychiatrist. But he knew the source of his sickness was not in his subconscious. He felt only a vague sense of embarrassment at having exposed so much of himself to Dorsey's clinical scrutiny. He terminated the narrative by getting up and prowling around the room.

"So now you know who I am—and why. What good will it do you?"

Dorsey looked at him stolidly. There was no compassion in either his eyes or his voice. "You know, of course, about the experiments with the rats in the maze. Eventually, through trial and error, they learn to find their way to food and water. Nobody knows whether it gives them a sense of accomplishment, but at least they build up a feeling of security because they know their way around.

"Then the maze is changed. Where they formerly found food, they get an electric shock. They expect pleasure; they get pain. It induces a neurosis in them. Some of them are strong enough to start hunting again. Others just huddle up and starve to death. The idea of the experiment, of course, is to determine the effect of frustration and disappointment on the nervous system. But, I've often thought, it parallels life in some respects.

"Not ten rats in ten million ever get shoved into the maze. The rest of them live a normal rat life. They probably experience some frustration, but they learn to cope with it. And nobody changes the rules on them. You happen to be one of the ten rats that got caught. I'd say that you have a basically stable personality. You seem to have responded quite well to the first two tests."

"And you're figuring on running me through one more time?"

"I suppose that's what it amounts to. But of course your reaction is entirely incidental as far as we are concerned. I might tell you, though, for your own sake, it won't do you any good to curl up in the fetal position and wait for the food to come to you."

"What you're telling me is that I have a basically stable personality, but it's been warped. Why the hell don't you just go through the Qual files and select a normal healthy American male. Why pick somebody who's a little wacky?"

"Because that might be helpful in the job we have in mind. We need somebody who's been through the maze and whose reactions we can pretty well predict. Besides, you have other qualifications."

"Like being able to kill somebody in cold blood?"

"Like being able to kill somebody in cold blood."

Vance stared at him in disbelief. "You don't need somebody who's a little neurotic. You need somebody who's insane. I don't think I quite fall into that category—yet."

Dorsey smiled. "No. You'd be no good to us if you did."

"Then what makes you think I'd even consider such an assignment?"

Dorsey rose from his chair, rested an elbow negligently on the mantel and gazed down speculatively into Vance's eyes. "There are a number of reasons. In the first place, as I told you, you would be performing a great service to your country. You are a man with a strong sense of loyalty, whether you know it or not.

"Secondly—and I don't think this would weigh too heavily with you—there would be a lot of money in it. A lot of money. If you pulled it off. Of course, as I mentioned, the chances are you won't be around to collect it.

"But then that shouldn't weigh too heavily either because you're not happy now and money wouldn't make you happy. I don't think it makes too much difference to you whether you live or die. You don't find too many people with that frame of mind.

"Finally," he added, turning over his hole card without a

change in expression, "it might help you regain your self-respect. So you could live with yourself—if you live."

"You go to hell," Vance flared. "That's one thing they didn't take away from me."

"Maybe not," Dorsey conceded. "Still it must shake you a little when nobody quite looks you in the eye."

Vance gave no sign, but the barb had struck home.

It hadn't quite registered the first time he noticed it. But then everything else was hazy too. He was still floundering in the mental fog he had wrapped around himself to blot out the nightmare of reality.

He had seen the look many times since, and it never failed to register. Even sometimes, he realized, when it wasn't there. Not contempt, not accusation, not pity, not even curiosity, yet a strange, searing amalgam of them all. Each time he saw it, it brought back with sharper clarity the scene that had transpired in the cool, aseptic conference room in the embassy in Rangoon. It was on the faces of the ambassador, the newsmen, the cameramen, the military intelligence officers (his friends)—even the faceless observers.

It had first begun to penetrate when Jerry Donaldson raised his equine muzzle from the folded yellow notepaper on the table and focused his red-flecked eyes on a point slightly abaft Cordell Vance's left ear.

Jerry Donaldson regarded Cordell Vance as his creature. He had nurtured the legend of "Gargantua, the Guerrilla Fighter." The strident, right-wing columnist had made Vance's name a revered word—if not throughout the country, at least among millions of kooky Defenders of Democracy. Many of them wrote to him with regrettable frequency and nauseous vapidity. He never answered. Jerry Donaldson had a proprietary interest in vindicating his minion. He fed him his cue.

"Major Vance, the Communist press around the world has made a lot of propaganda hay out of certain statements you are alleged to have made while in captivity in Sumprabum. Would you care to set the record straight?"

Vance blinked at the television lights and shook his head.

Donaldson switched to the mildly exasperated tone of a defense lawyer coaxing a confused witness.

"Are we to understand, Major, you do not repudiate the statements attributed to you by the Communist press."

Cordell Vance fluttered his hands in a helpless gesture— neither affirmation nor denial. "As I told the board of inquiry," he said in a thin, halting voice, "I don't remember making the statements, but they are in my handwriting . . . and I may have."

"They were obtained under duress." It was a statement, not a question.

"No. I wasn't tortured . . . or anything like that."

"Well," Arnie Cochran of UPI interjected impatiently, "do you subscribe to the views you allegedly expressed?"

"I . . . I . . . Some of them I would phrase . . . differently. . . . I don't remember anything about the first week or so of my captivity. . . . After that it was . . . kind of blurred."

"You were quoted as saying, 'I'm sick of slaughtering innocent people. These people don't know what they're fighting about and they don't care what kind of government they have. They just want to be left alone.' Did you say that? Do you believe it?"

"I . . . I may have."

"Did you admit participating in guerrilla activities against the People's Republic of Burma?"

"That's . . . where I was captured."

"You were an observer, the army says."

A shaft of annoyance pierced his lethargy. "In guerrilla warfare . . . there are no observers."

Lieutenant Colonel J. R. (Skinny Jimmy) Matoon, the army PIO, attempted to intervene. "He inadvertently became involved in a fire fight while observing patrol action."

Cochran brushed the explanation aside. "The dispatches claimed you were directing all guerrilla activities in southern Burma. Do you deny that?"

Vance's mind began to wander. He was getting confused as to who was conducting the interrogation. What were Jerry Donaldson and Soupy Cochran doing in a Burmese prison camp, firing questions at him? He switched frequencies from ratiocination to conditioned response. "I deny . . . I don't know."

"Let's get this straight." Cochran's tone was openly accusatory. "If you *were* engaged in hostile actions against a neutral country—a country with which the United States is not at war," he amended, "that is a pretty serious breach of international conduct."

The phrase lodged in Vance's brain. He raised his head and stared dully around the room at the intent faces, all focused on him. "Breach of international conduct . . . breach of international conduct . . . breach of . . ." He tried to pin down the meaning of the phrase. but it kept eluding him. He concentrated hard, knowing it was somehow important. His mind reached out for it, lunged and suddenly grasped it. He turned it over. It slowly collapsed, like a punctured balloon. A deflated nothing, with no more meaning or substance than his own life.

He heard himself mutter the words and saw the expression of shocked, incredulous outrage on the faces surrounding him: "Fuck international conduct."

Somewhat the same feeling toward life in general had dictated the decision (if it could be called a decision) which led Cordell Vance, by a circuitous route, to the frosty reception in the air-conditioned chamber in the embassy.

One sparkling spring day, near the end of the semester, he had awakened in his cheerful efficiency apartment three blocks from the campus with a vague sense of discontent. He sat through two morning classes, dutifully taking notes and scowling at the labored pedagogical humor of Assistant Professor Horace Wendhorne. He had a skimpy pregame lunch at the training table, and that afternoon he went three-for-four against Colgate. He returned to his room after the game, studied for two hours and that night went two-for-two on a sandy beach with a surprisingly knowledgeable sophomore coed from the fine arts school. All in all, it was an extremely satisfying day. It probably would never get any better. The next morning he went downtown to the recruiting office and enlisted in the U.S. Army.

There were times during basic when he wondered what had impelled him to do what he had done. He had no feeling one way or the other about the conflict in Vietnam, which was just then hotting up. He had always been a loner, and he had an aversion to sleeping in the same room with anyone else. If he had had any inclination toward a military career, he could have enrolled in the ROTC and qualified for a commission. He had no desire to give orders, and even less to take them.

Nevertheless, he and the army hit it off very well from the beginning. His aloofness and obvious intelligence at first aroused the suspicion and, to some extent, the antagonism of the noncoms and his barracks mates. He quickly proved himself the best soldier in the platoon, however, and once that was established and accepted, the resentments vanished.

For his part, the mindless existence and physical exhaustion satisfied, for the time being at least, his gnawing emotional needs. Shortly after they had begun to pall, he was assigned to Officer Candidate School and then was shipped to Vietnam.

He applied himself with diligence to mastering the techniques of his trade. He quickly grasped the basic concept—to kill without getting killed. He accepted it without any great ardor, but also without squeamishness. He became a skilled practitioner of his craft, and emerged with the distinction of having completed his tour of duty unscathed. He was awarded the bronze star, and his application for transfer to the Special Forces was approved.

When he returned to Vietnam a year later, it was with the feeling that he had perhaps discovered his niche in life. He found the work stimulating, the discipline not too onerous, the environment not too confining and his associates congenial. In short, he belonged.

When the tiresome, exasperating, dispirited war in Vietnam finally sputtered to an inconclusive halt, Captain Cordell Vance laid down the tools of his trade without regret and without relief. Lacking any firm convictions either way, he abstained from the endless alcoholic arguments as to whether the war was worthwhile. He did not join in the vehement denunciations of the goddamned self-serving politicians who wanted to end it and the goddamned self-serving generals who wanted to continue it. His own personal appraisal, which he rarely confided to anyone, was that it didn't seem to have served much purpose—but, then, what did?

He was waiting, neither patiently nor impatiently, for his orders home and his subsequent discharge when he received a summons to report to the office of the commanding general. To his mild surprise, he was ushered into the presence of Lieutenant General Christian C. Varnell himself.

"You realize," General Varnell thundered, slamming his fist down on a king-size green blotter, "this fucking war isn't over yet."

"No, sir. I don't suppose it is."

"We fought the damned thing wrong," the general declaimed. "We should have set up a strong point every fifty miles and fanned our own guerrillas out from there. If Charlie had had a hundred thousand guerrillas nibbling at his ass, he never would have been able to mount a frontal offensive. You people in the Special Forces did a good job, but you were on the defensive. You were trying to protect the populace. To hell with that. If you harass the enemy enough, they'll be too busy to harass the populace. The Commies think they've proved we can't cope with guerrilla warfare. These things are gonna be flaring up all over the world. We've got to beat 'em at their own game. To do that, we need men who know how to play it. They tell me you're a natural-born guerrilla fighter, Vance. We're gonna need people like you."

Vance shifted his eyes away from the general's. "I really hadn't planned to make a career of the army, sir."

"Why not?"

"I'm not sure I'm cut out for it. Oh, I like the army all right. But I can't say that I like killing people."

"People? They're the enemy. Killing 'em is just incidental to our main job. There are things about every job you don't like. And let me tell you, Vance, if we don't kill a few people over here now, in a few years a lot of our own people are going to be dying somewhere else."

The upshot of the discussion was that Cordell Vance reenlisted in the army—not to save his country from the dismal fate the general had prophesied, not out of any stern sense of duty, but simply because he had been asked. He was wanted, perhaps even needed. It gave his life a purpose. What it was didn't really matter.

He went from Vietnam to Thailand, from Thailand to
Malaysia, from Malaysia to Indonesia—wherever the home
office sent him. He no longer regarded himself as a soldier so
much as a professional troubleshooter, specializing in counter-
insurgency. The home office had learned that the business of
pacification could be more efficiently conducted through the
use of native labor.

In fact, after checking over the P & L statements for the
Korean and Vietnam conflicts, both the Communists and the
democracies concluded that unbridled competition on such a
massive scale was uneconomic. By tacit consent they switched
over to local-franchise operations, reducing the profit-making
potential, but also cutting the overhead. As a result, at any
given time there usually were three or four brush-fire wars
burning fitfully at scattered sites throughout the world, but
no major conflagrations threatening to touch off a global holocaust.

In theory Vance's job was to instruct and advise the government forces in antiguerrilla tactics. In practice he covered
the "anti" phase of the curriculum in two succinct sentences:
"The key to successful guerrilla operations lies in the element
of surprise. The element of surprise belongs exclusively to
the attacker."

He trained his army of cutthroats in cadres of twenty-five.
He accompanied each graduating class on its first full-scale
field exercise. From a professional standpoint he was gratified
to observe the skill with which they practiced their lessons in
butchery. From a personal standpoint he gradually grew to
dislike his students and to detest himself. He stopped going
on the field exercises after he began experiencing attacks of
nausea. He spent much of his spare time on aimless, solitary
helicopter flights. Then came another summons from General
Varnell.

"Major," the general said without preamble, "those boys

of yours over in Burma are sitting on their ass. I think maybe you'd better slip over there and put the prod to 'em."

In Burma the Communists had rudely violated the by now accepted pattern of uncivilized behavior. With only a token propaganda build-up, they had seized control of the established government and confronted the democracies with a *fait accompli,* affording them no opportunity to rise to the challenge of naked aggression. They were left with no recourse except to lodge an outraged protest with the United Nations.

Allowing a decent interval for discontent to ferment within the country, the Anti-Communist Coalition of Southeast Asia set about organizing an indigenous resistance movement. Since they would be less subject to distraction from mortar and small-arms fire there, the Burmese trainees were enrolled in the Cordell Vance School of Discriminate Slaughter in neighboring Thailand.

They proved to be not very apt pupils. Having missed the indoctrination of witnessing their female relatives raped and their male relatives disemboweled, they lacked the requisite motivation. Consequently, their grades were less than satisfactory in both ferocity and brutality. In the three months since they had completed the course and returned home to begin their practice, very little had been heard from them.

General Varnell's implied reprimand touched an exposed nerve. Vance did not try to disguise the resentment in his voice. "I'm afraid, General, those people don't have the stomach for this sort of thing."

The general looked at him coldly. "Nonsense," he said. "If they didn't want to fight, they wouldn't have come to us in the first place."

"I don't say they don't want to fight. They don't want to fight this way."

"For Chrissake it's the only way they can fight. Don't they understand that? What do they want—an invasion?"

Vance felt a listless sort of anger churning inside him. "General, there's a difference between dropping a stick of bombs on a bunch of ants and strangling a sleeping man with piano wire. Some people just aren't cut out for it. And even if they *can* do it, they eventually get so they either like it or they hate it."

"You don't like it, huh?"

"I've about had it, sir."

Surprisingly the general said, "I'm glad to hear it. I was wondering which way you'd go. You know," he added meditatively, "our business is killing, but we have to weed out the pathological killers—the people who are best at it. They're bad for morale. And sooner or later they crack up.

"Tell you what. You do this last little job for me and we'll find a soft staff berth for you. Better yet, I'll recommend you for the War College. How'd you like that?"

Vance shook his head. "I've had it all the way. How the hell can you justify spending your whole life destroying things?"

General Varnell leaned back in his chair and lit a cigaret. "I know how you feel. I think all of us in this business go through it at one time or another. You either get out of it or you adjust your thinking. The fact of the matter is, we're not just destroying things. We're preserving something. That's the way you've got to look at it. Of course," he added, "you've got to believe in what you're preserving. I happen to believe that the goddamned Commies are out to take over the world if we don't stop 'em."

Vance gazed bleakly out the window at the sandbags stacked against the steel fence. He straightened in his chair and met the general's bellicose stare.

"Very good, sir," he said in an exaggeratedly respectful voice. "When do I leave and how do I get there?"

The general looked at him quizzically, then hauled a map of the border region out of his desk drawer. He briefed him on the infiltration route, pointed out areas of suspected military concentrations, strategic bridges and munitions storehouses.

"Our people got clobbered pretty good on a couple of forays, and they've holed up since. It seems fairly certain the enemy was tipped off. The first thing you've got to do is find out where the leaks came from and take care of them," he said ominously. "Then get those people out of their goddamned dugouts and into the ball game. I don't want you taking any chances yourself. We don't want to create any international incidents. So don't, for Chrissake, get yourself captured."

The general's words rang in his ears, above the cough of the mortars and the staccato clatter of the machine guns as the ambush engulfed them. They were his last clear recollection before the haze began to lift in the American Embassy at Rangoon. . . .

Dorsey burrowed his meaty hands into the pockets of the too-tight pants and studied Vance's scowling face in the firelight.

"I've gone over the transcript of the board of inquiry pretty thoroughly. They were a little rough on you. I must say, though, you didn't put up much of a defense."

Vance made no reply.

"Actually," Dorsey continued as if it were a two-way conversation, "I didn't think the statements you made in the prison camp were too out of line. Of course the military is a bit more sensitive about such things. You say you were drugged?"

No answer.

"No, you said you didn't know. My guess is that you probably were, but that you didn't say anything you wouldn't have said among friends over the fourth martini. Unfortunately,

you weren't among friends. I don't think you were psychologically indoctrinated—brainwashed. If you had been, you would
have remembered something about it. Besides, it wouldn't
have served their purpose. The statements you made, coming
from a well-publicized hero, were more damaging than if you
had denounced the warmongering imperialists as a traitor.

"At any rate, I will tell you, after weighing all the objective
and subjective elements of your situation, we do not regard
your conduct or remarks as evidence of disloyalty—nor even
of weakness."

Having long since exonerated himself, on that score at least,
Vance felt no gratification at having his verdict confirmed.
He did, however, resent Dorsey's dragging up events of the
past which he had so laboriously buried, even though they no
longer rankled. He stirred in his chair and massaged his aching kidney.

"All right," he said, "so you have restored my citizenship.
What are you getting at?"

"The only reason I brought it up was because it does have
some bearing on why you were selected." Dorsey's tone was
businesslike again. "For one thing, if you will excuse my
saying so, you still have some taint of Communism in the
public consciousness. You would be an unlikely candidate for
a mission of supreme importance to the United States. Secondly, you are a man who has been wronged. You have reason
to carry a grievance against society."

"Screw society. They don't owe me anything. I don't owe
them anything. But I don't have any grievance."

"Whether you do or not is somewhat beside the point—
though I would say you do whether you admit it or not. At
any rate, you have reason to. That might be important. To
sort of flesh out your character and to establish a motive.
In case the question should arise."

"In case the question should arise, it probably wouldn't be too hard to determine whether I had a motive or didn't have a motive."

A wintry smile seamed the Negro's stolid face. "Presumably you wouldn't be around to testify."

"I see," Vance said. "For the same reason I might not be around to collect the bounty money."

Dorsey grimaced. "Let's just say it would be vital—to both of us—that you not be taken alive. And it would be preferable that you not be taken dead."

"To both of us."

Dorsey nodded soberly.

Vance stood up creakily, flexing the fingers in his right hand. The circulation was beginning to come back. "Let's drink to that," he said, gathering up the glasses. He started for the bar, then turned and remarked thoughtfully, "I can see how you might have a little trouble filling this job. You need a patriotic citizen with Communist leanings who is slightly insane—demented, I believe, is the word the newspapers use. He must be capable of killing in cold blood and willing to commit suicide—presumably in that order. He should have a grudge against society; be greedy but not too greedy, smart enough to carry it off and stupid enough to agree to do it."

"That's about the size of it. But the hours are good and you'd be your own boss."

Vance replenished the drinks and handed one to the visitor. "Well," he said, "it's been an interesting evening. I don't believe I want to do business with you, and I don't care to hear any more about it."

Dorsey swirled his drink around and took a sip of it. "You don't know what we want you to do—or why."

"Cut the shadow boxing. You want me to knock off somebody and take the rap for it if anything goes wrong. I don't know why and I don't *want* to know. It seems like a pretty shitty thing for the United States Government to be doing— if it is the government. But I don't even care about that."

"Would you care if it would save the lives of forty or fifty million people?"

Vance looked at him disgustedly. "Let's not run through that routine again. I know. We've got to draw the line somewhere. And somebody's got to do it. Well, I helped draw the line before. Right between my shoulder blades. If I'm going to commit suicide, I'll do it in my own time and in my own way."

"No, you won't. You'll serve out your time the hard way— if you have to—because you figure knocking yourself off would be desertion in the face of the enemy. You might go a little bit out of your way, though, to have an accident happen to you. That's why my proposition sort of appeals to you."

"You seem to have a pretty complete book on me. Does it mention in there that I've sworn off killing people? Regardless of what you may think, I doubt if a cold-blooded murder would do much for my neurosis."

"This one would," Dorsey said.

"Much as I dislike society," Vance said, "it's just as well there aren't too many of you brain-peepers passing out prescriptions like that."

Dorsey picked up the poker, stirred the fire, then lowered himself into the wing-back chair. "If you were in the insurance business," he said, "selling a fifty-thousand-dollar policy would do the same thing for you. But you're not. There aren't many things that would give you any real satisfaction. This would, I think. And you aren't ever going to be happy again until you're satisfied with yourself."

"I really appreciate your concern about my happiness."

"I don't give a damn about your happiness, except that it could be useful. Not that it would make much difference to you, but you may very well be one of the forty or fifty million people wiped out." He looked up at Vance. "You wouldn't mind that, huh?"

"You're the psychiatrist. You said I wouldn't."

"If you had something to live for, you would. Most of these other people have something to live for."

"Don't try to slip me a guilt complex, on top of all my other problems. You're not going to make me responsible for the death of fifty million people. I didn't even know they were in danger until you told me, and I don't want to hear any more about it."

Dorsey leaned forward, cradling his glass in his enormous hands, his round head sunk between his massive shoulders. "All right," he said. "You've pretty well got the picture. One egomaniac is going to blow up this country if we don't stop him. And you don't want to hear any more about it."

"Jesus Christ," Vance exclaimed, irritated but intrigued, "if the goddamned U.S. Government can't stop him, how the hell would I do it?"

"I've just explained to you. You're our best hope. I don't know how you would do it. That would be up to you. Don't you think that would give you some satisfaction?"

"No. If it's the way you say it is, it's a worthy cause. But I'm not buying any more causes, no matter how noble they are."

"What if you had a personal reason besides?"

"Don't be ridiculous. Not only do I not have a grudge against everybody; I don't have a grudge against anybody. At least, not enough to want to kill him."

"This is one you don't even know about."

"Then he isn't hurting me, is he?"

"He's already hurt you."

"Okay. So it didn't hurt too bad if I didn't feel it."

"You felt it. He ruined your life and your father's and your mother's."

Vance gazed into the fire, absently watching the yellow tongues lick at the charred log. He raised his head and looked over at Dorsey.

"Spearman?"

"Howie Ray Spearman."

Flashes of the past again filtered through the closed shutters of Cordell Vance's memory. His mother's bubbling laugh, her impulsive hug, her wide-eyed, little-girl faith that life was an inexhaustible storehouse of delight, full of surprises, all of them pleasurable. With searing clarity, he saw the stricken look on her face as he thrust the letter at her.

He remembered the Saturday mornings on the river with his father, their two-member secret society which was convened by hooking middle fingers together and uttering a password, the mellow evenings on the patio when the Plumed Knight would regale them with his robust account of that day's quest. He felt the juices of his own boyhood drain away as the luster faded from his father's eye and the gall of defeat seeped into his soul.

Vaguely he knew at the time that some powerful, malevolent force named Howie Ray Spearman was responsible for the thing that was happening to them. But he was an abstraction, a dark, unseen, evil presence, against which even his father was helpless.

Vance limped to the window, pushed aside the curtain and took in the silent, snow-covered valley. Over the past few months, the imperturbable peaks and the ceaselessly chattering stream had subtly begun to heal his ravaged spirit.

Thoughtfully, he rearranged the curtain and returned to the chair in front of the fire.

"It doesn't mean that much to me any more," he said

evenly. "I don't think it ever did. As far as I was concerned, it was just something that happened. I didn't really blame Spearman or anybody else. Except maybe my father."

Dorsey shook his head. "It didn't just happen. Spearman made it happen. And the people let it happen. Maybe they deserved what they got. Except your father. I'm not trying to tell you you owe it to him. I've spent years trying to convince people that revenge is a stupid, destructive emotion. I'm not going to try to incite you to avenge your father. I will say, though, that you could give some purpose to his sacrifice —as well as to your own life."

"I tell you, Dorsey," Vance said, "you can't pin this thing on me. You've got three million men who have sworn to bear true faith and allegiance to the United States. You can order any one of them to do it. My contract has expired."

"Naturally, we thought of them first, but the Pres—it was decided that no one connected with the government could afford to be involved in an operation of this type. You can understand why.

"I offered to try it myself," he added with a deprecatory shrug, "but obviously I would be at some disadvantage. I want to emphasize, this is not a suicide mission. We need someone who not only can pull it off but who also stands a chance of getting away."

"I imagine the premium on that kind of a policy would be pretty stiff."

"Yes. I'd say the odds are about a hundred thousand to one. We feel they are not prohibitive compared with the consequences."

"Who feels they are not prohibitive?" Vance said. "Some lard-ass computer operator who runs a balance sheet every night before he goes home to dinner? Some squarehead general who's got to save the country twice a week to earn himself another star? Sure, the world might be better off if Howie Ray Spearman wasn't in it. And if you can knock him off at the risk of one man, that's a damned sound investment. Who says he's out to destroy the United States? He sure as hell can't do it by himself. So why don't you just wipe out the Confederacy?"

Dorsey drew a deep breath and sat upright in his chair. "First of all," he said, "let me tell you there are only six people who have any knowledge of this . . . very tentative plan. It was left to my discretion, how much I should tell you. I'm going to tell you everything. Not so much to persuade you to do it. But so that if you do agree, it will strengthen your resolve to go through with it. That's where the real pinch is going to come. Nobody will be there to force you to do it. Nobody'll blame you if you don't. It'll be strictly between you and yourself. I'm not sure anybody has got that much control over himself. It will be interesting from a pathological standpoint."

Dorsey laid it out for him coldly and candidly, citing all the alternatives that had been considered and discarded. He related how Dr. Corfmann and he had assembled a psychological prototype of the consummate assassin and had then set out to find its closest living relative. Unsparingly, he dissected Vance's personality, singling out the qualities which would endanger the success of the project and which he would have to guard against.

"If you were to accept the assignment," he concluded, "it would be desirable for you to undergo a period of psychological reorientation to redirect certain nonconstructive thought processes."

When he had finished, he sat back and eyed Vance like a biologist observing a laboratory specimen. Vance slumped in his chair, fingers spliced on his stomach. The wind moaned fitfully through the pine trees behind the cabin. A blob of resin flared weakly, then sizzled into silence.

"From your standpoint," Vance said, not raising his head, "I can see that it might be justified. From my standpoint, I'm still just a bystander."

"A hundred and twenty million people in the Confederacy were just bystanders," Dorsey said grimly. "They're damned well involved now."

"Look," Vance said, shifting ground, "your computers picked me out of the pack because my slots happened to fit. There's one little thing you didn't have programed though. I happen to have sworn off killing people."

"But you could let fifty million people die."

"Yeah. If you want to put it that way. As long as it's not my responsibility. I could let fifty million people die easier than I could *make* one person die. I have nothing against dying. It's killing I object to."

Dorsey went to the window and looked out. The sky was beginning to pale in the east, outlining the ridge across the valley. He moved lithely back across the room and, almost without bending, reached down a long arm and plucked his coat from the floor. Vance watched him, not speaking.

"You've made up your mind?" Dorsey asked.

Vance rose painfully from the chair. "Yes. You haven't said anything to change it."

"One thing's changed. When I came here, you didn't have anything to do with the rest of your life but sit here and brood. Now you have a choice."

Vance listened indifferently.

"Think it over for a couple of days. I'll be back in touch with you." Dorsey hesitated. He sounded slightly embarrassed. "I had my doubts about this from the beginning. Entrusting a job like this to a . . . an amateur. I think . . . maybe you could pull it off as well as anyone."

Vance smiled and stuck out his hand. "Okay, Dorsey. Thanks for the free analysis—and the ruptured kidney. Let me know when you're stopping by again. I'll have the gun loaded."

Part Three

Chapter Six

Amerean Flight 219 slowed its descent, which had started over Omaha, with a perceptible jolt. The wheels whined out of their pods and thumped into landing position. The safety officer and a stewardess started their patrol down the aisles. Cordell Vance pocketed his book, pulled down his shoulder straps and fastened them to his seat belt. As the plane banked, he caught a glimpse from his center-section seat of sullen gray waves flecked with white streamers.

The voice of the aircraft communicator, depersonalized as it was by the public-address system, sounded discouraged: "Amerean Flight 219 will be landing at Daley International Airport in Chicago in six minutes. The temperature in Chicago is eight degrees, wind twenty-two knots from the northwest. Light to moderate snow is falling. There will be a slight delay in vehicular traffic crossing the causeway due to security measures. Please remain seated until the plane is anchored to the terra-transit. Thank you."

"Security measures my ass," the man in the next seat complained. "The damned thing is always jammed up whenever there's any weather. Who the hell but Chicago would put an airport in the middle of the lake?"

Vance gave him a perfunctory smile. As far as he was concerned, they should have put the city in the lake and the airport on the shore. Chicago was not his favorite town. He had spent a couple of besotted weeks there during his reconnaissance into depravity. His memories, what there were of them, were not happy. So what the hell am I doing here now? he mused.

Not, he told himself again, because there was the remotest possibility that he would accede to Dorsey's crazy scheme. The more he thought about it, the more bizarre the whole episode seemed. And it had seemed completely unreal when he awoke the day after the Negro's nocturnal visit. Until he rolled over. The aches and bruises were real enough.

With annoyance he had found himself idly ruminating how the deed might be carried out, even though he had no intention of doing it. He had concluded that there was no possible way it could be accomplished with any certitude of success, short of a suicidal close-range attack.

He had virtually dismissed the entire affair from his mind when he stopped at the post office in the Settlement a week later to pick up his mail. Although his correspondence with the outside world was even more circumscribed than his personal contacts, he did occasionally receive assignments from Foto-Syndicate for scenic mountain shots—a legacy from his late friend and benefactor Sid Rogenstein. The general delivery clerk handed him a plain envelope with a Baltimore postmark. Inside he found a round-trip plane ticket from Denver to Chicago made out to K. Saunders, and a typewritten note: "Call 301-266-4059." The note was unsigned. The ticket was dated the following day.

Inasmuch as it was the first personal letter he had received in two years, Vance had no difficulty surmising who had sent it. Slightly bemused by the cloak-and-dagger flavor of the correspondence, he nevertheless passed up the telephone office and placed the call collect from an outside booth, identifying himself to the operator as Mr. Saunders.

With no salutation, a woman's voice said: "Will you hold, please?"

She was followed almost immediately by a man. "Yes?"

Playing along, Vance said, "Vance."

"Vance who?"

"Cordell Vance."

"When is your birthday, Vance?"

"September 22."

"What brand of whisky do you drink?"

"Hudson Bay."

"What was your mother's maiden name?"

"Belcarine."

"Did you get the ticket?"

"Yes."

"Can you make it?"

"No."

"Why not?"

"I don't want to."

The voice at the other end of the line didn't sound like Dorsey's, but Vance suspected it was disguised.

"You won't be committing yourself."

"I've already committed myself—out."

"It is imperative that you be there on the sixteenth. A meeting has been set up."

"With whom?"

"I can't tell you that. I assure you you will be under no coercion. If you still don't want to do it, that will be the end of it."

"As far as I'm concerned, the other night was the end of it."

The impersonal voice at the other end thawed a trifle. "You'll be there."

"What makes you think so?"

"Because you can't resist it."

Vance considered the remark and realized it was true. "All right. I'll be there. What then?"

"Your name is Kenneth Saunders. There will be a room for you at the Driscoll Towers. Go directly there and wait. Don't leave the room."

So that was what the hell he was doing there, although he still didn't know why.

When the terra-transit delivered them at the terminal, he defied instructions by proceeding to the bar and lingering over two drinks. That was how long it took to reaffirm his antipathy to crowds—an antipathy which, on the few occasions he had tested it, was in no way diminished by his aversion to solitude.

He collected his overnight bag and hailed a taxi. The skepticism of his seat mate proved to be unfounded. Security measures were indeed in effect. A uniformed patrolman and a plain-clothes man halted the cab at the entrance to the causeway and inquired its destination. When the driver responded "Driscoll Towers," the plain-clothes man opened the right-hand door and swiftly ran an electronic detector over Vance's bag and his person. He asked to see his driver's license, noted down his name and description and examined his face to see that they tallied.

"Fuckin' Feds," the driver remarked, as they pulled onto the causeway. "They do it ever' time the President comes to town. You'd think only out-of-towners was allowed to bump him off."

As he walked through the lobby past the unobtrusive scrutiny of half a dozen hard-faced men in too neatly pressed dark suits, it occurred to Vance that Kenneth Saunders might have some difficulty in establishing his identity. Well, tough noodles, he thought ruefully. It's their responsibility. If they can't manage this little masquerade, they're not an outfit you would want to rely on too heavily.

At the registration desk, he gave the clerk his assumed name in response to an inquiry as to whether he had a reservation. The clerk flipped through a sparsely filled index file at his elbow, extracted a card and handed it to a thick-necked man who stood behind him, idly inspecting the incoming guests. The man stepped forward and pushed the registration pad across the counter.

"Glad to have you with us, Mr. Saunders. You'll be in Room 4287. It is ready for occupancy." The low-voiced announcement sounded more admonitory than informative. "We hope you will enjoy your stay with us."

Vance could feel the man's eyes boring through his scalp as he signed the register. Extemporaneously, he identified Kenneth Saunders as a petroleum engineer from Providence, Rhode Island, where, as far as he knew, petroleum engineers did not abound. His little whimsey was still-born, however, as the thick-necked apprentice desk clerk slipped the card in his side pocket, beckoned to a sharp-faced young man in a bellman's uniform and handed him the key. On the elevator trip, the bellman held the bag in front of him with his left hand and casually brushed his right sleeve over both surfaces, as if dusting it off.

The bellman led the way off the elevator at the forty-second floor, ignoring a heavy-set man sitting on a bench between the two banks. The lounger glanced cursorily at Vance as he passed, but his eyes followed them as they walked the length of a long, brightly lighted corridor. The bellman turned left into an intersecting corridor, scraped his knuckles lightly against a door on the right as he passed and halted in front of the next door. He opened it and preceded Vance into the room.

He conducted the conventional inspection tour, looking in the bathroom, the closet and checking the doors to both adjoining rooms. The curtains were drawn. He did not open them. He inspected the four dresser drawers, lifting a complete dining room menu from the top one. "Order anything you want," he said. "The bill will be taken care of."

He opened a cupboard in the night stand beside the double bed, removed a sealed bottle of Hudson Bay Scotch and a pony bottle of soda and placed them on the top of the stand. "You will find ice in the bathroom, of course," he said. "I trust everything will be satisfactory."

He moved toward the door, rested his hand on the knob, but did not turn it. In a less deferential tone he said, "It is requested that you not leave the room, nor use the telephone." For the first time he looked openly into Vance's eyes.

Vance returned the look without acknowledgment. He sauntered across the room, thrust his hand into his pocket and extended a dollar bill. The bellman darted a startled look at it, reached for it in confusion, pulled back, then accepted it gingerly between his thumb and forefinger. "Thank you, sir," he said, backing out the door.

Vance removed his coat and shoes, sandwiched the pillows and lay down on the bed. The room was larger and more elaborately furnished than most hotel rooms. In addition to the bed, it had a studio couch, three upholstered chairs, a coffee table, a couple of floor lamps, a cushioned window seat, a television-stereo recessed into a small alcove and a small but fully stocked bookcase.

Vance liked hotel rooms. They induced in him a sense of expectancy. He toyed with the thought of going down to the bar, picking up a woman and bringing her back to the room just to confound Dorsey's carefully laid plans. He dismissed the idea because it would destroy the sense of expectancy. And besides it was too much trouble.

He rolled off the bed, strolled to the window and looked out at the pasty city. Low-hanging clouds reflected a leaden glow from the blurred lights below. Fine snow, driven by a capricious, gusty wind, alternately swirled and pelted past the window. His muscles tensed in involuntary reflex against the bone-chilling cold outside.

He wandered over to the night stand, picked up the two bottles, carried them into the bathroom and mixed himself a drink. He stretched out in a maroon-colored easy chair and waited for the cloud of dark futility to drape itself over him. Instead, he found his omnipresent depression submerged by an almost pleasurable sense of suspense.

After half an hour he got up and mixed himself another drink. Glass in hand, he opened the door and stepped out into the corridor. Immediately, the doors on either side of his clicked ajar. A muscular, baldheaded man in shirt sleeves emerged from the one on his right and stood on the threshold, watching him impassively. Vance nodded to him. He nodded back. Vance stepped into his room and closed the door.

He paced across the room, then picked up the phone and punched the room-service button. Without consulting the menu, he ordered a filet mignon, rare, a baked potato, a tossed salad, coffee. Twelve years of field rations and army mess halls and two years of cooking for himself had severely circumscribed Cordell Vance's culinary horizons.

When he answered the subdued knock, he was not surprised to see the same bellman who had escorted him to his room standing self-consciously alongside a linen-covered cart. He wheeled the cart around the bed into the sitting area and looked about uncertainly. Vance regarded him impatiently, offering him no solace.

The bellman opened the table, uncovering dishes, smoothing the tablecloth, pondering his problem. Eventually he abandoned all pretense and stood in the middle of the room, frowning in undisguised perplexity. He glanced at Vance's neutral face and said, "Perhaps you would like to eat by the window, sir." Vance shook his head.

The bellman's eyes again roved the room, finally lighting on the half-opened door to the bathroom. With ruffled complacency, he stalked across the room and plucked a straight-backed chair from the dressing table. He returned, holding it aloft with one hand, and bowed Vance onto it with exaggerated deference.

"Will that be all, sir?" he said icily.

"For now. I'll ring for you if I need anything. Oh," he added as the bellman walked stiff-backed to the door. "You might bring me a paper. I'm sort of a shut-in, you know."

The bellman returned in forty-five minutes, silently handed Vance the newspaper, brushed aside the proffered tip and stonily wheeled the service cart out the door and down the hall. Vance sat down and skimmed through the paper. In the past two years, the major catastrophes and petty concerns of the outside world had ceased to have much relevancy for him.

He noted that the Air Line Pilots Association had condemned the Secretary of Transportation for issuing a certificate of convenience and necessity for the proposed intercity ballistic shuttle service between New York and Chicago; that India was protesting the intrusion of Pakistani marine harvesters into its hydroponic preserve; that President Lander was in Chicago to deliver an address before the International Consortium of Scientific Societies; that Argentina had defeated Colombia in the hemispheric finals of world soccer competition; that four persons had been killed in a skirmish along the Confederate-Mexican border at Nogales; that the temperature would drop to seven below zero at 3:40 A.M. Wednesday in Chicago.

Vance tossed aside the paper and strolled over to the book-case. He pulled out Gorall's account of the second Martian expedition—*The Stepping Stone*—and went back to his chair. He found it tedious, but persisted for nearly an hour. He flipped it closed, got up and wandered around the room in his stocking feet. He went to the window and contemplated the paralyzed city; a monument to a century and a half of man's incessant toil and inspired creation, helpless, obliterated by a contemptuous flick of nature's finger.

He felt a sudden, unbidden urge to be out in the storm, to lower his head and push against the wind. He was sitting on the couch, putting on his shoes, when a single, sharp rap sounded on one of the connecting doors. He looked up but remained seated. A key rattled in the lock and the door swung open.

A bulky man in a dark-brown suit stood in the doorway. He nodded pleasantly enough, but his eyes were unsmiling. "Excuse me," he said, stepping into the room. "Mind if I look around?"

Not waiting for an answer, he made the same inspection tour as the bellman, except that he looked behind the curtains as well as the three paintings on the wall. Vance heard voices in the other room, but saw no movement. He finished tying his shoes and leaned back on the couch. The silent visitor wound up his inspection by yanking the telephone jack out of the baseboard plug and carrying the instrument with him. He glanced once more at Vance as he closed the door behind him.

Vance clasped his fingers over one knee and waited. Two

minutes passed. The door opened quietly and two men entered. The first Vance recognized from his pictures as President Lander. Vance rose to his feet and automatically stood at attention. The President advanced toward him, seeming to bounce on his toes. His smile was warm but not effusive, his eyes friendly but appraising. He thrust out his hand, palm upward. "I'm Gordon Lander. You're Mr. Vance?"

Vance responded with something between a nod and a bow.

"How do you do, Mr. President," he said, not exactly flustered, but slightly discomposed.

The President peered at him for several seconds, as though memorizing his features. He stepped back and inclined his head toward the lank, bony-faced man who had followed him into the room. "This is Mr. Tazewell, Director of our Central Intelligence Agency."

Tazewell stepped forward and swung his long arm up in a controlled robot-like motion. He gave Vance a mechanical smile and a piercing look as they shook hands. "Mr. Vance," he said crisply.

"I want to apologize for imposing on you, Mr. Vance," the President said, sounding genuinely contrite. "Dr. Dorsey suggested I talk with you, and I thought Chicago might be a little more private than Washington. I trust it hasn't inconvenienced you too much."

"No, sir. It hasn't inconvenienced me. Mystified me maybe."

The President smiled. "Well, Mr. Vance, I can sympathize with you. That's the normal state of affairs in my job." He moved toward one of the chairs, sat down and stretched out his legs wearily. He glanced around the room and cocked an eyebrow at the bottle of Scotch sitting on the night stand.

"Is that drinking whisky, Mr. Vance? I might have a little libation. I've just delivered a dry speech to the International

Consortium of Scientific Societies, and that's almost as hard on the speaker as it is the audience."

"It was an excellent speech, Mr. President," Tazewell said. He followed Vance into the bathroom. "Let me give you a hand there. The President and I will have a little water with it."

Vance mixed two drinks and passed them to Tazewell, who added the ice and took a sip from each. He carried them into the other room and handed the President his glass.

Vance resumed his seat on the couch; Tazewell sat next to Lander. Vance had the feeling they were studying him like a rare insect. And he felt resentment welling up in him as it had in the white conference room in Rangoon.

The President took a swallow of his drink and sat twirling it in his hands. "I understand, Mr. Vance, that you have been given a general idea of what we have in mind."

"Yes, Mr. President. And I think I made it clear I didn't want any part of it."

"None of us wants any part of it, Mr. Vance." Lander's tone was regretful, as though he were discussing an increase in the cost of living. "Unfortunately it is a contingency which we may be forced to resort to. And I would like to stress that it is a last resort. We have considered a number of alternatives and they are unacceptable. We have no choice. You do, of course."

He paused, offering Vance an opportunity to speak. But Vance did not reply.

"I realize," the President continued, "that this is a despicable act we are asking you to perform. That's why I wanted to explain it to you myself. To assure you that the onus is entirely mine. You would merely be the instrument.

"I am told you are a man of some sensitivity, Mr. Vance. I imagine you would question whether the end justifies such disagreeable means. In this case I can only tell you, we feel it does. Rather, I feel it does. I am solely responsible for the decision."

Vance stared down at the patterned rug. "I don't doubt the necessity, Mr. President. I don't condemn your decision. It's just that I couldn't bring myself to do it. Even if it were possible. And I don't think it is."

Tazewell's pale-blue eyes fastened themselves on his. "You were a soldier, Vance. A damned good one they tell us. You know there are a lot of things a soldier doesn't want to do, but he does them. Because it's his duty."

Vance felt a welcome flutter of indignation. "Yes, I know that, Mr. Tazewell," he said respectfully. "Dorsey and I talked that over. The truth of the matter is, I don't really feel any sense of duty any more."

"I'm not saying you should." Tazewell dismissed the excuse as having no bearing on the subject. "I'm just saying you can force yourself to do something you don't want to do. We have checked you out pretty thoroughly, Mr. Vance, and we have satisfied ourselves that you are the man to do this job."

President Lander's face slowly clouded as he listened to the exchange. His lips tightened in annoyance.

"I think, Lawrence, we shouldn't pressure Mr. Vance. He really is under no obligation." He looked directly at Vance and said soberly, "More to the point, you couldn't possibly do it unless you were convinced yourself that it must be done. I gather Dr. Dorsey made it clear to you that the likelihood of your succeeding—and escaping with your life—is problematical at best."

Vance smiled. "I must admit, sir, that may have influenced my feelings in the matter."

"Well, Mr. Vance," the President said, "I'm sure you understand what is at stake here. I'm not going to tell you that the fate of the nation hinges on this mission. It doesn't.

If we must, we will destroy the Confederacy before it destroys us. Aside from the appalling bloodshed and misery that would entail, it would, I am convinced, have even direr consequences. It would inevitably pave the way for other nuclear conflicts and ultimately result in the destruction of civilization.

"But that is not your responsibility and I'm not trying to persuade you it is. I would, though, ask you to consider the dilemma with which I am faced. I suspect you feel the choice is not as clear-cut as I have made it out to be, that something will come up to alter the situation and make this decision unnecessary. That is entirely possible, of course, and I devoutly hope it will come to pass. But if it doesn't, I am going to take whatever steps are necessary to insure the survival of this country.

"The course I have suggested is revolting to me, as I know it is to you. I could in better conscience, I suppose, give the word to annihilate the Confederacy than to assassinate President Spearman. But I have reached the unhappy conclusion that this is a matter that transcends personal conscience. What I am proposing is a cowardly thing. But I honestly feel it would be more cowardly if we did not attempt it."

President Lander, still clutching his drink, rose from his chair and began to pace back and forth. He spoke more to himself than to his audience. "In times like these," he said, "it would be a comfort to rely on Divine Guidance. But I'm afraid old Abe Lincoln kind of shook my faith in Divine Guidance. He was a great believer in it, and look where it got us. He managed to postpone a war for one hundred and twenty years and now, Mr. Vance, the bill has come due."

"Gentlemen," President Lincoln said, peering myopically around the room at his advisers, some of whom he hardly knew, "I think we had best defer other matters today and take up the situation at Fort Sumter."

He shuffled through a small stack of papers on the table and extracted a single-page letter. "Major Anderson informs me that unless he is revictualed within ten days, he will be compelled to evacuate the fort. I would appreciate an expression of your views."

Full awareness of the gravity of the question was reflected in the faces of the seven men grouped around the table. The President, however, focused the issue.

"We need not delude ourselves. Evacuation is tantamount to surrender. And surrender of Fort Sumter will be regarded by our Southern sisters as an admission that we cannot or will not resist their secession from the Union. So, in a sense, the future of the nation hinges on that decision."

Secretary of State Seward raised his patrician head and inclined his beaked nose toward the President. He managed to convey by his tone a nice blend of homage to the office and condescension toward its occupant. "Mr. President, I do not impute quite so much importance to the defense of Fort Sumter. It has indeed become an unfortunate symbol of the differences between the North and the South. But I do not think we should permit a symbol to dictate what might prove to be a catastrophic course for our country.

"Even if we give up Fort Sumter, we by no means acknowledge the right of the Southern states to secede. We merely will have demonstrated our peaceful intent and our desire to settle this conflict without bloodshed. It will afford us time in which to pursue such a settlement.

"On the other hand, if we should attempt to reinforce the garrison—or even replenish its supplies—I fear we shall precipitate the open breach which we have so long sought to avoid."

"It is not we who would precipitate it, Mr. Seward." The President's voice was soft but firm. "Fort Sumter is federal property. There is no question about our legal right to supply

it. *Whoever interferes with us is the aggressor. It is of the utmost importance, of course, that that point be clearly established."*

"You're quite right, Mr. President," the Secretary of State replied indulgently. *"But I'm afraid the South is in no mood for legalisms. South Carolina regards herself as a sovereign nation. If we enter her territorial waters, she will no doubt claim she has been invaded. The other rebellious states will support her, and we have given them the provocation they've been looking for to justify their actions."*

Secretary of War Simon Cameron, *a sharp-faced political manipulator from Pennsylvania, grunted agreement.* "Make no mistake about it. Any attempt to relieve Fort Sumter will be regarded by the South as an act of war."

"I am under no misapprehension on that score, Mr. Cameron," the President said coolly. He looked around the table. *"Do any of you gentlemen think otherwise?"*

Gideon Welles, *Secretary of the Navy,* Caleb Smith, *Secretary of the Interior, and* Edward Bates, *Attorney General, shook their heads gloomily.* Salmon Chase, *Secretary of the Treasury, sat stiffly in his chair, giving no hint of assent or dissent.*

Postmaster General Montgomery Blair *brushed his prominent forehead with a quick, nervous gesture.* "Mr. President," he blurted, casting a dark, loaded glance at Secretary Seward, "I have no way of knowing what the reaction of the rebels may be. They have not taken me into their confidence. But whether or not they choose to seize upon the relief of Fort Sumter as a pretext for war seems to me to be beside the point. I believe it is time—"

"Yes, Mr. Blair," the President interrupted in his slow, high-pitched voice, *"it may be beside the point. But let us first make sure of the ground on which we stand."*

His dark, sunken eyes circled the table again. *"I take it, then, we are all aware of the probable consequences. Now we must decide whether the consequences are worth risking."*

"Is it not probable, Mr. President," the Secretary of the Navy said ponderously, "that a confrontation over Fort Sumter will drive Virginia, North Carolina and Tennessee into open alignment with the Confederacy?"

Lincoln nodded somberly. "It is entirely possible, Mr. Welles. And that is a contingency which we must of course weigh in reaching our decision."

"May I suggest, Mr. President," Seward interjected brusquely, "that we first consider the practical aspects of the problem. I think they may dispose of our dilemma. I believe Mr. Cameron has had some correspondence with General Scott and Major Anderson, touching on that subject."

The President turned a quizzical gaze on the Secretary of War. The latter shifted uneasily and fumbled in his pocket.

"As I mentioned to you, sir," he said, speaking hurriedly, "I thought it might be advisable to consult those most directly involved as to the feasibility of sending supplies and reinforcements to Fort Sumter. I have spoken directly with General Scott and have received an answer from Major Anderson."

He pulled an envelope from his pocket and extracted a single sheet of paper from it.

"If I may, I would like to read Major Anderson's letter, which is dated . . . April 5."

He glanced at the President's impassive face.

" 'To the Secretary of War, the Honorable Simon Cameron.
" 'Sir:
" 'I had the honor to receive by yesterday's mail the letter in which you inquire whether, in my judgment, it would be advisable and feasible to attempt to reprovision and reinforce the garrison under my command. Your inquiry surprises me

very greatly, as I was under the impression that Commissioner Crawford of South Carolina had been given firm assurances that Fort Sumter would be evacuated in the immediate future. I trust this matter will be at once put in a correct light, as a movement made now, when the South has been erroneously informed that none such will be attempted, would produce most disastrous results.

"'Even should a relief expedition reach our walls, the loss of life in unloading it would exceed the good to be accomplished. The truth is that the sooner we are out of this harbor the better. Our flag runs an hourly risk of being insulted, and I have not the power to protect it.

"'You are aware, sir, that I have endeavored with every resource at my command to discharge the difficult task which I have been assigned. I will continue to do my duty, though I frankly say that my heart is not in the war which I see is to be thus commenced. That God will still avert it, and cause us to resort to pacific measures to maintain our rights, is my ardent prayer.'"

Cameron folded the letter deliberately and returned it to its envelope as his eyes roved around the table. His colleagues sat in glum silence. Montgomery Blair's sharp features were compressed into a bellicose scowl. The Secretary of War turned his head and met the cold eyes of the President.

"Who gave assurances to the Commissioner from South Carolina that Sumter would be evacuated?" he demanded. It was a tone that none of them had ever heard from the President. They sat in uncomfortable silence. Montgomery Blair fixed his eyes on the starched countenance of the Secretary of State. As he watched, it underwent an imperceptible transformation from tight-lipped unconcern to studied concentration to bland reflection.

"It might possibly be, Mr. President," Seward said, "that

the Commissioner misconstrued something I may have said to Justice Campbell." His voice was not apologetic, but it was without its normal hint of haughtiness. "I have had several conversations with Justice John Campbell of the Supreme Court," he explained, glancing casually around at his colleagues. "I suspect he may have been acting as an intermediary for the Commissioners. Naturally, I wouldn't talk with them directly, but I did feel it might be useful to maintain some line of communication with them."

He addressed himself to President Lincoln, speaking more earnestly than was his custom. "Of course I filled you in on the substance of our talks. I told him we were anxious to avoid any inflammatory incidents. I did advise him that we had no present intention of reinforcing Fort Sumter, but I certainly gave no assurances that we would evacuate it. Justice Campbell hinted strongly that unless the Commissioners could report some positive progress in their efforts, Governor Perkins was resolved to open fire on the fort. I felt it imperative that we forestall any precipitate action on his part."

The President turned his brooding gaze on the Secretary of State. His quiet drawl held an abrasive edge. "It would appear to me, Mr. Seward, that you have forestalled any precipitate action on our part as well. And any action we take now will be regarded as precipitate. We have no choice but to relieve Fort Sumter or to evacuate it."

Seward's voice had regained its assurance. "Then, sir, I think our only choice is to evacuate it, in view of the testimony we have heard from Major Anderson. I don't see how such a move could be interpreted as weakness. It is obvious that the fort is militarily indefensible. If we abandon it voluntarily, I firmly believe it will be regarded as proof of our peaceful intentions. I feel it would have a most salutary effect on the other slaveholding states, and would cement their adherence to the Union."

Montgomery Blair could restrain himself no longer. "Poppy-cock," he exclaimed. Seward's Roman head snapped back as though it had been yanked with a bridle. His face reddened. His eyes blazed with outrage.

"I beg your pardon, Mr. Secretary," the Postmaster General said contritely. "I didn't mean to impugn your beliefs or your motives. I know you are as concerned as I am with the preservation of the Union. But, sir, we cannot preserve the Union by dismembering it."

The Secretary of State acknowledged his apology with a stiff inclination of his head. "I would hope," he said, "that we might decide this problem on the basis of reason, not emotionalism."

Montgomery Blair struggled to control his voice. "My God, if we could do that, we wouldn't have a problem. For four months we have been reasonable. We have done nothing. The South has been emotional. It has practically destroyed this nation." He lifted his arms, fists clenched, and cried out, "Mr. President, we have sat and talked too long. If we don't act now, there will be nothing to act on. Seven states have seceded from this Union and have formed a separate government. Every day it continues to exist, it will grow stronger and will attract more adherents. Every new conquest strengthens the rebels at home and solidifies their claims to recognition abroad. Millions of our own people will fight to preserve the Union now, but will they fight to restore it once it has been torn apart? I am convinced that the great mass of the Southern people are still loyal to the nation which belongs to them as much as to us. Their voice has been drowned out by the ranting of a handful of misguided zealots and power-thirsty demagogues. We must give them a standard to rally to.

"This country was founded on blood. If necessary, we must be willing to shed blood to save it. But I don't think it will be necessary. I believe Fort Sumter can be relieved with little

risk, if we move boldly. Such action, I feel, would fortify the resolution of our supporters—North and South—and would demoralize the rebellion. It would make clear the determination of the people and their President to maintain the authority of the government. That, in my judgment, is all it would take to restore it.

"In a matter of such moment, I don't think we can place too much reliance on the opinions of military commanders, who are naturally influenced by personal considerations. Should the attempt fail, I still think we would have accomplished our purpose. Should the attempt not be made, we will have disgraced ourselves and betrayed our children. We will have laid the groundwork for the same incessant strife and turmoil that have plagued the other continents of the world for centuries."

Blair folded his arms and glared defiantly around the table. His colleagues obviously had been impressed, if not moved, by the Postmaster General's fervor. Even Seward had listened attentively, if inscrutably. Lincoln's hooded eyes gave no insight into his thoughts. He turned his leonine head and looked questioningly at the Secretary of State, seated on his right.

Seward frowned and pursed his severe lips, but his words were more restrained and his tone less imperious. "I applaud the Postmaster General's lofty sentiments. If I believed that a show of force would be sufficient to quell the rebellion, I would heartily endorse it. But I do not believe it. Rather, I feel it is the one thing that would most likely provoke the conflict we seek to avoid.

"The South does not want war. Right now she is in the throes of an emotional fever. In a few months—or a few years —that fever will subside. In due time the slavery question will resolve itself. I am sure there is strong affection for the

Union throughout the South, an affection which will reassert itself if we do nothing at this crucial stage to strangle it.

"In addition, the South's economy is geared to ours. Emotion will not long prevail over material considerations. The firebrands and the flag-wavers are on stage now, but it is the merchant class which eventually will restore reason.

"Right now, Mr. President, the only real obstacle to a settlement of our differences is pride. The Southern states have maneuvered themselves—or have been maneuvered—into a position where they cannot honorably retreat. Time will ease that situation. Once they have demonstrated their independence, they will find a way to return to the fold. But they must do it voluntarily. That is why we must exercise forbearance during this period of stress. We are, after all, one people. I have every confidence that our common ties and our common sense will prevail, if they are not too severely strained."

The Secretary of State gave Montgomery Blair a challenging look and settled back in his chair, satisfied that he had clinched the argument.

"Thank you, Mr. Seward," the President said noncommittally.

Simon Cameron hitched his chair square with the table and ran a manicured finger inside his collar. "Mr. President, I realize that the decision to hold or to abandon Fort Sumter is of great political importance. But I do not think it would be prudent to make that decision without carefully examining the military consequences. I would be extremely reluctant to attempt to relieve Fort Sumter unless at the same time you were to issue a call for volunteers."

The President placed a bony hand on the table and abstractedly riffled his papers. "I'm afraid that would be out of the question. We are trying to reassure the Confederacy that we do not intend to resort to force except to counter aggres-

sion. Also, we have thus far refused to recognize that a state of insurgency exists."

He peered at the Secretary of War from under thick, black brows. "After all, sir, we do have a standing army. Do you not think it would be able to cope with disorganized militia and untrained recruits?"

Cameron squirmed uncomfortably and tugged at his collar. "As you know, Mr. President, the army is spread pretty thin. Our present complement is slightly under sixteen thousand officers' and men. Most of them are tied down in Indian country. It would be impossible, I am afraid, to attempt to secure all the federal installations in the Southern states, much less mount an expedition through hostile territory against organized resistance.

"As to the relief of Fort Sumter, I am not in complete agreement with General Scott and Major Anderson. I think it could be done. But I don't think it would be worth the effort. In order to hold it, we would certainly have to reduce the South Carolina batteries, which, as you know, have been greatly strengthened in the past few weeks. That would mean war, whether we fired first or they fired first.

"Mr. President, we are totally unprepared for war. I couldn't even guarantee to defend Washington against a determined attack. Particularly if Virginia throws in with the secessionists.

"As I see it, our only course now is conciliation. I think there is a very good chance, as Secretary Seward says, that the South may soon realize its error and return voluntarily. If not, we will at least gain time to build our defenses. In the long run, I can't foresee that they could ever be a serious threat to us. If, at some time in the future, it becomes necessary to undertake military action against them, we would certainly be better equipped to do it then than we are now."

The President went through the formality of polling the remaining members of the Cabinet, although he sensed that Seward's and Cameron's firm views had given them the justification they needed for postponing the fateful showdown. Gideon Welles, after first entering it on the record that the navy stood ready to sail to the rescue of the beleaguered garrison, allowed that the risks of such a venture outweighed any likely gains. Smith and Bates concurred.

Chase, the high-domed, austere Secretary of the Treasury, surprisingly had refrained from voicing an opinion throughout the debate, though he was a man who took little pains to conceal his confidence in his own superior judgment. He and Seward, both strong-minded, usually contrived to end up on opposite sides on any given issue. For that reason, perhaps, he cast a qualified vote for attempting to relieve Fort Sumter.

"Should actual hostilities result," he temporized, "it would perhaps be prudent to turn back. But we should at least assert our claim to sovereignty over federal installations, wherever they may be."

Montgomery Blair made a final appeal, but with less passion than he had previously displayed. "We cannot sacrifice principle for expediency," he said. "We have no right to pass our own troubles on to our children."

When they had finished, the President sat silent in his high-backed chair. The weight of his responsibility pressed down on every man in the room. Wearily he straightened his back, squared his sloping shoulders, raised his shaggy head, each movement distinct from the other like those of an uncoordinated puppet. The deep furrows, hollow cheeks and square jaw imparted a granite cast to his countenance, which was dissipated by the forlorn expression in his haunted eyes. His voice reflected both the harshness of his face and the sorrow of his eyes.

"I thank you, gentlemen, for your good counsel." He nodded gravely at Montgomery Blair. "Certainly our first concern must be for the future of the nation and those who will inherit it. It is our sacred duty to nurture and preserve for them those eternal rights of freedom, justice and opportunity which our fathers secured for us. We cannot shirk that responsibility.

"But will it serve our children and their children to pass on to them the bitter animosities that have racked our own generation? Perhaps intensified by fratricidal war? I have no doubt we can compel the allegiance of the dissident states if we are prepared to subjugate them by force of arms. But what kind of a Union will it be where one-third of our people feel themselves oppressed and coerced? And how soon will they rise up again? We do no favor to succeeding generations to bequeath to them a heritage of endless strife and turmoil.

"If I believed that we could wash out with blood the imagined grievances that have poisoned the minds of our brothers, I would not shrink from it. But history has proved it will not. The infection only festers and spreads.

"If we permit them to go their own way in peace, I fervently hope that in God's good time they will discover our destiny lies with each other. If they return to the Union of their own volition, it will bind us together with an inseparable bond of understanding and goodwill. If not, it is better to live apart in friendship, or at least tolerance, than to live together in hostility."

He turned to the Secretary of War. "Mr. Cameron, please instruct General Scott to arrange the evacuation of Fort Sumter as expeditiously as possible. Mr. Seward, please advise the Commissioners from South Carolina of our intentions and inform them we will hold the state of South Carolina responsible for the safe passage of the garrison."

The President ran a hand through his wiry hair. His

strained face had relaxed into its normal expression of gentle melancholy. He peered solemnly around the table. One by one, the members of the Cabinet gave a silent nod of acquiescence—even Montgomery Blair.

"We shall exert every effort," Abraham Lincoln said, "to dissuade the uncommitted states from seceding. I trust our restraint will have a salutary effect on them. I shall also ask the Congress to appropriate funds for a significant increase in our military strength. Should the Confederacy give any indication of aggressive intent, or should they attempt to incite rebellion in any state presently adhering to the Union, prompt and vigorous steps will be taken to suppress it.

"God grant," he added softly, "that our fellow countrymen may soon return to the fold; if not, that we may live eternally in peace with them."

A hundred and twenty years later his prayer was yet unanswered.

"The trouble is," Gordon James Lander said grimly, "there is always a temptation in a case like this to do nothing, because you can't really win regardless of what you do. If you act to prevent something from happening, and it doesn't happen, then there will always be the suspicion that it wouldn't have happened anyway. If you don't act, and it does happen, then it is obvious that you should have done something to prevent it from happening.

"We blame Lincoln for the break-up of the Union. But suppose he had taken a firm stand against secession. Despite what the historians say today, I believe it is quite possible that the South would have fought for its independence. Then Lincoln would have been blamed for precipitating a civil war. And God knows what our country would be like today if we had forced them back into the Union against their will.

"No," he went on reflectively, "in some ways I think the

choice we have to make is easier than his. We have made concessions and we simply can't make any more. At least the country is united behind us on that score. We know what *their* reaction is going to be, so we don't have to wonder about that. And we know what we are going to do to forestall them —if we have to. So really we have only one decision to make: whether we let events take their course or whether we try to change them."

President Lander placed his empty glass on the coffee table and sank into the easy chair.

"Conflicts between nations normally are based on deep-rooted animosities between peoples, as well as economic and territorial considerations. In this instance, none of those sources of friction exists. There have been long periods during the past one hundred and twenty years when we have gotten along very harmoniously with the Southern states. There is no reason why we shouldn't continue to do so. Except one.

"There have been many examples in history of wars that were more or less inevitable. There have been numerous other examples of wars that were completely without purpose, except for the glorification of one power-mad egomaniac. We can never know for certain, of course, but, in my opinion, the world would have been spared much suffering if Genghis Khan or Napoleon or Hitler had not been permitted to live. I am proposing to test that theory in the case of Howie Ray Spearman."

He paused and looked levelly at Cordell Vance. Vance squirmed like an unprepared schoolboy called upon to recite.

"Well, Mr. President," he said, "I can't argue with your theory. And, from your standpoint, I will admit that you would be justified in trying it out." He tossed out the statement and stubbornly let it lie there, with the inference that it was no concern of his.

Lawrence Tazewell frowned and started to speak, but the President picked up the discussion as though it were a casual dinner-table conversation.

"A good many years ago," he said reminiscently, "I was a district court judge right here in Illinois. That was in the dark ages when justice operated on the principle of an eye for an eye. In the course of my duties I was obliged to sentence eleven men to death. I didn't relish it, but I did it because they themselves had taken at least one life and the jury considered them a menace to society. Well, we don't do that any more. We rehabilitate them if we can, and confine them if we can't.

"I don't think there is any question that a jury would find Spearman guilty of the deaths of thousands and thousands of people, and certainly, from our standpoint at least, he is a menace to society. So I have rationalized it to this extent— that the moral and ethical grounds have been established. It is simply a matter of how to carry out the sentence. It is inconceivable that he can be rehabilitated, and it is impossible to confine him, so that leaves only one alternative."

He lowered his head and peered at Vance over the tops of his glasses. "Well, Mr. Vance, that is the case for the prosecution. Whether you agree to carry out the sentence or not, I wanted you to know that the judgment was not arrived at lightly."

Vance raised his eyes and met the President's probing gaze. "All right, sir," he said almost curtly. "You have convinced me it is something that should be done. But you haven't convinced me that it can be done—or that I should do it."

"No, I can't convince you of that," the President conceded without hesitation. "Only you can convince yourself."

Tazewell pulled his oversize feet back under his chair and thrust back his broad, bony shoulders. "If we didn't think it could be done," he said reprovingly, "we wouldn't ask you to do it. The Agency has drawn up several suggested approaches which we feel offer reasonable assurance of success, if carried through with determination."

"I thought you weren't supposed to have anything to do with it."

"Not with the actual execution of the deed. That will be up to whoever is chosen. We will, however, provide him with several alternative plans which he can adapt to the circumstances. The Agency will perform the necessary staff work and also provide all possible assistance short of direct involvement in the operation itself. We will see that you are—"

"Just a minute, Lawrence," the President cut in impatiently. "I thought it was made clear in our meetings with Dr. Corfmann that the success of an undertaking such as this depends entirely on the individual's resourcefulness and complete freedom of action. I would also remind you that the Agency is not to be involved, either directly or indirectly."

"I understand that, sir," the CIA Director said defensively. "But I feel we should let Mr. Vance know that he is not in this thing alone. That he has certain resources he can call upon."

"No," the President said firmly. "I think Mr. Vance should realize, if he agrees to do it, that he *is* in it alone. In extremity even the bravest man will call for help if help is available. I must tell you candidly, Mr. Vance, if you accept this assignment, you can expect no support, no thanks and no pity from your government. Let there be no mistake about that."

Strangely, Vance felt a rush of warmth toward the man who was condemning him so coldly. He nodded. "I understand, Mr. President. That's about what happened to me on my last assignment, but I didn't know the rules then."

"Yes," the President said. "I know. I intend to make that up to you some way."

"Uh-huh." Vance grinned irreverently. "You're going to give me a chance to redeem myself."

The President chuckled and stood up. "You know the story of 'The Man Without a Country.' I wouldn't blame you if you said 'God damn the United States.' But I hope you won't. Think it over, please. Dr. Dorsey will be in touch with you again."

He and Tazewell shook Vance's hand and disappeared into the adjoining room.

Vance mixed himself another drink and sat down on the couch. He tried to concentrate on the conversation he'd had with the President, but his thoughts kept wandering off onto irrelevancies, as though the subject were not of sufficient interest to hold his attention. He recalled his discussion with General Varnell in the compound at Muang Nau and how he had agreed to do what he had no intention of doing because it seemed to be the simplest way to end the feckless, futile argument. And just don't forget what that childish little impulse cost you, he reminded himself.

He swung his legs over the edge of the couch and sat upright, tossing off the remainder of his drink. He felt restless and listless, bored with himself yet satiated with company. He roamed over to the window and looked out.

Chapter Seven

The blizzard had stepped up its demonic assault on the cringing city. It swirled and screeched and howled through the vast, barren canyons. Cordell Vance plucked his coat off the bed, snatched his overcoat from the closet and went forth to challenge the storm.

He noted that the guardians of the corridor had abandoned their vigil. He strode across the sumptuous lobby, past a clump of shivering, stomping refugees, pushed through the revolving door and plunged into the teeth of the sleet-laden gale.

Forty-five minutes later he sat at the padded leather bar in the Carnival Lounge, savoring a Scotch and soda. He signaled the bartender for another and swiveled the low-backed stool around to survey the room. It was fairly crowded, considering the strong incentives for remaining home on such a night. The crowd seemed to be composed predominantly of well-tailored, self-assertive men of about his own age in business suits and too-shrill, self-conscious young girls in skirts and blouses. The storm, he surmised, had afforded a plausible excuse for those who were downtown to remain downtown. It was a world, he reflected with a small pang, to which he had never belonged.

As he turned back to his drink, he caught a glimpse of an ungainly figure lumbering across the table-cluttered floor toward the bar. He tilted his head and raised a hand to shield his face. Irrationally and impartially, he cursed the cruddy city of Chicago, the misbegotten impulse that had lured him to the Carnival Lounge and the arrogant oaf who was bearing down on him.

A beefy paw clutched his shoulder and a mocking voice rasped in his ear. "Well, if it isn't the old guerrilla fighter."

Vance revolved deliberately on his stool and stared into the corrugated face of Jerry Donaldson, wreathed in a gummy smile. "Hello, Jerry," he said.

Irrelevantly, he recalled his misstatement to Jo-Anne Christopherson that he didn't dislike anybody. Perhaps he should write to her and correct the record.

"I've been looking for you," Jerry brayed. "Nobody seemed to know where you were. You haven't kept in touch with your old buddies."

"No, I haven't."

"You getting along all right?" Donaldson leered. "Last I heard you were on the toboggan."

"No. I straightened up. Felt I owed it to my good friends who never lost faith in me."

"Glad to hear it," Jerry replied, ignoring the sarcasm. "I've got a proposition you might be interested in."

"I'm sure I would be. Your propositions are always interesting."

"This is a private matter. Stop by my room in fifteen minutes." He fished a key out of his pocket. "Three six one eight."

The imperious tone renewed Vance's loathing for this overbearing loud-mouth who fancied himself puppet master of the human race. He repressed an obscenity. He had seen Jerry Donaldson flay the skin from a foolhardy lieutenant who had had the temerity to criticize a column he had written excoriating the stupid politicians in Washington. His tongue was as venomous as his typewriter. Observing his tactics, Vance long ago had diagnosed his secret weapon as an unerring instinct for his opponent's jugular—the ability to goad his adversary into a frothing rage. So Vance launched a counterattack aimed at Donaldson's vulnerable point—his vanity.

"To tell you the truth, Jerry," he said, "I always suspected you were a bit of a fag—and I wouldn't care to go to your room with you."

The toothy smile faded, but the columnist responded affably. "Well, Major," he said, "I think I can refute that misconception. I've got a little piece over here I'd like you to meet. I'm sure she would be impressed by the great guerrilla fighter." He wrapped a salami-sized hand around Vance's biceps. "Come over and join us."

"I just stopped by for a nightcap. I'm on my way to bed."

A malicious glint flickered in Donaldson's red-veined eyes. "We can rehash old times and relive the glories of the past."

Despite himself, Vance felt a surge of his long-dormant lust for combat. He picked up his check and beckoned the bartender. "Okay, big operator," he said. "I'll go a couple of rounds with you."

Donaldson grinned complacently and plucked the check from Vance's fingers. "I'll take that, hero. It's little enough to do for a former fighting man."

He turned and plowed his way through the tangle of tables, tilting chairs without apology. Vance followed for a few steps, then veered over to the aisle fronting a row of booths. Jerry waved him to a semicircular booth in the extreme corner of the room near the service entrance and even with the orchestra platform, where a four-piece combo thrummed out monotonous rhythms. A dozen closely entwined couples marked time on a boxing-ring dance floor in front of the orchestra.

As Vance approached, Donaldson draped a long arm over his shoulders in a mock-friendly gesture. "Miss Fleming," he said, inclining his head toward a dark-haired girl sitting in the center of the booth, "may I present Major Cordell Vance, the scourge of Southeast Asia."

The girl coaxed her face into an indifferent smile. "Hello," she said with the prescribed quotient of enticing disinterest. Her hair was blue-black, her eyes a vivid blue, her eyelids light blue. She had a generous mouth, turned down at the corners, a petite nose, slightly tilted, a dark-skinned oval face, pronounced cheekbones and a determined chin. She looked to be in her early twenties—the finished product of a finishing school, lackadaisically shopping the male-merchandise counter.

Vance threw her slightly off balance by extending his hand. She accepted it without enthusiasm.

The two men seated themselves on either side of the girl. Donaldson reached out and blocked a waiter hurrying toward the kitchen.

"Sorry, sir," the waiter protested, "this is not my table."

"Well, buddy, you make it your table." His voice held a tinge of menace that punctured the waiter's professional hauteur. Muttering, he pulled out his pad.

"Double brandy, rye old-fashioned. What's yours, Vance? You still drinking that rice juice?"

Vance shook his head. "Not lately. Scotch and soda."

Donaldson thrust a bill into the waiter's hand. He turned and headed back toward the bar.

Jerry bent his head confidingly to the girl. "Cord here was a big hero in Thailand and Indonesia and Vietnam. I wrote several pieces about him. Gargantua, the Guerrilla Fighter, we called him."

"That must have been frightfully exciting."

"Yes," Vance said. "Frightfully." Then, turning away to face Donaldson: "What brings you to Chicago, Jerry?"

"Oh, Dancing Boy was out here making a speech to some scientists. I just thought I'd come out and see what he had to say about dismantling all our hardware and inviting the Commies into the kitchen."

"You don't approve of the treaty?"

"Well, now, if you read my column or listened to my broadcasts, you'd know what I think of the treaty."

"Oh, you still writing the column?"

"Yes," Jerry said tersely. "Maybe you ought to read it. Your name might crop up in it one of these days."

"Well, my clipping service would probably pick it up."

Donaldson scowled. The waiter brought the drinks and the columnist ordered another round. "Put this on my tab," he said, handing him Vance's bar check. He raised his glass. "Here's to the old guerrilla killer."

Donaldson turned to the girl. "He used to go out in the jungle and kill people with his bare hands. Killed scores of people, so they say. Course there was no way of keeping count." He looked across at Vance. "How many people you say you killed, hero?"

Vance fought back the spreading anger. The girl glanced at him, then said to Donaldson, "Let's dance."

"Not now," he replied brusquely. "The major and I want to talk over old times."

Vance stood up. "I'd like to dance with you, Miss Fleming. I'm a little rusty, but it doesn't look like we'll have to move around much."

She looked inquiringly at Donaldson. He nodded his assent and balefully watched the couple move to the dance floor.

They danced stiffly for a minute without speaking. Vance felt no urge to expand his acquaintance with the girl, and she extended no invitation to do so. She obviously was a self-centered dilettante—and a friend of Jerry Donaldson to boot. Since they could do precious little dancing on the packed floor, the silence was becoming obtrusive. He looked down at the top of her head. As far as he could tell, the shiny blue-black hair was natural. He pulled away from her and said, "Did you get caught in the storm, Miss . . . Fleming?"

She did not look at him. "No. Not exactly. I was having dinner with Jerry, but I didn't have time to go home and change."

Her tone was not apologetic, though the brown and green plaid suit she was wearing did not fit the hour or the occasion.

"Pretty raw out there," Vance said.

She ignored the remark. Having made the effort, Vance lapsed into silence.

She drew back and tilted her head slightly. She was quite tall. She looked at him and said matter-of-factly, "You and Jerry don't like each other much, do you?"

"Not much," Vance said.

"Why?"

"Well, as far as I'm concerned, you don't need a reason not to like Jerry Donaldson."

The girl accepted the answer without comment.

"You know him very well?" Vance asked.

"I've known him quite a while. I wouldn't say I know him well."

Beneath the veneer of sophistication, Vance caught a glimpse of a working intelligence. He wondered whether Donaldson was pursuing the flesh or the spirit.

They finished the dance and returned to the table. Another round of drinks had been delivered, and Jerry was halfway through his. He rose a trifle unsteadily and, with uncharacteristic gallantry, guided the girl into the booth. He stroked her arm as he seated her.

"Well, my dear," he said, "that's an experience you can tell your classmates about at your reunion. You danced with the famous Cordell Vance. He's a goddamned living legend, you know. Aren't you, Major?"

"I guess you could say that."

"And who made you a legend, Major Vance? I made you a legend, didn't I, Major Vance? And you made me a horse's ass, didn't you?"

Vance resisted the obvious retort.

Employing a patently practiced lecture technique, Donaldson switched his attention to the girl and continued professorially, "As I believe I pointed out in my talk to your class in communications arts, a symbol is worth ten thousand words. I made Major Vance the symbol of America's purpose. He was the sturdy Minuteman, the valiant defender of our fundamental beliefs. He knew why he was fighting, and who the enemy was. Unfortunately, Major Vance wasn't quite up to the role. Were you, hero?"

Vance lobbed it back to him. "To tell you the truth, I didn't care too much for the script."

"Oh, you didn't hurt me. I frankly confessed I had been taken in by you. But you did shake the faith of a good many people who identified with you, who were proud that someone was fighting for the things that America stands for." Donaldson's face was flushed. He could not resist reeling in his catch even though the fish was not firmly hooked. "The real tragedy was that you exposed the thinking element of this country to the ridicule of the bleeding-heart liberals." With an effort, he pulled back and tossed out the bait again. "Tell me, Vance, were you brainwashed or did you just sell out?"

Vance tugged on the line and turned it loose. "Or was I on their side all along?"

Jerry struggled to regain the initiative. "No," he said, "I don't believe that. You were a damned good soldier and you were killing Commies all right. But something happened to you. I dug into your record after you left Rangoon. It seems you stopped going out into the field about the time I wrote the pieces on you. General Varnell says you'd said some odd things just before you managed to get yourself captured. And it does seem a little strange that an old hand like you would walk into an ambush on your first patrol in a country where your presence would be damned embarrassing to the U.S."

Vance took a swig of his drink and gazed absently around the lounge. The crowd was beginning to thin out. The combo was on a break. The waiter sauntered toward their table, and Jerry signaled for another round. Vance stood up.

"Not for me. I've got to catch a plane in the morning."

"Sit down." Donaldson's voice held the harsh note of command that riled Vance more than anything he had said.

He edged his way out of the booth. "It's been real, Jerry. If you're ever in my neighborhood, be sure to look me up."

"Where's that?" Donaldson asked sharply.

"I don't think I said." He nodded to the girl. "Pleasure, Miss Fleming. Thanks for the dance."

Donaldson was suddenly placating. "Vance, I've always felt I may have been unfair to you. I'd like to hear your side of the story. Sit down and tell me what happened in the prison camp."

Vance shook his head. "I don't think that would serve much purpose. I told you what happened."

"Look," Donaldson said grudgingly, "I never blamed you for signing the statement. Maybe anybody would have done it under the circumstances. But why didn't you repudiate it when you got out?"

Vance shrugged and turned to leave. Jerry awkwardly disentangled his lank form from the booth and clutched his arm. He bent his head to Vance's ear and said in a low, urgent voice, "There's something I want to talk to you about. It's important."

Vance twisted his head in surprise and said coldly, "I haven't got anything to say to you. I don't give a damn what you write about me."

"It's not that. It's something that could make up . . . for what happened to you."

Vance started to brush the hand from his arm when he caught the eyes of the girl sitting in the booth. He read in them a helpless appeal. Reluctantly he returned to the booth and sat down.

Donaldson squeezed in beside the girl. He reached over and patted her hand. "Diane, why don't you run along? The major and I have a few things to talk over. I'll call you tomorrow."

She darted a glance at Vance's studiedly blank face. "It's blizzarding outside," she said lightly. "I can't go home now."

Vance felt mildly grateful that she had not seized the opportunity, that she had not merely been seeking succor from an importunate suitor.

"I'll grab you a cab," Jerry said. "Or why don't you get a room here for the night?"

The girl was suddenly serious. "Jerry, if I'm going to be in on it, I want to know what's going on."

Donaldson frowned, then twisted his ungainly head and gave her a searching look. "All right," he said, "but anything that's said here is between the three of us." He stared at Vance. "Understood?"

Vance had the feeling he had been this route before. "You know how I am," he said. "I've got a loose tongue."

Donaldson scowled at him, but his tone was conciliatory. "I think you'll be interested in what I have to say." He paused, obviously choosing his words with care. "Vance, you got a pretty bum shake, it seems to me, after what you had done for the U.S. of A."

He looked benignly across the table as though expecting an acknowledgment. Vance leaned back and shoved his hands in his pockets.

"But you got about what you could expect from a government that's been coddling Communists for five years. It's about time we got a government that will take a stand, and that will back up the people who are fighting its battles."

He waited for a response. Getting none, he went on: "It's not just the government. The whole damned country's gone soft. They won't elect anybody with guts. Any country that would elect a milksop like Lander twice is just asking for the Commies to come in and take over. And they'll do it unless somebody stops 'em."

That's not the way I heard it, Vance thought. "What's it got to do with me?" he asked. "I'm not in the hero business any more, you know."

"You saw how we pussyfooted around in Asia. The Commies just sucked us in deeper and deeper. We weren't hitting 'em where it would hurt. Either Lander and that intellectual idiot Barringer are just plain stupid, or they're selling us out on the installment plan. Unless we do something about it, the Commies are going to take over this country within the next three years—if they haven't already."

Vance was beginning to get interested, though he did not show it. "What do you propose to do about it?"

"We propose to stop them." He clamped his lips tight and glared at Vance.

"Fine. Then I guess there's nothing to worry about, is there?"

"Goddamnit," Donaldson snorted, "it's going to take the help of every able-bodied man and woman in this country who believes in the Constitution of the United States."

"I don't remember anything in the Constitution about over-throwing the government—if that's what you're talking about."

Donaldson's voice suddenly lost its abrasiveness. "I'm not talking about overthrowing the government," he said quietly. "I'm talking about picking up the pieces after it's knocked out."

"I doubt if the Communists would stand still for that."

"No, I doubt if they would," Donaldson said, as though addressing an obtuse schoolboy. "The Commies won't have anything to say about it."

Vance played the part assigned to him. "I thought you said the Communists were going to take over the country."

"Unless we do something about it," Jerry amended. "There are other people that wouldn't like to see that happen. We're not alone."

Again, Vance had the feeling he was repeating himself. "Spearman?"

Donaldson didn't follow the script. "The Confederacy can't afford to stand by and let the Communists take over this country," he said. "They'd be defending themselves. And, at the same time, protecting us."

"That's an interesting way to look at it," Vance said.

The girl suddenly leaned forward and spoke with an intensity that contradicted her façade of sophisticated aloofness. "Why do we have to be protected? Why doesn't everybody just mind their own business and leave everybody else alone?" She turned on Jerry. "You know I don't like the kind of materialistic society we live in. But I think we ought to change it ourselves. I certainly don't want anyone coming in here—Communists *or* Confederates—and telling me what to do."

Donaldson looked at her tolerantly. "You youngsters start out with a lot of half-baked ideas about living your own lives. Nobody lives his own life. He lives whatever kind of a life his environment shapes for him. The fact of the matter is, people don't really want to live their own lives. They're a damned sight happier if someone tells them what to do. Then they don't have to blame themselves if they screw up."

"Who's going to do the telling?" she flared.

"Spearman's worked out a very efficient system down South there." Donaldson spoke earnestly. "Everybody's got a job to do, and he does it. They're a lot happier than the great American consumer with his thirty-hour week and his five-dollar minimum hourly wage and his guaranteed annual income."

"Who does the telling?" the girl persisted.

"The people who are best fitted to do it. The people who have proved themselves by natural selection."

"Why wouldn't natural selection work just as well under our system?"

"Because nobody has got the guts to enforce it. So it deteriorates into favoritism." He smiled at her and said cryptically, "You'll see how it works. Those people down there are perfectly contented because they're doing what they are best suited to do."

The girl sat back, obviously troubled. Donaldson turned to Cordell Vance. "As I say, we don't plan to overthrow the government, so there's nothing subversive about what we're doing. But if there is an attack on this country from outside, we intend to be prepared to resist it . . . or to take advantage of it. There is a well-organized group of responsible citizens who share my views on the Communist menace. And there are elements among the military who are in full sympathy with the steps we are taking to meet it. I will tell you, confidentially, that General Varnell suggested we get in touch with you. He has a high opinion of your abilities—despite your little aberration. We need men with your skills."

Vance regarded him reflectively. "Let me get this straight. You want me to train a guerrilla force here in the United States?"

"Actually, it would be more in the nature of a pacification force. As far as you are concerned, you would merely be training groups of patriotic volunteers to defend the country against a possible Communist takeover. I can assure you, that is a very real danger. And if it comes, it will come with the connivance of certain members of the present administration.

"However, if a friendly power were to intervene to forestall such an eventuality, we would have to demonstrate that it was in support of a popular movement within this country. That's when we'd need your people. When the time comes, the political apparatus will be ready to function. Your job would be to guard against any counterrevolutionary activities on the part of the civilian population. You won't have to worry about the military. They'll have their hands full."

A pleasurable, uncomplicated anger washed over Vance. He tossed aside his carefully calculated game plan.

"Donaldson, you accused me of selling out to the Communists. What you're proposing isn't a sellout. It's plain, premeditated treason. Any way you slice it."

Donaldson's pulpy nostrils flared, his face purpled, his beefy neck seemed to overflow his collar. "You goddamned dupe," he exploded. "You can't see that this country has been sold for a mess of socialistic swill? That Lander is just a front for the Commies? That the moral fiber of the people has been deliberately eroded?"

He strove to control himself. "No, you wouldn't. You're basically a weakling yourself. When the chips were down, you didn't know what side you were on. You know why the Commies let you go? Because they saw you'd be no more good to them than you were to us. So they used you for the one thing you *were* good for—to discredit me!"

Vance smiled into Donaldson's maniacally contorted face. "Jerry, I always figured you for a dangerous bigot. But you're not dangerous. You're just a harmless, raving blow-hard. I can't see where a nut like you would fit into the evolutionary strata at all."

Donaldson uttered a strangled growl, and with his gorilla-like arms reached across the table, clutching at Vance's lapels. The girl raised a hapless hand to intervene, her eyes wide with astonishment. Vance sat motionless, his fingers still wrapped around his glass.

Jerry's gnarled fists closed on Vance's coat and yanked him forward and upward. Unresisting, Vance rose from his seat, bent awkwardly across the table. His left elbow suddenly cocked in a "V." The outer edge of his palm flashed forward and chopped into Jerry's throat just above the Adam's apple. The growl trailed off into a grunt and expired like a broken sound track. Donaldson collapsed into his seat, clutching at his neck, his face again turning purple.

Vance sat down, smoothing his coat. He twisted his head and looked at the girl. She was staring at Jerry's grotesquely swollen face, more in bewilderment than horror.

Donaldson's lips worked rhythmically, forming a succession of silent "O's," like a surfaced trout. His eyes bulged atop his craggy cheekbones. He was slumped forward, fighting for breath.

"Shouldn't you do something?" the girl stammered.

"He'll be all right," Vance said. He reached over Jerry's shoulders and hooked his fingers in his armpits. He gave a sharp jerk. Jerry's diaphragm rammed against the table. His chest heaved and he gulped in a lungful of air. He kept his head bowed, not looking at anyone.

"Are you okay?" the girl asked, placing her hand on his shoulder.

He raised his head toward Vance. "I'll get you, you son-of-a-bitch," he croaked.

Vance nodded at him, then edged his way out of the booth and stood up. Donaldson started to rise. Vance placed his palm on the sandy hair and thrust him back in his seat. He turned and walked unhurriedly away.

He retrieved his overcoat in the cloakroom, and as he moved toward the exit, the girl walked across the floor toward him. He waited for her. Without speaking, she reached into his side pocket, pulled out his room key, glanced at the plastic tag and dropped it back into his pocket. "I'd like to talk to you," she said. She gave him an impersonal look and headed back toward the booth.

Vance undressed, took a leisurely shower and stepped into his pajama bottoms. He poured himself a weak drink and stretched out on the bed. He felt fatigued and yet stimulated. For a man of his limited social proclivities, he reflected, it had been a large evening.

He reviewed the President's somber forebodings and Donaldson's incredible rantings. They seemed to tie in. All at once Robert Dorsey's fantasies seemed less unreal. He scowled at the thought of General Christian C. Varnell and Jerry Donaldson conspiring to direct the lives of two hundred million people. And particularly his own. Three years ago he had renounced control over his own destiny, but he did not relish turning it over to Jerry Donaldson.

He was suddenly struck by the paradox that he was exhilarated by the macabre prospects outlined by both the

President and Donaldson. Upon examination, he realized it was because he had been drawn into events that overshadowed his own dreary, joyless, corrosive existence. He had no intention of becoming involved in them, but at least momentarily they had swept away the fog of despondency.

His reverie was interrupted by a light tapping on the door. He had completely forgotten about the girl. He rolled off the bed and went to the door.

She stood in the hallway, elbows cupped in her hands, a fur-collared cloth coat draped over her arms. She looked coldly at Vance in his blue and white pajama trousers.

"You were maybe not expecting company," she said primly.

"I thought it would be nice if we just had an informal evening at home."

She hesitated as though debating whether to leave. Vance stepped out into the corridor, compromising her by his presence. She glanced uneasily down the hallway and hastily entered the room. Vance closed the door and extended a hand for her coat.

"Don't get any mistaken ideas," she said. "I wanted to talk to you. Nothing else."

"You weren't enthralled by my dancing?"

She walked to a chair and sat down demurely, knees close together. Her eyes roamed over his brown, sinewy torso.

"Where'd you get a tan like that in the middle of February?"

"Colorado, of all places," he said. "They've got lots of sunshine out there."

"I know," she said. "I've been skiing there. And the— punctures?" She rippled her fingers at the shrapnel scars.

"Oh, I picked them up here and there." He plucked his undershirt off the couch and slipped it over his head. "I'm sorry. I sometimes forget I'm disfigured. I trust," he said laconically, "they didn't upset you too much."

"Not at all. They're quite becoming."

Vance was vaguely irritated by the girl's air of restrained hostility. "What'll you have to drink?" he said. "Scotch and soda, Scotch and water or Scotch?"

"Nothing, thanks. Mr. Donaldson took care of me in that department."

"Mr. Donaldson has an extremely generous nature," Vance said, moving toward the bathroom. He mixed himself a drink. As he emerged, the girl said, "Oh, maybe I'll have just a small one. Soda."

He filled the order and handed her the glass without comment. She tilted it and looked at him over the rim.

"I think Jerry would kill you if he could," she said.

Vance pulled up a chair facing hers and sat down. "I doubt it. Jerry is a big talker."

"You think that's all he is?" There was an arresting note of concern in her voice.

Vance studied her face. Beneath the mask of indifference, she was worried.

"You came here to talk about Jerry?"

The girl nodded. "Sort of. Actually about me."

"Well, in case you're a close friend of his, I feel I should tell you—I'm not. Or perhaps you sensed that during our little discussion this evening."

The girl smiled wanly. "I'm not exactly a close friend of his. Maybe sort of a protégé. He conducted a seminar last year when I was in college, and he sort of singled me out. He usually calls me when he's in Chicago. I've been out with him a number of times. The past few months he's been taking me to meetings with him. That's what I want to talk to you about."

"What kind of meetings?"

"I don't exactly know. That's what bothers me. It's some

kind of political movement, but they're pretty mysterious about it. I've gotten in pretty deep with them, and it scares me after what he said tonight. I think Jerry is a brilliant man. And I believe in most of what he says. But I don't want to get involved in anything . . . subversive."

"What does he say that you believe in?"

"Well, he seems to realize that the people of my generation aren't satisfied with the way things are. The materialistic standard of values. That sort of thing. We're looking for some kind of a cause, I suppose. Jerry says everyone should have a place where he belongs, where he's contributing something. I believe that. But the way he explained it tonight, I don't think I want that."

"Look, Miss Fleming . . ."

"Diane."

"I'm not much good at giving advice. Or taking it either. So I don't feel I could be of much help to you. Besides, I happen not to like Jerry Donaldson, so I'm prejudiced."

"Do you think he was really serious—about what he said tonight?"

Unconsciously, she slipped off her shoes and crossed her ankles. She was no longer the blasé sophisticate but a troubled adolescent. Vance changed his tone.

"Yes, I think he was serious. And I think he would kill me if he could. I hate to say this, but I think Jerry is slightly insane. I never realized that until tonight. I think he and the other right-wing maniacs have got some harebrained scheme to take over the government. But I don't think anything will come of it. Those people have been ranting for twenty years, and all they ever do is scare everybody away. Servility is a pretty hard product to sell, even if you dress it up in a uniform."

Diane clasped her hands and looked at Vance like a child

with a guilty secret. "I don't think they're trying to sell anything," she said in a strained voice. "I think they're getting
ready to collect. You heard what Jerry said tonight."

"About 'a friendly power' intervening?"

She nodded tentatively, obviously debating how far to con-
fide in him. "I told you I've gone to quite a few meetings with
Jerry. It was exciting to sit in on the planning sessions, even
though I wasn't quite sure what they were planning. They
never talked about how they would come to power. Just what
they would do after they took over. And of course they never
talked like Jerry did tonight. It all sounded kind of idealistic.
Everyone would be doing what he was best fitted for, and it
would give him a sense of accomplishment. I was to be one
of the Youth Corps leaders. I told Jerry I was no good at
recruiting. He said there wouldn't be any recruiting. Everybody would be assigned.

"The last couple of meetings I attended, they had a man
from the Confederacy, who outlined the way their system
works. I began to see then where Jerry got his ideas. After
the meeting tonight, we went up to the man's room. They
talked about sending me to the Confederacy for a leadership-
training course. Apparently they've had this program going
for some time. The man said I would be sent to a 'resettle-
ment canton' in Oklahoma, where I would have a chance to
work under simulated 'reunification conditions.'

"Anyway, the whole thing seemed to be too carefully
planned—too final—for a sort of nebulous organization that
doesn't have any real prospect for putting its theories into
effect. Then when Jerry got so carried away tonight, I got a
little scared. What do you think?"

"It does appear you may be in over your head. I suppose it
would be difficult for you simply to pull out. I should think

the thing for you to do would be just to gradually lose interest."

The girl shook her head despairingly. "I don't think Jerry would let me. He never made me take any oaths, but when he took me to talk with the man from the Confederacy, they made it clear that I had gone too far to back out. You saw how he was tonight. He frightened me."

"Well, you could go to the police or the FBI, but I'm afraid they would probably brush you off. You haven't got anything very concrete to tell them."

Again the girl shook her head. "Jerry has told me they have a number of sympathizers among government officials—particularly in law enforcement agencies. I'm sure it would get back to him."

Reluctantly, he took a faltering step toward involvement. "I know someone who might be interested in Mr. Donaldson's little scheme. He might be able to help you."

He knew what Robert Dorsey's reaction would be if he tried to sidetrack him onto somebody else's problem. Dorsey would immediately suspect he had blabbed. Well, to hell with Dorsey.

"Tell me everything you know about this outfit."

She related to him how she had met Donaldson; how he had, over a period of time, picked out five or six members of the class and invited them to his apartment for "generation-spanning sessions." At first they talked about "life" and "values" and "the interrelationship of people."

Gradually, Donaldson began guiding the discussions into less ethereal channels. He contrasted the "bumbling antics" of President Lander with the serene wisdom of Plato's Philosopher King. Subtly but insistently, he made the point that the people were not equipped to choose their own rulers, that certain individuals were inherently destined to command, just as others were destined to follow. Casually drawing names from his own exalted circle of acquaintances, he ridiculed and lampooned the "goons" in Congress, whom the people, "in their inscrutable ignorance," had chosen to represent them.

The private seminars evolved into a sort of Socratic dialogue, with the students doing most of the talking and Donaldson pointing out the fallacies in their reasoning. He did not try to impose his ideas on them. Diane found the sessions more rewarding than any of her actual classes.

From time to time Donaldson would conduct a round-table discussion with his young seminarians on his syndicated television program. He called it "A Forum for the Future." Each of the participants was called upon to propound and defend one Utopian aspect of a theoretically perfect society. The Chicago *Tribune* praised the series as a "preview of the world of tomorrow." Diane became a bit of a celebrity in her own circle. She and another member of the panel were invited to debate with a pair of woolly-headed campus liberals. She felt her team came off very well. They had answers. The others had only questions.

Her disillusionment started when she was watching a rerun of one of the "Forums." She was suddenly struck by the uniformity of views expressed by the panel members and their resemblance to Jerry Donaldson's ideas. All the bold blueprints for the future, she perceived, were based on "harmony and order," which postulated a universal acceptance of what was harmonious and orderly. From then on, she was not entirely comfortable in her faith.

Shortly after Jerry returned to Washington, he wrote his apostles, announcing the formation of the Orderly Evolution Society and asking them to organize a chapter in Chicago. They did as he had requested. The response was extremely gratifying. In six months, twenty-four branches had sprung up throughout the city and the suburbs. Headquarters in Washington supplied the local units with "Discussion Topics," which, in toto, amounted to full-blown plans for remaking the social and economic structure of the nation. Diane was a bit uneasy about some of the suggestions. But more disconcerting was the discovery that she didn't like the people who were attracted to the movement.

On his trips to Chicago, Jerry gradually introduced Diane into the hierarchy of the local chapter. She accepted her role without ever fully embracing it.

When she had finished her recital, the girl turned her deep-blue eyes on Vance in a look of childlike appeal, anxiety mingled with relief. Inexplicably, her helplessness stirred an angry resentment in him.

"Tell me," he said brusquely, "why'd you come to me? There must be somebody else you could have told." Immediately he regretted his words.

The girl shrank back as though he had struck her. The mask settled over her face. "I'm sorry to have bothered you," she said coldly. "You seemed like somebody who could help me. I suppose because you stood up to Jerry. And I gathered you had gone through something like this yourself. I've tried to talk about it to my parents and a few other people. Nobody takes it seriously. They say nothing will come of it. Maybe it won't. I know it sounds fantastic. But they seem so sure of themselves. And nobody is trying to stop them."

Vance recalled the President's grim words and the CIA Director's stony face. "I'm sure somebody's aware of what they're up to. They'll stop them when the time comes. You can't take over a country with no more support than they have."

"I know that. But what about . . . what Jerry said tonight? What if they're conspiring with the Confederacy?"

"That's not your responsibility," he said curtly. That was for damned sure. And it wasn't his responsibility either. "You worry about saving yourself. Let somebody else worry about saving the country."

"I tell myself that, but I can't convince myself. I got into this because I wanted to do something . . . meaningful. Even if I could drop out, I'd just be back where I started. Worse. Because I had a chance to do something, and I ran away from it."

Vance scowled. That was Dorsey's line. Maybe he *should* put Dorsey in touch with the girl.

Diane saw the vexation on his face. She slipped her shoes on and stood up.

"Well," she said, "thanks for listening to my problem. It'll work itself out somehow."

Vance felt a sudden self-loathing. A frightened human being had reached out a hand to him for help and he had pushed it aside. Then the miracle slowly dawned on him. The hand had touched him. Nothing had ever really touched him since that dark night in the car when his father squeezed his knee and said, "You know you're not coming back here." That had been his last actual human contact.

He pushed himself up from the chair and stood staring into the cool blue eyes. She returned his gaze, at first questioningly, then with gradual comprehension. She smiled uncertainly. He moved toward her and clasped her in his arms. She lifted her head. They kissed. He held her loosely around the waist, marveling at the unknown taste of tenderness. Again he kissed her—gently.

"You know," she whispered, "I don't even know your first name."

He told her. "That's a nice name," she said. "You're a nice person."

He uttered a short explosive laugh. With the possible exception of his mother, no one had ever called him a nice person, and it was the last appellation he would have applied to himself. He led her to the couch, then refilled their glasses.

He touched his glass to hers. "To the beginning," he said.

He sat beside her and they looked at each other. She ran her hand up the side of his face and through his crisp black hair.

"Can you imagine?" she said. "When I first saw you tonight, I didn't pay any attention to you."

"That's good. You wouldn't have liked me. I was someone else then."

"Who were you?"

Surprisingly, he began to tell her. They lay side by side on the couch, talking, touching, occasionally kissing, but mostly just floating on a gentle current of euphoria. It was magical, incredible. And yet, now that it had happened, it was inevitable.

In time, without words, with no exchange of shy, questioning looks, they rose from the couch, undressed and got into bed. They explored each other's body as they had explored each other's thoughts.

She looked up at him with shining eyes. He smiled down at her, gave a final playful thrust and pressed his cheek against hers.

"I think," he said, "I love you."

When he awoke the next morning in Room 4287 of the Driscoll Towers, his body responded instinctively to the warmth of her firm haunches nestled against his groin. Almost as instinctively, his mind began erecting a barricade against the inevitable wave of revulsion that would ride in on the tide of consciousness. It did not come. Instead, he was suffused with a dimly remembered aura of childish anticipation, a feeling that he was awakening to a long-awaited day of delight.

Awareness came to him, yet he remained suspended in a web of wonderment. He opened his eyes and inhaled the fragrance of her hair. She rolled over and pressed herself against him. The world which she feared and he detested was suddenly warm and friendly and enchanted.

As though emerging from a chrysalis, they simply sloughed off the trappings of their old lives. Vance canceled his flight to Denver. Diane abandoned her classes at the University of Chicago's Graduate School. She did suggest that they might move to her apartment, but both of them knew intuitively that their new love was too fragile to be exposed to old surroundings, old routines and old acquaintances.

She picked up her car in the garage while he checked out of the hotel. He waited outside her apartment while she gathered together the multitude of feminine indispensables and stuffed them all into one suitcase. They drove north on Lake Shore Drive between ugly trenches of soot-stained snow. A snarling wind lashed fitfully at the small Jolo-Casta two-seater as it slithered through the sparse traffic. The grimy, brown-brick tenements on the left gazed vacantly across the leafless park at the ceaselessly churning lake. Dirty-gray clouds glowered from above. Inside the car, Cordell Vance and Diane Fleming held hands and basked in the radiance of their weatherproof, peopleproof timeless capsule.

Somewhere along the dreary façade of family-size containers, they came upon an old-fashioned *grand dame* of the twenties, set back from the Drive like a maiden aunt, relegated to the servants' quarters. A semicircular entranceway extended open arms from a stone-columned portico.

An elderly Negro in a worn uniform greeted them with

cordial dignity, as if they were house guests arriving at a country estate. He shepherded them through the registration ritual, then ushered them into a rickety elevator. He kept his back to them with elaborate unconcern during the slow ascent to the eleventh floor. They followed him down a wide, dusky corridor with a frayed carpet. He unlocked the last door on the right and invited them in with a courtly gesture.

"One of our nicest rooms," he said pridefully. "Used to be part of the Bridal Suite in the old days. They chopped it up some since." He shook his head disapprovingly.

It was not exceptionally large, but its high ceiling, curlicued cornices and tall, narrow windows gave it an air of archaic elegance. Its white-enameled walls had mellowed to a pale ivory. An old-fashioned fourposter without a canopy extended into the middle of the room. Sideboards enclosed a hip-high mound of mattresses and downy comforters, covered by a worn chenille bedspread.

The old retainer raised the blinds on the two slender windows, which were framed by faded blue curtains, draped in the middle. Snowflakes drifted down outside, blotting out the angry lake and the grimy city.

The bellman adjusted the thermostat, opened and closed drawers and shuffled into the bathroom. Diane and Cord were facing him as he came out, idly swinging an arm in front of him. Startled, he froze as he confronted them, hand upraised, two fingers extended as though bestowing a benediction on them. The lovers considered this an auspicious omen.

The days floated by in a kaleidoscopic blur—moments of sharply etched joy dissolving into long hours of tranquil, unfathomable content. The ugly, smelly, noisy city lifted its surly mask and opened up to them its hidden troves of pleasure.

They rose late and breakfasted, usually alone, in the sedate, high-ceilinged dining room in an atmosphere of genteel, decaying elegance. The weighted and dented knives and forks, bearing the hotel's monogram, and the snowy linen table-cloths mysteriously imparted a sense of permanence and solidarity to the gossamer unreality in which they lived.

After breakfast they would sometimes wander along the lake front, or drive north through the peaceful middle-class suburbs, or walk leisurely through the scurrying, stern-faced crowds in the Loop. Usually they would stop off in the late afternoon in a quiet neighborhood lounge—but never the same one twice.

Everywhere they went seemed to be invested with a quaint and gracious charm. Everyone they met was cheerful and friendly, as though sharing in the warmth of their love. The city itself took on the hearty, boisterous character of its legend.

They never spoke of the future, rarely of the past. Not that they deliberately avoided it—but there were so many timeless things to say; things they had thought and felt and never said, because there was no one to say them to; things they had never thought and never felt but which suddenly they did. They talked of everything and nothing, but always the topic was themselves, and the miracle that had happened to them. They didn't call it a miracle. They accepted it and relished it, but they did not dissect it or project it.

Once Diane suggested that she take Cord to meet her parents in Fort Wayne, Indiana. But he balked. "Look," he said, "I've got a mark on me. You may not see it, but other people do. They'd be polite to me, but they'd try to convince you that I'm not the one for you. And they'd probably be right."

The girl lifted the back of his hand to her lips. "If you're not the one, then there never will be one. And that's a pretty dismal prospect for a girl who has so much to offer."

Nothing in Diane's background could account for the bond between them. She was one of three daughters of a fairly wealthy banker. The family was prominent in Fort Wayne society, and she had suffered no traumas in her childhood or adolescence. Her stunning looks and her native intelligence attracted a number of eligible swains, and she seemed destined for admission into the young country club set as soon as she finished college and chose a suitable mate. In the normal course, she would have attended either St. Mary's of the Lake or St. Mary's of the Woods, but she did not follow the normal course. To the puzzlement of her parents, she insisted on enrolling at the unfashionable University of Chicago and living in an apartment by herself.

She devoted most of her freshman year to investigating the unfamiliar facets of adulthood. She sampled pot, LSD and more esoteric drugs. She breezed through a short course in conventional sex under the tutelage of a fairly competent premed student. She sat in on several sessions of various campus radical organizations, but joined none of them. She went to dances, the theater, music festivals, one orgy in which she did not fully participate and several demonstrations against the establishment. She derived no great satisfaction from any of her extracurricular activities, and she looked forward to returning to Fort Wayne. But she discovered she did not belong there either.

When she went back to Chicago for her sophomore year, she began to concentrate on her studies, more out of boredom with her laboratory experiments in living than because of any strong intellectual pull. She became tepidly interested in political science. Her interest quickened when she was exposed to Jerry Donaldson's stimulating dogma. She began to think. That unfortunate circumstance led her into the quandary in which Cordell Vance found her. While he offered few directions to guide her in her quest for meaning and fulfillment, he did give her the solace of knowing she was not making the journey by herself.

Actually, he learned more from her than she learned from him. She at least knew the recipe for a normal, dull, humdrum existence, though she did not find it to her liking. He had never even known the ingredients.

But mostly they learned about themselves and about each other. Vance was astonished to discover in himself an unsuspected strain of gentleness and an untapped reservoir of love. Diane was not astonished because she was not aware that before her they had not existed. She *was* aware that for the first time she was truly alive.

Each discovered in the other engaging mannerisms and physical traits which, to an objective observer, would have been merely peculiarities. As a result of too frequent exposure to artillery fire, Vance was slightly deaf in his right ear. When Diane spoke softly, he would sometimes tilt his head sideways in an odd, birdlike gesture which she found boyishly irresistible. The crooked little finger of his left hand—souvenir of an errant foul tip in college—impressed her as a "physiological improvement which should be incorporated in all male models" because it fit so nicely when they strolled down the street with little fingers entwined. She delighted in the lean, swarthy hardness of his torso with its pitted scars.

For his part, he was enchanted with everything about her, though he did not always put it poetically. He once remarked as she walked nude across the room from the bath, "You know, you've ruined my aesthetic judgment. Your legs are too long, your mouth is too large, you're a little sway-backed, yet to me you're the most beautiful woman in the world. Hereafter, I'll measure every other woman by how much she looks like you."

"There isn't going to be any hereafter."

Vance lay back on the bed and stared at the ceiling. "I wish to God you were right," he said.

Struck by the bitterness of his tone, she sat on the bed beside him and looked down into his face. "My whole world has changed," she said. "Hasn't yours?"

"Yes," he said. "My world has changed. But I'm not sure I have."

"You told me you were a different person than the one I first met."

"I am. I'm always kind of leery when something nice happens to me. Like Caesar said, 'The gods have been good to him that he may suffer more by the change in things.' " He pulled her down beside him. "But then," he murmured, "what's the use of trying to second-guess the gods."

The world did not intrude again. For ten days the spell lasted. On the eleventh, Cordell Vance awoke and marveled anew at the swift-rolling wave of joyous expectancy that engulfed him. He lay still and braced himself for the following swell of love and desire that he knew would come. And it did. But then suddenly he was plunging down into the dark, desolate trough in which he had wallowed for so long.

A low, stricken moan welled up from deep inside him. Not because of the return of the pain, which he had learned to endure, but because of the withering of the hope that had begun to bud.

Diane rolled over and enfolded him in her arms. He clutched her fiercely, but he knew with implacable certainty his love could not survive the malignant sickness of his soul. In the end he persuaded Diane—though he did not convince her—that only he could exorcise his private demon. That he must go away, and she must not follow him. He went back to the mountain. For three days he grappled with the black phantom. On the fourth day he called the Baltimore number. That night Robert Dorsey knocked softly on the door of his cabin.

Part Four

Chapter Eight

The sun-streaked blonde at counter "U-V-W" neatly inscribed her initials at the bottom of Cordell Vance's customs declaration and handed him the carbon copy, flashing what the manual no doubt described as a sincere smile.

"Thank you for coming to Fabulous Florida," she said, lowering her voice half an octave, thereby transforming herself from a brusque bureaucrat into a sexy greeter. "We hope you will enjoy your stay with us."

Vance grinned—not so much at her as at the incongruity of hardly-ever land. The sovereign Republic of Florida had never quite made up its mind whether it was a country or a country club. Actually, it was not quite either, but a creature of its own geography.

Separated from the North by the entire body of the Confederacy, Florida had, as a matter of course, been among the first states to secede—but without any great rancor. Insulated from the border frictions that rubbed raw the sores of conflict, it basked for half a century in the sun and surf, an island floating serenely away from the mainland.

It watched with sluggish envy the great convulsion that transformed the rest of the Confederacy into a newly hatched industrial nation during the latter decades of the nineteenth century. Geographically isolated, sparsely populated by the remnants of surly Indian tribes and clusters of equally surly

Crackers, the Florida peninsula offered no very tempting market to the new, impatient breed of Southern money-makers. By 1900 it had achieved the status of a sun-baked, snake-infested sand spit—good enough for the natives, but not good for much else.

For the next two decades it drowsed in the sultry heat, a haven for ne'er-do-wells and a mecca for nonconformists from both the North and the South. It was a place for people who liked to be left alone.

In the period of relatively cordial relations between the United States and the Confederate States of America following the First World War, the new rich and the old rich from both countries discovered the peninsula and invested it with a new resource—snob appeal. They were followed in short order by the would-be rich, and by 1920 Florida was in the throes of an enormous social and economic upheaval. Its population skyrocketed, its torpor evaporated and the Confederate States of America found itself harboring a colony of wealthy and poverty-stricken iconoclasts with no sense of fealty to its laws or traditions.

Those from the North arrived with an inherent distaste for the autocratic paternalism of the Confederacy. Those from the South were for the most part either mercenaries, malcontents or both. Neither element was inclined or equipped to contribute much stability to the emerging social order.

Attracted by quick profits and lush wages, investment money and skilled workers gravitated to the Land of the Big Boom, draining the entire Confederacy of both capital and labor. Egged on by their sister states, Alabama and Georgia imposed rigid restrictions on travel and trade across the Florida border. The sanctions infuriated the touchy Floridians, both natives and newcomers, and instilled in the motley populace a sense of outraged community interest. In addition, they stimulated the flow of men and money from the North. The Confederate Congress responded by banning all immigration and investment from the United States.

The Florida boom immediately collapsed. Overnight the state was plunged into bankruptcy. Its ebullient populace of freewheeling millionaires and empire builders, congenital con men and grifters, businessmen, speculators, laborers, salesmen and unreconstructed idlers was united into one vengeful citizenry. On December 15, 1925, the Florida legislature met in special session at Tallahassee. Two days later, after allowing time for sober reflection and a good deal of impassioned oratory, it passed a resolution of secession from the Confederate States of America, subject to ratification by a referendum of the people.

Deploring the "hasty and intemperate" action of their "esteemed neighbor," Alabama and Georgia rescinded their sanctions. Charitable and civic organizations throughout the South collected and shipped quantities of canned goods and used clothing to their distressed brethren. The Congress of the Confederacy rushed through a sizable "Southeast Area" relief appropriation, and authorized construction of a forty-million-dollar defense installation in central Florida. Southern railroads announced special half-fare excursion rates (round-trip) to any point in Florida.

On January 20, 1926, the electorate voted 1,324,605 to 112,-614 to sever the state's historic ties with the Confederacy, and to establish the sovereign Republic of Florida. The state legislature was designated the governing body pro tem, and Governor Conklin was invested with extraordinary powers to "maintain and preserve the security of the nation" during the changeover.

Two weeks later, on his orders, troops of the Florida militia occupied without resistance the naval base at Jacksonville, the naval air station at Dinner Key, Fort Pearson, the large army base near Cocoa and twenty-three armories throughout the state. The Republic promised repatriation of all military and civilian personnel and compensation for all property and equipment formerly belonging to the Confederate States of America.

On February 18 U.S. President Calvin Coolidge extended formal diplomatic recognition to the new nation and pledged "economic and military assistance, if necessary, to insure its integrity and independence." The Confederate States ordered a partial mobilization of its military forces and the United States followed suit.

Public opinion within the Confederacy was divided, as it had been seventy-five years earlier in the United States. A good many rabid "Preservationists" loudly insisted that Florida must be restrained, by force if necessary, from "deserting the sacred sisterhood of states." Their arguments were more rhetorical than logical, inasmuch as precedent was clearly against them. The Confederate Constitution plainly asserted the "sovereign and independent character" of the individual states.

President Underwood dawdled and procrastinated for nearly a year, trying by various stratagems to woo the defector back. By the time he got around to acknowledging Florida's right to secede, the matter had become academic, except to a few die-hard Preservationists. Actually, not so few. One enterprising flag manufacturer turned a tidy profit by continuing to produce fourteen-star flags for another twenty years.

In the succeeding decades, the "Playground of the Western World" sailed a precarious course between its sometimes bellicose neighbors, becoming increasingly adept at tacking with the prevailing wind. Its economy was at the mercy of the North, its security was dependent on the South and its heart belonged to neither. Eventually it managed to achieve the happy status of an American Switzerland—tolerated as a convenient market place for essential commerce and intercourse between two powerful antagonists.

Cordell Vance stepped aboard the pedestrian belt with his single bag and flicked his customs clearance at the guard as he moved through the electronic doors into the vast, round, bubble-topped terminal of Miami International Interchange. He rode the mobile promenade around the circumference of the huge arena, head bent, eyes lowered, not inviting any chance encounters.

At the Caribbean Causeway, he stepped off, set down his bag and pulled a pair of deep-aqua sunglasses from his inside coat pocket. He adjusted them on his nose, glanced casually around and walked through the exit into the purple twilight of the semitropics. He sucked in a lungful of the muggy air and exhaled slowly. Compared with the chill thin air of the Colorado Rockies, it was like breathing jellied consommé. But even here, adulterated with all the stench and fumes of a polluted civilization, it bore a faint fragrance of subtly mingled flowers. Though he had been here only twice before, briefly, Vance had been beguiled by Miami's languorous charm and stimulated by its frantic pleasure-seeking. It was a city with a dozen different flavors, custom blended to satisfy the most discriminating taste—provided, of course, the customer was willing to pay for it.

Vance strolled down the simulated-crystal sidewalk, tinted in a variety of pastel colors, past the taxi-loading zone to the Private Transport Area. A maroon Buick Executive pulled silently to the curb beside him. A burly Negro wearing dark glasses and a chauffeur's cap stepped out, walked around and opened the rear door.

"Yas-suh," he said with hearty servility. "Let me put yoh bag up front heah." He ushered Vance into the back seat and carefully closed the door. Not until he had cleared the loading area and turned onto the parkway leading to the airport gate did he glance at his passenger in the rear-view mirror.

"Y'all have comf-table trip, Mistuh Tre-mont?"

Vance met his eyes in the mirror. "You just tend to your driving, boy," he said. "Don't get uppity with me."

The Negro grinned and hunched his shoulders as though expecting a blow. A smile tugged at Vance's mouth. "You seem to have got yourself a pretty good tan since you've been down here," he said.

Robert Dorsey examined himself in the mirror. "It does seem to have firmed up some," he said. His voice became businesslike. "You didn't run into anybody you knew?"

Vance shook his head. "How are things going at this end?"

"Our man came out yesterday. He's got a five-day permit. You'll go in on Sunday. Everything seems to be in order."

A guard waved them through the gate at the airport boundary and Dorsey turned south on the Palmetto Expressway. Tall apartment buildings flanked the highway on either side. Behind them, acre upon acre of blue and pink and white stucco cottages dotted the sandy soil, like squat, wild-blooming shrubs. Pretty and peaceful.

Vance turned his head and focused his eyes on the back of Dorsey's thick-muscled neck, rooted like the base of a tree in powerful sloping shoulders. The sight was somehow comforting. Over the past six weeks he had acquired a deepening respect and even a contained liking for the imperturbable black giant, whose mind, he had discovered, was as formidable as his mountainous body.

Cordell Vance had lived as long as he had because he had heeded the basic precept of the risk-taking business: reduce the risk to the irreducible minimum. There didn't seem to be much he could do about the present situation—suicide was suicide, any way you sliced it. But Dorsey seemed to have done everything that could be done. Vance felt no sentimental gratitude toward him. After all, Dorsey was the one who had dragged him into this thing. And he had evinced no personal concern for Vance. But he had devoted as much care and competence to the preparations as if his own life were at stake. Vance's feeling toward him was ambivalent. Like a condemned man he was grateful to the executioner for arranging things as tidily and painlessly as possible.

He looked up into the mirror and saw Dorsey studying his face. That was one thing that did irritate him. Dorsey still apparently regarded him as an experimental weapon that might or might not prove out. If not, all the work that had gone into its development was wasted.

"How you feeling about it now?" Dorsey inquired with the solicitude of a physician making hospital rounds.

"The same as I've always felt. Like a sacrificial goat."

"It's not too late to pull out."

"I may just do that. You still planning the face-lifting?"

"The doctor'll be here tomorrow. You'd better make up your mind before then if you want to keep the one you've got."

Vance grunted. Dorsey dropped a steak-sized hand on the suitcase sitting beside him. "Anything in here you think you'll need?"

Vance shook his head.

"I'll pass it on to Tremont. Help him get a start in life. You've removed all identification?"

Vance nodded. "Does he know who I am?"

"No. Of course he *will* know your name when we give him your passport and visa. But he won't use it after he gets to the States."

The car had skirted downtown Miami, Coral Gables and Coconut Grove. Dorsey pulled off the expressway and angled toward the ocean. He followed the coast to Florida City, turned onto a side street and drove up alongside the Cantina Marina.

He got out and opened the trunk of the car. He lifted out a large suitcase, a gray metal attaché case and two cameras, each in a carrying case. He opened the door for Vance, but did not remove his bag. "Third boat from the jetty," he said, indicating a small hydroplane cabin cruiser floating high on the water. "Belongs to Mr. J. R. Smithson of Norton, Ohio, in case anybody should ask. I'll stash the car and get clearance. You wait here."

Vance started to collect the gear.

"No, suh, Ah'll come get that," Dorsey said. He drove off. Vance strolled over to the wharf and gazed out across the darkening bay. It was speckled with a variety of small craft, motor and sail; the time of day when office workers, salesmen, mechanics and teachers cast off their commonplace lives and set forth on voyages of high adventure and discovery. Voyages that would end predictably in a round of cocktails on the patio and an evening before the television.

A middle-aged couple in tennis shoes, dungarees and tight-fitting jerseys that accentuated the rolls of fat underneath were swabbing down the deck of a dilapidated Gazêboat two spaces from *The Smithsonian*. They paused and looked curiously over at Vance. The woman said something to the man in a guarded nasal whine. He snorted mirthlessly and went back to his chore. Vance took off his lightweight black coat, slung it over his shoulder and loosened his tie.

Robert Dorsey came around the corner of the marina office and ambled across the graveled parking lot in a stoop-shouldered shuffle. He picked up the luggage and deposited it alongside Vance on the wharf.

"Ah guess we may's well go aboard," he said. He reeled in the line attached to *The Smithsonian* and swung it broadside as it nudged against the sea wall. Vance stepped over the low brass rail and ducked into the cabin. Dorsey followed with the luggage.

They maneuvered cautiously out of the anchorage. As they emerged into the choppy waters of the bay, Dorsey advanced the throttles and the 440 Corsair engine responded with a throaty growl. The bow tilted sharply upward. Dorsey pushed a button on the control panel. Two slanted fins unfolded amidships. The bow arced downward onto the broad, slightly convex step and the stubby boat skimmed along the top of the waves on a level keel. Dorsey retracted the throttles gradually until the speed indicator settled at forty knots.

He looked over his shoulder at Vance, standing behind him. "You ever drive one of these things?"

"I checked out in an MTB," Vance said. "Didn't ride quite as smooth."

Dorsey slid out of the seat and motioned Vance to take over. "Just follow the shoreline about this distance," he said. "Course approximately 190." He offered no further instructions. After a minute he reached over and flicked on the running lights. Vance rolled the wheel to port, then starboard. The cruiser skipped over the water in a smooth slalom. Dusk slowly enveloped the land and the blue-green sea turned to purple. Vance throttled back to thirty knots. The swells rose and the boat began to bounce.

As they came abreast of Key Largo and passed under the Key Chain bridge, Dorsey touched Vance on the shoulder and indicated that he would take the wheel. He settled into the seat, pulled back the throttles further and punched the button to retract the fins. The boat sank abruptly into the water and bogged down to ten knots. Dorsey rigged the craft for slow-running and switched on a radar-chart monitor set into the center of the instrument panel. He twirled a numbered knob to "12" and depressed the selector button. The chart roll blurred past the viewer for several seconds, then focused on the offshore area at the tip of the peninsula. It was speckled with small islands and sand spits, and Dorsey maneuvered carefully through the narrow, shallow channels. Lights glimmered on some of the tiny islets. A pale melon-slice moon cast a faint halo over the shapeless tangle of the Everglades to the north. Its powerful engine muted to an almost inaudible mutter, the cruiser skittered among the flat gray discs like a spastic tadpole.

Obviously entering into familiar territory, Dorsey switched off the monitor, doused the running lights and headed toward a slightly larger island in the middle of an ocean pond. As they approached, Vance could make out a smoothly rounded dome rising fifteen or twenty feet above the shell-speckled beach.

Dorsey cut the engine twenty feet offshore, and the boat drifted stern first into a shallow concrete basin carved out of the edge of the island. They went on deck and guided it into its berth between four-inch rubber fenders. Dorsey reached up to the top of the retaining wall, pulled down a metal claw attached to a retractable chain and clamped it around the rail. He went below, handed up the bags and cameras and secured the cabin hatch. Standing on the deck, he placed both hands on the rim of the concrete shell two feet above his head and, with no perceptible spring, pulled himself up. Vance passed up the gear and hauled himself up.

The island was almost perfectly round, approximately a hundred yards in diameter, completely barren of vegetation and not more than five feet above water level at its highest point. The metallic dome was sunk into the center of it and occupied nearly half the total area. Dorsey led the way across the sand from the mooring basin. In the pallid light, Vance could see no seam or crack in the curved wall.

Dorsey put down the bags and pulled a pencil-shaped sensor from his pocket. He inserted the rounded end into a buttonhole dent. A sliding hatch opened noiselessly, exposing a narrow passageway and emitting a wisp of refrigerated air. Dorsey sidled through, holding the bags akimbo.

Vance followed, but halted as the door slid shut behind him and utter stygian darkness enveloped him. It reminded him uncomfortably of the "black holes" in Vietnam, Thailand and Indonesia, where men going on patrol were conditioned for night vision.

He could hear Dorsey moving quietly along the wall to the right. Presently a shaded overhead light went on. Vance found himself in a large, circular room, surrounded by a dozen closed doors and an open passageway leading to a kitchen-dining area. He was standing on a low, railed catwalk, from which steps led down at intervals to a sunken living room. The room was furnished with three large, imitation-leather couches, half a dozen easy chairs, assorted lamps and tables and two polished, backless benches placed parallel in the middle.

He followed Dorsey around the platform and down the

steps. Dorsey unloaded the bags and cameras and looked at him like a suburban homeowner showing off his new split-level. Vance gave it the standard inspection scrutiny.

"Mr. Smithson, I take it, is an eccentric millionaire with a passion for privacy," he said.

"Who?" Dorsey sounded genuinely uncomprehending. "Oh, that. I just thought that would save you having to make any lengthy explanations. No, actually the place is owned by the Smithsonian. It's sort of a lab for ichthyological and oceanic research. And it is convenient for people passing through Florida on unofficial business. It makes it possible for us to more or less handle our own security arrangements, and that's okay with the government down here. They're not too inquisitive."

"I would think a blockhouse in the territorial waters of a friendly nation would occasion a little comment."

"Oh, no. This is the conventional style of architecture down here. In the hurricane season this whole lash-up is under water half the time. It's hermetically sealed. There's nothing suspicious about that.

"As a matter of fact, this place is quite innocuous. Primarily it enables us to keep an eye on the traffic entering and leaving the Gulf. That irritates our Southern friends a bit, but there's nothing they can do about it. We have an elaborate sonar and laser setup in the basement, which the museum uses in its underwater research projects of course.

"The Confeds keep trying to egg the Republic into closing us down. They oblige by running spot inspections every now and then, but as long as we keep the operation clean we're in the clear. Actually, we get more heat from the museum than we do from the Republic. They really figure they own the place and they're very touchy about its being used for 'clandestine' purposes. They would object strenuously to your presence here."

Vance flopped into a chair. "All right. What's on the schedule?"

"I'll go pick up the doctor in the morning," Dorsey said, as if he were running over the agenda for a sales meeting. "I'll have him back here by ten. He thinks it'll take only a couple of hours—depending on how extensive the make-over is. We won't try for a complete match-up. Just so you look enough like Tremont to satisfy the ident pictures. He says he has no close acquaintances in Con City. Anybody else probably wouldn't tie the name with the face, and that's just as well. The boys from the Agency have got him doing his life story on tape so you can catch his inflections and phrasings. I'll run through it with you tomorrow night."

"How much does the Agency know?"

"Nothing about you. They collected the data on Tremont and arranged to bring him out. They know, of course, that somebody will be taking his place, but they don't know who. And they know you're not going to contact them and they're not to contact you."

Dorsey's tone was matter-of-fact, but Vance recognized the portent of his words. "There are six people who know about Cordell Vance and not that many who know about Peter Tremont. There's only one who knows about both of them. So— if anything happens to me, you won't even be a missing person. Unless you left a forwarding address with somebody."

"Goddamnit, I told you I didn't intend to see her again, and I haven't. Get it through your head. She has nothing to do with it."

"She has got something to do with it. She changes the emotional equation."

"Oh, for Christ's sake. A ten-day affair isn't going to change my emotional equation. You wouldn't even have known about it if I hadn't asked you to help her out of the jam she was in."

"I would have known about it," Dorsey said flatly. "And I also know it was more than a ten-day affair. In our neurogenic conditioning sessions I wasn't just planting things in your skull. I had to find out what was already there in order to correlate your responses."

He raised a placatory palm. "I'm not complaining about her, mind you. I know if it wasn't for her, you wouldn't be here. I'm still a little puzzled by your reaction. Normally, if a man has been locked up in solitary for a couple of years and somebody opens the door, he walks out. Instead, you closed the door again. Why?"

Vance stared belligerently at Dorsey. It was a question he had asked himself a hundred times. He didn't know the answer. All he knew was that he had done it because he had to.

"You're the psychologist. If you don't know, how the hell should I? Besides, what difference does it make?"

"It doesn't make any difference—and neither does the girl. Except insofar as she may have affected your survival quotient."

"Shoveling aside the pedantic manure," Vance said, "I gather you're afraid I might want to go on living."

"That's about it. One of the imperatives in the selection profile was a sublimated inclination toward self-destruction. I'm not sure you still possess that essential factor."

"So—you want to deal me out?"

"No. But I'd advise you to deal yourself out if you don't think you can go through with it."

"You son-of-a-bitch. You know you've got me on the noose."

Dorsey had done it indirectly, by degrees. There never was a time when Vance could not have turned in his suit and walked away. But there never was a time when it quite seemed appropriate. Vance was fully aware of what was happening to him, and Dorsey kept him advised each step of the way. When they were finished, given who he was, Cordell Vance was as committed to the assassination of Howie Ray Spearman as he would have been had he signed a pact in blood. Yet he had never even actually agreed to do it.

Robert Dorsey had exhibited neither surprise nor gratification when Vance announced he would undertake the mission. He set about planning the preliminaries with the meticulous attention to detail which gradually won Vance's confidence and guarded liking. On his own, Vance had spent two weeks on conditioning exercises, scaling fourteen-thousand-foot peaks, jogging for miles over rocky slopes and snow-covered ravines and hiking through tangled, trailless forests. The strenuous physical exertion served no real purpose except to occupy and exhaust him so he had little time to dwell on aching memories of the past or contemplate the uninviting vistas of the future.

When Dorsey next materialized on a blustery, pitch-dark night, he brought with him a coffin-size chest, crammed with an assortment of automatic weapons, all of foreign manufacture. Included were a lightweight Chinese machine gun with a skeletal stock, a three-barreled South African shotgun, a stubby Italian carbine, a Russian Lotka 16-mm rifle, a Czechoslovakian Zlants machine pistol with a revolving magazine and half a dozen hand guns, each equipped with a silencer. Three of them were Confederate models.

"Might as well acquaint yourself with these," he said. "No telling, of course, whether you'll get a chance to use them. But if it looks like you can, we'll get you whatever you need." One by one, Dorsey disassembled and reassembled them, pointing out the capabilities and idiosyncrasies of each.

Along with his aversion for killing, Vance had acquired a distaste for firearms, but he found himself inspecting the arsenal with schoolboy fascination. He cradled the carbine against his shoulder and was conscious of Dorsey's hooded black eyes on his face. Wordlessly he put the gun back in its slot in the trunk.

"I'll leave these with you for a couple of weeks," Dorsey said, "so you can get the feel of 'em. I don't think it will be necessary for you to fire 'em. I assume you know how to shoot. From now on it would be a good idea not to attract any more attention than you can help."

"How are you going to get these things through to me without implicating yourselves?"

"That will be taken care of. It's just as well for you not to know. You let us know what you want. We'll let you know where to pick it up."

Dorsey was systematic and unhurried. Vance asked few questions, assuming the answers would be forthcoming. When Dorsey had finished the weapons demonstration, he replaced them in the chest, fastened the lid with two hefty padlocks and handed Vance the keys.

"I know you don't have many visitors," he said, "but we'd better put this where nobody is likely to stumble over it. The darkroom probably would do."

Vance looked at him quizzically. Dorsey smiled. "When I visited you before, you remember, I had a little time to look around."

Together they carried the chest down the single flight of stairs to the board-walled cave Vance had excavated under the kitchen to house his photographic equipment. It must have weighed at least 250 pounds, he estimated. Dorsey had carried it in by himself, casually balanced on a muscular shoulder. They cleared a place for it on the cement floor under a shelf.

"I've got a few more bundles out here," Dorsey said, leading the way up the steps and out the back door. A battered panel truck was parked precariously on the steep incline behind the cabin. Faded lettering on the side carried the legend "MARGOLIS & SON. PUMPING-DRILLING."

Dorsey unlocked the rear doors and handed Vance a square wooden box nailed shut. "Homework," he said. He lifted out a tall, oblong metal cabinet and set it down carefully on the flagstoned area extending out from the entrance. He went back to the truck, picked up a black leather satchel and locked the doors.

Inside, he set the cabinet up on end, unlocked and opened its panels, exposing a multicolored cluster of dials, bulbs, tubes, switches and wires. "Cardioencephalograph," he explained. He squatted down and plugged a cable into a wall outlet. "I want to get a reading on your stability profile."

"You want me crazy, but not too."

Dorsey unwound his vast torso. "Uh-huh, and if things go wrong, we want to be able to prove that you were."

He gave Vance's chest and skull a thorough going-over with the machine and followed with a perfunctory physical examination. "You're in pretty good shape," he said. "You ought to live a long time if you take care of yourself."

He closed the cabinet, packed his instruments away in the satchel and sat down in one of the wing chairs by the fire.

"All right," he said. "Now's the time to call it off if you want to. From here on, after we start the indoctrination, it would be an—embarrassment to have you running around loose. You understand me?"

"I understand you. You're cutting my line of retreat."

"That's what I'm doing," Dorsey replied. "For your sake as

well as ours. Considering what we are trying to accomplish here, it would be preferable to work on you subliminally. But we don't have enough time, and I'm afraid you'd be a difficult subject. So I'm going to be candid with you and rely on your cooperation.

"What we've done, as I told you, is to compile case histories on every assassination for the past hundred years. From them we have distilled the essence of an assassin, eliminating those factors which were either irrelevant or potentially disruptive. You will find a monograph on each case in there." He indicated the box. "Also, a synthesis of those elements which they had in common and which, it would appear, contributed to their success. Putting it bluntly, our purpose now is to construct from these blueprints a working model of an assassin.

"You have all the external skills that are required. In fact, you're better equipped in that respect than any of the subjects we've studied. Of course, it's impossible to duplicate or even simulate the mental stresses which impelled them to act as they did. I believe we can, however, reinforce your motivation, which will in turn strengthen your resolution. That would involve a process of psychic reorientation, through both conscious and semihypnotic suggestion, which we call neurogenic conditioning."

"That's out," Vance snapped. "You're not going to make an automaton out of me. I'll either do it or I won't do it. If I do it, I'll do it of my own volition."

"It would in no way restrict your free will," Dorsey assured him. "It would merely help incline you toward the desired course of action. It would, in effect, dispel certain acquired moral inhibitions, and to that extent it would enhance the exercise of reason."

"You'd be eliminating my conscience."

"In a sense," Dorsey admitted, "but only in one selected area."

"One selected area. Sure. And I could then begin slaughtering people without any 'moral inhibitions.' That should make me a useful citizen."

"No. I'm afraid it wouldn't prepare you for a career. You would be motivated only toward one specific target, so to speak. Once that target was eliminated, you would have no further motivation."

"To hell with it," Vance said. "If I can't motivate myself, that's too bad. That's a chance *you'll* have to take."

"There would be one residual effect that doesn't particularly concern me, but might concern you. If it were successful, the conditioning would induce in you a conviction that what you were doing was of supreme importance. It would more or less expel everything else from your mind. You would be like a man in battle. He has very few other worries. And if you pulled it off, I can guarantee you would feel you had accomplished something. From what I know about you, Mr. Vance, that might be important to you."

In the end, Vance had consented. He was never sure whether the conditioning course had been effective or not. For the next two months Dorsey dropped in on him irregularly and unannounced, staying sometimes for two or three days, sometimes for only a few hours.

Each time he brought with him another box full of books, manuscripts, pictures and tapes. The literature ranged from a three-volume biography of Howie Ray Spearman to a minute-by-minute account of a week in the life of an unidentified agent.

Vance had always been intrigued by the history of the Confederacy, partly because he had never completely forgotten his birthright, partly because it somehow paralleled his own life. It followed no discernible course. It flowed along smoothly and peacefully for decades, then suddenly swerved from its banks and carved out a completely new channel.

For twenty years following secession the Confederacy drowsed along under the benign and paternalistic rule of the plantation aristocracy. Legalized slavery was abolished as a concession to world opinion and primitive technology, but it was succeeded by a form of economic serfdom which freed the slaveholder of his moral responsibilities and left the slave still fettered to the plow.

Lulled by the chauvinistic conviction that cotton was king, the South unwittingly and uncaringly lapsed into the role of supplier to the rapidly industrializing nations of North America and Europe. A series of world-wide depressions jolted it into the realization that it was a mere agrarian appendage of the great commercial powers, at their mercy, both financially and militarily. Playing a skillful duet on the pride and poverty of the lower middle class, a swashbuckling breed of financial privateers seized control of the drifting ship. In league with the ruthless money barons of the North, they built railroads and factories, pushed through the plebiscite by which the Confederacy acquired the Southwest territories, dug mines, launched ships, looted the treasury and brought the Confederacy to the brink of bankruptcy.

During the era of relaxed tensions following secession, when the North was the South's best customer, there was a growing sentiment for reunification. The North American League was a political force wooed by all parties. When the booming economy fell apart and the carpetbaggers and freebooters scuttled back across the border, a revulsion set in. A strident band of Yankee-baiters marched to power to the rousing, nostalgic strains of "Dixie."

Dispossessed landholders and unemployed tradesmen patriotically flocked to the colors as, in the time-honored tradition, the rattle of the saber drowned out the rumble of empty bellies. Paddle-wheel pleasure boats, putting in at ports of call on both banks, ceased to ply the Potomac. The new rulers of the Confederacy threatened to shut off the North's supply of raw materials, thus dragging the merchant classes of both nations into the growing conflict.

This time it was the North which ignited the spark that might have touched off the tinderbox. Fanned by the lusty bellows of William Randolph Hearst's yellow press, the spark flared into a warm-up war with Spain. When a United States expeditionary force invaded Cuba, ninety miles off the Florida coast, the Confederacy again issued a call to the state militias to rally to the sacred cause.

But this time it was the North that was gripped with martial fervor and the South that was divided. Occupied with the settlement of the newly acquired Western Territories, the states of the Deep South ignored the call, and in some instances passed resolutions of neutrality. As Secretary Cameron had foreseen, the day had come when the North was in a position to take up some unfinished business. And there were those in the North who were eager to do so, notably the fire-breathing former Assistant Secretary of the Navy, Teddy Roosevelt.

Shackled by the limitations imposed on him by the strong "States' Rights" provisions of the Constitution, Confederate President Gaylord Duncan muffled his militance and adopted a more conciliatory tone. Remorseful that he had been goaded into the role of bully by the jingoists, President McKinley gradually succeeded in abating the war fever in the United States. President Duncan saved face by demanding that the U.S. withdraw its troops from Cuba—after it became apparent that it fully intended to do so. By the time Theodore Roosevelt succeeded to the presidency, the North was no longer in a contentious mood.

The military bellicosity between the two nations was superseded by a less clangorous but more deep-rooted commercial rivalry as the South set about building an industrial base which would free her from economic dependence on her unpredictable neighbor to the north. For a decade both jockeyed with tariffs and duties and threats of embargo.

Even the mildewed skeleton of secession was resurrected when the Democrats nominated Woodrow Wilson as its candidate for President in 1912. Wilson, it was frequently pointed out by both his opponents—President William Howard Taft and ex-President Theodore Roosevelt—had been born in Staunton, Virginia. Therefore he was not a native-born citizen of the United States and was not eligible for the presidency. Reluctantly, the Republican-dominated Supreme Court ruled that since he had been born five years before secession—when Virginia was still part of the Union—he could not be disqualified on those grounds. His rivals, however, continued to question his loyalty in the event of a conflict between the two countries.

The Confederacy maintained a haughty detachment from the wrangling until after Wilson was elected. The Southern press then permitted itself some prideful reflections on the inherent superiority of Southern breeding and tradition and talked hopefully about improved relations between the two nations.

With the outbreak of war in Europe and the gradual alignment of the United States with the Allies, the Central Powers made strenuous efforts to woo the Confederacy into a secret alliance. Failing that, they strove to cajole her into a state of friendly neutrality. Initially, the Southern leaders were favorably disposed toward Germany and denounced the Allied blockade as "brigandage on the high seas." As the blockade tightened, however, and trade with the Central Powers dwindled, popular sentiment swung toward the democracies. When the United States entered the war, the Confederacy took advantage of the ready market to build a formidable war economy of its own.

It remained in being for some years after the disillusioned U.S. had dismantled its armies and its munitions industries and turned to a frantic pursuit of the dollar. Consequently, when the Florida crisis erupted, the Confederacy was prepared to back up its stern warning against interference in its domestic affairs. The issue never came to a showdown, and thus the challenge was never accepted or rejected. It did, however, give the professional military establishment in the South a chance to flex its new muscles.

Both countries agonized through the Great Depression, too mired in their own misery to worry about foreign threats or to brood about past frictions. The South suffered more because it was poorer to begin with. But it managed to export some of its woes. For the first time since slavery had been abolished, a torrent of Negroes began pouring across the border into the North. Some bore visions of freedom, equality and opportunity; others merely trudged along the dusty back roads toward the unknown, knowing only that it could be no worse than where they came from.

The United States made frantic but futile efforts to dam the tide of impoverished immigrants. Hundreds of thousands of the unemployed were mustered into a motley border patrol. Bloody clashes ensued between gangs of surly, frustrated whites and hordes of hopeless, despairing Blacks. Thus were sown the seeds of racial hatred which ripened thirty years later.

Since secession, a small but steady trickle of Blacks had filtered through the porous curtain between the two nations. At first they came via the Underground Railroad, which continued to operate until slavery was abolished. Later, they moved more or less openly, depending on the current climate in the Confederacy.

As long as they comprised but a trickle, they were admitted to the North without much resistance and were treated with somewhat less prejudice than the scruffy Irishmen then pouring in from their famine-stricken island. Since the refugees were, by and large, the more spirited and energetic specimens of their race, they found quick acceptance in the bustling cities of the North. For the same reason, the South was happy to be rid of them. Except for their color, they would have melted right into the pot along with the Micks and the Wops and the Polacks. Because they were powerless and easily identifiable, however, they became prime targets for the recurrent outbreaks of bigotry and pseudo patriotism that followed on the heels of every economic decline.

As the Great Depression deepened, they began to fight back. And as their ranks were swelled by the influx of ragged illiterates from the South, the amiable relations between the races began to curdle. In self-defense the Blacks congregated in ghettos in the big cities. Gradually their existence took on many of the aspects of the life they had left behind—except that there they had resigned themselves to oppression. Here opportunity lay within their vision but beyond their grasp. Their frustration vented itself in occasional riots throughout the thirties, forties and fifties, culminating in the bloody uprisings of the sixties. Goaded by the taunts of the Confederacy, which had solved its racial problems in short order, once the Party of National Resurgence came to power, the United States took stock of its shame.

Painfully, and not without repeated fittings and some alterations, it draped its vaunted mantle of freedom and equality over the shoulders of its black citizens. Even now it did not sit entirely comfortably. But underneath the ugly bulges, the pattern of democracy was taking shape.

Like the U.S., the Confederacy tinkered with social reform and flirted with Communism during the dark years of the depression. Under the weak administration of President Arthur Braxton, it copied many of the finger-in-the-dike tactics of Franklin D. Roosevelt. They proved largely ineffectual, but they did pave the way for the federal government to pry loose some of the sacred powers previously reserved to the States. President Braxton covered up his failures by intensifying his efforts to shoo the Negroes across the border. He was abetted by a night-riding gang of hoodlums called the Ku Klux Klan, which sprang up like a noxious weed throughout the South and which gained control of several state legislatures before it wilted as suddenly as it had sprouted.

Meanwhile, a bulb-nosed, redneck politician from Louisiana had come up with a number of novel policies which he lumped under the engaging slogan "Every Man a King." Huey Long appeared to be well on the way to putting his slogan into effect, at least so far as he was concerned, when a dissident doctor with an unprofessional disregard for his own health laid him low among the stately columns of the state capitol. The Confederacy continued to limp along under President Braxton. But Huey and the KKK had shown that its red-clay soil, properly cultivated, was congenial to the growth of fascism.

When the second great conflict erupted in Europe the Confederacy realized from the outset which side its bread was buttered on. It became the principal subcontractor to the "arsenal of democracy" to the north. A relatively liberal administration had succeeded the do-nothing regime of President Braxton, and President Roosevelt had made some gestures toward including the South in his Good Neighbor policy.

There was even talk of the two ancient rivals entering into a pact of "militant neutrality" to shore up floundering Britain after the fall of France. But there was enough latent rancor and suspicion in both countries to make it politically inexpedient.

When the United States was suddenly plunged into the war, the North American League made strenuous efforts to pull the Confederacy in alongside her. It might have succeeded had Pearl Harbor been in the Atlantic rather than the Pacific. The Confederate States had by then established themselves as an Atlantic power. But having no access to the Pacific, they were little concerned about Japan's domination of Asia. Consequently, they were not greatly aroused by the sneak attack on their neighbor. In fact, there was considerable satisfaction in naval ranks that the U.S. fleet had been whittled down to pregnable proportions.

Thus the North American League's insistence that "It's one continent" was offset by the Yankee-haters' clamor that "It's not our war." Furthermore, there was a good deal of stiff-necked resistance among Southern politicians to jumping into the conflict as a junior partner. As the war progressed, that role became more and more pronounced. Though it teetered on the brink several times, the Confederacy never quite got around to joining up.

Nevertheless, the possibility of an Axis victory impelled the South to take stock of its peculiar relationship with its stepbrother. Despite their intermittent quarrels, neither country would have tolerated the domination of the other by an outside power, for reasons of both security and sentiment. Although severed, they were still bound together, bodily and spiritually.

The North American League openly recruited a Confederate Legion, which fought through the hedgerows of Normandy and into the heartland of Germany. Although their valor had not been tested in more than a hundred years, the Confeds proved to be spirited soldiers, both on the battlefield and in the bistros. They gave a good account of themselves whether skirmishing with the Nazis or the Yanks—as the occasion demanded. The common cause served to dissipate some of the ingrained hostility between the two peoples, at least at the GI level.

A non-neutral by temperament, Royston Vance conceived a strong aversion to Hitlerism even before the outbreak of the war. As a youth he had absorbed the anti-Yankee sentiment which was fashionable in his circles. Characteristically, his convictions overrode his prejudices, and he joined the North American League in 1941. He was on the verge of enlisting in the Confederate Legion when he met Cathy-June and at the same time became embroiled in a political fracas with the Long regime in Louisiana. He could not bring himself to abandon either of them. One thing and then another deterred him from his intended course, until the arrival of Cordell and the armistice in Europe shelved it permanently.

Meanwhile, the South was producing vast quantities of ships, planes, tanks and guns for the Allies, and at the same time greatly strengthening her own economy and war-making capacity. When the conflict ended, a spirit of rare cordiality existed between the two American powers. Briefly.

The burgeoning military caste in the Confederacy was disappointed that it had not had an opportunity to display its might and test its weapons. In the face of cautious if not entirely passive resistance from the civilian authorities, it launched a series of probing operations to the south, under the guise of combating Communist influence in Central America.

Alarmed at the prospect of being encircled by a new

Gringo imperialist, Mexico appealed to her old adversary—
the United States. President Truman was attempting to restore peace and amity to the North American continent when
he suddenly found himself embroiled in a hot war on the
other side of the globe—in Korea. While his attention was diverted, the South continued to dabble in the affairs of the
Banana Republics, though it refrained from any overt aggression. By the time the United States had disentangled itself
from the Korean imbroglio, it found half a dozen tin-horn
dictators installed in Latin America, all of whom owed a certain amount of allegiance to the Confederate States of America.

In a pointed move to offset that threat and stabilize the
area, President Eisenhower and John Foster Dulles entered
into a mutual assistance pact with Mexico. That was the situation which prevailed when the Party of National Resurgence
came to power in the Confederacy. Since then the situation
had gradually deteriorated.

Obviously not wanting him to become too partial to the
Confederacy, Dorsey had provided Vance with history books
reflecting both the Northern and the Southern view of relations between the two countries. They showed quite a wide
divergence. Had he not, as it were, been more or less committed to shaping the future history of both countries, Vance
would have been inclined to invoke "a plague on both your
houses."

Dorsey spent hour after hour quizzing him on trivial aspects of Confederate idiom, mores, culture, behavior and attitudes. He memorized the names and style of the leading
pop singers, the batting averages of the top baseball players,
the advertising catch phrases, the training manual of the Citizens Protection Force, the culinary specialties of different

localities, the current songs and jokes, the faces and voices of the hierarchy of the National Resurgence Party. Much of the indoctrination seemed utterly pointless and nonsensical, as Vance frequently complained.

"That's true," Dorsey agreed amiably, "unless maybe you think there is some point in staying alive. Spearman runs a mighty tidy police state down there, and he has one minor obsession: that there's a place for everyone and everyone in his place. You'd better know where your place is."

Near the end of March Dorsey plucked a plastic-bound dossier from the wooden box and announced the reincarnation of Cordell Vance. "Meet Peter Tremont," he said. "That's you."

Vance read through the minutely detailed biography of Peter Tremont, finding it as dull as a personnel file:

PETER TREMONT: Born September 22, 1948, Macon, Ga. Parents— Marvin Sidell and Marietta Louise (Carswell) Tremont. Educated— Macon public schools (Central Grade School, Simms Jr. High School, Longstreet High School); two years National Classification Laboratory (#26); two years Civilian Technology Institute (#14); three years military service (artillery-civil pacification). Evolutionary Classification—Deserving . . .

Dorsey appeared to be sound asleep on the couch. He sat up as Vance skimmed through the final pages.

"I can't say I identify with the role."

Dorsey yawned. "I'm sure you'll find some interesting nuances once you get to know the character."

That night they began the neurogenic conditioning sessions. "For the most part," Dorsey explained, "you will be in a state of semihypnosis. You will be conscious and aware, but we will focus your mind only on the immediate subject and close off all extraneous thought. It will not require any active cooperation on your part, merely nonresistance."

He continued talking in a conversational monotone. Vance shifted his brain into neutral. Nothing happened, except that he lost interest in what Dorsey was saying. His mind wandered. He felt a mild sense of gratification at balking his omniscient tutor. He was aware that Dorsey was reading from Peter Tremont's dossier. The words registered, but he did not bother to associate them. A few minutes later, Dorsey suggested they knock off and go to bed. Vance noted abstractly that the sky was beginning to pale beyond the eastern foothills.

Dorsey was cooking breakfast when Vance walked into the kitchen.

"You like your eggs scrambled, don't you," Dorsey remarked, whipping a batch of eggs, butter and milk in a skillet with an incongruously delicate stroke.

In all the time Vance had been cooking for himself, he had never scrambled eggs, but they suddenly looked appetizing. "Yeah," he said. "You're kind of an expert at everything, aren't you?"

Dorsey half-turned, his bulk almost obscuring the stove.

"Yas-suh! A man got to learn to fend for hisse'f. Ain' nothing Ah cain' do, 'cept read 'n' write."

They ate at the small porcelain-topped table in the kitchen. Predictably, the scrambled eggs, hallmark of a good cook, were light, fluffy and delectable. Vance had a vague feeling of unfamiliarity, as if a misplaced memory were hovering at the back of his brain. The coffee was stronger than he was accustomed to but somehow tastier. Halfway through the meal, he realized he had forgotten to put cream in it. It didn't seem worthwhile going to the refrigerator.

Dorsey finished the eggs and ham on his plate and poured himself another cup of coffee. "You used to work in a restaurant, didn't you?" he asked.

"It was really just kind of a hamburger joint outside of

Macon," Vance replied. "When I was going to—" He almost gasped in astonishment.

Dorsey grinned at him. "When you wuz goin' to Longstreet High School, Mistuh Tremont?"

"God damn you," Vance yelled. "What have you done to me?"

"Nothing really," Dorsey said calmly. "I'm just sort of superimposing Mr. Tremont's personality on yours. It isn't going to hurt you to eat scrambled eggs and drink black coffee. You may get to like it."

"Christ almighty! I didn't think it was taking."

"You'd be surprised," Dorsey said.

He was. Under Dorsey's questioning, he recited the life story of Peter Tremont as precisely as and more facilely than he could have recited his own. He reeled off the names of uncles and cousins and schoolmates, descriptions of places he had never seen and events he had never experienced. Even more astounding, though, was the eerie feeling that they all were a part of his half-remembered past, shadowy but real.

In the weeks that followed, Dorsey insinuated into his brain bank a profusion of disconnected trivia, responses to hypothetical stimuli, speech mannerisms, latent prejudices, opinions on current topics, social attitudes and a festering resentment toward the rulers of the Confederacy. Cordell Vance and Peter Tremont remained two separate and distinct persons, and he was at all times aware of the distinction. Yet he found he could assume the personality of either almost interchangeably.

To further complicate his induced schizophrenia, he also gradually acquired a third personality—that of an involved but detached onlooker. In that role he could compare with judicial aloofness the emotional responses of his other two selves to stimuli from their respective pasts.

The memory of Diane Fleming still filled Cordell Vance

with a haunting sense of loss. To Peter Tremont she was merely a memorable lay. To Cordell Vance, Howie Ray Spearman was a tactical objective—an impersonal evil which he had been detailed to eradicate. To Peter Tremont he was a vicious tyrant who was in some abstract way responsible for his own failures and frustrations.

The third person had no strong feelings about either Diane Fleming or Howie Ray Spearman. He was a sort of emotional zombie who neither loved nor hated. His instincts and reflexes were completely pragmatic, impervious to moral judgments, physical cravings or spiritual yearnings.

As he grew to identify with his alter ego, Cordell Vance gradually acquired an impersonal liking for Peter Tremont. Either because he was unable completely to submerge his own personality or because they had arrived at similar destinations by different routes, he had little difficulty adjusting himself to the Southerner's outlook.

Peter Tremont had started out as a young man of considerable promise in the Evolutionary Order. He had scored well in his early aptitude tests and during his observation period in the National Classification Laboratory. He had been assigned to the Civilian Technology Institute, which was the traditional launching pad for careers in the space program. He had compiled an outstanding scholastic record, and had been recommended by the faculty board for enrollment in the elite Academy for Scientific Studies. But the screening committee for the Selective Process had not concurred.

Consequently, Tremont's military deferment was canceled, and he embarked upon his three years' compulsory service at the advanced age of twenty-three. He rose to the rank of first lieutenant, but not beyond it. Upon his return to civilian life, he was assigned to a minor research job in the space program. Here again, his natural brilliance asserted itself and he was quickly promoted to section head, and, in due time, upgraded to "Respected" citizen.

Though it was not clearly stated in his record, he apparently had differed rather vehemently with his superiors on the relative priorities to be assigned the military and civilian space efforts. Tremont was looking to the stars. The heads of the agency were only looking across the border. He was transferred out of the space program into the Department of Consumer Goods. He showed no great aptitude for his new work, and his discretion evidently declined along with his fortunes. In due time, he was downgraded to "Deserving" citizen again.

Where his earlier records had carried the notation "FMP" (Fortuitous Mutant Prospect), later documents bore the stark initial "E" (Established—a euphemism for those who had been placed in the niche where they belonged and where they would remain). At one point his Reliability Index dropped to "Suspect," but later was restored to "Questionable."

Peter Tremont made one last convulsive effort to redeem himself and, Cordell Vance surmised, to reassert his individuality. He applied for transfer to the Private Sector. In view of his record, it was readily granted. He drifted from one job to another without marked success. He was dickering to purchase an art and photographic supply house in Charlotte, North Carolina, when an anonymous agent of the CIA offered to smuggle him out of the country and find a job for him in the United States space program. Peter Tremont asked no questions. His bags were packed.

Even Robert Dorsey was fairly well satisfied with Vance's interpretation of the role. And he was a harsh critic.

"It's not enough to play the part," he insisted. "You've got to *be* Peter Tremont. Think like him. Feel like him. Otherwise, they'll trip you up somewhere. And once it begins to unravel, you're through. You've got him down pretty good, but you've got to absorb all his background and his environment. For instance, he is tolerant of the Blacks. He may even feel kindly toward them. But he's not going to treat them as equals."

The criticism came at the end of a long, tiresome session and Vance had had his fill—not only of Peter Tremont but of Robert Dorsey. "I could damned easy come around to that way of thinking."

"I wouldn't doubt it," said Dorsey, smiling mirthlessly.

Vance was surprised at the note of bitterness in Dorsey's normally expressionless tone. "You've got some hang-ups of your own."

"Aftuh all," Dorsey began to drawl, "Ah'm jus' a primitive —only six generations removed from the jungle. This is a hostile environment fo' me."

Immersed in his own miseries, Vance had given no thought to Dorsey as a person. Suddenly he was interested.

"You seem to have adjusted pretty well."

"Da's what ah'm try'n tell you. You got to adjus' 'f you wanna survive."

It dawned on Vance that he had overlooked the obvious angle. "You're the one with a grudge," he said accusingly. "You're out to get Spearman."

Dorsey shook his head. "No. It's true, I was born in the South. But my parents brought me out when I was a baby. Before Spearman appeared."

"But you've got a grudge against the South."

"No. Not really. I suppose if we were to dig into my id the way we have yours, we would discover I have kind of a thing about the white race generally. But it doesn't bother me. It's just there."

"They give you a bad time?"

"No. As a matter of fact, being black has probably been an advantage to me—in some ways. Even my parents weren't treated too bad down South. As long as they kept their place. My pop made pretty good money during World War II, when the Confederacy was turning out trucks and tanks and munitions for anybody who could pay for 'em. In the 1950's when automation came in and it looked like they weren't going to have much use for thirty million Negroes, the whites kind of encouraged 'em to migrate. As soon as I was born, my pop made up his mind I wasn't going to grow up in the South. Just like yours did."

Dorsey's teeth flashed in a brief smile. "Fact of the matter is, we emigrated before you did. Sort of unofficially, of course. We just headed west and strayed across the border into Kansas. The Confeds were very obliging at that time. They ran kind of an informal travel agency for Blacks, pointing out the tourist attractions in the U.S. and how to get there. Course they weren't selling any round-trip tickets.

"And the U.S. wasn't carrying a torch any more for the 'huddled masses, yearning to breathe free.' They'd been through the black-locust plague during the depression, and they weren't what you would call hospitable. But after the fuss they had made about the British keeping the Jews out of Palestine, they couldn't very well shut the gates completely. It would have been slightly ironic. They couldn't build a three-thousand-mile wall and preach the blessings of democracy all over the world. My family had some pretty tough years in Kansas City and Detroit and Cleveland. Half of the Blacks were here illegally, and that made 'em fair game for all the righteous, native-born Anglo-Saxon thugs and bigots in the country.

"Actually, Spearman was a godsend to us. When he came to power and invited the Negroes to 'return to their homeland,' the North naturally began taking a little different view of us. They weren't going to play Spearman's game. That's when they opened up the naturalization laws for Afro-Americans. Well, that made us legal, but it didn't make us any more popular. In fact, in some ways it made it harder on us. Now we were supposed to be as good as anybody else, and quite a few people took it into their minds to prove that we weren't.

"Like I say, though, most of this was going on while I was too young to realize it. My pop never let us get bitter. He kept telling us we were better off than the Negroes down South in their cozy Cloisters. I think he and your father would have hit it off pretty well. Anyway, by the time I grew up, the pendulum had swung back. The colleges were bidding for Black students. And if you were a Black football player, you had it made.

"No." He shook his head. "I've got no complaints. Except maybe that the whites feel so damned pious about what they've done for us. You know, it probably would have been good for your mental health if you had been black. Then you could have blamed what happened to you on discrimination."

Vance was not to be distracted. "If you've got this thing about the whites, how come you're in bed with the establishment?"

"You know how it is. That's really all we want to do, is bed down with you folks."

"How do I know you won't stick the shiv in me? That happened to me once before, you know."

Dorsey's black eyes glistened. "Listen," he said. "In the first place, I don't like what Spearman is doing to our people down there. You kill a man's spirit, he's just as dead as if you shot him in the head. In the second place, I'm responsible for you. I got you into this. I'm gonna take care of you—best I can."

Vance felt a sudden flush of comradeship toward the giant.

"Okay, Dorsey," he said. "I guess that's what I've always needed. A black mammy to look after me."

A slow grin creased the Negro's face. "Now you' talkin', Mistuh Tremont."

When not engaged in the process of reincarnation, Cordell Vance set about snipping the few strings that tied him to his own rootless existence. He consulted a real estate agent in the village about selling his cabin, and set such a low figure on it the agent himself snapped it up on the spot. He notified the New York syndicate for whom he did occasional photographic assignments that he would not be available for six months. There was no one to say good-bye to.

He had lost interest in money at the same time he lost interest in everything else. During his years in the army, when his expenses were virtually nil, he had accumulated a comfortable nest egg. Together with his disability compensation, the income amply covered his needs. He carried no insurance because he would not have known whom to name as beneficiary. To spare himself the bother of corresponding with banks and brokers, he had turned over all his finances to a Denver investment management firm with instructions to provide him with a drawing account, a yearly statement and nothing else. He supposed he should make some provision for his estate, but since money had meant so little to him alive, it hardly seemed worth disposing of dead. But the ubiquitous Dorsey raised the question one afternoon at the conclusion of a lengthy review session on Peter Tremont's financial status and history.

Dorsey pulled out a legal document, notarized but not dated, assigning power of attorney to one L. Joseph Parmenter.

"We'd better get your affairs in order," he said bluntly.

"In case something happens to you, we don't want anybody trying to track you down. There's nothing like a bundle of unclaimed money to attract a crowd of mourners."

Vance skimmed through the paper and eyed Dorsey skeptically. "L. Joseph Parmenter? Who's he?"

"He'll see that your money goes wherever you want it to and no questions asked."

"You don't mind if I ask a question," Vance said. "Why the hell should I turn over my worldly goods to somebody I never heard of? Why don't I just make a will?"

"This wouldn't be an appropriate time for you to be making a will. It would tend to substantiate any suspicions that might be directed toward you—which God forbid. Besides, in all likelihood, I'd be the only person who would be able to testify to your demise. And I wouldn't want to do that."

"Well, this strikes me as a damned sloppy way to do business," Vance said. "The odds aren't long enough, I should have L. Joseph Parmenter rooting against me too."

Dorsey gave him a brief smile. "You think I whipped this whole thing up to bilk you out of your life's savings?" he said. "Incidentally, I told you at the beginning there would be a good deal of money in it for you. So far you haven't shown much interest in it. I'm glad because when the moment of truth comes, that money isn't going to seem too important. But regardless of how our venture turns out, there'll be $200,000—in cash—waiting for you or your heirs. It will have to be handled discreetly, of course, but I give you my word it will be paid to whoever you want—if you can't collect it yourself."

Vance shook his head disgustedly. All his adult years he had spent erecting defenses against the outside world, making himself self-sufficient. Now here he was, confiding his life, his honor and even his security to a man he hardly knew and whose admitted purpose was to use him. He signed the paper authorizing L. Joseph Parmenter to dispose of his assets as he saw fit. He confided to Dorsey a private codicil naming Miss Diane Fleming his sole heir and beneficiary.

Late in April, with the soft breath of spring wafting across the greening valley, Dorsey appeared at the cabin with no papers or paraphernalia but with an air of subdued tension about him. He responded abstractedly to Vance's greeting, paced back and forth for a minute in the living room, then pushed on into the kitchen. He opened the liquor cabinet and pulled out a bottle.

"School's out," he said. "How about a drink?"

He filled two glasses, handed one to Vance and unceremoniously gulped his. Vance took a sip and glanced at him questioningly. Scotch. Peter Tremont was a bourbon drinker, and Cordell Vance had been weaned to it over the past months.

"One for the road," Dorsey said. He sat down on the couch and peered up at Vance, his face solemn.

"Looks like we'll have to go through with it. Howie Ray is moving his missiles into position. He'll be ready to hit us any time after the treaty is implemented. That gives us three months. You'd better get down there and look over the territory."

He reached inside his jacket and pulled out a ticket.

"Miami. Day after tomorrow. We'll do the face lift down there. Tremont is on his way out. You with it?" His tone was more questioning than challenging.

The familiar knot of dread gathered in Vance's belly and seeped through his veins. It did not concern him. It came in the darkness before every mission—to everyone. What did concern him was his next reaction. He waited. It had been a long time, and he was not the man he had been. With a sense of relief he felt, not so much his mind, but his professional reflexes taking command. His nerves responded. The muscles in his shoulders relaxed. A tight-reined calm descended on him, and with it a long-dormant stirring of excitement.

For the first time there was no trace of defensiveness in the level gaze with which he returned Dorsey's appraising scrutiny. Both realized their roles had been reversed. The power of decision had passed to the man in the field. They stared at each other silently.

The forgotten phrase came automatically to Vance's lips. "Let's move out," he said.

Dorsey lifted his glass in a restrained salute.

Chapter Nine

Cordell Vance awoke in his windowless, lightless cubicle to the sound of a recurrent muffled thump, like a distant artillery barrage. As soon as he had oriented himself, he identified it as the pounding of heaving swells against the insulated metal shell. He had a momentary feeling of being in a submerged cave.

In the interval between waves, he heard the catwalk creak outside his door. He switched on the light over his head and swung his legs over the side. The wedge-shaped room was compactly fitted out like a ship's cabin—or a prison cell—with a two-tiered bunk, one straight-backed chair, an imitation-walnut foot locker with a cushioned top and a shoulder-high chest of drawers.

Unhurriedly, he slipped on his socks and shoes and stood up as a knock sounded on the door. He moved across the carpeted floor and slid back the grooved panel. Dorsey loomed in the doorway attired in black oilskins and a crumpled yachting cap.

"Morning," he said affably. "I'm ready to shove off. Just keep buttoned up here until I get back. I shouldn't be gone more than three hours. You won't have any visitors on a day like this, but, just in case, I'd better show you around."

He led the way around the catwalk, down the companionway and across the living room to a squat television console pushed unobtrusively back against the wall. He opened the cabinet, disclosing two screens, and switched them both on.

At first, neither seemed to be functioning properly. The blank screens darkened into a swirling, dirty-brown maelstrom as though someone were sloshing water over the camera lens. On one of them Vance caught an intermittent glimpse of the dome through sheets of flying spray. The other showed snatches of towering waves and a roily, seething sea.

"Closed-circuit monitors," Dorsey explained. "The Confeds are a little suspicious of our lab, and we keep an eye on them. I doubt if they'll be snooping around today though."

Vance followed him around the catwalk to the passageway through which they had entered. Dorsey pressed a switch. The hatch slid open, revealing a thin slice of pallid light, sandwiched between lowering gray clouds and tossing gray waves. He stepped over the foot-high bulkhead, hunched his shoulders against the wind and waded into the murk.

Vance clicked the hatch shut and went back to his cell. He had checked out his new wardrobe the night before and found the fit adequate, the style and color only slightly distasteful. As a concession to the weather, though he was not likely to encounter it, he pulled on a high-necked green jersey and a pair of unpressed brown slacks. He picked up Peter Tremont's shaving kit and was heading for the bathroom two doors down when the insulated stillness was pierced by the sudden shriek of the wind. The sound cut off abruptly, but the salt smell of the sea filtered through the processed air like a whiff of ammonia.

Vance slid open the nearest door and ducked into the darkness. Dorsey emerged from the passageway, a rolled tarpaulin riding on his shoulder. He jerked his head around as Vance stepped out onto the catwalk. His eyes glittered with cold fury. He carried his burden down to the lower level and deposited it carefully at the foot of the steps. He crouched beside it, then gave an angry tug on the tarpaulin. It unrolled like a bolt of cloth, spilling a stiffened corpse out on the floor.

Vance gazed at it unfeelingly. Having lived on close terms with death, it held no horror for him. Indeed, it scarcely even seemed unnatural. He had become callous toward death long before he became squeamish about killing. His aversion to the cause did not extend to the effect.

Dorsey bent one arm of the corpse at the elbow and watched it slowly sink back to the floor. He lifted an eyelid, peered inside and brushed it shut. His fingers probed the skull and found an irregularity behind the left ear. He stooped over and examined it, then rolled the head from side to side between his huge hands.

He stood up and stared grimly down at the body. The dead man was about fifty years old, of medium build, fairly tall. A long strand of limp, yellowish hair was plastered over his high forehead. His narrow, lined face was frozen in an expression more of incredulity than terror. He was fully clothed in a soggy, powder-blue uniform, blue shirt and crepe-soled shoes. The patch on his left shoulder bore the letters "FCP" stitched over a speedboat emblem.

"Florida Coastal Patrolman," Dorsey intoned. "The Confeds must have left him as a souvenir. He was wedged in the boat basin."

"Why the hell would they do that?"

"They like to call attention to us whenever they can. CIA figures they're building up pretexts for a takeover. At any rate, they try to create friction between us and Florida at every opportunity, so we don't get too chummy. And then, of course, they'd like to shut down our operation here if they could."

"This seems a bit crude. You certainly wouldn't knock off a

patrolman and leave him floating around in your front yard. Who'd swallow that?"

"Nobody's going to swallow it. Florida is onto their game, of course. But they can't afford to raise a fuss about it. If the body is found on our premises, they'll at least have to investigate. And we damned well don't need an investigation right now. If anybody tags you, it'll blow the whole deal."

"You think they've got wind of it?"

"Hell, no. They just blundered into it. In the first place, there's no way they could have known anything. Take my word for it. In the second place, if they even suspected we were trying to smuggle somebody across, they'd let you through and then nab you there."

"That's a comforting thought. Well, I'd say the thing to do would be to keep our friend out of sight until I'm gone."

Dorsey grimaced at the body as though it were to blame. "We've got to get rid of it," he said. "The Coastal Patrol will be calling on us before long. The Confeds will contrive some way to point the finger at us. We not only have to get the body out. We have to get you out."

He strode over to the closed-circuit monitor. The gale was subsiding and the weather was beginning to clear. The ring of islands surrounding them was dimly visible through the mist. Dorsey cursed softly.

"They'll be watching us. We can't take you off in the boat. If we get stopped—and the Confeds will see that we do—we'd have a hell of a lot of explaining to do. We might be able to dump the body, but we can't dump you."

Vance looked at the heaving gray waves on the screen and shivered inwardly. "I might be able to paddle around for a couple of hours," he said. "Any of these other islands unoccupied?"

Dorsey shook his head. "The Coastal Patrol will be swarming over this place until they find their buddy. They'd spot you. I doubt if they'd believe you were just out for a morning swim."

He paced across the room, his bowling-ball head cradled between the muscular slopes of his shoulders. He turned, started back and suddenly halted.

"Come on," he said. He moved lithely to the body, flipped the tarp over it and lifted it in his arms like a log. He strode across the floor, mounted to the catwalk and opened a door opposite the entrance. Vance followed him into a semicircular room that curved around nearly a fourth of the circumference of the building. It was obviously fitted out as a laboratory. Fish tanks rimmed the outside wall. Three white dissecting tables were spaced in the middle under adjustable overhead lights. Tall metal cabinets lined the inner partition. A four-foot-square paneled closet extended into the room at one end.

Dorsey walked toward it, shifting his burden from his arms to one shoulder. He reached inside his raincoat, pulled out the sensor and fitted it into a small indentation in the side of the closet. A narrow door slid open, revealing a steep companion-way leading downward.

Dorsey maneuvered his own bulk and the rigid body through the opening. The steps descended into a rough concrete storeroom, twenty feet square, cluttered with boxes and cartons. As they reached the bottom of the steps, Dorsey turned and wordlessly transferred the corpse to Vance's shoulder. Vance accepted it with a twinge of revulsion but without protest.

Dorsey began pushing the heavy boxes aside until he had cleared a path to the corner behind the stairs. Again he inserted the sensor into a dent in the wall. A section of the wall revolved on a center fulcrum. Dorsey stepped through the aperture, and Vance followed him into a dimly lighted, fairly spacious cave, hollowed out of the coral that formed the island. Its sides were encrusted with salt and its damp air smelled of the sea.

A concrete apron ran in a "U" around three sides. The two prongs of the "U" rested against a solid steel bulkhead. Half submerged in a shallow cement berth in the center was a tiny submarine measuring no more than thirty feet from bow to stern. Protruding from the hull amidships, both port and starboard, were thick glass observation bubbles several feet in diameter.

Vance deposited his load on the apron and examined the trim little craft with interest. It was painted a light blue. It had a jaunty look about it, with none of the bloated menace of the working subs he had seen in Asian waters.

"The Smithsonian's pride and joy," Dorsey said. "They'd hang us for piracy if we took her out."

He picked up a boarding plank and snugged it to a support on the miniature platform deck. He climbed atop the vessel, opened the hatch in the squat conning tower and wriggled inside. As he stood on the deck, his upraised hands extended past the hatch cover.

"Hand me the package," he said in a low voice, which nevertheless reverberated through the cave.

Vance hauled the corpse aboard and lowered it feet first through the hole, then dropped through after it. He found himself in a cozy ball-shaped compartment with leather-backed chairs abaft the bubbles on either side, facing the control panel and steering mechanism in the forward bulkhead.

The body of the patrolman was propped grotesquely against one of the chairs, seemingly suspended in the act of rising. Dorsey was unlatching a small watertight door leading to the forward compartment. He opened it and squeezed through on his hands and knees, then reversed himself, peering out through the hole.

He gestured to Vance to pass him the body. "Take off the tarp," he instructed. Vance did as he was told, pushing the corpse through head first. Dorsey maneuvered it upright, as though he were guiding a broom up a chimney.

Vance stuck his head through the opening into a cramped triangle, narrowing to the point of the bow. Lines, nets and assorted fishing gear were racked neatly around the sides. In the middle, a black metal tube, three feet in diameter, extended from the deck to a hatch in the ceiling. Dorsey was engaged in stuffing the body inside it. He cursed as he removed his hand from its chest and its knees slowly sagged. He slammed the door shut, dogged it tight and with some effort pulled down a lever protruding from the side of the tube.

He turned and looked tensely at Vance, his chest heaving, sweat running in rivulets down his face. His eyes had the glazed, trigger-taut stare of a man waiting in ambush in the dark.

"D'you think you can run this damned thing?" Dorsey rasped. "I don't know much about it."

Vance squinted up at him from his squatting position. "I dunno," he said. "I've got twelve hundred hours in helicopters. I suppose the principle's the same. Is there a checkoff list?"

"I suppose there must be. I've seen the Smithsonian boys take it out without much practice. It must be fairly uncomplicated."

"I'll manage," Vance said.

He glanced around the compartment, the patrol leader studying his emplacements. Dorsey motioned him aside, but he hauled himself over the coaming and sidled past the big man to the cone of the bow. He examined a metal cylinder resembling a sawed-off bazooka barrel. Its muzzle extended outside the prow. A length of rope trailed from its hollow butt and coiled around a revolving drum fixed to the deck.

"Spear gun?" Vance asked.

"Looks like it."

Vance took a last look around and crawled back through the hatch. Dorsey joined him in front of the control panel.

"There's an electric eye here somewhere that opens the gate," he said, passing his sausage-size fingers over the panel, delicately, like a blind man.

"I'll find it," Vance said.

Dorsey flicked on a radar-chart monitor similar to the one on the hydro boat and punched the No. 12 channel. He pushed another button and a red speck glowed at the bottom of the blank screen.

"The spot will trace your course and record it on film," he said. "When you want to come home, just punch the reverse playback and follow the course."

He looked at his watch and reached for the conning tower ladder. "I've got to shove off. We'll be having callers any minute. The Confeds'll probably follow me. Wait until I'm past the first ring of islands."

He grabbed the tarp and swung himself up the ladder. As he stepped onto the apron, he snatched up the boarding ramp and secured it to three clamps cemented into the wall of the cave.

"Mustn't let Mr. Smithson know we've been joyriding in his sub," he growled. "Of course if you don't bring it back, he'll probably be suspicious."

He moved to the corner through which they had entered and switched on another closed-circuit monitor, sheathed in plastic and bolted to the floor. He pulled the sensor from his pocket, but then turned back to Vance.

"Oh, one other thing. There's a red navigation light on top

of the lab. Don't come back unless it's yellow. You're not color-blind, I hope."

Vance shook his head. The big man inserted the sensor in the wall and the door swung open. "Any questions?"

"Just one little thing. How do I get rid of the passenger?"

"Oh, yeah. That's the escape hatch he's in. Works by compressed air. It's loaded and cocked. Just release the lever on the side. It'll shoot him about ten feet in the air, so don't do it in front of an audience. But don't take him too far out. We want the Coastal Patrol to find him. Otherwise they'll be hanging around for weeks."

Surprisingly, his strained face relaxed in a lopsided grin. "I suppose it has occurred to you, if you screw up on this one, you're off the hook on the other deal."

"Yes, I've thought about that. But then I'd have the Smithsonian on my back."

"Believe me," Dorsey said. "You're better off with Howie Ray."

Vance stood in front of the monitor. The storm had blown over. Patches of blue appeared between the clouds, but the seas were still heavy and a brisk wind was blowing from the west. He watched Dorsey emerge from the hut, the tarpaulin slung over his shoulder. It was rolled up as if the body were still in it. He moved quickly to the boat basin and gingerly lowered his burden over the side.

After a minute the boat pulled away from the dock and headed northwest—the way they had come in. Vance watched as it threaded its way through the surrounding islands. As it disappeared into the thinning haze, another boat hove into view, following at a distance.

Vance turned off the monitor, cast off the single mooring line and leaped to the deck of the sub. Unhurriedly, he climbed down the ladder and dogged the hatch. He strapped himself into the portside seat and tested the helm. He discovered it moved backward and forward as well as revolving sideways, and concluded that the fore and aft movement controlled the diving planes as it would the ailerons in an airplane. He turned his eyes to the control panel and to his relief found a checkoff list pasted to a clipboard between the seats.

He ran through the list, paused before the next-to-last item, then punched the port starter button. The lights in the cockpit dimmed, the electric engine whirred for a moment, then caught and settled into an almost noiseless whisper. He started the other engine, checked the power output and took a deep breath. He reached for the toggle switch set into a bright red panel labeled "Flood Chamber." He flicked it up and waited. Nothing happened. He flicked it again and again. Still nothing happened. He ran through the entire checkoff list, stopping and starting the engines again. Still nothing.

He felt a faint stirring of panic. He thought of the dead man in the forward compartment, of Dorsey returning to find him sitting there stupidly, helplessly. Then, as he had learned to do in the fetid swamps of Asia, he cleared his mind and focused it like a laser beam on his predicament.

There was no use juggling switches and pushing buttons. Either the electric eye was not functioning or the receiving grid was not responding. If it was a mechanical failure, he had not the faintest idea how to correct it.

He unfastened his harness, mounted the ladder and opened the main hatch. He jumped to the apron, walked to the mammoth sea gate and examined the transom arm that should have rolled back on a trolley set in the ceiling. He could see nothing obstructing the one on the right. He started back around the "U" to the other side. On an impulse he stopped at the monitor and flipped it on. A hundred yards away,

making directly for the dock, loomed the unmistakable outline of a Coastal Patrol boat. A chill pierced his concentration. He stood for a moment, hypnotized.

Out of the corner of his eye some irregularity, some dis-
order registered vaguely on his brain. His attention snapped
to the wall. His eyes traced a small crack running from the
deck to eye level. The hidden door was ajar. He hurled his
shoulder against it and it snapped shut.

He ran back to the sub, leaped aboard and secured the
hatch. He threw himself into the seat, breathed a nondenomi-
national prayer and flipped up the toggle switch. The heavy
door slowly moved upward and backward. The sea surged
into the basin, spread across the apron and the submarine
gradually rose on its crest.

Vance engaged the twin screws and pushed the wheel gently
forward. The nose of the sub tilted slightly downward. He
eased the throttles forward. Slowly the craft moved through
the mouth of the cave and out into the rolling sea.

He gingerly tested the controls, trying to maintain a depth
midway between the surface and the shallow floor. He steered
generally west by south, away from the thickest cluster of
islands. Satisfied that he could hold the sub on a straight and
level course, he cautiously attempted a few elementary acro-
batics, rolling it from side to side and finally standing it
almost on its tail. It responded manfully but sluggishly, like
a willing but awkward porpoise. Grace and speed were not
its strong points. He glided along with no sense of motion for
nearly an hour.

When the chart showed him to be in relatively open waters,
Vance eased the boat toward the surface, raised the stubby
periscope and took a sighting. The heavy swells restricted his
vision. Figuring they also would conceal the low silhouette

of the sub from any casual observer on the islands, he hove to and surfaced. He climbed to the top of the ladder and stuck his head out of the tower.

The dotted line of the Florida Keys stretched off to his left, carelessly strung together by the Key Chain Highway. The dark bulk of the brooding Everglades squatted on the horizon to the north. Ahead lay the open waters of the Gulf. Aside from the toy automobiles gliding across the highway spans, there was no sign of life.

He took a last look around preparatory to going below and discharging his cargo. His stomach was beginning to flutter to the rhythm of the swells. Both it and his skittish nerves would be better off in the calmer waters below.

He reached over and grasped the handle of the hatch cover. The sub wallowed in a deep trough, rose smoothly on the frontal slope of a tremendous roller and rode up and up to its crest. From the ridge Vance gazed across miles of serrated waves. In the distance he descried the sleek, trim outline of a destroyer. As he started down the roller coaster, he caught a glimpse of a small boat, on a line with the ship, making directly toward him.

He swung the hatch closed, battened it and dropped to the deck. He shoved forward on the wheel even before he edged into his seat. The bow tilted sharply downward, toppling Vance forward against the wheel, accelerating the pitch even more. He regained his balance, flopped into his seat and leveled the boat off at a depth of twenty feet. His eyes leaped to the visual scanner. A stationary blip appeared at the two-mile divider and a moving one halfway between. As he watched, the gap steadily closed. He reached over and switched off the engines. The sub settled onto the sandy bottom at twenty-eight feet.

The small blip slowed its approach, passed slightly to starboard, circled back and stopped almost directly over him. Through the starboard porthole he watched a cable with a bulbous cup on the end of it lazily unreel. It snaked through the water like a questing tentacle, weaving closer and closer to the sub. As it neared the hull, the cable stiffened. The bulb ceased to dangle. It jerked around, darted toward the sub and clamped onto the topside of the bow. Vance waited. It could be just a marker line or it could be a charged cable which would transform his comfortable compartment into a death chamber. He dismissed the thought.

The Coastal Patrol surely would not resort to such drastic action against an unidentified and patently harmless vessel. It would be damned embarrassing to be taken into custody, but hardly fatal. That mildly comforting conviction was rudely jarred by a sudden concussion that rocked the sub on its side and seemed to squeeze the hull like a diaphragm.

The shock nearly hurled Vance out of his seat, despite his restraining harness. It also aroused his fighting instincts. Heedless of the possible damage to the thin shell, he reached for the starter switches. He engaged the screws, lifted the boat off the bottom and jammed the throttles full forward.

The small craft surged ahead and then sideways as another explosion convulsed the water where it had been resting. Vance yanked back on the wheel and fought toward the surface, where he calculated the blast effect would be dissipated, whatever else the consequences.

The stubby little craft almost leaped clear of the water, then flopped down and plowed forward at a straining ten knots, towing an orange plastic buoy in its wake. Vance twisted his head to look out the glass bubble in the side. A speedboat chugged up alongside and throttled back to keep pace with the laboring sub. Two men knelt along the low gunwale aft. Another was at the wheel in the cockpit. The boat was painted a grayish white. It flew no pennant.

This was not the Coastal Patrol. Who the hell were they to be harassing him? Vance resented being blown out of the water by anonymous busybodies. Then he remembered the mother ship and his resentment escalated into anger. He reduced power, and as his escort followed suit, he jammed the throttles forward and pulled momentarily ahead. Unobtrusively painted on the bow, he made out the Stars and Bars of the Confederacy.

One of the men in the stern was hunched over the cockpit, apparently talking with the pilot. He straightened up, scowling, and made a flat-handed gesture to Vance to stop. Vance stared at him impassively, then suddenly wrenched the wheel to the left in a clumsy attempt to ram his tormentors. The sub was too cumbersome. The speedboat quickly veered away and took station at a slightly more respectful distance.

The pilot turned his head and said something to the men in the stern. They stooped over, then stood up, hanging onto the rail with one hand, their other hand clutching a round, black object. The powerboat angled farther away from the sub. On command from the driver, the two men twisted half around and, with a stiff-armed motion, hurled the objects toward the submarine. One fell short. The other hit the hull and bounced off astern. It exploded in the air, rattling the topside with a hail of shrapnel. The first sent up a geyser of water and tipped the submarine over at a sixty-five-degree angle.

Without attempting to right it, Vance tilted the diving planes and the boat slipped under water like a crippled sturgeon. He leveled off only ten feet under the surface and turned toward his attackers, surmising that they would not want to use the grenades at too close range to their own boat. They pulled a short distance ahead, and he threw the engines into reverse. They turned and approached him slowly, and he thrust the sub forward, narrowing the gap. The game of cat-and-mouse went on for several minutes, during which they dropped no more grenades.

But Vance knew the outcome was inevitable. Grimly he worked out a last desperate gamble. Ignoring his pursuers, he spiraled the sub deeper and deeper until it settled in the sand on the ocean floor. Not knowing for sure what he was doing, he pressed a button labeled "Forward Ballast Tank." The nose of the sub rose at a forty-five-degree angle, and it started to drift upward. He adjusted a trim tab between the seats and cracked the throttles half ahead. The boat maintained a fairly even keel as long as he kept the wheel pushed hard forward. He plucked a mooring spike from the rack and wedged it in that position.

Two explosions rocked the sub again, but not so violently as before. Vance looked at the depth gauge. It showed forty feet. He surmised that the grenades could not reach that deep and that he was relatively safe so long as he stayed near the bottom. Or until the hunters tired of sport and set out in earnest to end the game. One business-sized depth charge from the destroyer, he reflected, would leave the Smithsonian bereft.

He unstrapped his harness and lurched to the hatch in the forward bulkhead. He swung it open and stepped through into the bow compartment. The violent maneuvers had dislodged some of the gear, leaving it strewn over the deck. Vance picked his way through the tangled lines and nets to the spear gun mounted on a ball swivel in the nose. He examined its trigger mechanism and rotated it to ascertain its firing radius. A cross-hair target locater was etched in the sight affixed to the barrel.

He stepped back and turned his attention to the escape chamber. The compressor lever was in the "down" position, as Dorsey had left it. Stenciled in urgent yellow letters at the top of the chamber were instructions to "DISENGAGE HATCH CLAMPS BEFORE RELEASING LEVER." Vance found the clamps and undogged them.

He bent over, one hand on the lever, and took a last look around. He shoved down on the handle, slapped it sideways out of its notch and jerked his hand back. With a muffled "whoosh" the lever slipped into the slot on the side of the chamber and shot up to the ceiling.

The submarine shuddered and reared back on its tail. Vance dove for the passageway to the steering compartment, scrambled through and pulled himself into his seat. He removed the wedge from the wheel, let the nose swing up and rolled the boat on its axis to give him an unobstructed view out the side window. He caught a glimpse of the corpse surging through the water ten feet behind the sub and twenty-five feet above it. As he strained to keep it in sight, it popped through the surface, disappeared for a moment, then splashed back and floated there, bobbing on the waves.

Vance made a tight spiral turn, keeping his eye on the body throughout. The nose of the sub was pointed upward at a seventy-degree angle. He adjusted the trim tab to keep it in that attitude without pressure on the wheel. He came about, aimed the nose at the corpse and eased the throttles back. The sub floated slowly upward. When the depth gauge showed ten feet, he reversed the engines and applied enough thrust to maintain that level. He took another bearing on the body, moved the helm two degrees left and lashed it in position.

With an effort, he pulled himself out of his seat and scrabbled toward the hatch, which was now almost overhead.

He clawed his way into the forward compartment, reached up and clasped his arms around the escape tube and hauled himself astride it. He reversed his legs and inched along the cylinder until he could grasp the butt of the spear gun. Lying almost prone, he screwed his neck around and applied his eye to the cylindrical sight. The body was in view, but at an extreme angle off to the right.

He cursed and weighed the advisability of crawling back to the wheel and swinging the nose around farther. The decision was immediately resolved as the powerboat nudged alongside the corpse. All three occupants stood at the rail looking down at it. One of them ducked into the cockpit and reappeared, carrying a grappling hook. He lowered the triple-pronged hook over the side and snagged the patrolman's blouse. The other two grabbed hold of the pole and heaved.

The upper portion of the body lifted out of the water. They pulled it toward the boat, and one of the men let go of the pole and reached out to grasp it. As he touched it, the coat tore loose. The body dropped into the sea and disappeared. It bobbed to the surface several feet farther from the boat and closer to the sub.

Vance held his fire. The man who had been in the cockpit during the pursuit pointed off in the direction of the buoy and snarled something at the other two. They nodded, and he again stepped down into the wheelhouse. He turned the boat around in a circle to come in downwind. The wash bounced the corpse five feet closer to the sub.

Vance trained the cross hairs on the patrolman's body. The boat drifted alongside, touched it and floated into the center of the target. Vance pulled the trigger. The spear lanced upward, trailing the rope behind it.

The point pierced the flat bottom of the boat just aft of the pilothouse, leaving half of the shaft sticking out beneath. Vance swung the barrel upward and caught a glimpse of the three men whirling around with the precision of a ballet team.

He jumped from his perch, snubbed the line around the stanchion, dropped through the door and scrambled into his seat. He ran the trim tab forward with one hand and with the other shoved against the wheel. As the nose of the sub swung downward, he walked the throttles to full astern. For a moment the vessel hung nearly motionless, then lurched backward.

Vance eased the throttles forward and moved across the aisle to peer out of the starboard porthole. The line swirled into view trailing the bent shaft, a jagged chunk of fiberglass impaled on the spear points. Vance felt a glow of triumph.

He slanted the submarine to the surface and slowly circled the capsized hulk with the three men clinging to it. Their life jackets were inflated under their oilskins, and they bobbed up and down in the swells like three glowering roly-polies in a bathtub. He throttled back, leaving the engines idling, and climbed out on deck. He stared at them silently, like a tourist on a sightseeing boat. They stared back at him, muttering to themselves but not raising their voices.

Vance went below and battened the hatch. He took another look out the window and spied the body of the patrolman floating some distance from the stranded seamen. He maneuvered the sub upwind from it, scooped it onto the trailing buoy cable and scraped it off on the upturned hull of the boat. That may take some explaining, he thought.

He stood off fifty yards from the wreck and hove to. He crawled forward into the bow compartment, rummaged through the equipment locker and found a pair of powerful binoculars and a crowbar. Unhurriedly, he climbed out on deck again and leveled the glasses at the destroyer. A group of sailors was clustered on the foredeck, lowering another launch. He swung the glasses around to the shattered boat in the water and studied the faces of the three men clinging to it. Their glowering expressions brought a grunt of satisfaction from him.

He stepped off the small platform onto the rounded hull and shuffled his way, spraddle-legged, to where the magnetic cup of the buoy line was attached to the bow. He succeeded in wedging the crowbar under it and wrenching it loose. It fastened onto the crowbar. He heaved cup and crowbar as far as he could toward the overturned boat, waved airily to the men in the water and went below.

He took the sub down to twenty feet, punched the reverse-course button and locked the auto pilot onto it. Then he sat back in his chair and emitted a short, gleeful chortle. Based on what Dorsey had told him, he doubted if the Confeds would report their clash with an unarmed sub. It would entail too many explanations and would not reflect much glory on their navy.

The return trip was without incident. He picked up a few small craft on his visual sonar and gave them a sizable berth. The engines sounded, to Vance's now practiced ear, to be laboring as the sub slipped between the surrounding islands into home waters. He had noticed the seams in the forward compartment appeared to have been strained, though they were not leaking. Dorsey could explain to the Smithsonian that he had taken their baby on a shakedown cruise.

Cautiously, he brought the boat up to periscope depth and inspected the other islands before heading for port. Sheltered though it was from the long combers of the open sea, the choppy surface of the ocean pond still was not conducive to pleasure sailing, for which he was grateful. He circled the domed island. The hydroplane was moored in the basin and a yellow beacon flashed atop the hut.

He ran through the landing procedure and checkoff list on the back of the clipboard, maneuvered the boat near the vicinity where he judged the cave to be and revolved the course monitor to zero in accordance with the instructions.

A green line appeared on the screen slightly to starboard of his position dot. He swung the boat around in a 180-degree arc, throttled back to idle and watched as the dot drifted over onto the line. Using just enough power to give him positive control of the rudders, he backed the dot down the green line. The sub slid through the mouth of the cave and came gently to rest between the padded sides of the apron. He looked out the window at the rough coral walls and cut the engines.

He flicked a green toggle switch on the control panel marked "Drain Chamber." The massive sea gate ponderously descended, closing the entrance. He watched the water level slowly recede from the ceiling. He suddenly felt weak.

He sat slumped in the chair, not even bothering to unfasten his harness. He did not move until the water had drained off the ramp and the sub had ceased its gentle rocking. He freed himself from the straps, stood up and flexed his leaden legs. He clambered up the ladder and threw open the hatch. The dank air filtered into his lungs like the first fragrant scent of spring. He heaved himself up and jumped onto the apron. His legs nearly gave way under him.

He twisted his torso around and his eyes swept over the grinning face of Robert Dorsey, standing inside the open doorway.

Dorsey walked toward him. "Have a pleasant trip?"

"Not very," he said. "The stiff and I have been sitting here playing pinochle." Somewhat volubly for him, he described his first encounter with the Confederacy.

When he finished, Dorsey gave him a long sober look. "Now are you convinced these people mean business?"

"I would have to say I thought so at the time. Why the hell were they so eager to knock me off if they didn't know who I was?"

"They weren't after you. The Coastal Patrol picked me up and frisked me. When they turned me loose, the Confeds must have figured you had the body on the sub. They've got us zeroed in with sonar and they could have tracked you. They didn't want to take you alive. You could have talked your way out of it. But with you and the patrolman both dead in the sub, we would play hell explaining it. To the Florida authorities *or* the Smithsonian. Incidentally," he added, moving toward the hidden door, "you put on a pretty good show. I think you may be ready for the main event."

Dr. Abranowitz was bustling, breezy and filled with professional zeal, but apparently devoid of curiosity. Dorsey had introduced him to Vance as a "plastic retreader," and Vance to him as "him." Completely naked, Vance lay on one of the dissecting tables in the lab as the doctor minutely examined him from scalp to soles.

The doctor was taken aback when he observed the shrapnel scars speckled from knee to neck. He looked at Dorsey despairingly. "For God's sake," he said, "it'll take me two months to sandpaper these down and even then he'll look like the moths have been into him."

"Forget 'em," Dorsey said. "He's not going to be entering any swimming meets. He's got a cover story."

The doctor pulled a thick sheaf of photographs from the false bottom of his bag and set about comparing sectional blowups of Peter Tremont's body with Vance's anatomy. He made notes as he went along. When he had finished, he stepped back from the table and shook his head dubiously.

"The face is not too bad. We'll round out the cheeks, lift the left eyebrow, give him a scar on the chin and open up his eyes a bit. It'll maybe pass with his wife, but it won't fool his girl friend."

"Just do the best you can," Dorsey said irritably. "Let him worry about the girl friend."

Dr. Abranowitz opened two black medical bags and laid out an array of scalpels, needles, clamps and other paraphernalia. He picked up an electrical needle and plugged it into a floor outlet. He slapped Vance on the buttock and motioned him to roll over.

"Now then," he said, "how about a nice hula girl on the left bicep and an Armenian flag on the right?" He pressed a switch in the handle and leaned over Vance's face. "I'll let you know when it hurts."

He tattooed a jagged, lifelike scar from the left corner of Vance's mouth to the middle of his chin, consulting a close-up of Peter Tremont's face from time to time, like an artist copying a portrait. When he had finished, he executed a strawberry birthmark on his right leg and a prominent mole at the base of his throat so realistic it almost seemed to have hair growing out of it.

He straightened up and inspected his handiwork. He glanced mischievously at Dorsey, hunched over a chair back watching the operation stolidly. "Ah, very good," he said. "I plan to submit before and after pictures to the *Journal of Plastic Surgery.*"

"You do that, Doc," Dorsey said. "We'll send along a death mask of the author."

Dr. Abranowitz opened the door of a portable sterilizer and

selected a small scalpel with a slightly convex blade. "Now you may bleed a little if you wish," he said to Vance indulgently.

He made a small incision at the corner of each eye, and a larger one extending from half an inch above the left eyebrow into the eyebrow itself. He stitched up the cuts, gathering the one on the forehead tightly so it gave a twist to the eyebrow. The flesh-colored stitches were invisible. He rubbed a cosmetic paste over the incisions and they too disappeared.

He handed Vance a hand mirror. "Take a look. You may not recognize yourself after I have wrought my next miracle."

He reached into the sterilizer and extracted a long, hollow needle with a bulb attached to its handle. He plucked a tube from his bag, snipped off the tip of its nozzle with sterile scissors and squeezed the contents into a valved opening in the bulb. He pricked the needle into the hollows of Vance's cheeks and squeezed the bulb. Rapidly and deftly, working simultaneously with both hands on both cheeks, he kneaded and shaped the congealing silicone foam, his eyes darting from the photograph of Peter Tremont to the live bust he was molding. As the silicone set, Vance could feel his skin taking on an unfamiliar pattern.

Dr. Abranowitz stepped back and brushed the perspiration from his forehead with the sleeve of his gown. "Don't open your mouth. Don't sneeze. Don't swallow. Don't breathe."

He crouched down and gazed at the contour of Vance's face from below. He circled him slowly from left to right, then from right to left. Once he stepped forward, placed a gloved thumb at the right corner of Vance's mouth and pressed upward.

He picked up the photo, held it over Vance's head and glanced from one to the other. Apparently satisfied, he passed the picture to Dorsey, anxiously watching his reaction. Dorsey studied the picture and its replica, then stood up and went through the routine of peering at the patient from all angles.

He turned to Dr. Abranowitz and handed him the photo. "Not bad."

The doctor broke into a broad smile. "The bone structure is similar, which makes for a good likeness. We will, of course, have to lighten the hair and eyebrows. If the subject could be trained to breathe through his mouth, it would soften the lines of the face even more."

The subject nudged the doctor's leg with his foot and gave him an inquiring look.

"Oh, of course," said Dr. Abranowitz absently. "You may talk now. I suppose you might be interested in seeing the results of my work." He handed him the mirror.

To Vance, accustomed to seeing the same countenance for thirty-six years, the transformation was startling—and a bit disappointing. He had always taken his good features for granted and, in his youth, when it seemed of some importance, had suffered some regret over his imperfections. The face that looked back at him seemed gross, vapid, characterless. Yet it did closely resemble the picture, which was not unattractive.

His cheeks were fuller, almost plump; his high cheekbones and the deep lines about his mouth were hardly discernible. His narrow, almost slanting eyes were round and wide and seemed to have taken on a look of naïve simple-mindedness. The crooked eyebrow and the jagged scar on the chin leaped out at him like hideous disfigurements. He shook his head distastefully and handed the mirror back.

The doctor rummaged in his smaller bag and pulled out a flat metal container resembling a cigarette case. He flipped it open, revealing a handful of capsules, the size of large vitamin pills. He spilled them out on the table and arranged them in an apparently prescribed order.

He took a small pair of tweezers from the case, pulled apart the pellet on the left and extracted from it a tiny wadded ball of tissue-thin material. Carefully he inserted the tweezers in it and opened the prongs. The material was so flimsy and so transparent as to be almost invisible.

"Little finger, left hand," he said, not taking his eyes off the tweezers. Vance held up his finger. The doctor slipped the tissue over it, rubbed it down and massaged it with his own gloved fingers. He picked up a razor-thin scalpel and ran it around the nail, then tamped the tissue down with his thumb. He held up the finger and inspected it. It looked exactly like Vance's other little finger—except that it had Peter Tremont's fingerprints on it.

"Artificial skin," the doctor said in response to Vance's skeptical glance. "Has the same elasticity and more durability than your own skin. Does everything but sweat. Just don't get yourself killed. Your own skin will deteriorate. This won't. It'll stand up under normal wear and tear. It locks into the pores, so you can't even sandpaper it off."

Deftly he fitted the artificial skin over Vance's other fingers. When he had finished, he examined them under a magnifying glass, then handed the glass to Dorsey.

"Good reproduction," he said. "Did it myself. Notice the hairline scar on the right thumb. Might come in handy for identification purposes."

"He's not going to need that much identification," Dorsey said.

Dr. Abranowitz took a bottle labeled "Instant Follicle Hair Coloring" from his bag and handed it to Vance. "Apply it about once a week," he said. "You don't have to be furtive about it. He uses it." He gestured toward the pictures of Peter Tremont. "You can get it over the counter, I understand. How's your face feel?"

"Like a chipmunk," Vance said.

The doctor looked pleased. "You'll get used to it. If you decide you don't like it, stop by my office when you get back. I can change it."

Dorsey said, "You finished, Doc?"

Dr. Abranowitz reached out one hand and gingerly squeezed Vance's new cheeks. "Yes. I guess so."

Dorsey gathered up the photographs and counted them. "I'll take care of these."

Vance showered and applied the coloring to his hair and eyebrows. They came out a dark brown. Dressed in Peter Tremont's second-best suit—a boisterous greenish-blue check he himself would not be caught dead in, he hoped—a royal-blue shirt and a figured tie, he reluctantly stepped to the mirror and scrutinized his new self. Strangely, he did not experience the same feeling of outrage, of being despoiled. At his first look into the hand glass he had felt like a mongrel— part Cordell Vance, part Peter Tremont, part faceless impostor. Now, as he looked in the mirror, he saw Peter Tremont —through the eyes of Cordell Vance.

When he entered the living room, Dorsey was seated in front of one of the polished benches, an array of cards and documents spread out before him. He looked up. His sleepy eyes widened minutely in what, for him, passed as a startled glance. He studied the strange face and nodded his head in satisfaction.

"Nice to have you with us, Mr. Tremont. Here're your papers. Look 'em over."

Tremont reached in his pocket, pulled out a package of Southern Prides and lit one. Cordell Vance had broken the smoking habit without too much discomfort in a Burmese prison and had never resumed it. In the Confederacy non-smoking was regarded as unpatriotic if not downright subversive.

"Wheah's the doctah?" His voice held just a trace of a Louisiana drawl.

"He's fiddling around in the lab. And in case you were wondering, he's a little gabby, but he's very good at forgetting faces and has no memory at all for names."

Peter Tremont sorted through the cards and papers on the bench. He frowned briefly as he inspected the Classification Catalogue, proclaiming Peter Tremont to be a "Deserving Citizen of the Confederate States of America." He gathered the documents together and stuffed them one by one into a compartmented pocket-size portfolio bearing the Great Seal of the Confederacy on its cover, with his name and central records number stamped underneath: passport, visa, civilian status, military status, mobilization assignment, driver's license, coded psychological profile and Reliability Index, employment clearance, violations record, financial rating and travel permit authorizing him to "proceed from Charlotte, N.C., to Confederacity or environs via Miami, Fla., between 21 April 1981 and 29 April 1981."

He tucked the last card into the leather folder and looked across at Dorsey. "Purchase permit?"

Dorsey rummaged in his shirt pocket and tossed another card on the bench. It bore Tremont's picture and the notation: "Authorized to purchase nonessential articles in Private Sector stores. Valid until revoked."

"This is the part I'm most concerned about at the beginning," Dorsey said, "your pretending to be a businessman. Of course Tremont isn't either—really—so that should be all right, even if you make a few mistakes. But you don't have any conception—other than what you've read—how the free enterprise system operates in the South. You'll have to feel your way along. If you run into any serious problems, you can call on the Intercontinental Import Company for counsel. That's part of their job," he added with exaggerated heartiness, "to help their distributors any way they can."

"How many distributors do they have?"

"It's a legitimate setup. Don't worry about that. There won't be any slip-ups there. They do business all over the world. However, I will be handling your account personally."

"That's mighty neighborly of you," Tremont drawled.

Dorsey rose from the bench and strolled over to a chair. "The Confeds are likely to be a little riled after what you did to them this morning. I don't think they'll do anything rash, but you never can tell. It might be a good idea to ship you out ahead of schedule. Maybe tomorrow night. I want to run you through one more conditioning session."

Cordell Vance reasserted himself, and Peter Tremont deferred to him. "Screw it. You just want to play Svengali. If I'm not 'conditioned' now, I never will be. You know damned well all this neurogenic crap isn't going to make any difference when the time comes. I'll either do it or I won't do it."

Dorsey eyed him coldly. "What would you say the odds are?"

"How the hell should I know? Right now, I'd say the chances are it can't be done without me getting myself killed. And right now I don't favor that. Even if I get an opportunity, there's a damned good chance I'll chicken out. So how do those odds strike you?"

"Right now," Dorsey said dryly, "we don't have a suitable replacement. So I guess we'll have to play along with them." Abruptly he dropped the sparring tone they customarily adopted with each other. His voice betrayed genuine concern.

"Look, if you get in any trouble down there, don't hesitate to call for help. We can bring you out all right without seriously compromising ourselves if they don't know what you were there for. Any time you decide you can't go through with it, don't be afraid to call it off. Just let me know. I've got the channel set up. Nobody else has used it—or will use it—so you'll be in the clear." He grimaced. "I shouldn't be talking like this. I shouldn't be giving you an out. But you're right. You'll either do it or you won't do it. I'm not worried. I know you'll give it a try—if you possibly can."

Peter Tremont looked at him suspiciously, wondering whether his solicitude might not be part of the psychological con game.

"Okay, Dorsey," he said. "You've been prowling around in my skull long enough you probably know what I'll do. But I don't. We'll just have to see." He paused, then continued self-consciously, "If something happens to me, you'll try to let the girl know I won't be coming back. So she won't be waiting around for me."

"Of course. And I'll see she gets the money."

Peter Tremont stood up and felt his unfamiliar face. "Well, boy," he said, "it's against my upbringin', but why don't you break out that ol' bottle an' we'll have a little drink togethah."

Part Five

Chapter Ten

"We will be landing in Confederacity in approximately eight minutes. Please have your passports and customs declarations ready for inspection. Foreign visitors use the front exit, nationals the rear." The lazy magnolia drawl held an undertone of command. "I wish to welcome you to the Confederate States of America. We hope you have had a pleasant flight and that you will enjoy your stay in our country. Please remain seated until the plane has reached the terminal. Thank you."

Peter Tremont glanced across the aisle at the passengers in the five-abreast center section. The four men in his row each had one hand thrust inside his coat as though performing a drill. The scrawny-necked, pointy-chinned woman was sitting upright, her hand in her open purse. Peter Tremont reached inside his coat and touched the leather document holder in his breast pocket.

The plane hit the runway, jolted to a stop to the roar of reverse blowers and taxied swiftly to the terminal. No one made a move to peek out the curtained windows. Everyone remained seated until the plane was at rest and the whine of the engines had ceased. A sign flashed on over the left aisle: "REAR EXIT," over the right aisle: "FRONT EXIT." The passengers sorted themselves out silently and efficiently, and meshed into their respective lines like cogs in interlocking wheels.

Peter Tremont stepped briskly through the rear exit and onto the elevated walkway. He raised his head to a star-sprinkled sky and inhaled the velvet fragrance of a spring evening. An elusive nostalgic memory flashed past on a soft warm breeze and was gone before he could grasp it. He marched stolidly to the brightly lighted bulk of the terminal, curving off to his right, and into the customs enclosure.

He collected his baggage and joined the small clump of travelers at the "S-T" section of the oblong counter. The three inspectors handled their duties with brusque competence, responding to the nervous pleasantries of the passengers civilly but curtly. One of the inspectors examined the baggage while another checked the papers. The third stood between them, observing with seeming disinterest.

All the travelers, Tremont noticed, grew tense and quiet as they approached the counter. All except a balding, stocky, moon-faced man who obviously was familiar with the routine. He extended his right index finger and rolled it expertly over the ink pad without being told, then held it out to the inspector as though presenting him with a gift.

"Gonna have to get a new set of prints," he chuckled. "You guys have about worn this one out."

The fingerprint man looked at him unsmilingly and rolled the print onto the form without comment.

The loquacious passenger chattered away to the inspector checking his papers, ignoring the one going through his baggage. He answered the routine questions good-naturedly and unhesitatingly. The luggage man finished his examination without challenge and snapped the two large suitcases closed. So far as Peter could tell, no words were exchanged behind the counter. But the observer-inspector stepped forward, gathered up the man's papers and said in a low voice, "Please step into the interrogation room. Wait for me there."

The chunky man caught his breath, started to speak, then turned obediently and walked away, his chalky face set in a frozen grin.

Tremont stepped to the counter, shoved his bag and two cameras through the opening at the bottom and glanced uneasily at the overseer. The official returned his look inscrutably. Peter dropped his eyes.

He extracted his passport, visa and travel permit from the leather folder and handed them to the document inspector. "Your other papers, please."

Tremont handed over the folder. The inspector nudged the ink pad toward him. "Right index finger."

Peter inked his finger and pressed down heavily as the print was transferred.

"You were traveling in Florida?"

"Miami."

"Jacksonville, Palm Beach, Key West?"

"Just Miami."

"You have been to Florida before?"

"No."

The inspector gave him a sharp look. "When one goes to Florida for the first time, he usually travels around."

"I was there on business."

"What was your business, Mr. . . . Tremont?"

"I'm just moving to Confederacity. I've bought a photographic supply shop here. I looked over a number of shops in Miami and bought a couple of cameras."

"Why would you buy cameras in Miami if you are in the business of selling them here?"

"I bought them from the supplier I will be doing business with."

"Why do you not do business with a supplier in the Confederacy?"

"Camera imports from Florida are approved under the currency exchange regulations. These are foreign cameras which I would have difficulty buying in the Confederacy."

"They were manufactured in the United States?"

Peter shook his head. "Italy, Liechtenstein." He pointed diffidently to the cameras. The baggageman, who had not been paying any apparent attention to the questioning, handed them across to his partner. The document man examined them cursorily and handed them back.

"Your travel permit is good until the twenty-ninth, Mr. Tremont. Why did you return two days early?"

Peter hesitated. "Well, the currency allowance doesn't go very far in Miami. Besides, I wanted to look around here before I take over the shop."

"You have lived in Confederacity before?"

"I've been here several times, but I never lived here."

"Where will you be staying, Mr. Tremont?"

"I have an apartment over the shop at 689 Granger Avenue. I'll move in there when I take over. I'll be staying at a hotel for a couple of days."

"What hotel?"

"Well, I don't know. I've stayed at the Beauregard a few times before."

The supervisor reached over the shoulder of the document inspector and picked up Tremont's folder. He riffled through it, studied the passport photo and raised his eyes in a feature-by-feature scrutiny of Peter's face.

"How long since you've updated your picture, Mr. Tremont?"

"Uh . . . I guess a year or so." He licked his lips and shifted uncomfortably.

"You're a photographer," the supervisor said caustically. "Take another picture of yourself." He flipped over the cards in the dossier. "Why aren't you working in the service of the State?"

"I did my three years' military and three years' compulsory," Tremont replied defensively.

"An able-bodied man your age has no business being in the Private Sector these days."

Peter was silent.

"Well, what's your reason?"

Tremont drew himself up with a show of dignity. "The Private Sector is an important element in the Evolutionary Order, as our President has frequently pointed out."

The inspector eyed him coldly. "What's your reason?"

"I was downclassified," Peter said in a low voice. "There didn't seem to be any future for me in the service."

"There is a future for everyone who adapts himself to the Evolutionary Order," the official said sententiously. "I would advise you to adapt."

He tossed Tremont's papers onto the counter in dismissal. The subordinates stamped his passport and customs clearance and waved him away. He took the monorail in to Jefferson Davis Square and walked the two blocks from there to the Hotel Beauregard.

He had no trouble getting accommodations in the second-rate hostelry. The creed of the Party of National Resurgence —"A place for everyone; everyone in his place"—did not allow for very much shifting about. Consequently, there was virtually no transient population in the Confederate States of America. And very little frivolous travel, inasmuch as an absence of more than a few days from one's accustomed domicile was almost certain to provoke inquiries from the Citizens Protection Force.

Though slightly unnerved by the inquisition at the airport, Peter Tremont was glad to have that one under his belt before coming up against the Seepees. The open contempt of the chief inspector had been reassuring—as well as exasperating. It tended to confirm an apparent flaw he had detected in Howie Ray Spearman's major opus, *The Inevitability of Social Evolution*: that the process of natural selection tended to ignore the mediocre as drones who constituted neither an asset nor a liability to the system. Thus it gave them a kind of protective coloration. They possessed neither the ability and ambition to disrupt the "orderly structure of society" from above nor the resentment and desperation to threaten it from below.

Like every police state in history, the stability of the Confederacy rested on the innate resistance to change of the plodding, put-upon, grumbling middle class. Though they had passively resisted the new order originally, they had eventually adapted themselves to it, and would passively resist any attempt to overthrow it. The keystone of Spearman's theory of social evolution was the nurturing of "fortuitous mutation"—the motive power that moved mankind ahead. However, it postulated the existence of a common denominator, against which the mutation might be measured. Spearman's Seepees were constantly on the lookout for mutations, either fortuitous or deleterious. The refuge for anyone seeking anonymity was in the common denominator. At the moment Peter Tremont's one objective was to achieve anonymity. Resisting the impulse to go out and scout the terrain, he went quietly to bed.

Having helped build one nation, and feeling it was at least as much their handiwork as the North's, the Confederacy suffered no chauvinistic qualms about copying the processes and institutions which had, by painful trial and error, established the United States as a world power in less than a century. So it was that, even in its infancy, the new nation determined to erect a magnificent monument to its glorious future. De-

spite the wounded feelings it aroused, and in the face of outraged imputations of ingratitude, one of the first acts of the
First Confederate Congress was to direct the removal of the
capital from the seedy little town of Montgomery, Alabama.

As an inducement to the kingpin of the border states to
stop vacillating over secession, it was agreed that the capital
would be transferred to Richmond, Virginia. No sooner had
that been done, and no sooner had the lawmakers endured a
torrid summer in that provincial backwater, than agitation
started to erect a great new city in more congenial surroundings. The decision was hastened by the increasing belligerence
in the North. Stung by accusations that he had cravenly
abandoned the Union, Abraham Lincoln had belatedly but
energetically set about building the nation's military might.

The architects of the Confederacy realized it would not be
politic to construct the symbol of secession a hundred miles
from the capital of a hostile neighbor. Besides, the touchy
Western states were beginning to grumble about being treated
as colonies and to mutter about creating a nation of their own.

The upshot of it was that a Congressional committee, composed of one member from each state, was appointed to select
the site. After nearly two years of deliberation, artful conciliation and rancorous altercation, the committee accepted a
joint offer by the legislatures of Alabama, Georgia and Tennessee to deed in perpetuity to the Confederate Government
a fifty-square-mile area encompassing portions of all three
states. It was located on the Tennessee River, near the bustling city of Chattanooga, in the rolling, forested foothills of
the Cumberland Plateau. The capital—Confederacity—was
to be situated in the center of a huge, natural park, dotted
with small lakes and stocked with wild game from the far
corners of the world. The entire enclave was to be called the
Commonwealth of Independence.

After months of heated debate, highlighted by Senator Ar-

nold P. Clatworth's daily recital of the mean temperature
during the previous twenty-four hours, Congress approved
the committee's recommendation. On February 8, 1870—the
ninth birthday of the Confederacy—the seat of government
was transferred to the raw new capital in the western wilderness. The mean temperature was twenty-nine degrees, prompt-
ing grizzled Congressman Lloyd G. Bannister of South
Carolina to comment, "What the hell! We might as well have
stayed in Washington."

Peter Tremont stood at the window of his dingy room in
the Hotel Beauregard and took in the clean green and white
city, bathed in the sunlight of a sparkling spring morning.
For the first time he felt a genuine bitterness toward the ruthless freebooters and fanatics who had seized the smiling land
and corrupted its gentle, friendly people. He repressed it for
the time being. His task now was not retribution but to stay
alive.

He dressed and went down to the coffee shop off the lobby.
He bought a paper and listened to the conversation at the
counter. It was no different from that in Chicago or Denver
or Hoboken—talk about bowling and television shows, women
and car payments and golf.

There was no mention of the bloody clash near Alva, Oklahoma, in which, according to the lead story in the paper, "ter-
rorist ginchoes" from Kansas had been routed in a "provocation raid" across the border. Nor was there any discussion of
President Spearman's annual summary of "Evolutionary
Achievement," nor of the "economic imperative of a Pacific
lifeline," nor of the breakthrough in missile-guidance systems
announced at Huntsville—all prominently featured in the
news.

It reminded Peter Tremont of the wars he had fought, in

which, outside of business hours, all talk of war was tacitly avoided. He got the impression that the people of the Confederacy were not bubbling with martial fervor.

He walked purposefully across the shabby lobby, through the old-fashioned revolving door and turned right on North Second Street toward the Grand Concourse of the Confederacy. Though he had never seen it before, his briefings had made him as familiar with the topography of Con City as with the Ban Phan Valley, where he had waded through every thicket and rice paddy on the guerrilla training ground.

The city was laid out on somewhat the same pattern as Washington, though without the diagonal streets. The Capitol stood on a high bluff overlooking the river. The Grand Concourse, lined by stately trees on either side, extended twenty blocks north through the heart of the city. At the far end, the Citadel of Justice—the Supreme Court—was perched atop a semicircular ridge, following the bend of the river. The ground sloped rather steeply down from both ends of the Concourse to Stone Mansion—the presidential palace—situated symbolically midway between the legislative and judicial branches of the government.

Resembling the Mall in Washington, the Concourse was a block-wide swath of greensward, dotted with plazas, fountains and landscaped gardens. A concrete bowl with a sliding glass roof was sunk into the center of Jefferson Davis Plaza at the foot of Capitol Bluff. It could accommodate twenty thousand people for concerts, entertainment or inaugurations.

The great gray pillars of Stone Mansion faced east. Broad, sweeping drives, like reverse parentheses, curved through the front and rear porticoes, leading to East and West Concourse avenues. A terraced roof garden covered the entire expanse of the South Wing of the mansion, the scene of informal receptions in clement weather. Protruding out over the south wall was a modest balcony, enclosed by a tasteful, wrought-iron, waist-high grille and an invisible, bulletproof glass shield.

The balcony was familiar to every television viewer in the Confederate States and particularly to the 300,000 National Service Workers in Con City. Periodically, they were granted the privilege of assembling in mammoth Spearman Square underlooking the balcony to hear major policy pronouncements from the lips of the President. Attendance was in no way compulsory, but it was considered to be advisable. Not that anyone's presence would be missed in the "Sardine Pit," but it would certainly be noticeable anywhere else in the vicinity when Howie Ray Spearman was speaking. Besides, Howie Ray always put on a good show.

The bulletproof shield was of course not visible to the viewers, but its existence had been well known to them since the time, four years before, when they had witnessed the puzzling row of pockmarks that unaccountably splayed across the screen in front of Spearman's face on the occasion of his fifty-eighth birthday. The crazed, would-be assassin was beaten and kicked to death by outraged citizens before the Seepees could seize him.

The avenues on either side of the Grand Concourse were flanked by massive, squat marble and granite buildings housing the government agencies. Whenever President Spearman paraded up to the Capitol and back, which was not infrequently, the buildings themselves were screened by a solid row of armed soldiers and the windows looking out on the avenue were shuttered.

The business section of Con City extended back six or seven blocks east and west of the Concourse. Although the same height restrictions were in effect as in Washington—no building higher than the Capitol—the slope of the terrain permitted considerably more leeway—up to twenty-five stories.

Peter Tremont walked briskly along Second Street across

the Concourse. He glanced up at the Capitol, but did not pause to inspect it. Presumably he would have visited it on one of his previous trips. He continued on to Granger Avenue, three blocks beyond East Concourse, and turned left toward the business area.

He slowed his pace to a saunter as he approached Sixth Street. He stood on the corner and gawked up at the teal-blue glass and aluminum building which occupied the northwest corner of the block. He moved across the street, counted its twenty-two stories and surveyed the pedestrian traffic passing in front of it along the avenue. He walked to the corner, re-crossed the street and strolled into the Granger Avenue Photographic Supply Shop next to the building entrance on the alley side.

A thin-faced, sharp-featured woman with scraggly gray hair peered at him through thick, rimless spectacles. "Yes? Can I do something for you?" Her voice was shrill and wavered on the edge of a whine.

Peter advanced toward her, ducking his head diffidently. Who the devil was she? He hadn't been briefed on her. He did not know whether he had met her or not.

"Oh," she said as he approached and cleared his throat. "It's Mr. Tremont. I didn't recognize you at first."

"Uh . . . yes," Peter said. "I'm a few days early. Is Mr. Tarlin in?"

"Yes, he's in the back. I'll get him." She disappeared through a curtained doorway behind the counter. She returned in a minute followed by a short, heavy-set, jowly man wearing a mustard-colored sweater. He shuffled around the counter and shook hands.

"Ah, Mr. Tremont, we weren't expecting you till Monday."

"Yes, I know. I finished my business in Miami and decided to come on over and get settled in."

"Well." The man's voice was on the edge of being contentious. "We weren't planning to move out of the apartment until Sunday."

"No, no. That's quite all right. I wasn't planning to move in till next week. My furniture hasn't arrived yet, I'm sure."

"No, it hasn't. Well, you want to sign the papers and run through the inventory?"

"I suppose we might as well."

They spent the remainder of the morning going over details of the transfer. Though no businessman, Tremont had been thoroughly briefed on the papers he should be familiar with. He did know something about the operation of a photographic supply store, thanks to Sid Rogenstein.

When they had finished the paper work, Harry Tarlin showed him around the shop. "Should make you a fair living," he said, "if you tend to business. If I was you, I'd try to build up some connections in the agencies."

Tremont feigned interest. "How would you go about it?"

"Oh, you know. Maybe a little favor for one of the section chiefs who has purchasing authority." The round man sounded meaningfully vague. "Take some pictures of his family—or girl friend. Get to know him. A lot of those people like to do a little business on the side." He gave Peter a knowing look. "In fact, I could put you in touch with a fellow I've had some dealings with."

"Fine. Fine," Peter said. "How about the Party?" he asked innocently. "Any chance of getting an in there? I'd think that'd be a good place to have a connection."

Harry Tarlin's manner changed abruptly. "Well, sure," he said guardedly. "If you know someone in the Party, you'll make out all right. Of course," he added in a carefully neutral voice, "they don't normally do business with the Private Sector. But I suppose it depends on the circumstances."

His tone, though correct, was no longer confidential. He

appeared to be in a hurry to wind up the transaction. He escorted Peter to the rear of the shop and quickly ran through the parts inventory. "I suppose you'll be doing most of your own repair work," he said. "Can't hardly make it on sales alone." His suddenly querulous manner was not one to inspire confidence in a purchaser taking over the business.

"Yes," Tremont said, "I like to tinker around. That's really the reason I picked this business."

"You'll need someone to help out in the front end. The missus probably'd be willing to stay on for a couple months anyway."

Peter shook his head regretfully. "I think I'd better try to handle it myself until I see what it's good for."

"She's good with the customers."

Peter looked over at the pinch-faced harridan who had greeted him and who presumably was "the missus." "Yes," he said, "I'm sure she is. But I want to try it alone for a while."

"You're not married?"

"Not now." Peter Tremont had been noticeably reticent about his two former wives, and his stand-in was doubly so.

The proprietor of the Granger Avenue Photographic Supply Shop reached into the drawer of a battered desk and pulled out a pair of keys hung together on a paper clip.

He handed them to Peter. "This one's to the shop, this one's the apartment. You saw it last time. Don't suppose you'd need to look it over again, wouldja? It's kinda messed up."

"No, no. Everything's fine."

"I'll leave the other set in the drawer here. I'll stop in and see how you're gettin' along next week." He walked Tremont to the door and shook hands perfunctorily. "The missus" gave him a purse-mouthed nod.

Tremont walked over to East Concourse and had lunch in a sidewalk café cater-cornered from the Stone Mansion. He spent the afternoon sightseeing, and the evening in an aimless tour of the taverns in the vicinity of the hotel. He was lying on his bed reading when the Seepee knocked on his door.

By its nature, a police state handicaps itself. It creates a universal furtiveness that cloaks the innocent and the guilty alike. Fear has many aliases but only one visage. Peter Tremont, assassin, opened the door with the same apprehension as a "distinguished" citizen of the Confederacy.

The Seepee was a nondescript, middle-sized man who undertook first to allay his anxiety and then to lead him into innocuous contradictions.

"Just a routine inquiry," he assured him. As far as Peter Tremont could tell, it was. It covered most of the ground he had been over numerous times in his neurogenic conditioning sessions with Robert Dorsey. Indeed, it was so familiar he was obliged toward the end to simulate more nervousness than he felt. "Don't be so goddamned phlegmatic," Dorsey had repeatedly admonished him. "Everybody in the Confederacy is jittery. Don't act too innocent. You'll stand out like a virgin in a whorehouse."

At the conclusion of the interrogation the Seepee handed him back his papers and moved toward the door. He reached for the knob, then glanced over his shoulder and said conversationally, "Of course we know why you're here." He smiled enigmatically, and closed the door softly behind him.

Chapter Eleven

On Monday Peter Tremont arrived at the photographic store an hour before opening time. He let himself in and locked the door behind him. He inspected the two rooms downstairs, then mounted the open stairway leading from the stockroom in the rear to the apartment above. Throughout the Confederacy, and particularly in Con City, the local police were notoriously lackadaisical about guarding the premises of private entrepreneurs. Consequently, the owner usually occupied quarters in the same building. Paying commercial rates for living quarters was one of the minor disadvantages of operating in the Private Sector in the Confederate States of America.

Although free enterprise had been proclaimed by the Party of National Resurgence to be a keystone of the "economics of evolution," it was a testament to the perversity of the human creature that it even continued to exist. Theoretically it afforded the ideal arena in which to test Howie Ray Spearman's concept of the survival of the fittest. The original action plan drawn up by the Party brain trust called for a return to unfettered competition "with all deliberate speed." Not only did it seem the proper vehicle to carry out the process of natural selection; happily it also fitted in perfectly with the rather elemental economic ideology of the Party patron, D. J. Cawthorn.

It was implemented immediately upon the Party's accession
to power. It worked out as the theoreticians had planned—
up to a certain point. Pragmatically, it was a smashing success. It spewed to the top an ambitious breed of financial buc-
caneers who quickly seized control of the country's economy
and modernized it with ruthless efficiency. As projected by
the manpower engineers, the weak, the hapless and the incompetent bounced around like pinballs and eventually settled
into their predestined holes.

But instead of the satisfied, stratified social structure
Howie Ray Spearman had envisaged, the Confederacy was
shaken by a ground swell of discontent, threatening to erupt
in open mutiny. Instead of order, chaos.

Applying his Darwinian insight to the problem, Spearman
soon detected the fatal flaw in the apparatus. The superior
species were not content with achieving the natural order of
things. They were working for their own aggrandizement. Reluctantly he set about purging those who were in actuality
best fitted to survive—those who should have been the fortuitous variants from which a higher civilization would evolve.

The upshot was that the Party was forced to take over
and operate the economic machinery of the nation. Fortunately, it had been brought to a high state of efficiency by the
departed "supeers." Furthermore, the "supeers" had discovered certain shortcomings in the free enterprise system. It was
wasteful, disorganized and unpredictable; in short, unwork-
able.

They were in the process of phasing it out and substituting
a much more sensible system of "managed monopoly" when
the Party of National Resurgence "selected them out." The
politico-administrators who succeeded them had the perspi-
cacity to see that a competitive economy was not compatible
with an orderly society. Consequently, the state undertook
to produce and market, at reasonable prices, all the goods

and services essential to the welfare and happiness of a contented people. The products were of uniformly high quality, they were available to rich and poor alike, and they were identical in every respect.

Surprisingly, there was still a brisk demand for imported items, which were for the most part inferior in quality and excessive in price. Their only selling point, specious as it was, was that they differed from the standard merchandise which everyone possessed. Such was the state of the free enterprise system in the Confederate States of America when Peter Tremont became an entrepreneur there.

It had taken a good deal of manipulating to find an inconspicuous spot for Cordell Vance's rather specialized talents. While he was an expert in death and destruction, and while there was a great demand for those skills in the Confederacy, his references would not have borne too close scrutiny. Also, his health required that he find employment which would allow him some freedom of movement without too close supervision.

In the course of his dissection of the psyche of Cordell Vance, Robert Dorsey had come upon a faintly pulsing ganglion in the glob of dead emotional tissue. He isolated it, nurtured it and tagged it as an interesting and atypical facet of Cordell Vance's moribund personality. It was more than that. It was, in fact, a rather weak antibody to the cancer that was devouring his soul.

After the proceedings of the board of inquiry in Rangoon had been duly reported in the nation's press and the findings filed away in Major Cordell Vance's qualifications jacket, his continued presence in the U.S. Army proved awkward and embarrassing, both to him and to that proud institution. He resolved the dilemma by submitting his resignation as an officer and a gentleman. The army gratefully allotted him 75 percent disability compensation for the assorted pieces of iron still reposing in his torso, and happily transferred his file to the Veterans Administration.

Upon his return to his adopted country, he immediately embarked upon the descent into semialcoholism and joyless dissipation which his circumstances seemed to indicate. His guerrilla battle against despair lasted for four months, during which period the situation steadily deteriorated.

One gray November morning, when the glorious paean of Christmas carols was issuing in full cry from every radio, department store and jukebox, he awoke in a characterless motel room in Wilmington, Delaware, with a mild hangover and a strong impulse toward self-obliteration. His eyes focused on a limp, broken cigarette butt, brown-staining the dregs of a whisky glass on the dresser. He contemplated the sight for several minutes. He crawled stealthily out of bed, teetered into the bathroom and vomited in the toilet.

He brushed his teeth. In the mirror he caught a glimpse of a flabby, fish-white body, speckled with scars, a sagging abdomen overhanging a spiritless penis. He raised his head and looked into red-veined eyes which returned his gaze with loathing.

He snatched up his shaving kit and stuffed his toothbrush and tube into it. He dressed and packed swiftly and silently, standing motionless for a moment as the plump-cheeked blond rolled over in the bed, exposing one pendulous breast. Weighing the aesthetics of the situation, he hesitated, then tucked two twenty-dollar bills in the cluttered purse lying open on the dresser.

He slipped out the door and drove across the country for two days and two nights, stopping only for food and fuel and an occasional nap. Across Pennsylvania, Ohio, Indiana, Illinois, Iowa and Nebraska. Across the brown brush-covered plains of eastern Colorado. He holed up in Denver for two days and sobered up to the stark realization that he could not flee fast enough to escape the incubus that rode with him.

He drove aimlessly into the mountains, insensitive to the magnificent panorama of peaks and valleys unfolding before him. He reached the crest of the foothills girdling the front range of the Rockies and gazed across a broad, snow-blanketed meadow, guarded by a semicircle of somber stone sentinels. Under their indifferent scrutiny, the turmoil within him ebbed to a dull, hopeless ache. Though it was only midafternoon, on an unreasoned impulse he registered at a motel on the outskirts of the Settlement and, without unpacking, wandered up a pine-covered slope to the base of a steep cliff.

He sought shelter from the cutting wind in a cluster of rocks, but there was no shelter from his thoughts. Unaccountably, he found himself crawling up the jagged face of the cliff, like a fugitive in a television western. He had no experience in rock climbing. Once he paused and looked down. His muscles froze and his joints locked at the sight of the terrifying void below. He could move neither forward nor backward. Paralyzed, unable to raise his hand to the ledge jutting out overhead, he felt a sudden desire just to let go. Where a moment before he had cringed at the sight of the rocks below, his imagining now did not go beyond the exultant feeling of falling through the air into oblivion.

His conditioned survival instinct took over. He pulled himself up to the ledge and continued to the top. As he stood at the summit peering down into the depths, he felt a small glow of accomplishment. He took an easy trail down the back of the cliff. It was dark when he reached the motel. He lay down on the bed and fell asleep without recourse to alcohol or sedative.

The next day he stopped at the real estate office in the Settlement and rented the cabin on the side of the mountain until May 1. Daily he tramped through the pine forests and waded through the snow-filled ravines. He chopped logs for the fireplace and laboriously dug a cellar in the stony soil. After the snow began to melt, he scaled each of the fourteen-thousand-foot peaks in the area. He went to bed every night exhausted. Gradually he rebuilt his body, but he could only stupefy his mind.

On his weekly excursions into the Settlement he made an effort to satisfy the small-town curiosity of the merchants and clerks, but his reticence about his past was noticeable. In his limited circle of acquaintances he was regarded as "a nice fellow but kinda strange."

Slowly, though, the companionship of the silent, towering peaks and the incessantly babbling streams penetrated the sealed-off corridors of his mind. He began to look at the beauty about him and to absorb the peacefulness of nature.

On a certain trip into the Settlement, he deviated from his usual tour of the supermarket, the drugstore, the hardware store and the gas station to include the Rogenstein Studio and Camera Shop at the far end of the main thoroughfare. A bell tinkled overhead as he opened and closed the door. The sound did not disturb the silver-haired, gnomish little man perched on a stool at the rear of the room, squinting into a viewfinder at a ground-glass image. "Be with you in a minute," he called out in a squeaky voice, not raising his head.

Cordell Vance strolled over to a display counter and peered through the glass at a dozen cameras scattered around the shelves. "Pick out anythin' you like," said the little man.

Vance said nothing. He gazed at the unframed blowups tacked around the walls, all of them scenic shots of the nearby mountains. His silence eventually infiltrated the concentration of the intent viewer. He slipped off his stool and padded around the counter.

"Don't believe I know you," he said, holding out a delicate hand and staring into Vance's face through bright china-blue eyes. "My name's Rogenstein—Sid Rogenstein."

"Cordell Vance."

"Glad to meetcha, Mr. Vance. Can I help you?"

"Well, I thought I might like to learn something about photography, so I suppose I would need a camera."

"Makes it easier," the little man agreed. "You come to the right place. Reckon I know about all there is to know about it."

He waved his hand at the pictures on the walls. "Shot those right around here. Do a lotta postcard work for Photo-Craft and the big companies. What kinda pictures you wanta take?"

"That sort of thing."

"Well, it took me twenty-five years to learn to do 'that sort of thing,' but I can start you out. You live around here?"

Vance nodded. Sid Rogenstein cocked his head and waited, birdlike, for him to elaborate. "Up on Brandy Mountain."

"Funny I never run into you before. You from Denver?"

"No. Back east."

"That's good. People from Denver been lookin' at these mountains so long they don't even see 'em. I'm from New Hampshire myself. We got mountains there, but not like these."

Apparently satisfied that Vance was in earnest, he slid open the glass front of the counter and pulled out the cameras one by one. "Pontiflex. Italian. Good for wide-angle stuff. Fine depth of field . . . Guerdon. Swiss. Good workmanship. Good for time exposures. Lenses of great resolution . . . Yokuda. Japanese. Versatile. Foolproof. All right for tourists . . ."

He ran through the entire display, more for his own edifica-
tion, obviously, than Vance's. All but two of the cameras were
of foreign manufacture.

"Americans are great on know-how, not so good on do-
how." He stated it as a fact, not an opinion. "They'd rather
give you a replacement than go to the bother of making it
right in the first place. I do all my own repair work. In fact
I made my own camera—outa the best parts of all the others.

"Here," he said, thrusting the Yokuda at Vance. "This's
what you need to start out with. Later on we'll see what you
can handle."

He bustled around filling a canvas bag with film, accessories and a fat paperback book entitled *Photography—Fine
Art.*

"If you stick with it," he said, "I'll teach you how to develop your own film. Only way to tell what you're doin'
wrong. That'll be $97.75 with tax."

Vance wrote out a check on a New York bank. Rogenstein
dropped it in the register without looking at it.

"When you've messed up those rolls," he said, "bring 'em
in and we'll look 'em over."

Vance went home and read the book. He shot the three rolls
of film, took them back to the little studio and got three more
rolls. He read the book again and it began to have some
meaning. When he returned to the shop the next time, Rogenstein went over his first batch of pictures print by print,
pointing out flaws in technique, composition and choice of
subjects. The next week he repeated the critique. The third
week he delivered his first encomium. "Not bad," he said of a
gnarled, wind-tilted tree, standing alone on a barren, rock-
strewn slope.

The fifth week he reached into the counter and pulled out
an English-model CY-12 Landrith. "Here, try this," he said.

"You've passed the tourist stage. You need a precision instrument."

At the end of his critique, he invited Vance into the back room and poured him a water glass half full of Scotch. Vance took his first drink since his arrival in the Settlement. On his way home he stopped at the liquor store and bought a quart. It lasted for three weeks.

Sometimes, when Vance entered the shop, the sprightly little man would not answer the bell at all. Not knowing who the customer might be, he would call in his piping voice from the back room, "Take what you need. Ring it up on the cash register."

Vance would wander back and find him at his workbench, his fingers sorting, fitting, assembling—seemingly without conscious guidance since they went right on while Rogenstein talked on totally unrelated subjects. One afternoon as Vance stood behind him watching, Rogenstein jumped up and motioned him to sit.

"The carpenter should know how to sharpen his saw," he said.

He took a camera down from the shelf and disassembled it completely, explaining to Vance where each part belonged and what its function was. Thereafter Vance would join him at the bench for several hours whenever he dropped in. He had always taken a craftsman's interest in the tools of his former trade and had prided himself on his ability to field-strip every weapon in the guerrilla's arsenal. Eventually, though, his phobia against killing had spread to the impersonal instruments of death themselves.

In the grubby back room of the Rogenstein Studio and Camera Shop, he rediscovered the pleasure of fitting things together for a purpose, and his hands worked their subtle therapy on his disturbed spirit. Under the old man's critical supervision, he learned to develop his own films and to understand the artful interplay of light and shadow. One day, when they were working side by side at the bench like two medieval guildsmen, the bell tinkled over the door and an unfamiliar voice called, "Anybody here?"

"Goddamnit," Rogenstein snapped, not looking up, "go see what they want."

Like an obedient apprentice, Vance laid aside his tools and waited on the customer.

A few days later Vance strolled into the store shortly after one o'clock. Rogenstein gave him his usual perfunctory greeting, then stepped into the back room. He came out pulling on an old mackinaw and carrying his camera of many parts. "Look after the place, will you," he said. "Here's an extra key. Lock up whenever you wanta leave."

Vance began stopping by more frequently, and gradually, without a word spoken between them, he became an independent partner in the business. He came in only when he felt like coming in and did only what he felt like doing, which fitted in very well with the proprietor's own operating methods. Sometimes neither of them would come in, and the shop remained closed. Vance did not enjoy waiting on customers, but he realized it kept open a tenuous channel of communication between him and the human species.

As long as he was occupied, either in the store or hiking through the mountains, he could keep back the black, billowing specter. But he could never completely exorcise its presence. And at night—and sometimes in the day—it rolled in like an ocean fog and possessed him.

One evening at the end of April, after Sid had locked the door and they were sitting in the workshop sipping warm Scotch from kitchen glasses, the white-haired little man reached into his shirt pocket and handed Vance a check for seven hundred dollars. Surprised, Vance glanced at it and handed it back.

Rogenstein pushed it away. "Take it. Take it. We're in business together."

Rogenstein's pale-blue eyes scowled at him pugnaciously from the chirpy, button face. "When the tourists come, they take up all my time," he said vexedly. "I give you half the profits. You do half the work. When I go—" he tossed his frizzy white mane—"you can have this if you want it. I got nobody else to leave it to."

Rootless all his life, Vance had never really considered the prospect of taking root. He considered it. It did not appeal to him. He smiled at the photographer and shook his head.

"No. I can't. I'll be moving on after May 1."

"Why? Where have you got to go?" The old man had never questioned him about his past or his future, but he was wise enough to know that a person who never mentions his past or future says a good deal about both. "You're running from yourself?"

"Maybe."

"Sometimes you have to. You never escape, of course, but as long as you keep running you at least think you might. It's better to keep running than to just hole up and die. But sometimes you don't die. Why don't you just rest a while anyway?"

Vance thought about all the dismal motel rooms in all the dingy cities he had drifted through, all the nameless women he had screwed and all the joyless whisky he had drunk.

With sudden stark clarity, he recalled the depth of his despair, and he realized he had achieved, if not serenity, at least a certain emotional insensibility. It was not much, but to a man who has been in hell, purgatory is not unattractive. He had no intention of staying at the Settlement, but he had no idea where he would go. Having been a wanderer all his life, the thought of permanence disturbed him as the thought of change upsets the normal sedentary citizen.

His friend's restless eyes were fixed on his face. "I'm sorry, Sid," he said lamely. "I appreciate your offer—very much. But I don't want to get tied down. I've got to be able to move on when I feel like it."

The old man planted his feet on the floor and shook his head impatiently, as he did whenever Vance's pictures displeased him. "You think you have to be free to run. All right. But you can never be free unless you are also free to stop running."

That night Vance pondered Rogenstein's words. Maybe he's right, he reflected. Or maybe I'm afraid to run any farther. In the end he compromised. He exercised his option to buy the cabin on the side of the mountain, but he declined to enter into any formal arrangement with the photographer.

"I'll come in and help out when I feel like it," he said, "but I don't want to be under any obligation and I won't take any money."

Rogenstein accepted his decision without parley. They went on as they had before, except that the photographer began sending some of Vance's pictures to the syndicate that handled his work. In due course, Vance started receiving magazine and commercial photo assignments himself.

When summer arrived, he discovered the unique advantage of being a resident bachelor in a resort town. By inclination, as well as by example, he had gone along with the historic army approach toward women: "If they will, screw 'em; if they won't, screw 'em."

Without applying himself too diligently, he learned several valuable corollaries to that basic axiom: one, that a woman's scruples loosen in direct ratio to the tightness of her slacks;

two, that indifference frequently makes the difference. The physical therapy worked its magic, and by the end of the tourist season his mental attitude had improved from a state of chronic depression to one of intermittent despondency.

After the troublesome tourists had departed, Rogenstein taught him to play chess. Though they usually played not more than two nights a week, it made the other nights less foreboding because Vance knew he could find refuge from his dark thoughts if he wished.

He grew to know and to understand Sid Rogenstein. One night a casual remark by the photographer, in combination with a raging blizzard and an extra tot of Scotch, loosened the seals on Cordell Vance's proscribed past.

Having immobilized Vance's remaining rook, the old man was in the process of stripping the pawn shield from his king by ruthless attrition. "They say," he observed innocently, bending his white head over the board, "that chess is a blood-less replica of war."

"That's a meaningless comparison. Blood is the essence of war. It's like saying sleep is a replica of death." He waved a hand at the board as Rogenstein set up a pawn exchange. "Would you send a man out in the open like that if you knew he was going to get killed?"

"I might. It would depend on the circumstances."

Vance took the pawn, and Rogenstein retaliated with his bishop, putting Vance in check. "You see," he said, "my man did not die in vain."

Vance moved his king to momentary safety. "That's what you say. How do you think he felt about it? Do you really believe he would consider the king's life more important than his own?"

"Not the king," said Rogenstein, moving a knight into position for the kill. "But perhaps a cause."

"Bullshit," Vance exclaimed with the annoyance born of imminent defeat. "Once you're dead you're dead. Who cares about causes then?" He toppled his king and reached for the Scotch bottle.

Rogenstein held out his glass. "For six thousand years my people have been slaughtered like sheep. They would have been better off to die in battle."

"Your people maybe," Vance conceded, "but not the ones that died. It wouldn't make a damned bit of difference to them."

"For a man who places so little value on living, it seems to me you overemphasize the importance of dying."

In support of his argument, Vance began recounting some of the grisly, heroic, meaningless epics of human carnage in which he had been a participant. As he talked, his bottled-up bitterness against the stupidity, futility and contemptible dishonesty of wars and the makers of wars poured out of him. Without intending to, he wound up with a recital of his own dreary semidisgrace.

"I suppose," he said, "if I had had a choice I would have died in the ambush. And what would my heroic sacrifice have accomplished? It would have saved face for the people who put the shaft in me. This is worth dying for?"

Rogenstein listened silently to Vance's tale. His eyes clouded in pained revulsion at the graphic descriptions of torture and savagery on both sides. When Vance had finished, he clasped his small hands in his lap and leaned back in his chair, his feet barely touching the floor.

"If you had died in the ambush, you would have thought you were dying for a cause."

"No. It was too late then. I was already fed up. I was just going through the motions."

"Well, then, I guess it would have accomplished nothing."

The stubborn glint came back into his eyes as he fought to hang onto his cherished conviction. "But I still say there are things worth dying for."

It was doubtful if he had proved his thesis when Vance found him two months later lying under his workbench with his head smashed in, his distant blue eyes staring vacantly at nothing. Recognizing death, Vance stood rigid for a minute looking down, not touching him. Without raising his head, he uttered one stricken incoherent howl of rage and frustration. He waited until the frenzy had ebbed. Then he called the local deputy.

The evidence pointed to robbery and senseless, unpremeditated murder. The small safe in the rear had been hacked open and its contents strewn around the workroom. Several of the more expensive cameras were missing. There were no real signs of a struggle, but Sid Rogenstein would not have been able to put up much resistance against a sturdy opponent. Vance was grilled rather thoroughly twice. In the course of the investigation some interesting facets of his past were brought out.

His connection with the case attracted the attention of the wire services and the national press and inspired a goodly number of the villagers to confess that they "always thought there was something strange about that fellow."

No firm suspicion was ever directed at Vance, though there was some speculation among amateur sleuths as to why a common burglar would have felt impelled to bludgeon the old man to death—unless, perhaps, it was someone he recognized. The speculation was heightened somewhat when a will naming Vance as his sole beneficiary was found in his safety deposit box. To persistent and sometimes pointed inquiries from investigators and newsmen, Vance replied uncommunicatively that he didn't know a damned thing about it. He did not bother to mention the conversation he had had with Sid Rogenstein the previous spring.

He went back to the store twice—once to go through the old photographer's personal effects, again to conduct a perfunctory inventory and pay the bills. As soon as the estate was settled, he instructed the real estate agent to sell the store and all its stock, except for the "Rogenstein Special" and a Swedish Loffgren movie camera, which Sid had once described as "the finest camera on the market."

He deposited the money from the sale in his investment account in Denver, courteously but firmly declining suggestions from the Settlement Improvement Association that he make a substantial contribution to the fund for construction of a Community Building. His inclination was to remove himself immediately and completely from the town and its, by now, politely aloof populace. But he realized that his summary departure would be interpreted as "running away" —and not just from himself. Furthermore, he had gone that route once before, and, for the time being at least, he preferred the knowing looks of the townspeople to the questioning glances of strangers.

He went back to his cabin on the side of the mountain and picked up his career as a recluse. It was there that Robert Dorsey sought him out a year later.

Chapter Twelve

By the end of the week Peter Tremont had settled comfortably into his role as a small businessman and second-class citizen of the Confederate States of America. As he had surmised from his initial encounter with the previous owner—who, incidentally, did not come back to "see how he was doing"—the Granger Photographic Supply Shop was not exactly a gold mine. During the first week the busiest day produced a meager harvest of twelve customers. They were, however, uniformly well heeled—as they would have had to be considering the disparity in prices between his merchandise and that in the State Service Stores. The entire inventory consisted of imported cameras and accessories, priced at slightly higher prices than those prevailing in the Settlement, Colorado, U.S.A. And there was no inflation in the Confederacy. Confederate-manufactured cameras of comparable quality sold in the State Stores for little more than half what Peter Tremont charged.

Almost at the outset, he discovered the paradox that his customers were willing to pay extra for the privilege of being overcharged. He tested it in his third week by raising the price of a Yugoslavian model which had previously sold for the same as a Dutch Grazkoop 12-Y-M. Although he assured his customers that they were virtually identical in performance, the Yugoslavian camera quickly outstripped the other in sales. He suspected the purchasers might leave the price tag on permanently.

The Private Sector Inspector, who stopped in every two weeks to go over his books, raised no objection to his pricing policies. There was a specific minimum price for every item on his shelves, but no maximum. The partial price-control system, Peter soon realized, was entirely sensible from the State's standpoint. It eliminated any mass competition between imported and domestic goods. Theoretically, the higher the price, the fewer the purchases. But even though the theory might not prove out, the State did not concern itself with exorbitant profits, inasmuch as it siphoned off 20 percent of the gross on every transaction. Thus, after the first month, Peter found himself beginning to show a tidy profit; and even more so after the word got around that his prices were the highest in town.

The customers, mostly wives of upper-echelon officials, were somewhat patronizing, but not offensively so. Although regarded by the government as an unnecessary evil, "enterprisers" were treated cordially by the general public and even with a certain respect. Virtually everyone was engaged in some illicit activity, and the enterprisers were looked upon as pros who were bold enough to openly buck the system. To his surprise, Peter Tremont found himself rather enjoying his status.

In accordance with the operational plan laid out by Robert Dorsey and reinforced by his neurogenic conditioning sessions, Peter Tremont spent an entire month immersing himself in the role he was playing. He deliberately blanked out the purpose of his mission and turned back any vagrant ideas on how to accomplish it. Basic to the success of his undertaking, Dorsey had dinned into him, was an open mind, capable of recognizing and seizing upon whatever opportunity presented itself. Any preconceived schemes, he had stressed, were virtually certain to lead to disaster.

Once he had accustomed himself to thinking as a shopkeeper, Tremont spent most of his spare time familiarizing himself with commonplace aspects of life in the Confederacy. Like any newcomer, he spent hours wandering around the city.

Confederacity was hailed by the Party of National Resurgence as "the laboratory of the Evolutionary Era." Except for historic structures such as the Capitol and Stone Mansion, it had been almost entirely rebuilt in the past twenty-five years. It was a completely planned metropolis. Its streets were broad and functional; its commercial area was plotted and zoned for maximum efficiency; its parks were numerous, spacious and meticulously landscaped; its residential sections were clean, convenient and of uniform construction. When viewed from the air, the perfect harmony of its planning was especially striking. It was a masterpiece of design, utility and sterility.

There were no slums, no blighted business sections, no garish honky-tonk districts, no blocks of decaying, converted apartment houses. Set in the middle of every residential area, and separated from the surrounding community by an attractive block-wide green belt, was a well-groomed, self-contained Black Cloister, which always seemed to be teeming with hubbub and ringing with shouts and laughter.

The middle-class white community was particularly proud of the way the racial problem had been solved almost overnight when the PNR came to power. When the bulldozers began leveling vast aging areas of the city, an acute housing shortage developed. To the disgruntlement of the white populace, the reconstruction started with the Cloisters. Negroes who had never ridden an elevator were soon ensconced in comfortable high-rise apartments while the dispossessed whites were living in makeshift barracks-type squalor.

The topsy-turvy state of affairs was soon redressed, of course, but the astonished Blacks never lost the conviction that Mistuh Howie was looking after them. To be sure, there was a considerable outcry and some violence when it was decreed that schooling for Blacks would be restricted to nine grades, except for the most promising Negro members of the Resurgent Youth Corps, who would be sent to the newly established Black Leadership Academy. The demonstrations and minor uprisings served to identify the malcontents and troublemakers. They were quietly removed from the happy Black Cloisters and sent to Enlightenment Camps in the Southwest.

Although they were required to live in one of the Compounds, the Blacks were free to come and go as they pleased. The State Service Stores in the shopping enclaves carried the same goods and charged the same prices as those in white sections; the green belts surrounding the Compounds were open to Black and white alike, though few whites availed themselves of the privilege; restaurants, recreation and amusement facilities, churches and hotels within the Black Compounds were in every way comparable to those in all but the Capitol Bluff section of the city, which was reserved for the highest-ranking members of the government and the Party. In short, though there were no formal restrictions on their activities, there really was no reason for Blacks to want to mingle with whites outside of their normal occupations.

Likewise, the whites were free to wander through the Cloisters, or even to visit Blacks in their living quarters. Naturally, too frequent visitations were liable to provoke comment and, eventually, inquiries from the Citizens Protection Force.

On his second Sunday, Peter took a sightseeing tour of the city, which included a complete tour of a Black Cloister. As far as he could tell, the Blacks appeared to be as cheerful and contented as their white neighbors claimed they were. The passengers lunched in a Black restaurant, specializing in fried chicken, collard greens and other native fare. The food was delicious, and the other patrons treated them courteously but not obsequiously.

The tour also included a stop at an observation point on the bluff overlooking the river. Off to the west the steep cliff mellowed into a rounded ridge that sloped down to the mud flats at the water's edge. The entire slope, spreading over an area of perhaps a square mile, was crammed with ramshackle buildings, tilted at crazy angles and bisected by narrow, un-surfaced streets, seemingly laid out without pattern. The buildings were mostly four or five stories. They resembled the worst tenement districts of Chicago or Cleveland or Man-hattan. Tremont recognized them from his homework.

A fat, moon-faced woman in a voluminous flower-print dress, whose accent identified her as being from the back country of Alabama, gazed at the sorry landscape and ex-claimed to the guide, "My sakes. What in the wor-ald is tha-at?"

The guide turned to look, then quickly turned back. "Prive Town," he said tersely.

"Oh." The woman ostentatiously swung her back upon it and gushed rapturously over the stately Capitol, majestically crowning the bluff downriver. Peter Tremont took several pictures of the great river and the wooded shore opposite, then climbed back into the bus.

Monday night he walked over to the armory on West Concourse Avenue, four blocks down from the Capitol, to report for duty with the Mobile Militia, composed of men who had served their time with the regular army but who were still on a semiactive status. His papers had arrived from Charlotte. He was interrogated briefly by an intelligence officer, fingerprinted and assigned command of a squad in the Domestic Tranquillity Section. The Domestic Tranquillity Section was charged primarily with crowd control on special occasions and with putting down civil disturbances on very rare occasions.

Major Wellbourne, commandant of the section, greeted Tremont with stiff cordiality. He waved him to a chair and shuffled through his service record.

"I see, Lieutenant, that you served in the tank corps in the army."

"Yes, sir."

"Well," he said with heavy humor, "I don't anticipate that we will have much use for your skills in the Domestic Tranquillity Section, but it's nice to know that they are available if we need them."

Tremont smiled wanly.

"Our job is largely routine—to handle parades, large gatherin's, that sort of thing. But that doesn't mean we are not goin' to be ready to handle anythin' that comes up. You follow me, Lieutenant?"

"Yes, sir."

"You checked out on all weapons systems and procedures?"

"Yes, sir. I may need a little refreshing on some of them, but I think I can pick it up without too much trouble."

"All right. I'll give you clearance to the magazine. You browse around in there. Let me know if there's anythin' you don't understand."

The major dropped Peter's dossier and started to rise when a notation on his civilian-status record caught his eye. "Uh . . . you're in the photographic supply business, I see."

"Yes, sir. Just since I moved down from Charlotte."

"I'm kind of a camera bug myself. They tell me this little Clayburn 2x-C is a honey. You think you could get ahold of one for me?"

"Well, sir, I'm not permitted to handle domestic products, but I could get you a Swiss camera that is just as good—if not better."

"You think you could do that, couldja?" He cleared his throat. " 'F course you understand I want to pay for it, Lieutenant. Those import prices may be a little steep for me, though."

"We'll work it out, Major."

Tremont saluted and wheeled to leave.

"Oh, by the way, Lieutenant, I suppose you take pictures yourself."

"Yes, sir."

"Do any movie stuff?"

"Why, yes, some."

"You've got movie cameras, of course."

"Yes, sir."

"Tell you what I'd like you to do. Bring along the camera on our field exercises—or actual operations too. Take pictures of the way the men handle the job. Keep 'em on their toes. Might be useful, too, in the follow-up critique. You think you could do that?"

"Yes, sir. I'm sure I could."

"All right, Lieutenant. Glad to have you with us. . . . Don't forget about that . . . uh . . . other matter I mentioned to you."

"No, sir, I won't."

Tremont took his clearance to a supply sergeant in the magazine which occupied the entire cavernous subbasement of the building. The sergeant accompanied him as he wandered through the arsenal. It contained every type of small arms and light artillery piece in the Confederate weaponry system. They were neatly racked in hundreds of individual reinforced-steel cubicles. Each cubicle was isolated from the others, not in rows, but apparently with no more pattern than trees in a forest. The vast room looked like an enormous maze.

"Man could get lost in here," Tremont observed.

"That's the idea, sir," the sergeant replied. "We don't want people wandering around loose in here. All the weapons personnel spend a week just learning to find their way around. Course there is a key to it, but we're not allowed to tell anybody. Care to try to find your way out, Lieutenant?"

Peter had followed the sergeant, not paying attention to where he was leading him. He studied the thicket of cabinets clustered around him. There were no windows. The recessed lights were scattered about the ceiling with no more uniformity than the cubicles themselves. It was impossible to proceed in a straight line in any direction. After walking for two minutes, Peter had no idea whether he was heading the way he had started or had doubled back or was going around in circles. In the jungles of Southeast Asia he had developed an unerring built-in direction finder, but here it was no more serviceable than a compass in a magnetic box.

The sergeant trailed close after him, a pleased half-smile on his red face. Peter tried sighting along a line at the most distant cubicle in view, then repeating the process when he reached it. After five minutes he gave up, baffled and defeated. The sergeant took over and in forty-five seconds brought them to the door through which they had entered.

He pushed it open, stood back respectfully and recited his practiced quip as Peter moved past him. "Bring a bag of popcorn next time, sir, and leave a trail—like Hansel and Gretel."

As the weeks passed, Peter Tremont found himself becoming accustomed to his new personality as he had to his new face. Whether because of the conditioning sessions or because he was making a conscious effort to be outgoing, he accumulated more acquaintances in a month than he had in the two years' estrangement from mankind. The congeniality which he at first simulated gradually became almost genuine. As he observed his transformation with a kind of wry astonishment, he wondered sometimes if Dorsey might not have miscalculated. Certainly he had not intended for Peter Tremont to begin enjoying life. Abstractly, Peter realized it would only make his task more difficult. But, in compliance with instructions, he shunted aside all thoughts about his mission whenever they intruded. The mission itself was beginning to seem unreal.

At the end of his first week he had filled out an order blank and dispatched it to the Intercontinental Import Company, Biscayne Building, Miami, Florida. He had received a prompt acknowledgment and assurance that the merchandise would be shipped immediately. The correspondence continued regularly and routinely. Peter Tremont was satisfied with the service he got from his supplier, and the supplier never failed to express its appreciation for his business.

On June 5 the *National Voice* announced in a boldface box on page one that President Spearman would address the people of Confederacity and the nation from the balcony atop the south colonnade of Stone Mansion at 9 P.M. the following night. Peter Tremont's alert box, which he was required to carry on his person at all times, buzzed as he was preparing to lock up for the day. He called the duty officer of the Domestic Tranquillity Section and was ordered to report to the armory for an operational briefing at 4 P.M. the next day.

When the twelve officers of the section were assembled in the briefing room, Major Wellbourne walked to the door, closed and bolted it. He strode to the rostrum and faced them solemnly.

"Gentlemen," he said, as though pronouncing a benediction

upon them, "once again we are called upon to perform the task for which we have been trained."

Peter Tremont was amazed at the portentous tone and the pouter-pigeon bearing of the rabbity major. He glanced around at the other officers. They were sitting at rigid attention.

"I remind you once more," Major Wellbourne continued, "that we are responsible for the safety of our beloved President. It is a sacred trust which we shall discharge with our lives—if need be."

Out of character though it seemed, the major's almost worshipful attitude was in keeping with the puzzling reaction Peter had detected in nearly everyone he had met. Southerners, as he remembered them from his childhood, were warm, generous, friendly people with a trace of irreverence in their nature. He found them to be so when he returned—except where Howie Ray Spearman was concerned.

His new acquaintances, mostly middle-echelon civil servants, spoke derisively of the regimentation and eternal surveillance to which they were subjected, of the PNR hierarchy and even the divinely ordained process of social evolution. They complained quite openly about the goddamned Seepees, the overbearing military, the officious bureaucrats. But not about Howie Ray Spearman. They seemed to regard him as the ancient Greeks regarded their capricious gods: with a kind of affectionate tolerance for their foibles, but never forgetting that they *were*, after all, gods. Peter Tremont never heard anyone blame Howie Ray Spearman for the brutal injustices of the police state. Like Moses, he was leading his people to the Promised Land; but unlike Moses, he was not held responsible for the hardships and suffering they endured along the way.

As an involved and yet detached observer, Peter Tremont

was annoyed but not surprised by the seeming contradiction in the national character. He had seen, through the eyes of Royston Vance, the alternating currents of arrogance and servility that pulsed beneath the smiling amiability of the South. He had been brought up on the legend of a benevolent aristocracy. He knew about the demagogues and charlatans who had, off and on for 150 years, played upon the character defects of their subjects, disguising them in knightly armor and rustling crinoline.

When the briefing was finished, Major Wellbourne signaled Peter to remain. "Y'all understand your duties, Lieutenant?"

Tremont nodded.

"I've stationed you up front where I can help out if you need it. You keep on your toes now, y'hear?"

"Yes, sir."

"Y'all got your camera, I see. Will it work all right at night?"

"I think so. I understand the square will be lighted. And I have an infrared laser-strobe that's actually better than natural light." He showed him the pencil-shaped attachment that fastened onto the extended lens.

"Ain' that likely to burn somebody?" the major asked dubiously.

"No, the rays are refracted."

"Awright. Now you understand this is just a collateral duty. Your first job is to look after the President."

"Yes, sir," Peter Tremont said with feeling.

He stood almost directly beneath and about ten yards in front of the spotlighted balcony, facing the vanguard of the enormous crowd, which was pressed against a waist-high iron railing. The camera hung from a strap around his neck. In his left hand he carried a two-way talker, tuned to the Domestic Tranquillity frequency. Holstered to his hip was a 9-mm Barstead automatic. In the slit pocket along his left thigh nestled a Sub-Due nerve paralyzer. His fifteen-man squad was strung out in front of him, also facing the crowd.

Tremont snapped to attention as the martial strains of the national anthem blared from the amplifiers, mounted on lofty steel poles spaced a hundred feet apart around the square. The poles were topped by shielded crow's-nests, manned by sharpshooters from the Domestic Tranquillity Section.

The throng stood in rigid silence as the anthem swelled to a crescendo of trumpets and drums, then faded into a wispy echo. The hush suddenly exploded in a great rumbling roar that swelled like rolling thunder, then gradually congealed into an accented chant: "Spear-MAN, Spear-MAN, Spear-MAN."

Tremont threw a quick glance over his shoulder. The President stood on the balcony, erect but not stiff, holding one arm straight overhead, fingers extended, in the evolutionary salute, symbolizing the upward course of the Confederacy. Flowing white hair, cushioning strangely pointed ears, curled into an abbreviated wave at the nape of his neck. A long, slender nose and wide, thin lips bisected a strong, square face. A high forehead slanted outward into craggy brows, overhanging dark, deep-set eyes. He was tall and solidly built, with long arms and heavy shoulders. His face showed the furrows of age, but his carriage was still youthful. He was the incarnation of the patrician ideal.

He stood for two minutes, arm upstretched, a faint enigmatic smile on his face. When he swung his arm down, the chorus ceased as though the sound had been switched off. The smile vanished. His hypnotic, brooding eyes roamed over the vast, silent throng for thirty seconds. Then he began to speak in a soft, sorrowful voice.

"My good friends. I thank you for paying me the courtesy

of your presence here tonight. I speak to you on a matter of grave importance, one which seriously concerns you and about which you therefore should be informed.

"Three days ago, I received from the President of the United States a communication which I truly believe can only be characterized as monumental effrontery. You well know the ceaseless efforts I have exerted over the past many years to arrive at a peaceful settlement of the unhappy differences that have divided our two nations. Those differences have been most painful to me—not only because they have created a continuing threat to the security of our own country, but because of the affection and esteem I have always held for our neighbors to the north, bound to us as they are by ancient ties of brotherhood and tradition."

He went on to describe, his voice suffused with humility, how he had made concession after concession, only to meet with rebuffs and intransigence.

"I do not blame the people of the United States," he intoned. "I pity them. For they are held in thrall by the same power-hungry clique that seeks to reduce the Confederate States to vassalage, the same greedy, corrupt gang that would deny to us our rightful share of the heritage which our forefathers hewed out of the wilderness. We do not ask favors. We do not beg crumbs from the table of gluttony. We *do* demand that which is rightfully ours. To do less would be to betray the principles upon which this great nation was founded.

"But I do not come before you tonight to plead the justice of our cause. That is manifest to all men of good conscience. I come to disclose to you the latest and most shameful affront to the sovereignty of a proud and independent people. The President of the United States has delivered an ultimatum to me—and to you—that we must cease to build the defenses of our country or face, and I quote, 'unforeseeable consequences.'

"Well, perhaps my vision is better than that of the President of the United States. I can foresee the consequences of any attempt, overt or covert, to interfere in the internal affairs of this country. Whoever does so will find himself faced with the righteous wrath of an unconquerable people. He will think he has invaded hell itself."

Imperceptibly, the President's voice had risen to an evangelistic pitch. His eyes seemed to glitter, his clenched fists were upflung to the heavens, his formidable jaw outthrust. Peter Tremont had not even noticed the transition from reason to ranting, so natural had it been and so hypnotic the effect of Spearman's words and delivery.

"Why? Why should a nation of 210 million people forbid the prudent efforts of a much smaller and weaker country to safeguard its integrity and its institutions? Why? Because they fear us! Not our military prowess—though, indeed, they will have reason to if they provoke us.

"No, they fear an idea—the concept of order. And well they should. For the society which we have built, and are continuing to build, stands like a beacon of salvation to the lost, straggling multitudes across our border. They wander blindly in a hopeless quest for meaning and fulfillment. While here—here there is a place for every man—and a man for every place."

There was no denying the sincerity of the President's words. He believed them with an all-consuming fervor. And because he believed, the people followed him. For it was easier to follow than to search for a belief of their own.

He had started reading from a script. His manner was one of patient forbearance. His words were temperate, even, conciliatory. He was a man possessed of the truth, not demanding conversion but only seeking understanding, not for himself but for the chosen people of the Confederacy, that they might live in peace and in conformity with the natural law.

The words on the paper were reasonable and compelling. There was nothing in them to which the alarmists in the foreign press or the provocateurs in the world chancellories could take exception. They were words his listeners would remember and to which they could point as proof of his peaceful intentions.

But the words on the paper were merely words. They could only penetrate to the intellect, and the intellect was circumscribed by reason. Midway through his speech, Howie Ray Spearman abandoned the words on the paper, bypassed the intellect and spoke directly to the heart and the emotions and the instincts of the human animals massed before him in the square. He thundered phrases which, to the outsider, were mere gibberish, but to the believer touched secret depths of passion; phrases which, through constant iteration, had acquired an impalpable meaning and the power to bind men together.

Even Peter Tremont, who was not of the faith and who had an abiding distrust of catchwords and slogans, was stirred by the mystical communion between the President and his audience. For though the phrases by themselves made little sense, he recognized that they touched a transcendental chord —the yearning of all men for purpose and direction in their lives and for harmony with the universe in which they lived. Or, in the words of Howie Ray Spearman, for "oneness and order."

Three days after the President's address, Tremont received an invoice from the Intercontinental Import Company, with an accompanying letter:

Due to an increased volume of business, we are obliged to reprogram our computer. It is therefore imperative that all accounts currently outstanding be settled in full not later than 10 Aug. 1981. We would be grateful for your cooperation in this matter. If you are unable to comply with this request, we would appreciate your so advising us, so other arrangements can be made. In the meantime, we shall be happy to continue serving you in every way possible.

Peter Tremont burned the letter and regretfully reopened the sealed recesses of his mind. His proximity to President Spearman at the convocation in the square with a gun on his hip would seem to bear all the earmarks of an unmistakable opportunity. Yet the earmarks were deceptive. Or were they? Was he really looking for an opportunity?

As a man who had faced similar decisions a dozen times before, he strove to divorce his professional judgment from his personal instincts, to view the problem from the perspective of the command post rather than the squad leader whose life was on the line. Did the probable gains outweigh the certain losses?

It was a foregone conclusion that an attempt on the life of Howie Ray Spearman in front of his followers would cost the life of the assailant. Despite Robert Dorsey's protestations to the contrary, Tremont was sure he would regard that as an acceptable if not minimal price to pay. Provided that the identity of the sponsor was not disclosed. And he had taken extreme pains to insure that that would not happen.

Peter suspected, further, that a principal if unspoken purpose of the neurogenic conditioning sessions was to instill in him an imperishable determination to avoid capture at any cost. If so, they had succeeded. He did not know if he was prepared in the ultimate event to lay down his life for an impersonal cause, no matter how fateful to the nation and to mankind. He did know that for strictly personal reasons he would rather die than be paraded before the eyes of the world as the perpetrator of a monstrous crime. Capture was no part of his calculations.

So the decision, from an operational standpoint, narrowed down to the question of whether he could kill Spearman before he himself was killed. If he could, he ruefully acknowledged, the decision was obvious. The only question was: could he? In all objective honesty, the answer was: no.

The shield precluded any rash frontal assault with a hand gun, even at point-blank range. The terrace behind the balcony, he had observed, was thronged with high-ranking officers of the Party and the military, and ringed by a cordon of Seepees. The chances of his getting close enough for a shot from that direction were virtually nonexistent.

Furthermore, there was no assurance—indeed, little likelihood—that Spearman would make another public appearance before August 10. Finally, there could be only one attempt. If it failed, it would be the end not only of him but of his mission. That would serve nobody's purpose. With an uncomfortable sense of relief, but also with a professional conviction that he was right, he scrubbed the balcony as a prospective site for an assassination.

Relegating the distasteful task ahead to his subconscious, he turned his attention to the immediate necessity of remaining alive. The August 10 deadline had at first chilled him. But upon reflection he found some cold solace in it. First of all, he doubted if his resolution would sustain an indefinitely protracted siege. Second, if no opportunity presented itself in the next two months, he was, in a sense, relieved from duty.

Dorsey had, in fact, offered him a chance to resign. Although he had been momentarily tempted, he had not accepted. Instead, he had notified the Intercontinental Import Company that he would strive to meet their terms, but that it would depend to a large extent on how his own business prospered in the meantime. He presumed they would proceed with "other arrangements" regardless of his response.

The deadline did, however, dissipate the unexpected enjoyment he was beginning to derive from playing at being a businessman. At first he was annoyed at the sense of satisfaction he experienced when he balanced the books at the end of each week. He feared he was showing bourgeois tendencies. But since he was hardly in a position to enjoy the fruits of his enterprise, he exonerated himself on that score. The satisfaction, he concluded, was in competing successfully against the government monopoly with all of the odds stacked against him.

And yet it was surprisingly easy. Being completely untutored, not only in accepted business practices, but in the police state environment, he quickly recognized the customer demand that was not being met. The State Service Stores were equipped to supply every conceivable consumer need. But along with their meat and potatoes, the Southerners hungered for an occasional French pastry. Little by little, Peter began branching out into nonutilitarian items like musical door chimes and pastel kitchenware and oriental trinkets. Little by little, his trade increased. Indeed, it soared when he hit upon the idea of ordering a gross of catalogues from the Intercontinental Import Company and passing them out to his regular customers to whet their appetites.

The more outlandish the item, he discovered, the greater the demand for it. Gradually it dawned on him that among the people of the Confederacy a great craving existed to possess something their neighbors did not have. It occurred to him that that perverse human passion might be another fatal flaw in Spearman's vision of universal order.

Tremont continued to mind the store, attend drills twice a week at the armory, broaden his circle of acquaintances and improve his performance in the role of the harried shopkeeper.

But over all his mundane activities hung the specter of August 10. And as it drew nearer he was haunted by a growing sense of guilt and urgency.

Nearly every evening he strolled up and down the Grand Concourse, pausing to gaze at the majestic spectacle of the Capitol and the fortress-like towers of Stone Mansion. Several times he took guided tours of those historic shrines. He indulged his passion for guns. After duty every militia night, he would roam through the magazine with the attendant, picking out a different weapon and experimenting with it on the firing range at the south end of the drill field on the roof. His eagerness earned him the approbation of Major Wellbourne, who had taken a liking to him, and to the Swiss camera which Peter had contrived to obtain for him at considerably less than the prescribed minimum price. Occasionally he joined Peter on the firing range and invited him to his office for a drink afterward.

Major Wellbourne was about Peter Tremont's age. He was the type of zealous but pedestrian officer who supplies the dedication and mental flab that is the fiber of any military organization. He was enamored of his uniform, delighted in giving and carrying out orders and would have preferred to be serving in the regular army. Unfortunately, his native stupidity exceeded even the broad tolerances of that service, and he was shunted into permanent active status with the militia. Peter Tremont did not enjoy his company, but he realized that it might someday prove useful.

At 3 A.M. on the morning of June 22, his alert box on the night stand beside his bed aroused him. He called the duty officer and was transferred immediately to Major Wellbourne. The major was in a state of near-hysterical excitement.

"Get your ass over here, Lieutenant. This is the big one!

We're goin' out and kill ourselves some Prives. Your squad is assemblin' now. I've sent the staff car down for you. You hurry on over here."

Peter Tremont sat alongside the driver in the cab of the personnel carrier as it careened off the Capitol Bluff highway onto a narrow graveled road leading to Prive Town. It wound through a haphazard tangle of shacks and jerry-built apartment houses and skidded to a stop halfway down the slope at a roadblock manned by two militiamen with rifles at the ready. They saluted self-importantly as Peter stepped from the cab.

"Right over there, Lieutenant," one of them said, sweeping an arm toward a ramshackle brick building which was lit up by a circle of high-powered searchlights. "Keep your head down. They's some shootin' goin' on."

Tremont led his squad down the road to the cordon of militiamen sheltering behind an irregular string of shacks on top of which the searchlights were mounted. The target of the lights was an oblong, barracks-type brick building, five stories high and in better condition than any of the other structures Peter had observed on the slope. The militiamen were enthusiastically blazing away at the shattered windows. Peter could detect no return fire, but the besiegers were keeping themselves well covered.

Major Wellbourne had set up his command post on the flat roof of one of the shacks. He held a bullhorn in one hand and a .45 in the other. He alternately bellowed into the bullhorn and waved the .45 in great sweeping circles as though directing a symphony orchestra in a cavalry charge. Peter climbed to the roof on an aluminum ladder leaning against the wall. He looked placidly around at the compounded confusion.

When Major Wellbourne spotted him, he turned the bullhorn on him, though Peter was standing not more than twenty feet away.

"Lieutenant Tremont. Y'all take your men over there opposite the entrance. Captain Terwilliger is gonna storm the buildin'. You give him coverin' fire." He suddenly noticed that Peter was armed only with his pistol, still holstered. "Goddamn, Lieutenant. We're in a shootin' war here. You high-tail it over to the weapons truck and arm your men with machine guns."

"What's going on?" Peter inquired blandly.

"Hell-fire, Lieutenant, I ain' got time to give you no situation report. You jus' do what I told you to do." Relenting, he aimed the bullhorn in the direction of the sergeant standing at his elbow. "Sergeant, you fill the lieutenant in on what's happenin'."

The sergeant, a pot-bellied retired regular, followed Tremont down the ladder, away from the din of the bullhorn. Laconically he outlined the events which had precipitated Major Wellbourne's big moment.

Informed that an arms cache was concealed in the apartment house, a detail of Seepees had raided the building shortly after 1 A.M. Five men had entered. None came out. After a half-hour, two of the four men stationed outside went in to investigate. They, too, failed to return. The other two called for reinforcements. A squad of Seepees arrived with riot guns and tear gas. They marched up to the entrance and were met with a volley of rifle and small-arms fire. They retreated and put in a call for the militia. The full complement of the Domestic Tranquillity Section was dispatched to the scene. They had lobbed tear gas and grenades into the building and were now preparing a frontal assault on both entrances. That's where matters stood at the moment.

Tremont led his fifteen-man squad to the weapons wagon, where they were issued machine guns and ammunition belts. He deployed them in a cluster of shanties, where Captain Terwilliger's men were assembled, tensely awaiting the order to attack.

Their objective was approximately seventy-five yards distant, across the road and a barren patch of ground. There was no cover. From the command post off to the right came the bellow. of the bullhorn. "Captain Terwilliger. You may advance when ready."

Captain Terwilliger blew a whistle. His warriors straggled forward out of the dark into the shadows cast by the searchlights. They moved silently. There was no sound from the building. Even the sporadic fire from the surrounding militiamen sputtered out. The attackers had crossed the road and were advancing in skirmish formation across the bare patch of ground into the glare of the searchlights.

The silence was shattered by the sudden blare of the bullhorn. "Lieutenant Tremont! Goddamnit, give 'em coverin' fire!"

Tremont raised his left arm, then let it fall. A torrent of machine-gun slugs sprayed the face of the building. The attackers instinctively hunched over as the fusillade whizzed over their heads. They broke into a lumbering trot.

"Up. Keep your fire up," Tremont shouted through cupped hands. His own weapon was hooked over his elbow. He had not fired it.

Terwilliger's men had emerged into the bright area and were beginning to converge toward the doorway. A single shot rang out from the ground floor of the building. Captain Terwilliger sprawled on the ground and lay there, his shoulders twitching spasmodically. The ragged line slowed, then halted. For a long moment they stood, frozen, gaping at their fallen leader.

The frenzied voice on the bullhorn set them in motion again. "Move, goddamnit. Charge. Forward." The major's howl was punctuated by the bark of his .45, echoing through the horn.

The squad surged forward. Sheering through the rattle of the machine guns came a sharp concerted volley from behind the low parapet on the roof. Half of the advancing men performed a grotesque pirouette and toppled over. The others turned and raced back toward the shanties. A ragged fusillade, seemingly coming from all parts of the building, pursued them and overtook two more. The terrified remnants scurried like mice into the narrow spaces between the shacks. Tremont's men, no longer playing at being soldiers, poured lead into the dark sockets of the building with belated ferocity. Peter himself traced a line of shattered bricks along the top of the parapet. Ammunition exhausted, the besiegers suddenly broke off, and silence again descended on the improbable battlefield.

Staring in disbelief at the shapeless clumps dotting the open ground, Tremont's men gathered around him in a shocked huddle. Reflexively, he studied their faces, weighing their reactions. First blood was a fairly accurate indicator of the killing potential. Although they had all done their three years' compulsory service, they were scarcely out of their teens. None of them had ever witnessed the finished performance, for which they had so long rehearsed. Two of them were ashen-faced, trembling on the edge of panic. The grim mask of the fledgling warrior had begun to settle over the strained faces of the others.

Automatically, Peter Tremont asserted the first principle of command—to command, to give the followers a route to follow.

"Jennings, Lakin, Piatkowski. Over to the weapons wagon. Three belts for every man. The rest of you spread out. See if you can spot the snipers' posts. Carrington, you're in charge. I'm going to see the major."

He strode off, not waiting for his orders to be carried out.

Surprisingly, the shock of battle seemed to have brought a semblance of order to the command post. Major Wellbourne had set aside the bullhorn. He was issuing orders in crisp, clear tones. His manner was composed. He looked up as Peter approached and waved him over to the small group surrounding him.

"All right, Armistead," he was saying to one of the officers. "I'm not gonna move the perimeter back and take a chance on any them possums gettin' away. You got to lay it right in there first time, y'hear? Y'all pour it on 'em till I tell you to stop.

"Rest of you get back to your positions and plunk 'em off as they come out. I don' figure to take no prisoners. We'll just consider this as live target practice."

The officers dispersed. Peter lingered behind.

"Major, I think I could take my squad around to the left there and slip in through the south end of the building without too much problem. Once we get 'em pinned down inside—"

"Nope, Lieutenant. We're gonna do this nice and neat, like it says in the manual. In about five minutes, Cap'n Armistead is gonna open up with the mortars. We gonna see them Prives come runnin' outa there like rats, and we gonna pick 'em off one by one."

Tremont saw the blood lust in his eyes. He saluted and walked back to his squad. They were clustered around the ammunition detail, reloading. "Don't shoot unless you have something to shoot at," he told them.

The first mortar shell landed in the clearing in front of the building, jarring a couple of the bodies nearby. The next was a partial hit on the northeast corner of the building. After that, Armistead walked them systematically from one end of the building to the other and back again. He was firing from the top of the slope directly above the target.

Peter gazed thoughtfully at the winking flashes on the hillside.

The barrage continued without interruption for twenty minutes. The building gradually disintegrated into a smoking caldron of rubble. Tremont could picture the frantic Prives, scurrying from room to room, trying to guess where the next shell would land. Armistead apparently was using antipersonnel explosives. The walls remained standing, and there were no great bursts of flame.

The mortars did their work with deadly effectiveness, but with disappointing results from Major Wellbourne's standpoint. The Prives did not come pouring out of the building. Midway through the bombardment, three men appeared at the entrance, each of them waving a white handkerchief. They stumbled forward a dozen paces. When they were clear of the building, every gun in the perimeter opened up on them. Except Peter Tremont's. He closed his eyes for a moment, then turned them back to the flashes on the hillside.

Finally the barrage ended. A sickly silence enveloped the smoking ruin and the surrounding ring of steel. Major Wellbourne suddenly marched out of the darkness into the eerie half-light beyond the focus of the searchlights. He walked across the clearing, past the sprawled corpses almost to the entrance. He turned and signaled the medics. They trotted out with the stretchers and began their grisly task. Major Wellbourne strutted back to the perimeter.

"Lieutenant Tremont," he called. Peter stepped forward.

"All right. Take your men in there and clean that place

out. I don't think you gonna meet much resistance. Bring me back four, five prisoners. That's all, y'hear? The rest, you just gimme bodies."

Tremont assembled his squad, formed them in a skirmish line and led them across the open ground. They reached the entrance without incident. He signaled the men to close up. He formed them in two ranks on either side of the double doors. "Cover me," he said.

He pulled open one of the doors and stepped back. A smell of charred flesh and cordite wafted from the opening. There was no sound within except a faint crackle of fire. He stepped inside. The squad crowded in after him.

A long corridor extending the length of the building was brightly lighted by the searchlight beams shining through the empty windows and glowing through the holes in the roof. It was flanked on either side by twelve-foot cubicles, separated by metal partitions. The roof had literally been blown to pieces. Scores of gaping holes pitted the intervening concrete floors like Swiss cheese. Most of the partitions had been blown apart, and nearly the entire interior of the building was visible from the small foyer where they stood.

Tremont divided his squad into three-man details and assigned a floor to each. "Count the dead. Leave them where they are. Bring the rest down here. No shooting unless you have to. Is that clear?"

Several of them had heard Major Wellbourne's instructions. They seemed relieved to have them countermanded.

The open stairs at either end of the building appeared to be reasonably intact. Those in the middle were a jumbled mass of iron. There was no elevator shaft. The squad dispersed. Peter set off toward the south wing at the head of the ground-floor detail.

Both corner rooms were charnels. At least a dozen bodies—the precise number could only be determined, literally, by head count—were strewn about each. Obviously the victims had assembled here in hopes of making a desperate sortie to the near-by cluster of shacks. It was just as well, Tremont reflected, that the major had vetoed his plan to gain entry here.

Arms, legs, entrails were scattered about in jumbled heaps. Shreds of bloody tissue and stringy tendons spattered the walls. Lumps of flesh and splintered fragments of bone littered the floor like hunks of marble in an untidy sculptor's studio. Tremont felt stirrings of an old nausea. He stepped out into the corridor.

"Get a count," he said over his shoulder. "I'll start at the other end."

He walked the length of the corridor, flexing the muscles in his legs to steady them. Then he started back, forcing himself to look in every cubicle for a sign of life, closing his mind to the profuse signs of death. In the third room facing the front of the building he came upon a man and a woman, both fairly young, both breathing. The lower part of the man's face was blown away and his right hand was missing. Blood was seeping from the open end of an artery. His remaining hand was clamped over the stump of the wrist in a pitiful effort to stanch the flow of blood. His eyes were glazed with pain and shock, but as he stared up at Tremont a feeble gleam of hatred shone through.

Peter turned away to avoid his gaze. The woman's body, surprisingly, was unmarked, although her clothes had been blown off. She lay on her side, quivering. Peter leaned over to examine her. A sliver of shrapnel protruded from her temple, almost concealed by her tousled brown hair. He reached over and touched the piece of jagged steel. It was firmly embedded in her skull.

She moaned, jerked twice and stiffened.

Peter straightened up, and his eyes again met those of the young man. He obviously was struggling to speak, but he had nothing to speak with. Then he lost consciousness. Peter stared for a moment at the horrible half-face. He leaned over and removed the fingers from the mangled wrist. Blood spurted from the artery.

Tremont counted nineteen corpses in the north wing. No survivors. Three, he suspected, had finished themselves off. He pondered the extremity that would impel several hundred people to docilely accept extermination rather than hurl themselves either at the feet or the throats of their enemies.

For the most part, the Prives—the identifiable ones—looked like what they were: derelicts. Yet there was about them a diversity seldom seen in a single stratum of society. They were young, middle-aged, old; male, female; husky, frail; intelligent-looking, stupid-looking; handsome, ugly. Indeed, they had only one thing in common—two now. They were discards—people who, for one reason or another, had failed to measure up in the process of natural selection. And they were dead.

Peter sat on a mound of rubble in the foyer, fighting the queasiness in his stomach and striving to look composed. The squadmen began bringing in a few survivors, all of them wounded. They laid the mangled bodies on the floor and fled back to the dead, who were not capable of reproach. Peter watched as the number mounted to ten and willed them to die so they would not exceed Wellbourne's quota.

He dispatched two men to report to the major and to bring stretchers for the wounded. The fifth-floor detail finished its rounds first, since there was very little left of that floor. He sent them to the basement. They returned shortly to report seven bodies on the floor of the laundry room, each with a bullet hole in the head. Presumably the Seepees.

Tremont went down to look at them himself. They were laid out in a neatly spaced row, their arms folded across their chests. Each had a small hole at the base of the skull and a missing frontal lobe. He knelt beside the man on the end, flipped open his coat and extracted his document dossier. Engraved on the back of a blue leather cover was the crossbar emblem of the Citizens Protection Force.

"Leave them here for the time being," he said. "Go up and carry out the survivors."

The leader of the detail swallowed and turned a white face toward him. He looked as though he were about to cry. "How many, sir?"

"All of them."

The boy soldier looked relieved and hustled his men up the stairs.

Peter inspected the dingy basement. Surprisingly it was still lighted, though poorly, by a dozen bare bulbs dangling from cords fixed to the walls. He heard a hum in the far corner and spied a battered generator, which obviously supplied the power. In fact, the basement was relatively undamaged. He wondered why the Prives had not sought refuge here. Apparently they preferred to die on the barricades. He glanced again at the row of bodies on the floor, then started up the stairs to the foyer.

A shot rang out on one of the upper levels, followed by a stampede of boots pounding on bare concrete. He met the fourth-floor detail clattering down the stairs at the second landing. Private Leader Barstow, brandishing his machine gun at arm's length above his head, was nearly overrun by his two followers as he came to a screeching halt six inches from Peter's scowling face.

"There's somebody up there ... alive," he gasped. "He shot at us."

"Why didn't you shoot back?" Tremont replied coldly.

"He's ... he's ... we thought he was dead."

Peter pushed past them and paused at the fourth level. "Which way?" Private Leader Barstow gestured to the left. "Sixth door down, I think."

Tremont slipped the strap off his shoulder and moved stealthily down the hall, machine gun at the ready. As he approached the shattered door of the sixth cubicle, he stopped and motioned the militiamen against the wall. From long-ago instinct he brushed his hand against his belt for a grenade. He had none.

He glanced back over his shoulder at the three petrified youths flattened against the wall, their eyes fixed on him. He inched back toward them and said in a taut whisper, "What kind of weapon has he got?"

"Rifle, I think."

Tremont reached down and picked up a grenade-size chunk of concrete. He moved away from the wall. He hurled the concrete through the doorway, head-high, and dived in after it. He caught a flying glimpse of a gray-haired old man peering down the barrel of a gun resting on the edge of an over-turned table. Tremont twisted in mid-air, landed on his shoulder and rolled up against the flat bottom of the table. In the same motion he reached up and grabbed the protruding barrel of the gun and yanked down. It pinwheeled through the air and thudded down on a body sprawled beside the door.

Tremont leaped to his feet and trained the machine gun on the gray head. The man, who had been kneeling behind the table, rose slowly. His hair stuck up ludicrously on one side. His face was grimy and powdered with plaster. One arm of his coat was torn off. His left eyelid fluttered open and shut in a comical wink. Yet there was about him an indescribable air of dignity. He glared defiantly at Peter with no trace of fear.

Tremont stared at him. "Papa," he whispered.

The old man blinked bewilderedly. A look of mingled incredulity and suspicion came into his face.

Tremont raised the machine gun and fired a burst into the ceiling. With an admonitory gesture he motioned the old man to silence. He turned and strode out of the room.

The squadmen were huddled in the hall, guns trained on the doorway. Peter waved the snout of his weapon at them. "Get downstairs and start carrying out the prisoners. I'll finish up here."

He watched them trot to the end of the corridor and scramble down the stairs. He turned back into the cubicle and gazed unbelievingly at his father. Royston Vance's eyes roamed over the militiaman's face and rejected it. He raised a hand to still the fluttering eyelid and stared balefully out of the other. "Shoot," he said contemptuously.

"Papa, it's me. Cordy."

A shadow of doubt returned to the old man's eyes. He leaned forward and studied the other's face. "No, it's not," he said positively.

The flat contradiction was so incongruous under the circumstances—and so typical of Royston Vance—his son could not stifle a laugh. The old man scowled.

"It is, Papa. It's me. Cordy. I've ... My face has been changed."

"I ... I couldn't have forgotten my son's face." The old man's voice broke. Tears welled in his eyes.

"I know you couldn't, Papa."

The old man's face suddenly hardened. "If you are my son, what are you doing here? What are you doing in that uniform?"

"Papa . . . I can't tell you."

Royston Vance said nothing. His eyes held the same withdrawn look as when Cathy-June had upbraided him for ruining their lives.

"Trust me, Papa," Cordell Vance said. "I'm on your side."

"Well," Royston Vance said, "I guess it doesn't make any difference now."

"Yes, it does. I'm going to get you out of here."

"No." Royston Vance looked at the bodies scattered around the room. "I got these people into this. I'm going to die with them."

"What good will that do?"

"What good would it do to live?" Royston Vance's voice held a note of hopelessness Cordell had never heard before. "We thought we could at least ignite a spark of resistance and maybe it would spread. They caught us before we were ready."

Along with the note of defeat there was a faint echo of the stubborn defiance that had destroyed Royston Vance and his family. Emotional arguments were futile, his son knew. The only appeal the old lawyer would listen to was hard logic. To hell with Robert Dorsey.

"Papa, I was sent down to . . . do something. Maybe you could help me."

His father stared at him suspiciously. "What?"

"I can't tell you right now. But it's important. To both of us."

The old man gestured toward the white glare of the searchlights. "There's no way out of here. I won't be taken alive."

The professional guerrilla fighter seized the opening. "If I can get you out of here, do you have someplace you can hide?"

A wintry smile creased the weathered face. "I've been doing it for fifteen years."

"Are you hurt? Can you walk?"

Royston Vance raised his left hand to the side of his head. The gray hair was rusty and matted with blood. "I was unconscious. I must have been grazed." He tested his legs. "I'm all right."

"Okay. Now listen to me and do as I tell you." The old man looked up in surprise at the brusque tone. "You've got a bunch of bodies down in the basement. Seepees from the looks of them."

Royston Vance nodded.

"If I can get you loaded in the dead wagon with them, you think you can take it from there?"

A little of the hopelessness faded from his father's face. "Maybe." He still sounded resigned.

"You've got to," Cordell Vance said harshly. "I need you. And if you get caught, it'll be my neck."

A glint of the old ferocity shone in Royston Vance's eyes. "All right," he said. "What do I do?"

"Come around here."

The old man picked his way through the litter and the mangled bodies. Cordell stooped over and lifted him to his shoulder. "Stiffen your legs a little. You're dead."

He met one of his patrols on the stairs, carrying a wounded Prive to the foyer. "I've got one here that looks like a Seepee," he said. "I'll take him down to the basement. You ask Major Wellbourne to hold a couple of ambulances for the Seepees."

He lugged his father to the basement and set him down. "Wash up and strip," he said. He looked over the row of dead

Seepees, lifted the oldest one to his feet and started undressing him. "He's got papers in his pocket. They might come in handy."

Royston Vance put on the Seepee's clothes, and they both set about dressing the dead man in his torn rags.

"Papa," Cordell said, "what happened to Mama?"

"She died. Four years after you left. I don't think she ever forgave me. Did you?"

Their eyes met. Cordell caught a glimpse of the suffering his father had endured. "I have now," he said. His tone became military again. "Where can I get in touch with you?"

His father hesitated. "I'll have to get out of Prive Town. Obviously there was an informer. They'll be looking for me. I have friends outside, but I couldn't take a chance on your contacting me there. Where can I reach you?"

"I run a little photographic store downtown on Granger Avenue between Sixth and Seventh. Next to the alley. My name is Peter Tremont. Come in there Monday morning if you can. If you can't, don't send anybody. Don't tell anybody. If there's any chance you're being followed, stay clear away from me. You understand?"

The old man looked hurt. "I understand," he said coldly.

Royston Vance lay down in the middle of the row of cadavers and folded his hands over his breast. Suddenly, it was as though he really were dead. Silently, Cordell Vance damned those who had drained the joy from his father's life.

Lieutenant Peter Tremont hauled the body of the Seepee upstairs and dumped it in the corner room with the other corpses. He returned to the foyer, where his squad was loading the last of the prisoners. "How many?" he asked.

"Fourteen," Private Piatkowski said apologetically. "Five of 'em died. The major said not to bring out any more."

"All right," Tremont said. "I'll handle the major. Take these out and bring back the stretchers. The rest of you round up some blankets. Take 'em down to the basement and cover up the Seepees. Then start carrying them out."

He went back downstairs, and when the militiamen came with the blankets took one and tucked it around his father. The men, no longer squeamish, performed their grisly chore with insensitive haste, wanting only to get it over with.

Tremont led the somber procession across the brightly lighted ground to the ambulance and stood by as the medics stowed them on narrow racks, fastening straps across their chests and legs. He observed with relief that none of the attendants moved to ride in back. He watched the ambulance with Royston Vance in it pull away, then walked back down the slope to find Major Wellbourne.

The major was in a jovial mood. He did not mention the surplus prisoners. "I understand you counted a hundred and eighteen bodies, Lieutenant. That's not a bad night's work. Let's go take a look at 'em."

Peter started to beg off, then reconsidered. He set off across the clearing again at Major Wellbourne's side.

The stench of death hit them as they entered the building. It interrupted the major's gleeful rehash of the operation in mid-sentence. He almost gagged, then pushed on into the slaughterhouse. Obviously it was his first encounter with the end product of his trade.

He toured the first floor, growing progressively less loquacious. Peter followed, standing outside in the hall as the major gaped at the gruesome results of his night's frolic. Midway on the second floor, the major had had enough. "Let's get outa here, Lieutenant," he said, shoving past Tremont and moving briskly down the corridor.

Tremont turned to follow him. Idly his eye brushed over a cluster of steel slivers forming a saucer-size circle in the plaster, as though someone had been playing a macabre dart game. He paused and came back to them. For no reason, he plucked them out one by one and slipped them into his shirt pocket.

Part Six

Chapter *Thirteen*

The free enterprise system, what there was of it, functioned rather casually, not to say lackadaisically, in the Confederate States of America. Since they were for the most part one-man operations, the shops opened at the proprietors' convenience. If they remained closed for a day—or permanently—it occasioned little comment. The customers were accustomed to it.

When Peter Tremont returned from the massacre of the Prives, he hung a "Closed" sign on the door and went to bed. When he awoke in midafternoon, he lay staring at the ceiling.

At six o'clock, his normal closing time, he got up and dressed and brewed himself a cup of coffee. Unsurprisingly, he was not hungry, though he had not eaten for nearly twenty-four hours.

He descended to the tiny cubbyhole which he had partitioned off in the workshop to serve as an office. Consulting the catalogue, he filled out an order form from the Intercontinental Import Company. In addition to the usual camera replacements, he requisitioned an assortment of unrelated items, including an astronomer's telescope (412-6R34) and a surveyor's transit (#68-3J25). He appended a note at the bottom of the form in the space reserved for "Special Instructions": "Some of the merchandise I have received from you recently has been of rather poor quality. I would appreciate your giving this order special attention."

He took his customary constitutional up and down the Grand Concourse, pausing in front of the armory to gaze down the magnolia-scented mall at the spotlighted Stone Mansion, standing in isolated splendor at the bottom of the sloping green carpet.

There was no mention the next morning in the *National Voice* of the Prive uprising, nor of a missing Seepee. Business was a little brisker than usual, due to the fact that the store had been closed the previous day. No one commented on that fact, nor on the extraordinary fireworks display, which must have been clearly visible from across the river.

It was a regular duty night for the Domestic Tranquillity Section. Major Wellbourne assembled the entire complement on the roof of the armory in full battle array for a critique on the recent field operation. He deployed each of the companies in their respective positions and re-enacted the whole operation with relish, pointing out to the officers where their performances could have been improved.

"Cap'n Armistead," he said, "you did real good once you got sighted in on the target, but that first round landed right out in the open. Coulda killed somebody."

"Well, Major," the captain said defensively, "shootin' down like that, it's hard to figure the exact elevation and windage. You've just about got to fire a couple of guide rounds to make your corrections on. The correlates on No. 3 gun didn't jibe with the other four. We had to redirect it manually. I think the computer digestion system is out of sync with the range-finder."

"Well, Cap'n, you just better get it in sync. Y'all take it out on the range next Saturday and find out what's wrong with it. We got maneuvers comin' up here in September, and I don' aim to have you shootin' off the general's head."

By and large, though, Major Wellbourne was well pleased. At the end of the critique, the section broke up into weapons seminars. Each company was rotated to a different weapons category for familiarization lectures and demonstrations. Tremont wandered over to Armistead's mortar seminar.

The captain looked at him sourly, evidently ruffled by the major's reprimand. Peter soothed him by listening with rapt attention to his lecture. He hung around afterward and asked several patently unknowledgeable questions about the aiming device. Armistead answered them tolerantly, and thawed further when Tremont helped him load the mortar and four dummy shells on the little electric-powered ammunition cart. They rode down on the elevator together to the magazine. Armistead cursed when he saw the line in front of the weapons check-in stand.

"Son-of-a-bitch," he said, "I got some quiff waitin' for me, and that goddamned Wellbourne has already kept us overtime."

Tremont volunteered to return the mortar and ammunition, although it was contrary to regulations. Armistead, it turned out, didn't give a damn about regulations, and gratefully accepted the offer. The supply sergeant noted an objection, but signed the receipt.

Tremont accompanied him into the magazine to pick out a machine pistol for target practice. The sergeant pulled the cart by hand, since operation of any electrical appliance was prohibited within the magazine. Tremont tagged along after him, trying to establish a bearing from the entrance to the mortar cabinet. When they reached it, he was hopelessly lost.

Peter helped him hoist the compact little 60-mm mortar off

the cart and into the cubicle. While the sergeant was stowing the mortar away, Tremont lifted two of the dummy shells and handed them in to him.

Awkwardly he scraped one of them along the outside of the cubicle. It left a tiny scratch in the black paint.

"Jesus Christ, Lieutenant," the sergeant exclaimed, "be a little careful, will yuh. These ain't beer cans, y'know. They got a percussion cap on 'em even if they ain't live."

"Sorry," Peter said contritely.

The sergeant locked the mortar bin and started off with Tremont close on his heels. Peter noticed that overhead two of the thousand recessed lights which blazed down day and night from the ceiling, bathing the magazine in a constant glare, were out. Together, they provided a rough directional line.

The elderly man in the dark suit entered the shop just before closing time, as Tremont was unpacking the weekly shipment from the Intercontinental Import Company. The telescope and the transit he had shoved under his workbench without uncrating. He had opened the other boxes and was checking their contents against his order form.

When the door buzzer sounded, he stepped to the curtained partition and called, "Be right with you." He pushed a couple of empty cartons in front of the two under the workbench, put on his suit coat and walked into the front room.

"Yes, sir. What can I do for you?"

A pair of alert brown eyes studied him from behind lightly tinted glasses. Thick, snow-white eyebrows stood out in sharp relief from a ruddy, wrinkled face. A dark, broad-brimmed hat shaded the weathered countenance. The tie was loosely knotted and slightly askew.

"I'm planning to take a trip in a couple of weeks. I'd like

to take some pictures. Scenic pictures. I don't know much about photography. What kind of a camera would I need?"

"Still or movie, sir?"

"Oh, just snapshots."

Peter moved to the middle of the room, away from the two microphones he had spotted shortly after he moved in. The Seepees had taken no great pains to conceal them. It was common knowledge that they monitored all Private Sector establishments. To have tampered with them would have aroused suspicion.

"I think this might be what you're looking for," Peter said, opening the center display counter. "It's a German make. Good workmanship. Built-in strobe."

Royston Vance glowered at his son when he heard the price, but fished in his pocket and extracted four bills from his wallet, leaving it bare.

"Fine, sir," Peter said. "The price includes the carrying case and four film cartridges. Here, I'll show you how to load it. Since you're not going for several weeks, I would suggest that you try it out and, if you're not entirely satisfied, bring it back. Walk over to the Concourse and take some pictures of the flowerbeds. That'll give you a good test. Wait until it's dark, so you can check out the strobe."

He rang up the purchase on the cash register and handed his father back the four bills. "Thank you very much, sir. We develop the first set of prints free."

Royston Vance studied his son's altered face for a long moment. Peter smiled. His father shook his head doubtfully and left the store.

They met at nine o'clock that evening at the Garden of the States. They sat down on a bench. Peter took the old man's camera and ran through the instructions again.

"Did you have any trouble the other night?" he asked, holding the viewer to his eye.

"Not a bit."

"Is there any reason the Seepees would be hunting you? Do they know you were involved in the shooting?"

"Yes, they'd know that. But they don't know I'm not dead. Nobody tried to identify the remains. They just dug a pit and dumped 'em in."

"How long can you hide out?"

"Indefinitely, if I don't try to do anything else. I've moved out of Prive Town. I didn't live there all the time. I was doing some organizing." He paused for a moment. "You going to tell me what you're doing here?"

Peter lowered the camera and turned his face toward his father's. "I'm here to assassinate Spearman," he said with a friendly smile.

Royston Vance stared at him. He reached out a hand and squeezed his son's knee. His grip was surprisingly firm, as firm as it had been on the night they parted forever. His voice, however, was shaky.

"It can't be done. We've tried half a dozen times. We have an organization. Men who would sacrifice their lives. We have a committee that does nothing but draft plans. What could you do by yourself? There's no way."

"I'm not by myself," Tremont said. "I've got you to help me."

Tremont rose and snapped a couple of pictures of the garden. "A good dependable camera," he said. "Let's try it out under different lighting conditions."

They strolled across the grass toward the floodlighted Capitol on the crown of the bluff.

"Tell me about Mama," Cord said.

His father looked stricken. "She just didn't want to live any more," he said in a strained voice. "Actually, I killed her. I had something to live for. She didn't. She wasn't even very sick. I think she died simply because she wanted to."

"Couldn't you have bent a little? To save her?"

"I did. After I was downclassified to 'Noncooperative,' I stopped all activity for a year. We were both miserable, but we could have stuck it out—I think." His voice faltered. "Then—I had to make a choice. . . ."

They had moved to a small, run-down clapboard house on the dilapidated fringe of the downtown section. The area was populated largely by former businessmen who had, one way or another, run afoul of the regime. They constituted the bulk of Royston Vance's sparse practice.

When the two Seepees came to the door shortly before midnight, both Royston and Cathy-June assumed that the day of reckoning had come. They faced it defiantly—together. But the Seepees were unaccountably polite, even considerate.

"You come with us," they said to Royston Vance. "You may want to pack a bag. You might be gone for a couple of days."

The crusty lawyer was puzzled by their respectful tone and baffled by the suggestion that he pack a bag. People who went with the Seepees in the middle of the night rarely took a bag —and rarely returned in a couple of days.

Surprisingly, it was Cathy-June who faced up to them. "Where are you taking him?" she demanded. "I'm going with him."

The Seepees were amused. "No, ma'am. I'm afraid you can't do that."

"I *can* do it. I'm going to do it," she declared, locking her thin fingers around her husband's arm. "Where are you taking him?"

To the astonishment of her husband, who knew an inadmissible question when he heard one, the Seepees ended up telling her. Probably because they themselves were not sure of their ground. Or his.

"Mistuh Spearman wants to talk to him. We're takin' him to Confederacity."

Royston Vance had his doubts—until he was loaded aboard the plane. When it became apparent they really were taking him to talk with Spearman, he was even more perplexed. He had never met Howie Ray Spearman, who was still Commissioner of Internal Development and Security, though he felt he knew him very well indeed. Before muting his tirades against the regime, he had become convinced that Spearman was the evil force behind the Party of National Resurgence and the Evolutionary Concept. He had much to say to Howie Ray Spearman—though he resolved he would not. But he had no idea what Howie Ray might have to say to him.

Even though he had no preconceptions, he was surprised.

Howie Ray greeted him with courtly cordiality, striding halfway across the vast carpeted expanse of his office to grasp his hand. "This is indeed a pleasure, Mistuh Vance," he said in his soft drawl. "I've heard a good deal about you."

Royston gave him a narrow look and a tentative handshake.

After they were seated and Howie Ray had delivered the conventional blandishments about the beauty and friendliness of Baton Rouge, he came obliquely to the point.

"And how is Mrs. Vance? I understood her health was not too good." The drawl was less pronounced.

Vance assured him that Cathy-June was well.

"And the boy? I understand he is not with you now."

"No. He's away at school." Royston Vance did not elaborate.

"Well now, that's too bad," Howie Ray commiserated. "Let's hope you'll be back together again shortly. We feel that the family is the basic unit in our system, that it strengthens and solidifies the nation. Though I do understand, Mr. Vance," he continued after a barely perceptible pause, "that you are not in complete accord with our system. Or were not at one time."

"That's right, Mr. Commissioner," Royston said, leaving Spearman's unspoken question hanging in air.

"Well now, I do hope you've come around to our way of thinkin'. We need men with your kind of vision. There's a place for you in the Selection Process. I hope you find it." The drawl had returned.

"I hope so, Mr. Commissioner," the lawyer said noncommittally.

"I hope I can help you find it, Mr. Vance."

Royston studied the heavy gray face, shaggy eyebrows converging in concern. He felt annoyed that Spearman did not fit the Machiavellian image he had molded for him. "I'm sure you'll do your best."

Spearman smiled. "That's why I asked you here. You can render a real service to the Confederacy, to the cause of Evolution and to yourself."

He paused and gazed expectantly at Vance. Vance did not reply.

Spearman was suddenly businesslike. "I am familiar with your activities in the past, Mr. Vance. I trust you have now adopted a more cooperative attitude. In the beginning there were a good many people like you who resisted the Evolutionary Concept. Happily, most of that resistance has died down. However, I suspect that a certain ... antipathy remains. If we are to fulfill the Evolutionary Concept, we must be united. Not only in deed, but in thought.

"You were one of the most vocal critics of the new order, Mr. Vance. It would be most helpful if you were to demonstrate—in some positive way—that you have undergone a change of heart. That you fully embrace the process of natural selection and support what we are trying to do."

A steely note crept into Spearman's voice. "It would, of course, be mutually beneficial. To achieve the impact we seek, it would be desirable to show that our system rewards the deserving, regardless of their previous . . . uh . . . derelictions. I could use a man with your talents in my own department, Mr. Vance. In fact, I have a place in mind which I think you would find very attractive. For appearances' sake, of course, it probably would be advisable to work you into it gradually. The first step would be for you to join the Party of National Resurgence."

He sat back in his chair, his strange eyes boring into Vance's.

Royston Vance could not suppress his advocate's instincts. "Wouldn't that contradict the process of natural selection? I have done nothing to merit such distinction."

"Quite the contrary. It would demonstrate that the process works. I'm not just trying to seduce you, Mr. Vance. The great mass of the people do not have any strong convictions. They will do whatever they think would be to their advantage. The process of natural selection takes that into consideration. There are a few people who are born zealots. I am one of them. From what I know of you, Mr. Vance, you are another. The zealots are the people who get things done. Their opinions are firm, but they are not irrevocable. The most convincing anti-Communists are those who were the most dedicated Communists. You are an intelligent man. All we are trying to do is to provide a climate in which superiority can assert itself. You belong with us, Mr. Vance."

Howie Ray's appeal was so forthright—so genuine—Royston Vance could not condemn it. But neither could he accept it. He took refuge in the sanctuary of caution to which he had retreated. "I'd have to think it over. And talk it over with my wife."

The missionary spark faded from Spearman's eyes and was replaced by a look of veiled calculation.

"You do that, Mr. Vance." His tone was meaningful if not menacing. "Just remember that we appreciate the value of zealots. We also appreciate their danger."

Royston Vance returned home without the Seepee escort. Oddly moved by Cathy-June's unexpected reaction to the confrontation with the Seepees, he told her, without embellishment, of his talk with Spearman. She listened in silence. He had girded himself to explain why he could not accept the offer, perhaps secretly hoping she might persuade him. She surprised him again.

"You couldn't do it," she said in a hopeless voice. "We'd be worse off than we are now."

"If I don't do it, we'll be worse off than we are now," he said.

"Royse," she said. It had been years since she had called him "Royse." "I hate what has happened to us. I don't know why it had to happen, but I guess it just had to. I know you can't change. And if you did, it wouldn't be any good. I don't care any more. You do what you have to do."

For six months he didn't do anything. He did not notify Howie Ray of his decision because he had made no decision. Howie Ray did not press him. After Cathy-June died, Royston gradually picked up the threads of his old associations. In due course he was notified he had been "deprived" of his citizenship. He became a nonperson. He and his son had that in common when they met again.

Cord's face softened as he listened to his father's recital. But his voice still held a trace of reproach. "Papa, why didn't you ever try to get in touch with me? You knew where I was."

"Yes, Cordy, I always knew where you were. Until you vanished two years ago. Mr. Sievers sent me regular reports on you. But I made him promise never to let you know what happened to me. If he had, you would have felt you should come and rescue me. If you didn't you would have felt guilty. And there was nothing you could have done. There's still nothing you can do," he added flatly.

"We'll see," said Peter Tremont.

The telescope was carefully packed in excelsior. Tremont assembled it according to the directions and attached it to the tripod. He sat down in the battered easy chair in the workshop and skimmed through the astronomical handbook. It showed the relative positions of the planets and major constellations at different seasons of the year. He had a skimpy knowledge of astronomy, gleaned from a celestial navigation course he had once taken in the army.

When he had finished the book, he stuck it in his pocket, hoisted the telescope and collapsed tripod over his shoulder and walked through the passageway leading to the foyer of the building in which his shop was located. He crossed the foyer to the elevator bank. Two Negro maintenance men and a late-working civil servant looked at him incuriously as he entered the elevator and pushed the top button.

He got off at the twenty-first floor and climbed a flight of stairs to the roof. He had inspected the premises a couple of days before during the noon hour. A portion of the area had been fitted out as a sun deck, with plastic reclining chairs and awnings. He walked to the extreme southwest corner of the building and commenced setting up the telescope. He sighted in on the moon and then, consulting the handbook from time to time, sought out the visible planets.

He heard the door of the utility blockhouse open and close softly, but kept his eye glued to the telescope. He sensed a silent presence behind him. He straightened up, turned around and feigned a startled "Uh!"

The building superintendent, an ex officio Seepee monitor, stood watching him displeasedly. "What's goin' on, Buster?"

Tremont sized him up as an officious functionary, the kind who would exceed his modest authority if given any encouragement. He twitched his head at the telescope. "Doing a little star-gazing."

"Ain't nobody allowed up here after dark."

"Who says?" His tone was harsh.

The superintendent took a step backward and said a shade less belligerently, "That's the rules."

"I've got a copy of the rules, and they don't say anything about that. I'm a tenant in this building, and the rules say I have access to all the facilities. They don't set any time limit. If I want to come up here and eat my lunch at midnight, I'll do it."

"That's different. They don't say you can come up here and spy on people."

"For Christ's sake what's to spy on around here? There aren't any bedrooms within two miles. Here, look for yourself."

He motioned the other toward the telescope. Chastened, the

superintendent accepted as a peacemaking gesture. He moved the barrel around the skies, then leveled it at several nearby buildings.

"Guess you're right," he said. "There ain't much to see."

He stood around for a few minutes, then left. Tremont returned to his scrutiny of the skies. Before folding up the tripod, he lowered the telescope and panned over the city before him. Satisfied, he packed up his gear and returned to his quarters below.

He returned to the roof every night when he didn't have militia duty, usually arriving shortly after eleven and staying for about forty-five minutes. Several times the superintendent opened the door and looked out at him, then went quietly away.

Meanwhile, he unpacked and assembled the surveyor's instruments in the privacy of his apartment. The transit screwed into a plotting board, which was bolted to a tripod. It was not as powerful as the astral telescope, but to Tremont's inexpert eye it seemed to be a reliable instrument.

The following Monday, after he had locked up, he brought the transit down to the workroom and set it up. He removed the plastic sheath from the telescope and fitted it over the smaller transit, stuffing rags around it to hold it firm. When he was finished, he had a transit disguised as a telescope. Finally, he removed a folded astral chart from the handbook and pinned it tightly to the plotting board. Thus equipped, he took the elevator to the roof and set up in his customary spot at the corner of the building.

He wasted no time surveying the heavens. He trained the transit on the base of the spotlighted flagpole set in the railing of the balcony overlooking Spearman Square. He made a tiny pinprick in the astral chart, noting that it pierced the star Bellatrix in the constellation Orion. He swung the transit-telescope around to the flag flying from the parapet atop the east front of the armory. He previously had computed the flagpole to be twelve feet tall, and the top of the parapet to be six feet above the drill field on the roof. He made another pinprick in the chart.

He took sightings on the flagpoles atop the Capitol and the Citadel of Justice to cross-check his bearings, knowing them to be on an exact north-south axis with Stone Mansion. He packed up his instruments, returned to his workshop and restored the sheath to the telescope. He unscrewed the transit and the tripod, packed them away in their box and carried the plotting board upstairs to his apartment. He laid it down on the kitchen table and, after some searching, located the pinpricks in the astral chart. With a needle-pointed hard-lead pencil, he connected up his coordinates. His calculations showed the flagpole on the balcony of Stone Mansion on a relative bearing of 002°, 4′, 9″ from the flagpole on the parapet of the armory, distance: 928.36 meters, elevation: minus 27.15 meters. He sat down and committed the figures to memory. Then he burned the pad on which he had jotted them down and tore the chart into shreds, carefully effacing the pinholes.

During the next several weeks, Peter Tremont diligently tended to the business of the Granger Avenue Photographic Supply Shop, taking time off only to fulfill his militia duties and to indulge his proclivity for tramping around the city. Now and then he would take the telescope up to the roof, but his interest in astronomy had waned. He continued to experiment with the divers weapons in the Confederate arsenal and had frequent occasion to visit the magazine, always accompanied by a supply sergeant. He still could not fathom the mystery of the maze, but he was beginning to acquire a general sense of direction.

His acquaintance with Captain Armistead ripened into an off-duty camaraderie, usually winding up in one of the rather sedate State Service cafés on the periphery of the government complex. There were a handful of livelier spots, operating under a Private Sector permit, but attendance at them was not advisable for anyone desirous of being classified upward in the natural selection process.

In fact, Tremont discovered, deviations from the evolutionary path were readily available to anyone who wished to seek them out. Houses of prostitution, gambling casinos, even narcotics dens existed with the tacit consent if not the official sanction of the government. The theory was that in order to prove his fitness to rise under the selection system, the individual should be exposed to temptation so he could choose the course of rectitude of his own volition. The wages of sin were clearly understood. But a surprising number of people chose to accept them.

Captain Armistead proved to be one of them. He was an engineer by profession and held a supervisory job in the Department of Physical Resources. Engineers were categorized as "skilled technicians" in the Manpower Catalogue, along with automobile mechanics, chemists, pharmacists, etc. They did not normally rise above the "Accomplished" classification. Having achieved that rank, Captain Armistead was no longer bucking for advancement. He exercised enough discretion to avoid demotion, but, like a veteran noncom, he played the angles for all they were worth. Several times he suggested to Tremont that they sample the fleshpots of the Private Sector, but Peter declined. As a parasite, existing on the sufferance of the regime, he strove to maintain a maximum level of obscurity.

Despite his moral shortcomings, Captain Armistead was indeed a "skilled technician." He did not disguise his contempt for Major Wellbourne and the "chicken-shit outfit" of which he was a member, but he performed his duties competently and even with a certain abashed enthusiasm. To Peter's naïve questions, he responded with a detailed explanation of the computer-controlled range-finder, which operated with uncanny accuracy. Simple though it was, Peter could not seem to master the procedure. Eventually he lost interest.

Other than minding the store and fulfilling his militia obligations, Tremont led a sedentary life. He spent a good many hours lying on his bed, studying the ceiling. After one such lengthy period of contemplation, he rolled off the bed and strolled down to his workroom. He picked up the movie camera he used to record the activities of the Domestic Tranquillity Section, took it over to his workbench and detached the infrared laser-strobe. He removed the inner components and peered through the hollow casing. He rummaged around in a drawer and pulled out the souvenirs of the Prive massacre, wrapped in a facial tissue. Without unwrapping them, he stuffed the steel slivers into the empty cylinder, capped it at both ends and clamped it back in its brackets on the camera.

Before opening up the next morning, he changed the modest display in the window fronting on Granger Avenue. In the left-hand corner he inserted a German Gondar 2-YM, similar to the one he had sold his father.

They met that evening at the same bench in the Garden of the States. Each had a camera strung around his neck.

Tremont greeted the old man warmly and inquired how his pictures had turned out. The old man said he had not yet had them developed. Peter leaned over to inspect the camera, and the old man removed the strap from around his neck and handed it to him. Peter opened it and held it on his lap.

"Do you, by any chance, have a machinist in your club?" he asked, adjusting the shutter setting.

"Yes, a very good one. He has turned out some very ingenious . . . toys. Would you like to have one?"

Peter shook his head. "I was wondering whether he could broaden the beam on my laser-strobe." He pulled the strobe off his own camera and exchanged it with the one on his father's.

"I need it for close-ups," he explained. "I don't think it would require any new parts. If he could just reassemble those that are in there."

"I'll ask him and let you know." He signaled his son with his eyes and they rose and strolled through the flowerbeds. They squatted down to examine the petals on a Corolanthis orchid.

"Do you have a plan?" Royston Vance said between his teeth.

"Not a plan. More of a hazy idea. There's a slim chance it would work. It'd depend on circumstances."

"What can I do?"

"Nothing. It's too risky. I can't take a chance on involving anyone else."

"Cordy, you think I haven't been involved for twenty-five years?"

"I didn't mean that. I mean they must never find out who's involved. That means whoever does it can't be taken alive. The more people who know about it, the worse the odds."

"What do I have to live for? If I can't do something to help, my life has been wasted."

Tremont could read in Royston Vance's eyes what it had cost him to send his son away—and the only way his son could repay him. Tremont would not be sacrificing a life, he would be salvaging it. Besides, he *would* need help if his nebulous scheme materialized, and Robert Dorsey sure as hell wasn't going to be around to give it.

"Do you think you could get a Confederate officer's uniform?" he said curtly. "A colonel's or maybe a general's?"

"I can have one made. Mr. Spearman keeps us supplied with a great many skilled craftsmen," he added with a touch of irony. "When will I need it?"

"I don't know. Just get it and keep it handy. I have instructions to move by August 10. After that, I don't know what may happen, but I would advise you to get out of Confederacity."

"I don't care what happens," the old man said. "I plan to be wherever Howie Ray Spearman is."

They parted, and Tremont watched Royston Vance trudge off through the flower gardens. Unaccountably, he felt confident that they would somehow pull it off—together.

Time began pressing down on him. The minutes and the hours passed in their normal progression, but the weeks skittered by. He wrote the Intercontinental Import Company, requesting an extension on his account and explaining there was some indication that business might pick up in the fall. They informed him, regretfully, that they could not alter their schedule. They suggested if he was unable to meet the deadline that he come to Miami to discuss other arrangements. He notified them that would not be possible, but that he would make every effort to comply with their instructions.

On the evening of July 23 time—and everything else—suddenly came to a jarring halt.

Major Wellbourne was winding up one of his long-winded discourses on evacuation procedures in Lecture Room "C" before the entire complement of the Domestic Tranquillity Section. Colonel Farrington, the armory commander, opened the door in the rear and marched down the aisle to the rostrum, where Major Wellbourne was holding forth. Behind him, arms swinging and backs rigid, marched fifty young men and women in Resurgent Youth Corps uniforms.

In response to an order from the colonel, they peeled off right and left and stood at attention in front of the class. The colonel spoke to Major Wellbourne, then walked to the microphone.

"Gentlemen," he said. "These young men and young ladies standing before you are visitors to our country from a number of foreign nations. They were invited here by our government to see for themselves the conditions that exist in the Confederate States of America. It is our hope that when they return home, they will be able to refute some of the canards and slanders that have been circulated by foreign propagandists and enemies of our country.

"While here, they have been attached to the Resurgent Youth Corps so that they will have an opportunity to participate directly in the evolutionary process. As part of their indoctrination, they will spend some time studying the organization and training of the Mobile Militia. They will be assigned to the armory here, and will perform a variety of duties. I trust you will extend to them every courtesy and will help them gain an understanding of the proud traditions of our service."

The colonel went on to outline for the visitors the functions of the Mobile Militia and its vital role in the Confederate defense system. The members of that proud service listened more or less attentively, the colonel's bombast being less familiar and therefore more tolerable than the major's rambling lectures.

Except Peter Tremont. He was not listening at all. He was completely unaware that the colonel was speaking. His entire attention was riveted on the tall, black-haired girl standing third from the end on the right with a remote expression on her face. He shielded his face with his hand and gazed at Diane Fleming.

The youth group did not stay for the remainder of Major Wellbourne's talk. The colonel marched them out the way they had come. Peter Tremont did not watch them go. He was engaged in conversation with Captain Armistead, whose eyes wandered over Peter's shoulder as the trim young women swung down the aisle.

Tremont stood woodenly through retreat, dismissed his squad and joined the pell-mell rush of enlisted men for the stairs. The duty officer stopped him as he was signing out, and handed him a purple mimeographed slip. It said: "All officers on duty Tuesday, 23 July will attend a reception in Colonel Farrington's quarters immediately following retreat. The reception will honor a group of foreign students serving temporary tours with the Resurgent Youth Corps. Signed: Colonel A. J. Farrington. CSA/MM."

Tremont tossed the slip aside and resumed signing the register. "Can't make it," he said. "Got a pressing engagement." He started toward the exit.

"Just a minute," the duty officer said curtly. "This isn't exactly a social invitation. You will note it says, 'All officers *will* attend.'"

"Hell, Brad, I've got an important date. They'll never miss me."

"I'll miss you. My orders are to see that all officers attend."

Tremont turned resignedly toward the elevator. One thing about the Confederacy, he had learned. An order from higher authority was an order to be obeyed, whether in the military or the bureaucracy. He thought for a moment of hiding out, but Major Wellbourne was sure to notice his absence.

He slunk through the door of the ballroom adjoining the colonel's quarters and sidled over to a bar in the corner. Counting the guests of honor, there were eighty or ninety people present. He spied Diane standing silently in the midst of a group of youths and three or four officers. He kept his back to her, glancing at her out of the corner of his eye, moving when she moved. Captain Armistead, he noted uneasily, had attached himself to her crowd and seemed to have singled her out.

He was drifting toward the exit, planning to ask the colonel's permission to leave, when Armistead spotted him. He started across the floor, tugging Diane's hand. Characteristically she was moving without haste. Tremont veered away from the colonel and headed directly for the door. He nearly made it. But Armistead called out to him and a couple of officers standing by the door intercepted him.

He turned, shadowing his face with a nonchalant wave. "I've got to go, Armie. See you Thursday."

"Hold up, boy. You got to help our guests gain an understanding of the proud traditions of our service."

Defeated, Peter turned and faced the captain, an arm's length in front of Diane. He did not look at her.

"Meet the enemy. This here's Miss Fleming—Diane Fleming—from the United States. Lieutenant Tremont."

Peter nodded, but did not shake hands. He could not tell whether she looked startled or not. She did not sound startled. "How do you do, Lieutenant—Tremont, is it?"

"Yes, ma'am." His drawl was a bit more pronounced than usual.

She gave him the quick, sidelong scrutiny which he told himself was natural to her, meant nothing.

Armistead was chattering away in what he called his

"quail-hunting accent." Peter gave him his full attention, but he was aware of Diane's detached appraisal.

He was relieved when she said, "You remind me of someone I once knew, Lieutenant."

"I'm a common type, ma'am," he replied. "People are always mistaking me for someone they know. Either that or I just have a friendly way about me." If there was anything Cordell Vance did not have about him, it was a friendly way.

"Have you ever been in Chicago, Lieutenant?"

He forced a vacant, round-eyed stare. "Not hardly, ma'am. Ah reckon ah'd be a little out of place up theah in Yankee Land."

She gave him a small smile. "Oh, I don't know. We're not that different from you. I don't feel out of place down here."

"Glad to hear that," Armistead broke in. "If you goin' to be around a while, we'll make you feel right at home."

Reassuringly, she dismissed Peter Tremont with the same cool indifference she had displayed at her first meeting with Cordell Vance. "I don't know how long we'll be here, Captain," she said.

Peter Tremont was anxious to break away, but Cordell Vance could not. What was she doing here? Obviously she had fallen in with Jerry Donaldson's crackpot movement—either out of weakness or conviction. A sickening wave of disillusionment swept over him, like a lover betrayed. He hadn't really cared before because he had no strong feelings about it one way or the other. Now, he discovered, he did.

"... show you some real Southern hospitality," Armie was saying. "Course if you're really a spy, you can't afford to pass up an opportunity like this, 'cause I spill all sorts of secrets when I get a few drinks in me."

Peter Tremont looked at the girl. Her eyes were focused

in the vicinity of his left hand. Casually, he put both hands in his pockets. She raised her head and looked pensively into his face. He grinned, puffing out his cheeks, and said chattily, "Tha's foh shuah, Miss Fleming. Armie and I grew up togethah. He ain' kep' a secret since he was fahve yeahs old."

She glanced toward the doorway behind him and murmured something he did not catch. Reflexively he tilted his head and turned his left ear in her direction. Her eyes suddenly snapped back and burned into his. He forced himself to meet her gaze impassively.

She turned away and resumed her conversation with Captain Armistead. Tremont waved a negligent farewell and sauntered to the door.

As he walked home, he tried to analyze her manner—and his own feelings. He was more disturbed by his reactions than by hers. She might have noticed some resemblance, but she could not have recognized him. Any more than his father had. Although, he conceded, she had seen him more recently. And more intimately. He put it out of his mind, since there was nothing he could do about it—except avoid her in the future.

There *was* something he could do about his own feelings. Or was there? Despite the neurogenic conditioning, despite his total extinction of old memories, old associations, even his old self, the mere sight of her had torn down all the painfully erected barricades. The ache was back—as fierce as ever.

He concentrated on her defection to Donaldson. That would give him a reason to forget her and would strengthen his resolution never to see her again—regardless of what happened.

He did not see her again for two days. Then she and five other youths showed up on the roof while the D.T. Section was staging a population-evacuation rehearsal. For the past month drill periods had been devoted almost exclusively to precautions of one kind or another against simulated nuclear attack. In the light of the deadline he had been given, Tremont supposed that that was significant; and that he should perhaps advise the Intercontinental Import Company. But he did not.

The Youth Corps contingent—three boys and two girls—sat in the small enclosed stands on the north side of the drill field. The stands normally were the preserve of army brass, who conducted frequent sneak evaluations of militia readiness. The appearance of a regular army general invariably touched off near-panic among the permanent officers of the armory's complement, including Major Wellbourne.

At the conclusion of the drill, Peter maneuvered his squad toward the ramp at the west end of the parade ground and prepared to bolt down it. But Diane Fleming was waiting for him. He nodded and started past her, but she fell into step beside him. She was alone.

"D'you mind if I walk with you, Lieutenant? I don't know my way around here very well yet."

He slowed his pace. At the third floor she placed a hand lightly on his arm and steered him toward the exit. "We've been assigned quarters here. Will you see me home?"

"I imagine it's off limits to base personnel," he said brusquely.

"No, no. Just one corridor, and it's at the other end of the building." She had the supercilious tone which had repelled him when he first met her.

Guardedly, he followed her through the doors and down the hall. She obviously was playing some kind of game with him. He was in no position to be playing games—even innocent ones.

They reached the corridor, which was blocked off with a sign saying: "Off limits to all personnel except on official business."

"Well, I guess I have no official business down there," he said, warily watching her reaction.

She flashed him a smile which he interpreted as coquettish, and which unreasonably annoyed him. She stepped back and opened a door onto the main hallway. "We have kind of a reception room here—for unofficial guests," she said.

The room was dark and empty. She snapped on an overhead light and stood with her hand on the knob. The room, normally a lecture room, had been sparsely outfitted with easy chairs, coffee tables and a divan. He entered with more nonchalance than he felt. He heard her close the door behind them—and lock it.

He turned and faced her, his eyes probing hers. Unhurriedly, she moved toward him, put her arms around him, pressed her body against his, closed her eyes and raised her lips. He almost responded instinctively, then checked himself. He kissed her. But his lips were taut, his body stiff. He raised his hands and awkwardly clutched her shoulder blades.

It was an old theatrical device. The lover exposes himself because he cannot disguise his love-making. Well, any resemblance between Peter Tremont and Cordell Vance would be wildly coincidental. He did not try to break away. He opened his eyes and successfully fought back his straining desire.

He was wearing his summer field uniform. No blouse. He felt her pulling his shirt out of his trousers, and he discovered he was oddly jealous of himself. He tried to pull away. She held him. She writhed against him in unmistakable passion, despite his lack of response. She jerked up his undershirt and ran her hand sensuously over his bare back.

Suddenly he realized her deceit. He grabbed her shoulders and almost hurled her away. "Your back seems to be a bit chewed up, Lieutenant," she said evenly. "You have an industrial accident or something?"

Suspicion, jealousy, anger now drained away from Cordell Vance, and nothing remained but an all-consuming hunger for the love he had denied himself. He clasped her to him. For a moment she resisted. Tears welled in her eyes. She surrendered. They were back in their private world.

They pulled apart, and Cordell Vance spoke in a flat, husky voice. "Did you . . . track me here?" His life might rest on her answer, but he didn't really care.

"I didn't have the faintest idea where you were. I finally broke down and hunted for you in Colorado. But you'd completely vanished. I gave up."

"But how did you find me?"

"I didn't find you. You were just here."

"How did you recognize me? I've got to know."

She lifted his left hand and flicked his little finger. "That helped. That and your bird imitation when someone talks into your right ear. I still wasn't sure until just now. Now I'm pretty sure," she said, drawing him close. He forced himself to say it: "You went back to Donaldson."

"I suppose," she said hesitantly, "you have a reason for being here. And for changing your appearance." She looked at him expectantly. He did not answer. She turned away and paced slowly toward the divan, then turned back and said firmly, "I won't ask you. But I'll tell you why I'm here.

"Your friend called me three days after you left. He didn't tell me his name. The next day I met with a CIA agent. He listened to my story. He asked me to string along with Jerry and find out as much as I could. I didn't like it very well, but you were gone and it was something to do. Well, they finally sent me down here for indoctrination in the Resurgent Youth Corps."

"How long have you been here?"

"Six weeks in the Confederacy. I was in Oklahoma for a month. I just arrived here the day I met you."

"How long will you be here?"

"About two weeks."

"Then what?"

"I don't know. They're kind of vague about that. It seems a little strange, but all the others are going home. The ones from the United States are being sent to a staging area. For some reason they don't seem to want us to go back right now."

"Tell me," Vance said, "what do you think of Howie Ray's Evolutionary Order now?"

"Well, I guess one of us has to commit himself. And I guess I have more faith in you than you have in me. I like the people down here and I like the country. I hate what the Party of National Resurgence has done to them. That's how I feel. Are you going to turn me in?"

He smiled, kissed her lightly and led her to the divan. "Look," he said seriously. "You get up North as soon as you can. Not later than August 10 at the latest. I can't tell you why I'm here. If it works out, you may be able to guess. If you do, keep it to yourself. Don't tell *anyone* you saw me—including the CIA. Keep away from me the rest of the time you're here. Maybe I'll be able to join you in Chicago in a month or so. If I don't show up there, forget me."

She gave him a quick peck on the cheek. "Yes. Well, I've already done that—as you can see. Actually, Lieutenant—Tremont?—I've already been jilted once, and I can't chance its happening again. Now that I've found you, I'm not going to let you out of my sight."

"Listen to me, Diane. There's something I've got to do. It's damned touchy. If you hang around, you'll be jeopardizing not only yourself but me as well."

"Don't be so melodramatic. I suspect we're practically in the same business. After all, it was your friend who got me involved in it. What *are* you doing here?"

"I can't tell you."

"All right. I can't leave you. I tried to forget you and I couldn't. Now that I've found you again, if something happened to you, I'd never forgive myself if I wasn't with you. If you love me as much as I love you, you'd feel the same way."

He said it bluntly, brutally, to shock her. "I'm going to try to kill Spearman."

Her eyes widened slightly, but she showed no other sign of surprise. "How can you? It's impossible. I've seen how he's protected."

"I don't know. I'm working out a plan. I may never get a chance to try it. If I don't, I'll slip out and join you. I think I'm all right now."

"If you are, then why don't you come back to me now?"

He shook his head decisively. "I've got to try it. If I didn't, I'd be worse off than I was before."

"You'll be worse off anyway," she said tonelessly. "You'll be dead."

"Diane, I'm not doing it for myself. Well, maybe partly for myself. But there's a more important reason."

"All right. I'll stay away from you. But I'm going to stay here. I've got to know what happens to you. If it goes wrong, nobody will ever know."

"Nobody must ever know—regardless of what happens. You've got to promise me that."

"When . . . how soon do you . . . ?"

"Pretty soon. Or else it's all off."

They kissed without passion. To each of them, it was a farewell kiss, but neither spoke of it.

The death warrant appeared in the Sunday edition of the *National Voice*. It did not specify whose, but Peter Tremont had a premonition it was his. Still, it was a relief to him.

The announcement said: "President Spearman will address the nation at 7 P.M., Wednesday, August 1, in observance of the implementation of the Nuclear Treaty. He will speak from the balcony of Stone Mansion overlooking Spearman Square. The talk will be carried on the National Television Network."

Elsewhere, the paper was filled with imprecations against the United States: border atrocities, stepped-up war preparations, an unattributed charge that the U.S. was concealing several of its thermonuclear bombs in violation of the treaty. Reading between the lines, Tremont could surmise why the Intercontinental Import Company was getting ready to balance its accounts.

Though the shop was closed, he busied himself restocking the shelves and rearranging the displays, including the one in the window. His father was sitting on the bench when he arrived, his camera in his lap.

Tremont sat down beside him and said without preliminaries, "Was your friend able to fix it?"

"He fixed it as good as he could. But he says it would only be effective at a distance of a foot or two. I'm afraid that won't be of much use to you."

"It does work, though?"

"Well, it works up close, but what good is that?"

Tremont removed his own camera from the carrying case around his neck. He detached the laser-strobes from both cameras and held them up side by side. His father's had a tiny slit in the cylinder with a small, round-headed steel pin sticking out of it. Peter pushed it down as far as it would go and notched it in a slot at the bottom.

"Compressed air?"

"Yes. And quite powerful, he tells me. But it scatters."

Tremont carefully released the pin, holding it with both forefingers until the pressure eased. He clamped the cylinder on his own camera and passed the other strobe to his father.

"You can't," the old man hissed fiercely. "It would be suicide. And it wouldn't do any good."

Tremont stood up. "Let's walk up toward the Capitol," he said. "I've been cooped up in the store all day."

They strolled through the gardens, which were nearly empty.

"Have you got the uniform?" Tremont inquired.

Royston Vance nodded. A thought suddenly struck him. "It wouldn't fit you. He made it for me."

Peter smiled. "Of course. You'll look good in it."

They walked past the armory, flanked by the army and navy buildings, and on either side of them, the air force and Citizens Protection Force headquarters. The other buildings were much taller than the armory, enclosing it on three sides. After they had passed "Military Row," they paused and looked back at the brightly lighted Stone Mansion, nestling in the trough of the green slope eight blocks away.

They resumed their walk, Tremont talking, the old man listening. They halted on the rim of the amphitheater at Jefferson Davis Square. They turned and faced each other.

"Well, that's about it," Peter said. "If anything goes wrong, I don't try to save you. You don't try to save me. Do you understand?"

The old man squared his shoulders. "I understand," he said.

Peter Tremont looked affectionately at the man who had tried in vain to shield his son from his own murky fate. Suddenly, he was grateful for the grim errand that had brought them together.

The regular Tuesday night drill was devoted to a full-dress rehearsal of security precautions and crowd-control tactics in preparation for Spearman's address the following evening. It did not go well. Major Wellbourne grumbled and raged throughout, though trying to conceal the foul-ups from the Resurgent Youth Corps observers sitting in the VIP stands. Tremont caught a glimpse of Diane, sitting between two tall blond youths, who were paying more attention to her than to the exercise.

At the conclusion of the drill, Wellbourne ordered the officers to remain for a dressing-down in the briefing shack at the west end of the parade grounds. Tremont turned over his squad to Private Leader Criswell and trudged toward the shack. He detoured around the weapons range, and as he passed by the door of the target control hut, he opened it and slipped inside. He yanked the two-way talker off his shoulder and buried it in a carton of paper target covers. He shoved the carton under the control desk, stepped out of the hut, closing the door carefully behind him, and continued on to the briefing shack.

Major Wellbourne delivered a forty-five-minute harangue on the grave responsibility that rested on those who protected the President. It apparently made little impression on Captain Armistead.

"Man," he said, as he strolled beside Tremont across the drill field. "I'd like to be responsible for protecting that babe we met the other night."

"Who's that?"

"You know—that tall brunette I introduced you to. Fleming."

He chattered on about the curve of Diane's calf, which, he averred, was a sure indication of sexual drive. Tremont expressed no opinion.

Half a dozen Youth Corps couples were still strolling about the roof under a three-quarter moon. As he approached the ramp, Peter spied Diane out of the corner of his eye, leaning against the parapet, conversing with the two blond boys and another girl. He ignored them, but she detached herself from the group and walked toward him.

"Oh, Captain Armistead."

Armistead did a right oblique without breaking stride and stopped in front of her. Tremont hesitated, then edged toward the ramp. Diane glanced coolly at him. "Oh, Lieutenant Tremont—isn't it?"

He gave her a perfunctory smile. Unobtrusively she herded Armistead toward him. The blond young men turned and looked at her, masking their annoyance.

Armistead reached out and rubbed his hand familiarly up and down her arm. "We were just talking about you. How about joining us for a drink down in the canteen?"

She glanced at Peter, a message in her eyes. "I don't think I can tonight. I'm with some friends here."

She threw out her hand in a gesture toward them and her bag went skittering across the floor. Captain Armistead gallantly moved to retrieve it.

"I've got to talk to you," she whispered urgently to Tremont. "It's something you should know."

"Same place. Twenty minutes," he murmured.

The two officers walked down the ramp together. Armistead stopped off at the second floor, urging Peter to join him for "just one quickie." Tremont excused himself on the ground that he had some book work to do at the store and "that whinnying son-of-a-bitch has already kept us overtime."

He walked down to the first floor and signed the "out" register. Six or seven other officers were standing at the entrance, chatting. He joined them; then, as though suddenly remembering something he had forgotten, he hurried across the foyer and jumped into a waiting elevator. The duty officer did not glance around.

He. rode up to the Youth Corps floor and walked through the empty corridors to their wing, testing the doors on either side as he approached the restricted section. He found an unlocked room three doors down and across the hall from the makeshift reception room where he had met Diane. He left it dark and the door barely ajar. She came along ten minutes later and he pulled her silently inside and locked the door.

His eyes had accommodated themselves to the darkness. He led her to a circle of straight-backed chairs clustered around a wooden table. They sat down. He stared at the outline of her face.

"Well?" His voice was neutral.

"Jerry Donaldson is here."

That tears it, he thought. Every operation he had ever been on which went wrong had started with some insignificant miscalculation.

"Where?"

"He was here in the building tonight. He came to see me. I was afraid you'd run into him."

"D'you think he would recognize me?"

"No. I don't think so. I wasn't at all sure myself, and I must know your face as well as anyone. But he might. He tried to find you after that—incident in Chicago. He knows you disappeared. If he saw you, he might at least be suspicious."

"What's he doing here?"

"He came down to cover Spearman's speech. He's going to be on the terrace with him tomorrow night."

Oh, that's really lovely, Tremont thought. Well, he would have to play the hand out, regardless of what was showing on the board.

"I'm glad you warned me. At least I can be on the lookout for him. I guess there's not much more I can do." He put Jerry Donaldson out of his mind.

She reached for his hand. "Cordy, I want to help you."

"You can't, really."

"You're going to try it tomorrow?"

She saw his head move in the darkness.

"I'll be in the crowd. Nobody could suspect me. But surely I could help you get away."

Oh, what the hell, he thought. We're in it together, no matter what. If we come out of it, we might as well come out together. This one is for me, Dorsey.

"All right," he said. "Maybe there *is* something you can do. You'll be here in the armory tomorrow?" He told her what to do.

Tremont looked at his watch: 0300. Diane had gone back to her room three hours before. He had stayed in the empty conference room. It was as good a place to wait as any. He heaved himself up off the table, opened the door a crack and inspected the vacant corridor.

He walked silently down the hall, then turned left into an intersecting passageway which led toward the bowels of the armory. He passed the third, or inner, ring of offices and continued on to the fireproofed emergency stair well in the dead center of the building. He crept down four flights of concrete steps and halted at the dimly lighted well in the basement.

Slowly he turned the knob on the heavy, fireproof door and pushed with his shoulder. He peeked through the crack into the magazine supply room.

The two duty sergeants were laying out their lunch on the steel counter which completely encircled the round room. The door to the magazine itself was directly across from where he stood. The two men were halfway around to the left, near the main entrance leading onto the ramp. The munitions elevator was opposite them. In his frequent visits to the magazine, Tremont had made a careful study of the layout, and he wasted no time inspecting it. He kept his eyes on the sergeants.

As was to be expected of two men who had spent numerous dull hours in each other's company, they did not engage in idle conversation. They finished unpacking their lunches and arranged them on plastic mats.

As though at a silent signal, each man reached into his pocket and slapped a coin down on the counter. They peered at them, picked them up and repeated the ritual. The tall sergeant with the thin bony face raked in the two coins and put them in his pocket. The other swung down from his stool, unlocked the ramp doors and went out, pulling the doors shut. Timing his entrance to coincide with the other's departure, Tremont crouched down and noiselessly slipped in behind the counter. He squatted there for a minute, listening for footsteps. Hearing none, he unhurriedly worked his way around to the right, keeping well below the rim of the counter. He halted in front of the door to the magazine and waited. He heard the main entrance doors swing open again. Without looking, he shoved the bottom of the door behind him and slipped into the magazine. He ducked into the first row of cabinets and stopped, his eye on the door, his hand on his gun. He did not move for several minutes. Slowly he relaxed.

He took the canister of Sub-Due nerve paralyzer out of the pocket on his thigh. He stepped out of his hiding place and moved silently over the plastic cork floor to the asbestos-covered wall of the supply room, where a dozen rubber-tired munitions carts were lined up. He pulled a cart over to the small loading area in front of the door and climbed cautiously onto its upper deck. He pointed the spout of the nerve para-lyzer at the recessed ceiling light almost directly overhead and pressed down on the release button, keeping well clear of the drippings. A thin stream of pink fluid sprayed over the transparent plastiglass shield. The paralyzer contained an indelible skin stain to provide ready identification of its targets.

Tremont pulled the cart a few yards into the maze, keeping within sight of the pink-colored light over the door. He sat down on the floor and swept his eyes slowly over the eight or ten metal lockers surrounding him.

The magazine covered the entire block-square basement of the armory, except for the circular supply room in the center. The munitions cabinets were spaced irregularly, not in rows, to provide a series of buffers against a possible explosion. Anybody penetrating beyond the supply-room stockade would have no way of telling which direction he had come or where he was going. The supply sergeants delighted in telling stories, perhaps apocryphal, of men who had lost their minds in the maze.

There was, undoubtedly, a simple key. The sergeants had no trouble finding their way around. Peter Tremont sat on the floor and searched for the key. Each of the twelve-by-twelve cubicles appeared to be identical in every respect with the others, except for the white numbers stenciled on the door just below the padlock. But the numbers seemed to be in no discernible order. The steel cells were bolted into concrete slabs at each corner, leaving a six-inch space underneath which would permit the blast effect to dissipate downward as well as sideways and upward.

Tremont stretched out flat on the floor and peered through the supports, thinking he could perhaps establish a directional line. The blocks blended into a solid concrete wall.

After half an hour he abandoned his efforts to decipher the puzzle and set about devising a solution of his own. He returned to the entrance, and, sighting past the pink globe, pushed as far into the maze as he could while still keeping it in view. He then climbed up onto the cart and sprayed the light directly overhead. Keeping two painted lights in view at all times, he repeated the procedure at intervals of about twenty feet. An hour later he arrived at a black-painted wall. He sprayed an "X" at that point, turned right and followed the wall to a corner. He followed the second wall the length of the building, counting his paces.

Dividing that figure in half, he sprayed an arrow at what he calculated to be the mid-point of the third wall, pointing in the direction he was walking. He did the same at the mid-point of the next wall, and at the halfway point of the original wall where he had started out, he sprayed an "N," establishing an arbitrary north. Twenty-five paces farther on, he located his original mark.

He sat down and looked at his watch. It was 0535. Mornings, he knew, were devoted to housekeeping duties by the permanent personnel of the armory. The first detachment of Mobile Militiamen would not arrive until 1300. He had plenty of time to work out the problem—if he could work it out at all.

He had previously concluded, while lying on his bed, that he could eliminate the south (so to speak) half of the magazine. On the occasion when he had helped return Captain Armistead's mortar, they had plunged directly into the maze without circling the supply room stockade. The guides, he assumed, would not travel in a circle. Furthermore, they had angled off to the right from the entrance. He therefore determined to concentrate his search in the northeast quadrant. The original line of pink lights he had blazed ended approximately eight degrees east of north.

He pulled out a small pocket notebook and sketched in the cardinal compass lines. The supply room, he knew, was in the approximate center of the building. Recalling how long it had taken the sergeant to return from the mortar locker to the entrance, he penciled in two arcs, covering that approximate area and extending from north to east. Allowing for an indeterminate amount of zigzagging, the space between the two arcs should offer the most fruitful area to begin the search.

First, however, he must blaze a straight trail along the north and east lines. Laboriously, he set about doing that, carefully triangulating the first two lights perpendicular to the wall. If his calculations were off appreciably, he realized, he ran the risk of missing the stockade completely. They weren't. The north line ended up almost exactly at the entrance to the supply room. He repeated the process with the east line, using the north-south line as a base.

When he had worked out the cardinal compass lines, he marked off the termini of the two arcs, one-third of the way in from the ends of each directional line. The mortar locker should be somewhere in the area of the remaining one-third.

Knowing the approximate angle between his original trail and the north-south line, and using that as a rough reference, he painted the first arc and came out nearly on target at the east line. He then blazed the second arc. It was 0914 as he started his search. He was sweating profusely, although he knew the temperature was thermostatically controlled at a precise seventy-two degrees.

At 1047 he spied a gleam of bare metal beneath layers of

black paint and ran his finger over the tiny scratch on the side of one of the cubicles. He stooped over and checked the number under the lock: 2-739-4. It matched. He exhaled heavily and slumped wearily to the floor.

After a while, he stood up and removed his automatic from its holster. He hit the base of the padlock a sharp blow with the weighted butt. The prong sprang loose. He disengaged the lock from the hasp and swung open the door. Lined up on the floor in two neat rows were eight mortars; on racks above them, ten rounds per gun.

Carefully fixing his position in relation to the stained lights, he worked his way down to the east-west line, sprayed a mark on the floor and followed it back to the stockade. He retrieved the cart he had abandoned during the actual search and threaded his way back to the mortar bin. He loaded the mortar and three shells on the cart, and replaced the broken lock so it would pass casual inspection. It was 1125. He stretched out on the floor and turned off his mind.

He awoke precisely one hour later and ran through his agenda, still lying on the floor.

The Op Schedule posted on the bulletin board called for the Emergency Evacuation Section to assemble in Auditorium "B" at 1315 for a run-through on vehicle mobilization. Before that time, his presence would be noticed. After that time, he might run into someone he knew. It was risky either way, but it was a risk he could not avoid.

He weaved his way through the maze once more, pulling the cart behind him. He plucked a tarpaulin from a large pile in the loading area at the entrance and tucked it securely around the mortar and the ammunition. He backed the cart into the parking row with the others, and returned to the door. He grasped the heavy asbestos-covered handle and pulled. For a moment he thought it had been secured, although he knew it was never locked—to permit quick egress from the magazine in case of fire.

It inched open. Three supply sergeants were at work, loading forms into the cubbyholes under the counter. One was the ruddy-faced sergeant who had gotten so chummy with him. He cursed softly.

The two guards in dress uniforms snapped to attention as the two-star general strode up the broad flight of steps at the main entrance to the armory. One guard stepped forward and swung open the massive door. The general marched across the marble floor to the duty desk in the center. Lieutenant R. A. Cadwallader glanced up nonchalantly, then sprang to his feet.

"At ease, Lieutenant," the general said crisply. He wore the blue-gray uniform of a regular in the Confederate States Army, gray silk gloves, gold epaulets.

The lieutenant reached for the phone. "I'll notify Colonel Farrington you're here, sir."

"Negative, soldier." The general's deep-set brown eyes were shadowed by bristly steel-gray brows. He swept the silent foyer with a slow, imperious stare. "Carry on with your work."

The seven or eight loitering militiamen who were standing at various degrees of attention went about their business.

"Sit down, Lieutenant," the general said less brusquely. "This is a readiness inspection. Do not alert anybody to my presence here. Is that understood?"

"Yes, sir." The lieutenant reluctantly lowered himself to his chair. "Will you sign the register, sir?"

The general gave him a chilly stare. He whirled and marched to the ramp.

Peering through the slit in the door, Peter Tremont heard

the three sharp raps at the entrance to the supply room, saw the red-faced sergeant unlock it and stiffen. He watched as the general strode in and made a flinty survey of the room. Tremont let the door slide shut, moved to the parking area and pulled out his cart.

When he peeked out again, the sergeants were standing sideways to him, facing the fire exit. The general pulled the door open and inspected the landing at the foot of the stairs. He stepped through and the sergeants followed him.

Abandoning concealment, Peter Tremont pulled his cart through the door and around the counter to the munitions elevator. He released the hold lever and slid back the three-thickness steel door. He yanked the cart in and pushed the single control button. The door slid shut.

The munitions elevator shaft had no access except in the basement and on the roof. It was probably the most pampered piece of machinery in the armory. It rose so smoothly its movement was almost imperceptible, and Tremont was not certain it had stopped when he pulled the hold switch.

He waited, aware that his palms were beginning to sweat. A minute crept by on his watch. Another and another. He imagined he could see the outside indicator light over the elevator shaft shining through the triple steel door. It was a flagrant violation of regulations to leave the elevator at the roof stop, and its absence in the basement would inevitably be noticed. Something was wrong, Diane was supposed to give him the "all clear." When the second hand reached sixty again, he shoved the cart to the back of the elevator and flipped off the hold switch. The door slid open.

He stood in the back of the elevator, shielding the cart. Within his restricted range of vision, the drill field was bare and empty. He moved forward and looked out. At first glance, he thought the roof was vacant. Then he saw two figures in the shadows at the mouth of the ramp: a man and a woman, hands clasped. He pulled back and watched them stealthily. They shifted and he saw Diane's face upturned, laughing. She tossed her hair in the exultant gesture he knew well. She moved toward the man—one of the muscular blond Youth Corpsmen he had seen her with before. They wrapped themselves in a long embrace. She broke away and pulled him toward the ramp. They disappeared.

Tremont grabbed the handle of the cart and yanked it out onto the roof. He reached back in and pushed the control button. Relieved, he watched the door slide shut and the yellow light blink out.

Restraining himself, he trudged unhurriedly across the expanse of the drill field, tugging the cart behind him, feeling like a naked, one-man parade. He did not look around. Eventually, he reached the shelter of the target-control hut. He pushed open the door and shoved the cart in. Two yellow panels of light filtered through the louvered peepholes facing the target bunker. He groped for the carton under the desk, and unearthed the two-way talker. He shoved it under the tarp and pushed the cart into the darkest corner of the hut.

As he straightened up, a light rap sounded on the door. He swung it open and Diane stepped in.

She was white and frightened. Her voice trembled. "He followed me up. I didn't think I would ever get rid of him. I . . . didn't know any other way."

Peter Tremont smiled—a genuinely amused smile. "Well," he said, "that's about the best way there is. You don't think he'll be back?"

She shook her head, relieved. He kissed her.

"I'm afraid I wasn't much help," she said.

"When the word gets around, the whole Youth Corps will be up here."

She looked up worriedly into his face. "Your father?"

"He's on the scene. He was cut out to be a two-star general."

He kissed her once more. "Maybe you'd better go out and keep the coast clear for him. Introduce yourself. He doesn't know about you."

She opened the door and stepped out. Tremont flipped the tarp off the cart and squatted down beside the mortar. Swiftly, he cranked in the coordinates he had memorized on the aiming computer—bearing, range, elevation. Compensation for the specific deviations of the gun itself were already locked into the system. He made an estimate of the temperature and windage. Captain Armistead would have been surprised at his backward pupil.

When he had finished, he sat down in the target controller's chair and conducted a solitary tactical briefing. Step by step, he ran through the entire operation. Beside those items that had already been taken care of, he made a mental check mark. Those remaining he examined one by one for flaws and omissions. Mechanically, he followed in precise detail the procedures set forth by Cordell Vance in his definitive manual on guerrilla warfare. In only one particular did he depart from the book. He made no provision for withdrawal in case the plan miscarried. If the plan miscarried, there was only one place to withdraw to. He wasted no time contemplating that possibility.

He heard footsteps approaching the hut. Automatically, he loosened the gun in its holster.

Two quick raps sounded on the door. Tremont opened it and admitted his father, resplendent in the general's uniform. He threw him a swift, respectful salute. The old man's stern face relaxed in a fleeting grin.

"Any trouble?" Tremont inquired.

"Not yet. I just about had to keep those sergeants on their knees until that damned red light went out."

"Nobody asked any questions?"

"No. I attracted some attention," he said dryly. "They'll know I was here."

"Colonel Farrington is the only one we have to worry about. One nice thing about you Confeds, you're not nosy."

He led the old man to the mortar and motioned him to sit on the floor. He pointed to four indicator knobs set into the range-finder. "Left, right, up, down," he said, touching each one in order. "It's sighted in and loaded. This is the firing button. Just touch it off and drop in another round. Then make the corrections when I give 'em to you. You've got three rounds there. I don't figure we'll have time for more than two. Don't move it out until he begins to talk. I'll open the transmitter. You'll be able to hear him on the public address. Fire when you're ready.

"I'll mark off two spots directly under the flagpole, fourteen inches in from the parapet. Set the right-hand shocks squarely on the spots. Any questions?"

"It's all perfectly clear."

"You'll have—" Peter Tremont looked at his watch—"about five hours to run through it. The range is secured now, and there's no reason for anybody to come in here." He stood up and led the way to the target-control desk. "This switch activates the targets and turns on a red light over the bunker. The D.T. Section will assemble up here at 1630. If you run into any problems, pull the switch. I'll try to contact you."

The old man said, "I'll manage all right."

Tremont looked at the general's clenched jaw. He unbuttoned his blouse and began to pull his shirt and undershirt out of his trousers. He rubbed his fingers exploratorily over his lean stomach to the left of his navel. Pinching his thumb and finger together, he squeezed up a small welt of skin. With the thumbnail of his other hand, he tore it loose, exposing the dark pit of a shrapnel scar underneath. His father stared in bewilderment at his body and then at his face.

"Artificial skin," Peter reassured him. He held it out. Stuck to the underside was a tiny tablet. "I want you to take this. In case anything happens, it will kill you within ten seconds."

Royston Vance reached for it, then drew back. "No," he said. "You keep it. They won't be able to break me."

"Take it," Tremont commanded. "I'm not worried about you or me. I told you what's at stake. Neither of us can be taken alive. I've got the gun."

Tremont pasted the strip to the old man's skull behind his right ear. The small protuberance was hidden by his thick hair.

Tremont moved toward the door. He thrust out his hand. "I guess that's about all."

Royston Vance took his hand and held it firmly for a moment. "I never wanted you to get mixed up in this, Cordy," he said. "But I can't tell you what it means to me to have you with me."

"Papa, it's where I should have been all the time."

Tremont opened the door a crack and peeked out. Diane was lounging against the parapet near the exit ramp. He stepped out where she could see him. She closed her hand in a beckoning gesture. He looked once more at his father, shut the door and walked quickly across the drill field.

Paying no attention to the girl, he headed directly toward the flagpole. He pulled out the canister of Sub-Due, squatted down and measured two lengths of the can out from the parapet. Holding the nozzle close to the surface so the liquid would not spread, he sprayed two dime-size splotches on the concrete. He stood up, glanced idly around the roof and moved toward the ramp. As he passed in front of the girl, their eyes met but they did not speak.

Tremont walked at a normal pace down to the first floor and out the door without encountering anyone he knew. He opened the shop for business and waited on half a dozen customers, making a special effort not to appear preoccupied. At 3:45 he locked the door and posted the "Closed" sign on it. He went up to his apartment, showered and changed uniforms. He loaded the movie camera with fresh film and packed three extra cartridges in the carrying case. As he passed through the store on his way out, he paused at the central display counter, reached in and pulled a camera from the bottom shelf. He removed the infrared laser-strobe from its cradle and dropped it in his pocket. He replaced the camera, took a last look around and let himself out the door.

The Domestic Tranquillity Section assembled in the main auditorium on the third floor. At the conclusion of his familiar exhortation on the sacred trust that was theirs Major Wellbourne unfurled a large wall chart showing Spearman Square blocked off into numbered sectors. As though outlining the tactical plan for a major battle, he assigned a sector to each squad. Lieutenant Tremont's "Handy" squad was stationed on the western perimeter toward the south end of the square, three hundred yards distant from the balcony. Peter dutifully drew a small sketch on his operations pad.

The assembly broke up, to fall in on the roof for inspection. The major, surrounded by his "Plans Staff," strode up the ramp as though leading an infantry charge. Defying military decorum, Peter galloped on ahead, turned and set the camera grinding as the group of officers advanced toward him. Major Wellbourne clamped his face in the classic military scowl and slowed his pace. Lieutenant Tremont retreated backward ahead of him.

"Hold it, will you, Major," he called. "I want to get a pan of you and your staff."

The warriors obediently halted. Peter slowly swept the camera from left to right, zooming in on the major. He waited for them to overtake him and fell into step beside Major Wellbourne.

"What I would like to do," he said, framing his hands into an imaginary screen, "is a documentary showing an actual operation from beginning to end: the planning, the briefing, the inspection, and then the whole D.T. Section in action."

Major Wellbourne swiveled his head and gave him a curt, approving nod. "Good idea," he said. "I'll assign Captain Burns to take over your squad."

"That won't be necessary, sir," Tremont said. "I think I can handle it. It probably would be better, though, if I was up front. I want to weave in some shots of the President speaking—to establish the gravity of the occasion and the importance of the work we do."

The major grunted assent. He consulted his clipboard, and signaled an officer on the fringe of his escort. "Lieutenant Cormack, y'all switch assignments with Lieutenant Tremont here. That means you'll take over Sector Low."

"Yes, sir."

When they arrived on the roof, Tremont gazed across the drill field at the range bunker. A red light showed above the shadowed interior. He ran his tongue over dry lips. Again he felt the premonition of disaster.

During the inspection, he detached himself from his squad and busied himself taking pictures of the assembled ranks. He ran out of film as he was shooting a close-up of Major Wellbourne at the head of his command.

"Goddamnit," he exclaimed. "I've gotta slip into the hut
and change films, Major. Hold 'em in formation till I get
back, will you."

Tremont hustled over to the hut and rapped twice. "Papa,"
he whispered.

The door opened and he stepped inside. The general was
sweating.

"The talker," he said in a strained voice. "I think it's
dead."

Tremont snatched it from him and flicked the switch both
ways. There was no background sputter.

Tremont unfastened the shoulder harness on his own
communicator.

"Take this one," he said, exchanging it for his father's.
"Wipe off the fingerprints." Quickly he slipped a new film
cartridge into the camera, switched off the light over the
bunker and stepped to the door. They exchanged a look in
which there was no sentiment, but one which touched a chord
in each, the look of two men going into battle together.

Peter stopped off at the general supply room on the second
floor to trade in his faulty talker. While the supply sergeant's
back was turned, he slipped a new canister of Sub-Due off
the shelf and replaced it with his old one, scrubbing the
surface with his handkerchief. He took his place at the head
of his squad as it formed for the march down the Grand
Concourse to Spearman Square.

Peter Tremont opened the transmitter on his two-way
talker as President Spearman let fall his upraised arm and
the rhythmic chant of the crowd abruptly ceased.

The President stood for a moment in solemn contemplation
of the vast throng. Peter raised his camera and focused on
the leonine head, outthrust jaw, hypnotic sunken eyes. Then

he lowered the camera, removed the strobe cylinder and sub-stituted the one in his pocket. He twisted it so the slit along its side and the retracted release pin lay alongside the ex-tended lens of the camera. He moved a dozen paces to the left of the balcony, where he could get a profile shot of Howie Ray Spearman. The camera whirred as the President began to speak.

"My good friends," he said in his deep, soft drawl. "I speak to you this evening on an occasion of great moment to the world and to our beloved country. At seven o'clock on the night of August 1, 1981, the nations of this earth have entered on a new era and a new relationship. At seven o'clock tonight the long, dark saga of nuclear blackmail and the domination of the world by nuclear tyranny came to an end.

"From this day forward, the peace-loving peoples who have pleaded in vain for justice and the righting of ancient wrongs stand on an equal footing with those arrogant malefactors of power who have so long denied them. We will continue, with patience and forbearance, to seek an amicable and an hon-orable solution to the serious differences which divide us from those whom we once called blood brothers. But we will no longer plead."

Tremont could sense Howie Ray Spearman's mesmerism taking hold of the crowd, while at the same time it fed the flames of his own fanaticism. His voice rose gradually to a shrill, frenzied pitch, then dwindled to a barely audible murmur.

"And so I appeal once more to the generous and fair-minded spirit of our neighbors and our brothers who share a common heritage with us. Let us cease bickering and quarrel-ing over the patrimony bequeathed to us by our forefathers. Let us divide this rich land between us with equity and justice, so that we may live in peace, side by side."

Tremont suddenly realized that the President was nearing the end of his speech. He would finish it and nothing would have happened. Except that the plot would be exposed. And he and his father would die senselessly—"not with a bang but a whimper."

A sickening paralysis engulfed him, and his brain did not register the sibilant "whoosh" of the mortar shell. It passed over the terrace and exploded in a screaming hail of shrapnel against the central façade of the Mansion. Lethal slivers rained down on the dignitaries on the roof, and a blackened hole appeared in the massive wall of the Mansion behind them.

A stunned gasp swept over the crowd. Tremont bent his head and muttered into his own transmitter: "Down three, left two." A great shout erupted from the crowd, and turned to a bestial roar as Spearman, standing straight and tall, raised his arm above his head, palm out, fingers rigid.

Peter Tremont turned his back to the balcony and screamed at the three militiamen nearest him. Motioning them to follow, he whirled and ran toward the small door directly in front of him, guarded by two members of the Presidential Protective Brigade, the uniformed branch of the Seepees. As he ran, he threw back his head and saw a mass of government and Party leaders swarming toward their leader. He uttered a howl of rage, which was drowned out in the paean of rejoicing from the crowd.

He and the three militiamen were sheltered by the wall when the second shell exploded in the middle of the terrace. Three bodies hurtled through the air and thudded into the cleared space in front of the crowd. Shrieks of pain came from overhead.

The dazed guards made an uncertain effort to bar the militiamen from entering.

"Medics," Tremont shouted, brushing past them.

The door opened onto a raised landing, from which a wrought-iron spiral stairway ascended to the floors above. Tremont took it two steps at a time. The squadmen clattered after him. At the third level, the stairs led onto a broad hallway, extending the full length of the Mansion. To the right of the stairway, ceiling-high French doors opened onto the terrace. One door was missing. The other hung drunkenly from one battered hinge. The hallway was littered with shards of glass.

Tremont waited for his white-faced troops at the top of the stairs. "Get everybody inside," he commanded.

He led them through the shattered doorway onto the terrace. Bathed in a crimson sunset, clumps of government officials, military leaders, other dignitaries and a sprinkling of women stumbled dazedly through the shambles, pausing here and there, as in a macabre minuet, to bend over a stiffening corpse or a moaning survivor. Half a dozen frenzied Seepees were attempting to herd them toward the doorway.

Tremont led his men toward the largest clot of people, gathered at the far end of the terrace, near the balcony. He thrust his way through the crowd, grasping generals, admirals, disheveled women and Cabinet members by the arm and pushing them toward the entrance.

"Everybody off the roof," he ordered. "There may be another explosion."

The leaders of the Confederacy, schooled in obedience, recognized the voice of command and did not stop to inquire from whence it came. A bemedaled air force general with tattered trousers took up the cry. "Everybody inside."

The militiamen implemented the order with the unceremonious crowd-control tactics they had been taught, breaking the group up into segments, pushing them to the rear.

Tremont shoved his way into the center of the cluster. Three men in civilian clothes were kneeling beside the tall figure of Howie Ray Spearman, stretched out on his back. One of them held the President's wrist in his fingers.

"He's not badly hurt," he said. "Let's get him inside."

Tremont squatted beside him. "You a doctor?" he asked brusquely.

The man looked around at him and shook his head. "Go get a litter," Tremont ordered. The man, whom Peter recognized as Secretary of the Treasury Orenthal, bridled at the peremptory tone. He gave Peter a scathing look, but rose to his feet.

Tremont saw two Seepees approaching. "Get those men to help you," he snapped. Orenthal hesitated, then turned and walked toward the Seepees. The other two men lingered, looking down at the body of their fallen leader.

"Get inside," Tremont barked. "It's dangerous out here. Keep everybody off the terrace."

Given an assignment, they marched off to carry it out.

The Seepees and the militiamen were herding the last of the onlookers off the roof garden.

Tremont crouched over the granite-faced form on the floor. A small trickle of blood oozed from Spearman's mouth and dribbled down his chin. He was breathing heavily but evenly. He obviously was not mortally wounded.

Tremont glanced over his shoulder and saw a cordon of Seepees spreading over the terrace, three of them heading toward him. He reached over with his left hand and raised the huge head off the carpeted floor. As he did so, Spearman opened his eyes and gazed blankly into his face. For an instant they stared at each other.

In that moment, the President read Tremont's intentions in his cold gaze. He tried to twist his head away from the hand clamped at the base of his skull. A low snarl of frustration burbled from his throat. His dark, hypnotic eyes now bored into Peter's, charged with the paralyzing voltage of his fierce will. But Cordell Vance felt neither triumph nor remorse, vengeance nor pity.

He tightened his hold on the back of Howie Ray Spearman's head and cradled it on his knee. With his other hand he felt for the tiny release lever on the side of the laser-strobe cylinder. He leaned over until the lens of the camera dangling on his chest was pressed against the side of Spearman's face. He twisted the head slightly, but Spearman's eyes did not leave his. He flicked the lever with his thumb.

A soft hiss issued from the cylinder as the air burst from the compression chamber. Two small steel slivers sprouted in the thicket of gray hair behind the President's ear. Blood oozed from a minute hole in his eardrum.

He gave one vicious jerk, nearly tearing loose from Tremont's grasp. His eyes revolved in their sockets, but still seemed to remain fixed on Tremont's. He emitted a strangled moan, then his massive shoulders slumped against Peter's leg. A dull glaze passed over his eyes, dimming forever the hawkish glitter of defiant fury.

Peter Tremont gently lowered the leonine head to the floor as the trio of Seepees converged upon him. He remained kneeling beside the body.

"I'm afraid he's dead," he said.

"He can't be," the Seepee leader exclaimed, squatting down and reaching for the President's wrist. "Orenthal said he was all right."

Tremont shrugged and rose to his feet. He flexed his knee to unkink his leg muscles, his hand resting casually on the butt of his gun. He looked sorrowfully into the faces of the Seepees.

He raised his hand from the gun and removed the camera strap from around his neck. "Do you want me to take pictures of the body?"

The Seepee chief looked up at him. "Naw," he said, "we'll take care of it. What's your name, Lieutenant?"

"Tremont. Peter Tremont."

"You stationed over at the armory?"

Peter nodded.

"We'll get in touch with you later," he dismissed him.

Peter walked toward the rear of the terrace, half-expecting to be called back. Civilian hospital attendants were starting to load the wounded on stretchers. The dead still lay where they had fallen. As his eyes wandered over the shapeless, twisted lumps of flesh, Tremont felt a stab of remorse. He counted six bodies, not including those blown off the roof.

He found his squadmen standing near the door, listening to instructions from an officer of the Protective Brigade. The officer turned around as he approached. "This your detail, Lieutenant?"

"Yes, sir."

"Have 'em gather up the bodies and put 'em over there by the wall."

Tremont's legs suddenly went weak. A reminiscent taste of nausea rose to his mouth. He could feel the blood draining from his brain. He stiffened his muscles against the postbattle tremors and fought against the impulse to rush down the stairs and fling himself on the first available patch of green grass.

He saw the Protective Brigade officer looking at him quizzically. The expression triggered an associative vision. For an instant he was staring into the black face of Robert Dorsey. He clamped a grip on his emotions.

Disguising his repugnance, he turned away and motioned

the three militiamen to follow him. They picked up a litter
and trudged out through the carnage. Tremont forced himself
to assist in loading the bodies on the litter.

The grisly chore was nearly finished when they approached
a lank form, lying face down, a matted clump of reddish-
brown hair not quite concealing a caved-in section of the
skull. The militiamen gingerly rolled the corpse over. Peter
Tremont looked into the sightless eyes of Jerry Donaldson.

Chapter Fourteen

Donald Barringer glanced down at the sheaf of papers neatly aligned in the recessed compartment of the dispatch case, then raised his eyes to meet the calm scrutiny of the President.

"As was to be expected," he said, "there has been a good deal of saber-rattling and bellicose talk. It might be advisable for us to make some concessions to strengthen the hand of the moderates. But I sense, Mr. President, from the attitude of the negotiators that the Confederacy is no longer psychologically prepared to go to war."

"What kind of concessions do you have in mind, Donald?"

"Well, I think they would now jump at the offer of an internationalized corridor and a free port. If they don't get it, it's always going to be a source of contention between us."

"How would that affect our foreign trade?"

"It probably would cut in on it slightly at first. In the long run I think it would be to everybody's advantage. But the important thing is that we encourage the Confederacy to return to a normal system of commerce in the world community. They can't possibly compete with their present restrictions. They would have to change them. And that would mean they'd have to change their whole system."

"That would be helpful, unless they really set out to cut our throats economically."

"I believe, Mr. President," Barringer went on earnestly, "our restraint during the recent weeks of crisis has dispelled much of the public hostility Spearman had built up toward the United States. There are hopeful indications that the war faction is being quietly dispersed. If they were going to attempt a coup, they would in all probability have acted before now."

"What hopeful indications, Donald?"

"Well, sir, as you know, the Military Council has pledged itself not only to uphold the constitutional process of orderly succession but to support Vice President Darby for the remainder of his term. They wouldn't have gone that far if they were just paving the way for a takeover.

"The Military Council is made up of professionals, and, as Harmon says, they know what the odds would be in a war with us. There has been some reshuffling of commands, and, as far as we can analyze them, the most militant officers have been shunted into posts where they can't do too much harm. It looks also as though the military is quietly taking over some of the powers of the Seepees. That's the thing that would precipitate a showdown, if there was going to be one—and so far there hasn't been."

"What about Darby? Do you think we can deal with him?"

"Well, he's a confirmed Evolutionary Order man. Otherwise he wouldn't have been there. On the other hand, Spearman wasn't one to build up anybody who might constitute a threat to him. Darby stands in pretty well with the Party of National Resurgence, but he can't control it the way Spearman did. And if you don't control the Party, you're not going to be able to control their kind of system very long."

"What do you think might happen?"

"It's hard to say, of course. My guess is that sooner or later there's going to be a split in the Party. When that happens, there's bound to be a move to toss out the Selective Process. By definition, the Selective Process creates a power elite from which the mass of the people are excluded. So you can pretty well figure what would happen if it ever came to a vote. Mr. President, I feel a little patience and understanding at this crucial time could go a long way toward re-establishing the bonds that once existed between us and the South."

President Lander bobbed his head in noncommittal acknowledgment and turned to the Secretary of Defense. Harmon Thomas pushed himself up to a semiperpendicular stance and removed the pipe from his mouth.

"Well, Mr. President, I won't presume to guess what the Confeds' intentions may be, but my people estimate that their capabilities have declined at least 25 percent in the last month. A surprise attack of any kind entails certain last-minute preparations. We keep a close eye on those indicators. Not only have they not moved in that direction; they seem to be slacking off on some of the preparatory measures they had already put into effect before Spearman's demise.

"But most important, as Donald pointed out, the people just aren't of a mind to go to war now. Even the military realize you can't jump into a full-scale war these days unless you have the nation united behind you. The Confeds never really wanted to fight us, but I think Spearman could have hypnotized them into thinking they did. Nobody else can, though. In my judgment, Mr. President, we are no longer in any imminent danger of attack by the Confederate States of America."

Lawrence Tazewell assembled his papers as Thomas concluded his remarks. He was ready when the President turned to him.

"Essentially, I am in agreement with the Secretary of State and the Secretary of Defense," he said. "Our calculations indicate that the immediate danger is past. I would like to suggest, though, Mr. President, that the present period of unrest affords us an unprecedented opportunity to incite the people against the regime which led them to the brink of war. Already there is a certain amount of open opposition to the Party of National Resurgence and even the Evolutionary Concept. I am confident we can guide that opposition into channels which would be advantageous to us. In fact, Mr. President, I believe we are faced with a God-given opportunity to redeem the tragic error of 1861—to lead our wayward brothers back into a united family. In my opinion—"

President Lander raised a restraining hand. "I'm sorry, Lawrence," he said firmly, "I don't want you stirring up trouble in the Confederacy during this difficult period. I think we had better let them work out their own problems. And as for bringing them back into the Union, I think old Abe Lincoln may have had a point. If they don't come back of their own accord, we would have nothing but trouble with them."

The President looked over at the remaining member of the group gathered in the lead-lined cavern. Where his manner had previously been detached, it now was keenly interested.

"Dr. Dorsey, what can you tell us about our . . . friend?"

Dorsey made a vain attempt to minimize his huge bulk by sinking his neck between his mountainous shoulders. He shook his head disparagingly. "Not much, I'm afraid, Mr. President. As far as I know, he's still down there. At least we keep getting orders from his camera store. Actually, of course, that's the wisest thing he could do—continue as he was. But it must be a terrible strain for him."

"Mr. President," Tazewell interjected, "it would be no problem at all for my agents to run a discreet check on him. And I think it would be advisable from our own standpoint.

After all, we don't even know that he had anything to do with the . . . incident. In fact, the news reports make it clear that he could not have been responsible for the shelling, since he was on the other end of it."

"Excuse me, Mr. President," Dorsey rumbled. "You gentlemen don't know for sure that he had anything to do with it. And I think it's probably just as well to leave it at that. But I think it would be most ungrateful of us to persuade ourselves that this nation does not owe Cordell Vance a tremendous debt, one that it cannot possibly repay. The least we can do for him, it seems to me, is to abide by his wishes, whatever they may be." He looked at Tazewell sternly. "I think I can assure you, sir, that when Cordell Vance wants to get out of the Confederacy, he will manage to do so."

Peter Tremont and Diane Fleming strolled lazily through the fading glory of the Garden of the States. A hot end-of-summer sun shone down from a cloudless blue sky. The green mantle of the Grand Concourse stretched before them to the graceful towers of Stone Mansion and beyond.

"I know it doesn't make sense," Peter Tremont was saying. "I think it's something in the air that addles the brain. Or maybe it's because the people down here want to live in a fantasy world, so they do. . . . I was born here—perhaps it's hereditary."

"What's crazy about a fantasy world?" Diane said. "If it's better than the real one. I think it makes sense."

"But you never actually got to know the real world. You might like it."

"Not if you weren't in it," she said simply.

"Look. I don't know whether this is truly what I want or whether I feel guilty. I do know there is something worthwhile down here to work for. These are decent people. They should have a decent country to live in. I think I'd like to stay here and help build one. Besides, I owe it to my father."

"Have you heard anything from him?"

Peter shook his head. "I don't expect to. It was understood there'd be no contact between us until the investigation is closed."

"Have there been any developments?"

"Plenty," Peter said. "The Seepees have rounded up everybody with a mark against them. If they don't catch the culprit, they'll sure as hell use the assassination as the pretext for a purge. But it could backfire. Every time they remove one 'obstructionist' they create two more. There's been a lot of pent-up hatred of the Seepees. Without Spearman to front for them, it may not be pent up much longer."

"Are they making any headway in the investigation?"

Tremont hesitated. "You can't really tell, of course. The Commission hasn't made any announcements. I gather, though, they are working on the theory it was a large-scale conspiracy. They have plenty of suspects."

"Have they questioned you again?"

"No. They're still grilling everybody at the armory, of course. But I seem to be in the clear, since the Seepees know where I was."

"Where do you think your father is?"

"I'm sure he's back with the Prives. That would be the safest place for him now. But we'll be hearing from him. You can bet on that." He smiled. "I'd like for you to get to know him. He's a born reformer. He'll shape you up in a hurry."

"Speaking of reform, there's one I intend to institute. I'm going to change your face back to the way it was before. I feel—promiscuous."

"I fix myself up to please you and you complain about it. Besides, I don't think Dr. Dorsey would approve. But really

—if we stay, I'm afraid you're stuck with Peter Tremont. I like him better than—that other fellow. As far as I'm concerned, Cordell Vance is dead. I don't even want to try to collect the money. Although I'm sure Dorsey would get it to us some way if we asked him for it."

"Who needs it?" Diane twined her fingers in his. "This is the land of opportunity."

70 71 72 73 10 9 8 7 6 5 4 3 2 1